INTERSTELLAR
PATROL

INTERSTELLAR
PATROL

CHRISTOPHER ANVIL
COMPILED AND EDITED BY ERIC FLINT

Copyright © 2003 by Christopher Anvil.
"Strangers to Paradise" was first published in *Analog*, October 1966. "The Dukes of Desire" was first published in *Analog*, June 1967. "The King's Legions" was first published in *Analog*, September 1967. (These three stories were later combined and issued as the novel *Strangers in Paradise*, Tower 1969.) "A Question of Attitude" was first published in *Analog*, December 1967. "The Royal Road" was first published in *Analog*, June 1968. "The Nitrocellulose Doormat" was first published in *Analog*, June 1969. "Basic" was first published in *Venture Science Fiction*, November 1969. "Test Ultimate" was first published in *Analog*, October 1969. "Compound Interest" was first published in *Analog*, July 1967. "Experts in the Field" was first published in *Analog*, May 1967. "The Hunch" was first published in *Analog*, July 1961. "Star Tiger" was first published in *Astounding*, June 1960. "Revolt!" was first published in *Astounding*, April 1958. "Stranglehold" was first published in *Analog*, June 1966.

A Baen Books Original

Baen Publishing Enterprises
P.O. Box 1403
Riverdale, NY 10471
www.baen.com

ISBN: 0-7434-3600-8

Cover art by Mark Hennessey-Barratt

First printing, April 2003

Library of Congress Cataloging-in-Publication Data

Anvil, Christopher.
    Interstellar patrol / by Christopher Anvil ; compiled and edited by Eric Flint.
    p. cm.
    ISBN 0-7434-3600-8
    1. Life on other planets—Fiction. 2. Space warfare—Fiction. 3. Space ships—Fiction.
I. Flint, Eric. II. Title.

PS3551.N9I58 2003
813'.54—dc21

                              2003040348

Distributed by Simon & Schuster
1230 Avenue of the Americas
New York, NY 10020

Production by Windhaven Press, Auburn, NH
Printed in the United States of America

10 9 8 7 6 5 4 3 2 1

CONTENTS

INTERSTELLAR
PATROL

INTRODUCTION

by David Weber

I'm delighted that someone is making Christopher Anvil's work available once again. Especially the Interstellar Patrol stories. Vaughan Roberts, Morrissey, and Hammell have always been three of my very favorite characters, and I've always loved Anvil's . . . peculiar sense of humor.

I suppose, if I'm going to be honest, that Roberts' J-class ship is another of my favorite characters. In fact, although I hadn't realized it until I sat down to write this introduction, I suspect that there was a lot of the Patrol boat's computer hiding somewhere in the depths of my memory when I created Dahak for the *Mutineers' Moon* series. After all, Dahak is simply another self-aware ship kidnapping itself a captain on a somewhat larger scale. They even have a few personality traits in common.

The characters themselves are always a delight in an Anvil story or novel. Like most good character builders, Anvil creates his memorable people for the reader through their interactions, and the edge of zaniness which seems to creep into almost everything he writes only makes them even more interesting. His pronounced gift for building larger-than-life planets and environments for them to interact in sometimes seems to slip past almost unnoticed, yet it is a constant in almost all of his stories, and I think it is one of his strongest building blocks. He also has more than a touch of the Eric Frank Russell school of "poor aliens" in his work, because whoever sets out to oppose or overcome one of his characters has all unknowingly set his foot on the first slippery step of the slope of doom. The only question is how big a splat the villain is going to make at the foot of the cliff. This shows strongly in the first volume of Anvil's work from Baen Books, *Pandora's Legions*, but it makes its appearance in this volume, as well. In this instance, however, most of the "poor aliens" are actually "poor humans," with a sizable smattering of unfortunate master computers, robotic police units, and nasty extraterrestrial fauna thrown in for good measure.

In many ways, Anvil's storytelling style has always reminded me of the historical romance novels by Georgette Heyer or Lois Bujold's Miles Vorkosigan stories. Like Heyer and Bujold, Anvil's characters always have a perfectly logical reason for everything they do, yet they slide inevitably from one catastrophe to another in a slither which rapidly assumes avalanche proportions. A Keith Laumer character triumphs through an unflinching refusal to yield which transforms him, permits him to break through to some higher level of capability or greatness. An Anvil character triumphs by shooting the rapids, by caroming from one obstacle to another, adapting and overcoming as he goes. In many ways, his characters are science-fiction descendents of Odysseus, the scheming fast thinker who dazzles his opponents with his footwork. Of course, sometimes it's a little difficult to tell whether they're dazzling an opponent with their footwork, or skittering across a floor covered in ball bearings. But Anvil has the technique and the skill to bring them out triumphant in the end, and watching them dance is such a delightful pleasure.

The stories in this volume are science-fiction in the grand, rip-roaring tradition. Anvil throws around powerful bureaucracies like the PDA, huge space navies like the Space Force, and deviously capable guardians of the Right and Good (although said guardians may be just a mite tarnished around the edges) like the Interstellar Patrol. He delights in creating obscure, complex, often many-sided conundrums for his characters, and then taking us with him as they unravel the problem one strand at a time. I see a lot of the Golden Age in his stories, echoes of Williamson's *Legion of Space*, or of John Campbell's Arcot, Wade, and Morey in the scale and the sweeping, half-laughing scope of the problems he inflicts upon his characters. And most delightfully of all, in our post *Star Trek* universe, there isn't a trace of the Prime Directive. There are only characters with wit, humor, courage, and rather more audacity than is good for them.

While it is inevitable that any volume which is going to deal with Vaughan Roberts & Co. has to start with "Strangers to Paradise," that story—excellent as it is—was never really my favorite Interstellar Patrol story. I'm not sure why. Perhaps it's because the "want-generator" is a bit too much like Williamson's AKKA super weapon in the Legion of Space stories. Or perhaps it's because the "want-generator" is a little too much of the one aspect of Anvil's stories which sometimes disturbs me on a philosophical level. His characters, by their nature, are the sort of people who set out to fix problems, yet sometimes the means they embrace fringe just a little too closely upon a sort of intellectual totalitarianism. Not in terms of ideology per se, but in the willingness to manipulate and control in ways which cannot be resisted. At the same time, however, Anvil is always careful to show the pitfalls of such an approach, as in "Strangers to Paradise" itself, when the subjects of our heroes' "mind control" stubbornly persist in doing something their controllers never counted on.

Yet whether or not "Strangers to Paradise" would make my own list of top five Anvil stories, it is most definitely the direct and necessary progenitor of what undoubtedly *are* my two favorite IP stories: "The King's Legions," which is included in this volume, and the short novel *Warlord's World*, which is not but which I hope and expect will be along shortly. It's always seemed to me that, just as Laumer's novella "The Night of the Trolls" captures the essential Laumer hero perfectly, "The King's Legions" and *Warlord's World* capture the essential Anvil.

For those of us who have known Anvil for years, this book is a most welcome reunion with old friends. For those not already familiar with him, it offers an introduction to a writer and to characters very much worth knowing. In some ways, I rather envy the reader who is about to experience his or her first, concentrated dose of Anvil-dom. If you're one of those newcomers, welcome aboard. Whichever Anvil tale winds up *your* favorite, at least you'll have a rich and varied selection to choose from. This volume contains many of my favorites, but there's a lot more Anvil out there, and I hope that Baen will bring more of it to us. In the meantime, you hold in your hands an excellent starting point.

Buckle up tight. It's going to be an . . . energetic ride.

EDITOR'S PREFACE

Without a doubt, Christopher Anvil's richest and most developed setting was what he and John Campbell—who edited *Astounding/Analog* magazine where most of the stories originally appeared—called "the Colonization series." Anvil wrote over thirty stories in that setting, ranging in length from short stories to the novel *Warlord's World.*

At the heart of the Colonization series are the stories concerning the Interstellar Patrol, which are the best known. But Anvil wrote a number of stories in the same setting, in which the Interstellar Patrol does not figure directly. These stories often involved such organizations as the Space Force, the Planetary Development Authority and the Stellar Scouts, the Space Navy—and a wide range of civilians, from big businessmen to merchant spacemen to colonists on the ground.

Often enough, characters who appear in cameo or minor roles in the Interstellar Patrol stories are the protagonists of other stories. An example is the ruthless businessman Nels Krojac, who is only mentioned in passing in "The King's Legions" and "The Royal Road" but is a central figure in "Compound Interest" and "Experts in the Field."

In this volume, we are reissuing the first two major episodes of Anvil's Interstellar Patrol adventures, as well as—in Part III—a number of stories which give the reader a sense of the setting as a whole.

—Eric Flint

Part I: *Paradise*

STRANGERS TO PARADISE

Vaughan Nathan Roberts, captain of the fast interstellar transport *Orion*, stood in the huge room amidst all the wheeled and antennaed metal shapes, large and small, and thought of his ship orbiting the planet with its drive knocked out. The idea of coming to this place, he told himself stubbornly, was to get repairs. Not to get eaten alive, mobbed, or bundled around by roboid functionaries, but to get repairs. The question was, how?

Roberts was flanked by metal boxes nearly as tall as himself, much wider and thicker, with whip antennas on top, bicycle wheels below, and the words "Law Enforcement" blazoned on them front and back.

Directly in front of Roberts stood a far larger metal box, on low massive wheels, with a variety of antennas sticking up, and mouthpieces, viewscreens, and receptor heads thrust out toward him under the glowing letters: **CRIMINAL COURT.**

From this maze of screens and speakers, a voice was murmuring: " . . . Fingerprints, palm prints, retinal patterns, total body index: not on record. Conclusion unavoidable that this individual is not native to this planet."

"I've been trying to tell you," said Roberts, "we had gravitor trouble. We headed for the nearest repair facility, got here crippled, couldn't raise any response on the communicator, and half-a-dozen of us came down in the ship's tender. The tender cracked up in a forest forty miles from the spaceport. Three of my men were badly hurt. One of us stayed with them, and two of us hiked out for help. When we reached your city, here, we got garbage dumped on us, tin cans and chunks of cement slung at us, a gang of kids went for us, and then your iron gendarmes arrested us for causing a riot."

"Unsuitable attire," snapped a voice from the metal box to Roberts' right.

"We are dressed as spacemen," said Roberts shortly. "Now, I've got three injured men in the tender, and a ship in orbit with the rest of my crew trapped on board. We'll gladly pay for medical help and repairs. *Where are they?*"

A general murmur and clack rose from the big metal box in front of Roberts. On the screens, human faces and metal forms of various sizes and shapes rapidly came and went. From somewhere in the room, Roberts could hear the voice of Hammell, his cargo-control officer, raised in anger.

Then a speaker in front of him was murmuring, "On basis of correlation of statements of both accused, overall probability of guilt is 0.2, necessity of making examples 0.1. Therefore, adjudge innocent, transfer to Immigration."

At once, a loud voice announced, "We find the accused *innocent* of all charges brought against him."

From Roberts' roboid captors, to either side, came low murmurs of discontent.

A new voice spoke with authority. "The prisoner will be released at once, and escorted to Immigration for disposal."

Roberts blinked. "I don't want to immigrate. I just need repairs for my ship!"

The words **CRIMINAL COURT** faded out and the words **IMMIGRATION HEARING** flickered on.

"Name," said the box.

Roberts said, "I've been *through* all that. What I want . . ."

"*Name,*" said the box sternly.

To Roberts' right, one of the smaller boxes explained. "You *were* at the Criminal Court. Now you are at the Immigration Hearing."

"I don't *want* to immigrate!" said Roberts.

The big metal box said sternly, "This case has been transferred to Immigration for disposal. Relevant information of interest to applicant: 1) No individual not already a citizen will be compelled against his will to become a citizen.

2) Due to food and material shortages, technological break-downs, and attendant malfunctions, no one not a citizen will be fed, sheltered, clothed, or otherwise allowed to become a charge on the planet, unless otherwise decided by the due and constituted authorities." There was a brief pause. "Name."

Roberts blinked. Apparently he would have to become a citizen in order to exist while arranging for repairs.

"Name," snapped the box.

"Roberts. Vaughan N. Roberts."

"Sex."

"Male."

"Age."

"Thirty-six."

"Height."

"Six feet one-quarter inch."

"Weight."

"One hundred seventy-five pounds. Look . . ."

"Occupation?"

"Spaceship captain. Listen, all I want . . ."

"Inapplicable occupation. Demand for spaceship captains on this planet: Zero. Correction: Occupation: Unskilled. Years of experience?"

Roberts stared. "Experience? As a spaceship captain?"

"As unskilled," snapped the box. "This is your occupation."

Roberts said, "I have no experience as unskilled. I . . ."

"No experience," said the box disapprovingly. "Any physical defects?"

"No. Look, all . . ."

"Convicted of how many crimes the last three years?"

"None. All I . . ."

"Formal education?"

Roberts blew out his breath. "Twelve years of general schooling, six years training in the Space Academy, one year at the Tactical Combat Command Advanced Training Center. *And all I want is to get some repairs done!"*

"Seven years college training. Equivalent fourteen years experience credit. Excellent. Raise your right hand."

Roberts exasperatedly raised his right hand.

"Repeat after me," said the box, and rolled off words in short incomplete groups, so that Roberts had time to repeat the words, but not to understand their full meaning. Then the box said, "You are now a citizen of the planet Boschock III, known as Paradise, and entitled to all the rights and privileges appertaining thereto, and subject to all the laws, regulations, and customs thereof, so help you God, Amen. This hearing is closed."

The words **IMMIGRATION HEARING** faded out.

Before Roberts could say a word, he was rushed up a gravity-lift, down a hall, and shoved into a room where he was weighed, measured, photographed, fingerprinted, palm, toe, and foot-printed, retina-graphed, his mouth pried open and teeth examined, and then he was presented with an identification card, and run down the hall to a window where ration books popped out of slots onto a counter. Next he was hurried out to a store full of huge vending machines, and outfitted with a new set of clothes.

Roberts and Hammell now found themselves outside, holding their own clothing wrapped in big bundles, and each wearing a kind of loose long-sleeved blouse, loose long pantaloons, ill-fitting shoes, and long-billed high-topped floppy cap.

Roberts looked sourly up the street at the milling crowd, then glanced at Hammell. "Do *you* have any ideas?"

"I wouldn't know an idea if one banged into me," growled Hammell. "I'm so mad I can't see straight."

"We need to get in touch with someone in authority—if any human on this planet *has* authority."

"Yes," said Hammell. "But how?"

Roberts said, "If they have any kind of public communications system here, there ought to be a directory."

While they were trying to think where to look for one, a large mobile metal box stopped in front of them, and abruptly shot its antenna to full height. Metal covers on its sides snapped back and a dazzling yellow light flashed in their faces. A set of long flexible metal arms whipped out, a mesh-covered speaker snapped "Spot check," and with a quick flip of the metal arms, the robot emptied their pockets onto the sidewalk. Next, it rapidly felt them all over, then jerked loose the bundles they were holding, so that they spilled open in the street.

"Nonexplosive. Clothing. But nonstandard. *You have receipts for these?*"

For the moment, Roberts was speechless. He heard Hammell snarl, "They're our own clothes."

"Uncitylike behavior, one count: lying to roboid police officer under direct interrogation during spot check; these are not clothes permissible for a citizen to wear, hence they are not *your* clothes. They can only be *costumes,* and costumes can only be purchased by registered entertainers. You are not dressed as registered entertainers." The yellow light flashed in Roberts' face. "*You.* You have receipts for these? Your answer? *Do not lie.*"

"We're new citizens," Roberts began, "and—"

"Not asked. Do not evade the question. *Do you have receipts for these costumes?*"

"Of *course,*" said Roberts. "Yes, *certainly.*"

"Produce the receipts."

"They're on board the spaceship *Orion.* We wore these clothes on board *Orion,* came down to arrange for repairs, got sent to Immigration, and then bought the clothes we're wearing now. These clothes in the bundles are the clothes we wore when we came down."

"Spaceship visits are rare, improbable. It follows, this explanation is improbable. *Arrest on suspicion of shoplifting.* You will come with me for immediate interrogation while investigation proceeds."

The two men were separated, placed under bright lights for a long series of questions, then put into a cell with two cots, a light bulb, a toilet, a 3-V set that didn't work, and a decorative design on the ceiling that obviously incorporated the pick-up heads for a sight-and-sound recording system.

As the robot-jailer rolled off down the corridor, Roberts and Hammell eyed the ceiling, and lay down on the cots without a word.

Several hours crawled by, then a tall gray-haired man wearing dark-blue blouse and pantaloons, of good material and narrow cut, walked down the corridor, and stopped outside the cell.

"Which of you is Roberts, Vaughan N.?"

"I am."

"You represent yourself as a spaceship captain?"

"I'm captain of T.S.M. *Orion,* Interstellar Rapid Transport

Corporation. The ship is now orbiting this planet with a nonfunctional main gravitor. I came down here to arrange for repairs, but our tender went out of control, we cracked up, two of us hiked in to get help, were attacked by a gang, arrested, dragged into court, given to understand we would immigrate or starve to death, then arrested again because we couldn't produce receipts for the clothes we'd worn down, and here we are."

"I see. And this other individual . . . let's see . . . *Hammell?*"

"He's the cargo-control officer assigned to *Orion.*"

"As which," said Hammell coldly, "it is my duty to tell you that *Orion* has a spoilable cargo. This planet is supposed to have a Class II commercial repair facility. We've been trying to get in touch with it for days."

"I see. My name is Kelty. I'm assistant-chief of the Law-Enforcement Department, acting under the planetary computer, which technically is chief. I'm afraid I have some bad news for you gentlemen."

"Not surprising," growled Hammell.

Roberts said, "This planet has been nothing but bad news since we got here."

"Then why not go to another planet?"

"Our gravitor burned out. We had to strip the coils of the tender's gravitor, to make emergency repairs. Then, to come down here, we had to scavenge from the main gravitor, to get the tender to work."

"Where did you land?"

"We didn't land. We crashed about ten miles inside a forest belt, between a couple of wide tracts of cleared land. The spaceport was about forty miles to the east of where we crashed."

"Then," said Kelty, watching Roberts alertly, "you were well inside the killer forest. I'm surprised you got through alive."

"Yes," said Roberts, "we're a little surprised, ourselves. We'd scarcely started to set foot outside the tender when a thing like an oversize gray tiger jumped us. We fought that off with guns from the emergency kit. Our communications officer got in contact with your city here—we hadn't been able to raise it while we were in orbit—and while I was trying to arrange for help, another of these overgrown tigers showed up. Meanwhile, it turned out that I was talking to a mechanical answering device of some kind, so I gave that up. We fought off this second animal, the sun set, and something started taking cracks at the far side of the tender. This thing forced its way into the tender's cargo compartment. We managed to get in touch with someone else on the communicator, but before we could make our position clear, the tender got heaved around, and the communicator was smashed."

Roberts shook his head. "The next morning, Hammell and I started through the forest, got into some kind of a thicket that folded big clinging leaves around us like wet sheets, and while we were fighting clear of this, a pile of insects came pouring through the trees, tumbling over each other, and spreading out to eat everything in sight. We managed to get out of their way, and saw that when the horde passed, all the insects left behind jumped and flew after it to catch up and pour forward again. They were traveling southeast, which suited us, so we walked along close behind, and believe me, nothing bothered us. When they hit the cleared ground, they changed direction, and we got out of the forest and hiked the rest of the way in the open."

Kelty was listening intently. His look of suspicion had disappeared, and now he smiled. "You used your heads. Such good sense deserves success; but I'm sorry to have to tell you, we have no way to go after those men, and the repair facility you're looking for is no longer here."

Roberts looked at him blankly.

Kelty said, "You've apparently assumed that the population of this planet grew up from a beginning with a few tough settlers to its present size. In that case, if there was cause for a repair facility in the first place, it wouldn't disappear overnight. But it isn't so. The city was designed and built as a man-made paradise, through the beneficence of a tax-free foundation. The foundation was under legislative investigation. To get out from under, an accumulated surplus balance of several trillions had to be unloaded quickly, and it had to be done somehow for the demonstrable benefit of mankind. A planetary-utopia project was dug out of the files, and right here is the final result. This city was built, and staffed by highly-trained technicians, with a computer in overall control, then the foundation opened a campaign on half-a-dozen overpopulated worlds, gathered from their slums millions of 'socially-disadvantaged individuals' and used the last of its excess money shipping them here. *That* is how this planet was settled."

Roberts grappled with the mental picture this created.

Hammell said, "Where did a repair facility *ever* fit in?"

"It looked nice in the plans, and it did a good job when the populace was coming in here. After that, there wasn't much use for it. When a mob looted and burned it, the computer had what still remained reprocessed to fill more urgent needs. There's nothing left now but a plot of ground where the facility used to be."

Hammell shook his head and glanced at Roberts.

Roberts finally said, "There's no way to get the repairs done here?"

"Not without the equipment and the technicians. The equipment was looted. About that time, the technicians saw the way things were sliding, and made recommendations, which the computer, in compliance with its built-in directives, rejected. The technicians got fed up. One fine morning, they pulled out, leaving the computer programmed to neither produce nor maintain air-travel mechanisms. The technicians went to the far side of the killer forest, and set up independent farming communities over there. This planet being what it is, they're evidently having plenty of trouble, but they prefer it to the city. We can't reach them to bring them back. We have no air transport. And the computer couldn't be programmed to restore the repair facility except by these technicians."

Roberts said, "Could the technicians be persuaded to come back temporarily, just to program the computer?"

Kelty's eyes glinted. "If so, they'll never get away again. They broke their contract. Now the whole roboid police force is on the lookout for them. Naturally, I will obey the orders of the planetary computer, and seize them the instant they show up." Kelty saw Roberts' expression, and smiled. "Don't worry, Roberts. They know this. No, you could never possibly persuade them to come back here. We've tried to hire people to take their place, but without success. Who wants to spend his time struggling with the frustrations of a gigantic slum-city? Everything you do here fails. Put up a light bulb, and someone will smash it. Install a water pipe in the afternoon, and it will be ripped out by next morning. Bare maintenance is all the computer and its mechanisms can manage. For most specialists, the work is solid frustration. My job is a little different. It's quite a challenge to use limited force in such a way that a measure of order is maintained. But I do it, and I aim to continue to do it."

Roberts thought it over. "I can see what you're up against. But unless we can get the computer and the technicians together, how can we get the ship—or even the ship's tender—repaired?"

Kelty shook his head. "In the present setup, it's impossible. The computer can't divert the effort to rebuild the repair facility, because of the widespread disorder and destructiveness of the populace."

"I can't leave my ship in orbit," said Roberts, "and the men trapped on board, helpless."

"But, you see, unless some order can be brought out of this chaos, we have no choice in the matter. And to do that would take a change in the attitude of the populace. There's only one other way."

"What's that?"

Kelty studied him speculatively. "*If* you and your men, who have considerable technical background, will first consent to devote your time and training exclusively to work for the City, from now on, *then* we might be able to work something out." He straightened up, and then stepped back. "Then, you see, it might be worth the computer's while to rebuild the repair facility."

Roberts stared at him.

Kelty smiled. "Meanwhile, since you're citizens, you have guaranteed rent-free cost-free housing. If you should decide to join us, your work would naturally require that you live in close proximity to the Planetary Control Center. Until you do, it would, of course, be unfair to discriminate against the other citizens by giving you special attention. Since we've found you innocent, you will now be released. You'll be given a routing ticket on the way out, to take you to your quarters. You'll find them airy, with an exceptional view."

Kelty turned, gestured, and a roboid-jailer wheeled with a hiss of tires down the corridor.

Kelty gave them a final smiling glance. "Think over what I've said, Roberts. If you decide to join us, let me know."

That evening found Roberts and Hammell in a five-room apartment on the sixth floor of a ten-story building. The building had emergency staircases littered with cans, broken bottles, garbage, and large rats, which disputed the passage with them on the way up. The gravitor-drop had a chain across the entrance, bearing a dented "NO POWER" sign. There was not a whole piece of glass to be seen in the building. The empty window frames looked out over a park, where dead half-grown trees had four-letter words carved in their bark, and the spindly grass sprouted amidst heaps of rotting garbage.

From down in the streets came a scrape and rumble as battered cleaning-machines picked up trash. From the building above came a chorus of yells:

"*Kill* the lousy mechs!"

A fusillade of bottles smashed down on the machines' armored tops. Loudspeakers broadcast appeals for law-abiding cooperation, and the air shook with curses flung back in answer.

Roberts and Hammell stared out the window at the buildings and parks, laid out like the alternating squares of a checkerboard, and stretching off to the horizon. In the distance, lit by the setting sun, the buildings looked almost magical. Nearby, rats scurried amidst the trash in the park. From overhead, a bundle of garbage plummeted past the window, opening up as it fell.

Hammell turned away from the window. "*Now* what do we do?"

"The first thing is to get out of here. Kelty seems to think a little experience of this will make us eager to join him. I wouldn't want to stay in this place on *any* terms."

"The forest is murderous. The City won't help. That leaves the technicians."

Roberts nodded. "If we can get them to help, maybe we can straighten the mess out yet."

"If they haven't *already* helped, it's too bad for Matthis, Warner, and Cassetti."

Roberts nodded soberly. The three men had been too badly hurt in the crash to carry out. "Well, if we get out of here early in the morning, we should avoid getting waylaid by a gang. I hope we can find where we cached our packs, guns, and canteens. Then we can start back."

"Personally, I'm half-dead from the last hike."

"If we stay here, we could be all-dead before we know it."

Hammell glanced around. "There's truth in that, all right. Well, while it's still light, let's get set. This could be a rough night."

The two men blocked the apartment door with a battered bedstead and a bureau with all the knobs broken off its drawers, then cleaned out a small room and collected in it all the bottles they found in the litter, just in case they should need ammunition. They carried the wreck of a mattress into this one room, stuffed the baseboard's ratholes with smashed glass and the bent lids of tin cans, and jammed another can into the hole where the corner of the closed door was gnawed away.

The night started out like a bad dream. The mattress was lumpy, the room damp, and the garbage smell overpowering. Toward morning, someone began to scream, and someone else began to laugh hysterically. The louder the screams rose, the louder was the laughter.

Roberts came dizzily awake to find the room faintly lit by a reflected glow from below, where powerful street lamps stood protected by big metal shields and heavy wire mesh. From the walls came a twang of metal as the rats wrestled with the tin shoved into their holes. From the door came a scrape that Roberts interpreted as a rat trying to move the can jammed between the door frame and the gnawed corner. Then the scrape came again, louder, and Roberts sat up. He reached out carefully, and closed his hand around the neck of a heavy bottle.

Wide-awake now, he could see that Hammell was out of bed, but he couldn't see where he was. Carefully, Roberts got up.

From the doorway, came a louder, longer scrape.

Slowly, the door swung open.

From the darkness of the next room, a stooped figure eased in, the faint light glinting on the edge of a broken bottle in its hand.

From behind the door came a brief glint of reflected light.

There was the rap of glass striking bone. The intruder dropped. There was a crash and the sound of splintering glass.

A long moment passed, and nothing else happened.

Hammell stepped out from behind the door, glanced toward Roberts, and waited a moment. The screams and laughter overhead rose to a peak, then died away.

Hammell said, "How much rest are we going to get in this place?"

"You're right." Roberts felt carefully along the floor. "Here, help me turn the mattress over on top of this broken glass. All we need is a cut foot."

They gathered their bundles of clothing, carefully checked to make sure they had everything, and eased out into the next room. Around them, there was the scurry of feet as rats went across the floor. Then they found the door, eased out into the pitch-black hall, and a low voice spoke, close to Roberts:

"You get their ears?"

Roberts shifted his bottle, landed a solid blow, heard something thump to the floor, and groped forward toward the steps. As he carefully felt his way forward, something ran across his foot. He eased onto the steps, and started down. The slow descent to street level seemed to take all eternity. Then they reached the lower hall, found the front door, and eased it open.

Outside, the street was brightly lit.

A roboid policeman, whip antenna up, rolled past with a silvery flash from its swiftly-turning wheels.

Roberts waited, then carefully pulled the door wider. The policeman was a dwindling speck in the distance. Roberts and Hammell slipped out, walked quickly down the block, and turned left, toward the west and open fields.

Up under one of the streetlights, a loudspeaker blared:

"Halt, thieves! You are detected on the central board! Mobile police units are already on the way. You cannot escape!"

"Run!" said Roberts.

From overhead, someone shouted happily, "Hunt! A hunt!"

Roberts and Hammell ran, hampered by the bundles they were carrying. Overhead, fresh loudspeakers blared. There was the sound of banging, shouting, and a concerted rush to the windows. Screams of "Hunt! *There they go!*" rang out. A bottle crashed into the street just behind. The next bottle hit to the right and in front, scattering broken glass over the street. "Thieves! Thieves! *Kill* them. Look out! *Here come the mechs!*" There was a pause, then a loud jeering, and a deafening rattle and smash further back.

Urgently, the loudspeakers boomed, "You must cooperate! Do not obstruct the law-enforcement officers!"

Straight ahead, the brightly-lighted street abruptly came to an end, a garbage-filled park on one side, and a high building on the other side. From this building, streaks of light flashed down, the reflections from hurtling bottles, as Roberts and Hammell sprinted past.

"Look out!" screamed someone overhead. "You're headed Out!"

Roberts and Hammell shot over an embankment in a headlong rush, heard a squeal of rats as they plunged knee-deep in a mass of garbage, then slammed forward on their bundles. As they pulled free, they glanced back, to see the police robots, bottles bursting and splintering in a dazzle of light from their metal tops and sides.

Roberts and Hammell stumbled across the dump, fell forward on soft earth, and looked back to see the robots spreading out along the edge of the embankment. But they didn't go down the steep bank, where they might overturn or mire down in the piles of garbage.

The loudspeakers blared, "You have left the City! Before you is only bare ground and the killer forest!"

The hail of bottles had let up. Voices shouted from the buildings, "You're Out! *You can't live out there!*"

"Come back!" shouted fresh voices.

"Return!" blared the loudspeakers. "Here you have Universal Care. Out there is only the Wild."

Roberts glanced at Hammell. "You hurt?"

"No. By some miracle, I didn't step on any glass."

"Neither did I. Let's get further away from this place."

By daybreak, the voices and lights had long since faded into the distance. In the gray light of dawn, they located the cache, changed to their own clothes, checked their guns, slung their packs, and headed toward the forest. At an irrigation ditch, they stopped to drink, refilled the canteens, and munched emergency-ration bars from their packs. Then they went on. Late that afternoon, the forest came into sight far ahead, barely visible across a flat field with endless rows of small, geometrically-spaced plants.

"Better stop here," said Roberts.

Hammell nodded. "We don't want to hit that forest at night."

Worn out, they lay down in the soft earth, to fall asleep at once, and wake early the next morning, stiff, chilled, miserable, and dumbfounded that the night had somehow passed already.

Today they had the forest to get through.

By noon, they found themselves looking across a wide dry ditch at the mingled trees and shrubs of the forest. The forest edge ran in an almost mathematically straight line, north and south.

"Now," said Roberts, "we can't just walk into that mess. We've got to find the cleared path we came out on. Is it to the north or south?"

Hammell looked around. "Why didn't we follow our own footprints back?"

Roberts glanced back. In the enormous field, the only irregular feature was their fresh footprints in the soft soil.

Roberts said, "There weren't any footprints near the cache. Whatever cultivates this field must have wiped out the prints." They turned back to the forest.

"Well," said Hammell, "Which way?"

Roberts looked around thoughtfully. "South."

"South it is."

For the next hour-and-a-half, they trudged south, and had just decided to go back north when, in the distance ahead, they saw the open end of the angling track through the forest.

Simultaneously, they saw, far away and straight ahead, a low cloud of dust. Out of this, there speedily resolved a low broad frame, straddling the rows at the edge of the field, with an angled wing thrust out into the wide ditch. The frame was rushing toward them at high speed, suspended above the earth on antigravs, with the low cloud of dust rising behind it.

Hastily they looked around, took half-a-dozen steps toward the center of the field, then saw another dust cloud coming fast behind the first one, and further back, still another cloud of dust.

They whirled, looked back.

Already, the frame loomed larger. It was coming fast.

Roberts plunged toward the broad, dry ditch, rushed across the bottom of it with Hammell close behind, and scrambled up the far bank. A roaring hiss was now audible, and growing louder fast. Breathing hard, Roberts forced himself up the last of the slope into a patch of brush at the forest edge. The brush gave way before them. An instant later, the cultivator roared past.

Wind swept over them, and they looked out through a whirling cloud of dust. "That was close!"

"Sure was. But—"

Suddenly, Roberts grabbed for his sheath knife.

All around them, the brush was unfolding large leathery leaves that swung up to blot out earth and sky. At a touch, the leaves wrapped themselves around Roberts and Hammell, and clung tighter with every movement.

Roberts barely had time to reach his knife. As the leaves wrapped around him, his arms were pinned to his sides down to the elbow. The clinging velvety surface drew snug across his face, tight against his nostrils, and shut out the air. Only from the waist down was he free. He turned, felt a stem draw tight like a stretched cord, reached out with his knife, and cut it. With his free lower left arm, he tore at the big leaf across his face. At once, fresh leaves wrapped snugly around his arm and chest, pinning his arm. He sucked in desperately, bit through the leaf as it pressed into his mouth, then dragged in a breath of air that stopped as abruptly as a slammed door when a new leaf wrapped around his face.

Roberts struggled to concentrate on that sharp knife held in his right hand. He turned slowly, cutting away each stalk as it grew taut. Carefully, he stayed in the same spot, lest he bring himself within reach of fresh leaves. Meanwhile, his need for breath was growing. Already, his chest was straining in a spasmodic effort to draw in air. He cut and turned, cut and turned, then strained desperately to free his left arm. The clinging leaves, slashed loose at the base, reluctantly pulled free, and for an instant, all he could do was drag in great gasps of air.

Hammell, working the same way, managed to free himself a moment later. The two men stood breathing deeply, then cut their way out through the few remaining leaves.

"That's the *eighth* time," said Hammell heavily, "that this planet has almost killed us."

Roberts looked around. "I know. I've had nightmares I liked better than this." Behind them, clouds of dust were blowing into the forest. Atop the bank, the thicket folded its leaves, and the stalks pulled together to give the appearance of a place only sparsely overgrown and easily crossed. As the last big leaves folded out of sight, the rib cage of a large animal came into view, white and smoothly polished, just a few short steps from the edge of the clearing.

Hammell grunted. "There, but for the Grace of—"

"Don't talk too soon. We've still got the forest to get through, and the ship to find."

"That's right."

They found the straight wide path cut by the insects, and holding their guns warily at the ready, they started into the forest. Stretching out in front of them was a patch of devastation that stretched as far as they could see. There was no blade of grass, no tiniest small plant in sight in front of them, but only an occasional tree, stripped leafless and bare. They walked through an eerie silence between clumps of vegetation to right and left, but nothing bothered them. Nothing came near, save a small mouselike creature that blundered onto the path, looked in both directions, gave a desperate squeak, and vanished back into the undergrowth with desperate kicks of its hind legs.

After a few hours, they found where the horde of insects had first poured into view. In another hour, they found the clearing, and near one side of the clearing, the wrecked tender. The large flattened metal spheroid on its three stubby legs looked like home. They shouted, and a tall lean individual with sandy hair and electric-blue eyes looked out. This was Morrissey, the communications man.

Morrissey beamed and waved as they ran over.

Roberts called, "How are Cassetti and the others?"

"Those technicians we got in touch with the first night dropped down in a grav-skimmer and picked them up. They've got doctors and medicines, and they think everything will be all right. But believe me, that bunch was all business. If we hadn't had anything to trade, it would have been no go."

"Could they offer any help getting anybody down from *Orion?*"

Morrissey's smile faded. "They said they didn't have the equipment. They said the City has the equipment, and they'll fight to the death before they go back to the City. What's wrong with the City?"

Roberts and Hammell described their experiences, and Morrissey shook his head in disgust. "Then, the brains to do the repairs are one side of this forest, the equipment is on the other side, and never the twain shall meet?"

"That's it," said Roberts exasperatedly.

"How do we get around that?"

"I don't know."

Morrissey shook his head. "In time, we'll have a ship full of corpses orbiting the planet."

Hammell said, "Even if we somehow fix the tender, and get everybody down here, *then* where are we? We never wanted to get marooned on this planet. The idea of coming here was just to get some repairs done."

Roberts nodded. "Maybe if we could talk to those technicians some more, we could work out something. Have you got the communicator working?"

Morrissey gave an odd laugh. "It's *working,* all right. But it doesn't *communicate.*"

Roberts frowned. "What *does* it do?"

"Come on inside," said Morrissey, "maybe you can settle a problem that's been bothering me. The question is, whether or not I've gone nuts."

The communicator's case had been removed, exposing the works, and Morrissey pointed out a timer unit between the set and the power supply.

"I put that timer in there when I started work. I wanted to check the hatches again, and be sure everything was secure before nightfall. I knew if I just started work, I'd forget everything else, so I set the timer to cut off the current and give a long loud ring."

Roberts and Hammell nodded.

Morrissey said, "I got working on this, and saw after a few minutes that it would be no great problem to fix it—just a matter of a few connections that had jarred loose when the set was knocked to the deck. I thought what a sloppy system it was to use these pluggable connections, instead of permanent connections that couldn't come loose. Then I thought that this *was* quick and convenient, though, and handy when you wanted to hook something up temporarily. Then it occurred to me I had plenty of time, and nothing to do, and for the first time in a long time I *could* just fool around if I wanted to. Well, I was visualizing the circuit, and the action of the different parts, and suddenly I wondered what would happen if I fed the current to an interface that's ordinarily left unconnected in this kind of circuit. I made a few adjustments, so I wouldn't wreck anything, and then I tried it. The next thing I knew, the timer went off."

Roberts and Hammell looked blank.

Morrissey paused.

Roberts said "What of it?"

"I'd fallen asleep. I figured I must have been more tired than I'd realized. I checked the ship, and came back, still curious about this circuit. I reset the timer, and switched on the set. The next thing I knew, the timer was going off again, and this time I was picking myself up off the deck. Again I'd fallen asleep. This began to seem peculiar. I checked the ship, came back, cut the current to the interface way down, set the timer for ten minutes and switched on the set. Right away, I wanted to go to sleep. I wanted the worst way to sink deep asleep, sound asleep—and then the timer was going off and I came awake again."

Hammell stared at the circuit.

Roberts frowned. "What did you do then?"

"I cut the current to the interface to the barest trickle. I reset the timer, snapped on the circuit—and yawned. I didn't exactly feel *tired*, but I wanted to go to sleep. I fought it off till the timer went off, then the feeling that I wanted to go to sleep faded away, and I just sat there in a cold sweat."

"And," said Roberts, "you're wondering whether it really happened or you imagined it?"

Morrissey nodded. "That's it."

"Let's try it."

Morrissey bent eagerly over the timer. There was the snap of a switch.

Roberts yawned.

Hammell put his hand to his head, swayed against the nearest bulkhead, massaged his eyes and forehead.

It came to Roberts that he had walked miles and miles today, and miles and miles yesterday, and no wonder he was tired. He was worn out. What he needed, what he wanted, was a long quiet sleep.

Hammell was already stretching out on the deck.

Morrissey was fighting off a yawn.

Roberts turned toward the tender's control room, and its soft comfortable pilot's chair. But it looked a long way away. He didn't want to go all that distance. He wanted sleep *now*, not after a long hike. He wanted to sleep long and deep, and he took a step toward the control room, and then felt the soft cozy deck drifting up toward him as he slipped off into warm sleep, and swirling darkness and sleep.

Something was shaking him violently.

Roberts dizzily opened his eyes. The swirling scene steadied. There was a big face looking down on him, that resolved into Morrissey's face, the electric-blue eyes worried.

"Sir, I'm sorry. I never realized it would hit you so hard."

Roberts remembered the circuit, and pulled himself to his feet.

"Don't blame yourself. Hammell and I were worn out." Roberts' head was throbbing where he'd banged the deck, but that was a minor matter. "You've got a new discovery here. This could be important."

Hammell was bent over the circuit, his expression awed.

Morrissey said, "If only this had happened some other time, instead of down here, with hardly any equipment to work with."

Roberts looked down at the circuit. "You were able to vary the *current* to the interface. Are there *other* circuit characteristics you can vary?"

"Sure. Until I had witnesses, I was afraid to try it. But let me just mark this, so I know roughly where I was—" Morrissey bent briefly over a variable condenser, straightened, said, "I'd better set the timer for a shorter interval, just in case." Then he twirled a knob, snapped on the set, and—

Roberts felt jolted. He looked at Morrissey angrily.

Morrissey glanced at Hammell, still bent over the set.

"Give me a little room, will you?" snapped Morrissey.

Hammell straightened up. "I'll give you all the room you want."

Roberts became aware of an intolerable lapse in discipline. He said shortly, "Drop it. Both of you."

"Sir," snarled Hammell, "this juice-jockey is trying to shove me around."

Morrissey's eyes flashed. "*'Juice jockey'?*" He cocked his fist.

Somewhere inside of Roberts, there seemed to be a little figure, jumping up and down, crying, "What's happening?"

Aloud, Roberts said with grating emphasis, "That's *enough!* Morrissey!"

Hammell eyed Morrissey's cocked fist. He clenched his own fists.

Roberts glared at them. He would like to smash them *both* in the teeth.

The timer went off.

Roberts' ill-temper evaporated.

Hammell and Morrissey stared at each other foolishly.

Morrissey lowered his fist.

Hammell suddenly laughed, and said, "What have we got here, anyway?"

Morrissey got out a small notebook, and began writing in it. "That's what *I'd* like to know. Let's try something else."

Excited now, and more than a little scared, they tried setting after setting, with the current low and the timer set for less than a minute.

For less than a minute, Roberts looked at Morrissey and Hammell, and despite a fierce struggle to control himself, he wanted to blow their brains out.

Then the timer went off. Morrissey whistled, and tried another setting.

Roberts realized suddenly that his life had been a failure. He wanted money. With enough money, what couldn't a man do? Stacks of crisp green bills seemed to float tauntingly before him. In his mind's eye, he could see piles of gold and platinum bars and soft leather bags of diamonds. He wanted *money*.

Morrissey changed the setting.

Roberts felt a desire for self-sacrifice. What, he asked himself dizzily, could be nobler? With a hard effort, he fought off the desire to offer himself to science for experimental purposes, then an urge to volunteer himself as a human bomb-carrier. Not out of hatred of the enemy. No, not that. Out of love for mankind. Out of—

Morrissey changed the setting.

Now Roberts felt the urgent desire to do right. What mattered most in life was the knowledge that he was doing right. He stood straighter. He asked himself, *Was* he doing right? Suppose—

Morrissey changed the setting.

In his mind's eye, Roberts saw a lovely woman in a closely clinging dress. He saw her move her long legs as she walked toward him, smiled sweetly, and lifted her arms—

Wham!

Morrissey, Hammell, and Roberts hit the switch at the same time.

Hammell grinned. Morrissey swore. Roberts said, "Well, Morrissey, *now* we know what you've got here."

"That's more than *I* can say. What is it?"

"It's a want-generator, that's what it is. A desire-stimulator. And if we can't get a stranglehold on this planet with it, and lever the population around so we can get that ship repaired, I'll be surprised."

Morrissey blinked. *"How?"*

"Why, what's the cause of the trouble? The people here are destructive, and they're disinterested in work. They hinder, not help. Right?"

"Right."

"Then all we have to do is get them to *want to create,* rather than destroy, and to *want to work,* right? And *here* we have a *want*-generator, that plays the range of human desires like the keys of a piano. Once we find the right settings, where's the problem?"

You're right," said Morrissey. "Here I've been complaining because we happened to find this when we're stuck in this miserable place. It never occurred to me this might get us *out* of here."

"It shouldn't be any great problem" said Roberts. "Let's keep trying till we get all the settings we need."

In the next few hours, they felt one desire succeed another in seemingly endless variety, and then abruptly Roberts was filled with the undiluted urge to achieve.

"That's it!" he said.

"You've hit it," Hammell agreed. "There's one setting."

Morrissey carefully noted it, and went on, until suddenly they had a sensation they'd had before, of eagerly wanting to do something, *make* something, create—

"That's it!"

Hammell nodded. "That gives us what we want. That is, what *they* should want."

"Now," said Roberts, "we've got to find out the range of this device, whether it can broadcast, or whether the set has to be physically present to work. We may have to make other sets—"

"If so, we're hung up," said Morrissey. "We don't have the spares here to make another of these."

"The technicians may have spares."

"Their having them and our getting them are two different things. I had to trade them two guns from the emergency kit, and a lot of ammunition to get them to look after Cassetti, Matthis, and Warner. They'll want something in return for spares, and they're hard bargainers."

Roberts looked at the set thoughtfully. "You don't suppose there's a 'desire to be cooperative and helpful' there, do you?"

"Hm-m-m," said Morrissey. "Let's see." He reached for the timer, and suddenly Roberts had a distinct urge to take poison.

Hammell swore. "That's not it."

Morrissey tried again.

A peculiar murky indefinable longing none of them had experienced before came across.

Morrissey said, "I hope we can find something better than that." He tried again, and again, until at last Roberts said, "Hold it!"

He had never felt more agreeable and obliging in his life.

Hammell sighed. "Right on the nose."

Morrissey noted the setting, then glanced at his watch.

"It's getting pretty late. We'd better check again to be sure everything's tight."

Once they checked the tender, Roberts and Hammell again realized how tired they were. While Morrissey eagerly went back to work, Roberts and Hammell went to sleep.

The next morning saw the start of a bout of painstaking experiment. Where the first work had gone smoothly the next steps were maddening.

"Damn it," said Morrissey, "it's just *impossible* to broadcast this signal, or aim it, or focus it. At this rate, we'll have to take the set into the city, and *hide* it there somewhere."

Roberts had another worry. "If we trade with those technicians, we've somehow got to block out our own reception of that generosity signal. Otherwise, we'll probably end up by giving them the set."

Another week crawled by, and then in desperation, they discovered that a supertranquilizer pill, several tins of which were in the emergency chest, not only stopped them from worrying how long the delay would last, but also solved the problem. It stopped them from feeling any perceptible want or desire, natural or induced, at all. Once they took the pill, they were as good as vegetables for the next four to six hours.

"O.K.," said Roberts. "Now, how are we going to work this?"

Morrissey said, "We'll take apart the want-generator, and make a communicator, then I'll tell the technicians we've got some extra guns, ammunition, protective suits, and so on, to trade. I'll ask for circuit components, and also some things we don't especially want, so we have a little leeway in trading. Before they get here, we'll make the circuit back into a want-generator. When they land, I'll take a pill, and turn the want-generator on them."

"We'll need to be very sure it's on the right setting," said Roberts.

Morrissey nodded. "Don't worry about that. I'd probably turn it on low, and then gradually step up the power, so they don't notice it. Meanwhile, you and Ham will have taken pills—"

Hammell objected, "The trouble with that is, we won't be able to react right. We're going to act like zombies."

Morrissey thought it over.

"When I set up the meeting, I can say we've been knocking ourselves out, can't think of any solution, and so on. They'll expect us to look depressed."

Roberts nodded. "That ought to help, anyway."

Hammell said, "What about when they leave?"

"Before that, I'll start to cut down the power. After they leave, I'll step it up again, so they don't come to their senses the minute they get out of the clearing. If we work it right, and try to make reasonably decent trades with them, they may never guess a thing."

Roberts nodded. "Just so *they* don't skin *us.*"

It was just a few days later that the technicians came, in two medium-sized skimmers. They were bearded, bristling with guns, and gave the impression of watching in every direction at once.

As soon as the skimmers dropped into the clearing, Roberts and Hammell each dutifully chewed up his pill. They'd scarcely swallowed the last gritty bits when a layer of glass seemed to slide down over the world. They could *see* through the glass, but nothing out there really meant anything, ever had meant anything, or probably ever would mean anything. So there was no point getting excited about nothing.

Tranquilized into two-legged vegetables, Roberts and Hammell trudged outside, while Morrissey bent at the set.

The technicians climbed out of their skimmers.

Roberts and Hammell shambled across the clearing. Morrissey dropped out the hatch, and drifted after them.

The technicians stared at them, looking bemused.

"Poor guys," said one.

"Yeah, you can sure see *they've* been clobbered."

"Remember what it was like for us last winter? It's hit them already." Roberts and Hammell listlessly raised a hand in greeting.

A burly giant with a bristling red beard, said, "Ah, fellows, we're all in the same boat. Do we have to *trade* with these poor guys?"

The rest of the men shifted their guns in embarrassment.

"After all," suggested a small wiry technician with a rifle in his hand, a knife on his belt, and a pistol butt protruding from under his armpit, "we're all human."

"Sure, why be greedy?"

Someone mumbled, with a catch in his voice. "They'll have trouble enough, anyway, no matter what *we* can do for them."

Roberts had the impression of looking out through a glass wall, and sensing invisible forces that beat powerfully on the other side.

A technician with a scar down the side of his face, and a tough, no-nonsense cast of countenance, suddenly shut his eyes. Tears ran streaming down his cheeks.

Roberts' brain sluggishly added up two and two. He reached back and shook Morrissey by the arm.

"Turn it down."

Morrissey nodded listlessly, and headed back for the tender.

The technicians were now choking, trembling and struggling to keep control of themselves. Roberts said nothing, because the technicians were clearly too choked up to talk.

Morrissey disappeared into the tender.

The red-bearded giant thrust his right hand out, palm up. He began, *"Anything* we can do—"

Roberts, through the dull placidity imposed by the supertranquilizer, sensed a sudden lessening of force outside the glass wall. Suddenly there was no force there at all.

The red-beard frowned. "Within *reason,* of course—"

Another of the technicians wiped his eyes with his sleeve. "After all, *we* have to live, too, you know."

Roberts glanced around.

Morrissey was just coming out of the tender.

The scarred technician said flatly, "Those that are fit to survive, *survive."* He eyed Roberts and Hammell. "Nature weeds out the incompetent."

By now, every eye amongst the technicians was drying fast.

"These supplies weren't easy to get," growled the red-bearded giant. *"If* you have something to trade, we'll be willing to *consider—"*

Morrissey paused, halfway out from the tender, with a strange expression on his face. Then he turned around, and plodded back again.

The small wiry technician shifted his gun around, and alertly watched Morrissey go back into the tender.

"What's *he* doing?"

Roberts struggled to get some kind of idea through the glass wall.

"He . . . he's got indigestion."

Hammell, with a look of painful effort, said carefully, "Can't keep anything down."

"Could be ten-day fever. Has he got spots on the backs of his hands?"

The air outside the glass wall seemed to suddenly thicken again, then get thicker yet by graduated stages.

Tranquilizer or no tranquilizer, it came through to Roberts that Morrissey was botching the job.

Tears were spurting out of the technicians' eyes. The short, wiry technician rushed forward and emotionally offered Roberts his gun. The giant red-beard, weeping uncontrollably, clasped Hammell like a brother. Before Roberts could figure out what to do, he found himself surrounded by piled-up supplies, with the technicians wringing their hands tearfully; and then, apparently unable to bear their emotion, they all piled into one of the skimmers.

"We'll be back! We'll bring you more axes, and seeds, and everything. Just tell us what you need! We really *want* to help!"

The skimmer shot up over the trees, and vanished.

Morrissey, watching at the personnel hatch, faded back inside. A moment later, the air seemed to thicken like glue. Roberts still felt no emotion, but he found it hard to think or move.

Hammell, carrying a gun in each hand, looked stuporously at Roberts.

"Wait till they get out of range—not that it matters, of course."

"Nothing matters."

"No."

Hammell dully picked up more of the supplies. "Probably we ought to take in everything we can carry."

Roberts took an armful, and followed Hammell. Just as they reached the hatch, the swirling thickness outside the glass wall let up.

Out beyond the clearing, there was an outburst of snarling, thrashing noises.

It occurred to Roberts that if the device affected the local animals, there could have been half-a-dozen predators out there, taking mercy on their prey.

But that was all meaningless. Roberts climbed in, set own his load beside Hammell's, then stood waiting, sunk in blank tranquility. Finally, they roused themselves long enough to go into the control room and sit down, torpid and stupefied, till the pills wore off. By that time, it was starting to grow dark outside, and Roberts and Hammell were asleep, unaware of the opening and shutting of the hatch, and the sound of a pair of feet traveling back and forth past them.

Early next morning, as the first glow of dawn began to light the portholes of the control room, Roberts came awake.

A blaze of light was pouring through the slightly opened door of the general-purpose room between the control room and the inner air lock to the cargo compartment. It was in that general-purpose room that Morrissey was working on the communicator.

Roberts, feeling almost fresh for a change, sat up, stretched, peered at the lighted doorway, and asked himself what Morrissey was doing.

Roberts got up, opened the door wide, and looked in.

A wooden frame, made apparently of odd scraps from the cargo compartment, met Roberts' gaze. On different levels of the frame sat a variety of electrical circuits, connected by loops of wire. Roberts could recognize three separate circuits that looked like the want-generator.

Morrissey straightened, bemused.

"Those technicians brought along a good selection."

Roberts looked at the frame. "What have we got here?"

"Why, I wondered if it would be possible to make two or three of these sets, and get them to reinforce each other. There were more than enough components out there, so I tried it, using very low power, and trying first one set, then two, then three together."

"What happened?"

"Well, with two, I seemed to get less than twice the effect, and with three, there was no effect at all."

"None at *all?*"

"No, it was the same as turning them all off. It occurred to me they might be interfering with each other. I tried gradually stepping up the power on one of the sets, and turning down the others. Nothing noticeable happened. I had them set to create desire for sleep, and I was sure I'd notice that. But nothing happened. While I was mulling this over, there was a buzz from the communicator. I snapped it on, and the voice of one of the technicians snarled, "What kind of gas did you use on our people?"

"I was stupefied," said Morrissey. "I didn't even realize what he was talking about. 'Why,' I said, 'What do you mean?'

" 'You know damned well what I mean.'

" 'No, I *don't.'" Then all of a sudden I did know.* I'd been so stupefied by the tranquilizer that I'd done a clumsy job, and they'd sensed it. But I kept my mouth shut, and he said angrily, " *'What did you use?'*

"I said, 'Can we help it if we've had so much trouble they were sorry for us?'

" 'Oh, they were, were they? Suppose *you* tell *me* these troubles, while I'm out of range of your gas or whatever it is. Go on. Let's hear it.'

"Well," said Morrissey, "that gave me a chill. If I couldn't convince him, there was no telling what might happen. And he didn't sound very easy to convince. I could only see one possible way out. It seemed to me that there *had* to be *some* effect from these three circuits. Certainly, they weren't doing anything here. Could they, then, be producing an effect somewhere else? It was worth a try. I started telling him all the trouble we'd had—and meanwhile I varied the current to the three linked sets, and listened for some response.

"I told him all about how the accident happened, how the gravitic field distorted and held the circuit breaker shut till a section of coil burned out and vaporized, and how the next distortions knocked half the storeroom, and the spare gravitor wire, out through the hull. Then I told him what a desolate part of space it happened in.

" 'Tough,' he said.

"It was obvious I hadn't got through yet. Next, I told him how we jury-rigged the main gravitor, using wire from the tender's gravitor. I told him about all the trouble we had, from then till we got to this planet. I told him how the gravitor had knocked out the ship's communicator, so we had to use the one in the tender, and we couldn't get any response with that. I told him how we rewound the tender's gravitor, came down, and, at the last minute, it malfunctioned, and we missed the spaceport and smashed down in the forest.

"About this time, he said it was too bad we hadn't just fallen into a sun and got it over with quick. I kept readjusting the circuit. I told how Cassetti risked his life to try and fix the tender's gravitor, and how Matthis and Warner tried to save Cassetti, and all three were all but hashed when we hit. I described the trouble we had when the gray cats tried to get us, and when the bats got in here, and the giant thing with the big head, long snout, and battering-ram tail. He said he was getting bored, and hurry it up. All the time, I kept varying the current. In my mind, I had a picture of the want-generator sweeping the surface of the planet, the field moving from place to place as I readjusted the controls. I had an idea how this might work, but was beginning to wonder if this wasn't just wishful thinking.

"Meanwhile, I was telling how you and Hammell trekked all the way to the City, and there wasn't a repair facility there any more. How you came back and the cultivator almost got you.

" 'And then,'" I said, 'they jumped out of the way of the cultivator, and a big patch of smother brush unfolded its leaves—'

"He interrupted. 'Shorten up this tiresome tale, will you? I couldn't care less if they fell into a gangbat nest.'

" 'Well,' I said, giving it up, 'that's about it, anyway. They stumbled out of there, came back to the ship along that path the swarm of bugs had made—"

" 'Say,' he said, 'that *is* too bad, isn't it? They had to come back on a bug trail, because there was no other way.'

"I couldn't figure out if this was sarcasm," said Morrissey, "or sympathy. I sat there holding my breath. I didn't dare change the setting.

" 'That *is* something,' he said, a funny catch in his voice. 'All that trouble, and now when they try to come back, they've got to come back *on a bug trail*. No wonder the guys wanted to help! Buddy, we're *all* people. We've got to stick together. Why, I'd give you the shirt right off my back, now I see what you've been through. *I never wanted to help anyone so much in my life.* If I can get away, I'll be out there tomorrow, early. I want to help. I'll—'

"He went on like this so it embarrassed me. I started juggling the current to the different circuits, trying to cut it down gradually all around without changing the relationship too much. I'd figured out that it was the *relative* power to the three circuits that probably changed the focus, while the higher the overall power, the greater the effect."

Roberts said eagerly, "Could you check that, too?"

"When I got it cut down far enough, he stopped babbling, and when I cut it down further yet, he finally just sounded sympathetic. I told him we'd gladly trade for the goods we'd gotten, and I said how grateful we were for their help and sympathy, and we'd cheerfully pay for the help, but he wouldn't even think of it. I was in a sweat by the time I got through talking to him."

"Then," said Roberts, "we can use the thing *from a distance.*"

"The only trouble is, we don't know what it's aimed at. We only know the right setting to hit the *technicians.* And once they should move, we'd lose them."

"Never mind that. They left one of their skimmers for us. Hammell and I can go up in it—one of us can keep a lookout for flying pests, and the other can guide it. It has its own communicator. We can go to different places, and you can try different settings. When we feel the effect, we'll say a few words to let you know where we are. When we have enough of the settings plotted on a rough map, we should start to understand how to set the device to aim it anywhere."

Morrissey beamed. "And *then* we can go to work on the city."

They spent the next few days making a map, and plotting the settings that induced wants when they hovered close to any given territory. The city, they charted at night, moving low over the darkened buildings, lit from below by the heavily shielded streetlights. Meanwhile, Morrissey developed a method for focusing the device more accurately, so as to concentrate the effect or spread it over a wide region. Then they decided that they were ready to go to work in earnest.

"You can see," said Roberts, studying the completed chart, "that we can hit any or all of the city with one exception. The computer itself is apparently unreachable."

"Stands to reason," said Hammell. "Desires are *emotional.* The closest thing that computer has to an emotion is its set of built-in directives."

"So," said Roberts, "we have to work through the *people,* not the computer. Now, the technicians left the City for exactly the same reasons that the computer has been driven to supplying only bare necessities. The people are destructive, and uncooperative. What we have to do is to correct that, right?"

"Right," said Hammell.

Morrissey took out a sheet of paper with a list of settings. He read: "Desire for achievement, desire to excel, desire to cooperate, desire to make friends, desire to learn, desire to work hard, desire to help others. Once we get started, that computer will have the easiest time it's had since it was made."

"Then," said Roberts, "it ought to be possible for the technicians to go back. And once we get the technicians back there, and the populace cooperating, *then* there should be no trouble getting the tools made to repair the ship."

"Q.E.D.," said Hammell cheerfully.

"When shall we start?" said Morrissey.

Roberts said briskly. "Right now. Why not set the want-generator on 'desire for achievement,' and give the whole city a good jolt for the rest of the day?"

Hammell nodded. "They certainly could use it."

"O.K.," said Morrissey. He set up "desire for achievement" on the generator, and snapped it on. "No use making a simple thing complicated. After we let them want to achieve for a while, then we'll hit them with 'desire to work hard,' and then 'desire to learn.' We'll have them snapped into line in short order."

Hammell grinned. "Do you suppose we'll notice much difference if we take the skimmer up late this afternoon, and look them over through the glasses?"

Morrissey nodded. "Should."

"I don't see why not," said Roberts. "They'll doubtless be out cleaning those streets. We might even see them carrying off parts of the dumps to get that out of town."

Morrissey said, "We might be able to see without even going up in the skimmer. Some of the components the technicians left look to me like they'll work the 3-V on the comset here. All I have to do is put them in, set up for one-way viewing so we don't get snooped by mistake, and—*Voila!*—we can pick up the City's own 3-V news broadcast."

Roberts nodded. "O.K. Set it up."

"Good as done," Morrissey said.

Roberts and Hammell spent the rest of the morning hunting from the skimmer, and came back with an animal like an antelope, and two smaller animals, like large wood-chucks. The afternoon, they spent strengthening the cargo section, and refitting its hatch. By now, the big cats had learned to be wary of the tender, and the rest of the daytime carnivores were in awe of the strange three-legged beast. But the nighttime animals appeared to be in awe of nothing.

While Roberts and Hammell worked on the tender, Morrissey, in the general-purpose room, could be heard whistling cheerfully.

"O.K.," said Roberts, when they had the big cargo hatch tight, and the sun was dropping toward the horizon, "want to take a look at the city?"

"Sure."

Roberts called cheerfully to Morrissey. "Want to come along? We're going to take a look from the skimmer."

"Go ahead. I've almost got the screen done."

Roberts and Hammell got their guns, climbed into the skimmer, and watched the clearing drop away below. The ground flashed past, forest giving way suddenly to neat rows of crops. Far off to the south, a dust cloud crawled across the ground, and they realized it was the cultivator coming north again.

"Good to be up here," said Hammell.

Roberts glanced around, to see no flying predators nearby. "It sure is." He pointed up, toward *Orion,* orbiting unseen far overhead. "And let's hope we're up there again pretty soon."

Just then, far ahead, the City rose up over the horizon, and seemed to flow swiftly toward them.

Eagerly, Roberts raised the high-powered glasses.

The City sprang closer, clouds of smoke pouring up near its center. Frowning, Roberts adjusted the magnification.

The scene visibly enlarged, and grew clearer as they rushed toward it.

In the streets, rioting mobs battled lines of roboid police.

Hammell said eagerly, "Have they accomplished much? Does the City look improved?"

Roberts swallowed.

Hammell said, "Let's see."

Speechless, Roberts handed over the glasses.

Hammell stared through them at the city. His mouth opened and shut.

Roberts swung the skimmer further north, toward the center of the upheaval.

Hammell handed back the glasses.

A second and closer look corrected Roberts' impressions. It wasn't a riot. It was a war. The police robots were being overturned, and smashed with sledge-hammers and lengths of pipe. The humans were steadily forcing their way into the center of the city.

If the roboid police were destroyed, there would be nothing to protect the computer. If the computer were destroyed, the ship would *never* be repaired.

"Hang on," said Roberts. He whipped the skimmer around and streaked for the forest.

Hammell said, "Did Morrissey set it up wrong?"

"I don't know. But God help us if that mob wrecks the computer."

The sun was sinking toward the horizon. To their left, a flying cloud of roughly hand-sized gangbats appeared, and turned with a flash of white teeth to intercept the skimmer. The skimmer pulled ahead, streaked along over the wide cleared lane through the forest, then Roberts located the clearing and dropped down beside the tender's cargo hatch. A few moments later, they were inside, pulled the skimmer in and locked the hatch.

In the personnel section of the tender, the communicator was turned up high.

". . . Now being driven back along the main avenues leading from Planetary Control. Again we urge all citizens to remain indoors and avoid joining in this disturbance.

Unnecessary loss of life can be avoided only if all law-abiding citizens remain in their assigned quarters . . ."

Roberts and Hammell climbed the ladder to the air lock, stepped in, pushed open the inner door, and found Morrissey in a glare of light, staring at something out of view from the door. Roberts stepped forward. By the communicator screen, a pair of whirling hypnotic spirals seemed to briefly catch his gaze, drawing one eye slightly to the right and the other to the left, till a scrambled chaos of light and shadow on the screen suddenly took on depth and sprang out into the room, and now Roberts was looking at a fleeing mob, their discarded weapons rolled over by police robots sweeping in rigid lines down the long straight avenues from the center of the city.

Morrissey said shakily, "That was *close*. If I'd been an hour later getting that 3-V fixed, I wouldn't have known what was going on till too late."

"What happened?" said Roberts. "They acted like they were set up to 'want to revolt.'"

"I checked that," said Morrissey. "What I had set up was 'desire for achievement,' all right. What we overlooked was, what *kind* of achievement? Suppose they think the greatest achievement would be to *overthrow the computer and the robots?*"

Hammell turned to Roberts, "Remember what they yelled when they threw the bottles at the maintenance robots? '*Kill the mechs!*'"

"Ye gods." Roberts glanced at Morrissey. "What did you do to stop them?"

"Set the want-generator for 'desire to give up,' and beamed it at them, full power. Naturally, the computer and the roboid police weren't affected, so in almost no time, they had things under control. I've been cutting down the power since then."

Hammell swore. "There goes *that* setting. We won't get much help from 'desire for achievement.'"

Roberts was frowning. "It's worse than that. It means we don't know how they'll react to *any* desire."

Morrissey nodded. "Look at this." He hit the "Replay" button, and a recorded view appeared, showing an apartment house door coming slowly open. A crafty individual with a knife eased out, carrying a cord, on which was strung about a dozen odd objects. As he peered around, something flicked into his neck from the side, he clawed at this throat, staggered to the sidewalk, and a moment later a second figure greedily took possession of the string, bent over the fallen figure to take it by one ear, pulled out a knife, briefly tested its edge with a thumb—"

Morrissey hit the "Replay" button.

Black smoke poured out of a building. A set of scurrying figures ran past carrying a torch, sprinted down the block, hurled the torch through a window, threw half-a-dozen bottles in after it, and dove into the gutter. A yellow flash and flame roared out the window, to climb high up the side of the building.

"Accomplishment," said Morrissey dryly. "Collect ears, burn buildings, smash the town to bits."

Roberts snapped the switch, to see what was happening now.

At once, a mob appeared, racing in full flight down a street where no roboid police were anywhere in sight. Screams of terror mingled with the blare of loudspeakers:

"Be calm! *You are in no danger!* No punishment is intended for those who took part in this disturbance!"

Someone screamed. "They're after us!"

The loudspeaker boomed. "Be calm!"

Someone screamed.

"HERE THEY COME!"

Roberts glanced at Morrissey. "Better turn that thing down."

"I've *already* got it turned down almost all the way."

On the screen, the mob was running so fast that anyone who hesitated was immediately trampled underfoot.

"The trouble," said Morrissey, "is that once they get going, they go faster and faster all by themselves. They build up a kind of inertia all on their own."

The communicator was saying, "This view is typical of the streets in a twenty-mile ring around the Planetary Control Center. All citizens are urged to remain indoors. Repeat, all citizens are urged—"

Roberts said, "We've got to stop it."

"What would you suggest?" asked Morrissey.

"How about 'desire to fight'? That ought to nullify the panic."

Hammell nodded. "They can't be scared and mad at the same time."

Morrissey didn't say anything, but glanced at a list of settings tacked on the want-generator frame, then bent over it carefully. He straightened and glanced at the screen.

The screaming mob rounded a corner and there was another terrified mob coming from the other direction. They fled headlong straight into each other, hit like two avalanches in collision, and were strewn all over street and sidewalks by the impact. They then suddenly looked furious, and sprang to their feet.

"Quick!" shouted Roberts. "Shut it off!"

"Done," said Morrissey.

On the screen, the mingled remnants of the two mobs waded into each other savagely.

"For—" Roberts looked on, speechless.

"It's *started*," said Morrissey, "so it *goes on by itself*. Each one of them saw someone else glaring at him. That was on account of our want-generator here. We turned that off. But already, they were swinging at each other. And the punches connected. Well, what would *you* do? Now they've got *real* reasons to be mad. You want me to set it up for 'desire to flee' again?"

"No. This is just one scene. For all we know, on other streets they're still fighting and running at the same time. Set it up for 'desire to sleep.' I don't see what harm *that* can do."

On the screen, the combatants gradually seemed to run down. They looked around, yawning.

"Quick! said Roberts. "Shut it off!"

"Off," said Morrissey. "I'm getting quick at turning this thing off."

Hammell said, "Why not leave it on. Get them quieted down, and—*Oh.*"

Fire was crawling forward up the block, and now burst out the windows fronting on the nearest street.

"I was afraid," said Roberts, "they'd get caught in the fire."

"This disgraceful riot," the communicator was saying, "has caused damage that may not be repaired for years. Your city administration, human and roboid, will attempt to rectify the situation as rapidly as possible. But any improvement will be contingent upon your cooperation. This upheaval has cast doubt upon many fundamental beliefs firmly held in the past, and in future it may be necessary for your administration to use stronger methods to maintain law and order. It is fervently hoped, however, that—"

"Shut it off," groaned Roberts.

Morrissey reached over and snapped the switch.

"Great space," said Hammell. "*All* we did was beam 'desire for achievement' at them for a few hours. How did all this mess come about?"

"Obviously," said Morrissey, "their idea of achievement just wasn't what we had in mind."

"Sure, but that isn't what I mean. Look, it was only a *little time.* A few hours, that's all. How did a full-fledged revolution get going *in that length of time?*"

Roberts shook his head. "What's the big problem in getting anything changed? Creating *desire* for the change. To get a reform pushed through, for instance, there has to be a lot of argument just to get people headed in the same direction. With *this* device, we may get through that stage in a few minutes."

"Only," said Morrissey, "we don't know what will happen till we've done it."

"The trouble," said Hammell, "is that they just aren't *educated.* If they were educated, they'd want exactly the same things *we* want. Let's set up 'desire to study.' We've got that, haven't we? *Sure* we have. I remember."

Dubiously, Morrissey said, "I don't know. It seems to me—"

"Yes, we *have,* I remember when we hit it. All at once, I got an urge to study circuits, memorize formulas—"

"Yes," said Morrissey, "I *know* we've got 'desire to study' on the list. *Sure* we can hit them with that. But then what? I've had enough of being sorcerer's apprentice for a while."

"What harm could it possibly do?"

"I don't know. But that doesn't prove it *won't* do harm."

"The trouble," said Roberts, "is that we just aren't used to this thing yet. We need more practice. This is like stepping out into space for the first time, when you've grown up on a planet. The thing is strange. But that doesn't mean you won't master it, with practice."

Morrissey looked slightly encouraged. "It *is* true that this is the first time we've used it."

"Sure," said Hammell. "We were bound to have trouble."

"But," said Roberts, "already we're getting used to it. We know, for instance, that the effect builds up a lot faster than we thought. And we also know that, once started, there's a sort of inertia—the thing tends to keep going by itself."

"Well," said Morrissey, "when you put it that way—maybe things aren't as bad as they looked. But I think we'd better lay off for a while, anyhow. I'm about done in."

Roberts nodded. "They're about done in in that city, too."

"But *tomorrow*," said Hammell, "we can start educating them."

Early the next morning, they tuned in the city. The scene on the 3-V looked exactly like what it was—the morning after a small war. Roboid fire-fighting equipment battled fires in buildings and smoldering dumps, while first-aid crews shunted riot victims into big many-wheeled ambulances that rolled away with a dozen patients at a time. Whole buildings, and long stretches of street and park, were like mountains of white foam, but more fires still burned, and the prostrate forms in the streets plainly numbered in the hundreds, if not thousands.

"Whew," said Morrissey, glancing from the 3-V to the want-generator. "I don't know. I'm almost afraid to touch this thing."

"Don't worry about that," said Hammell, "a little education will straighten everything out."

"How do we know they can get anything to study? Does the place have a library?"

"It's bound to," said Hammell. "Come on. Let's get on with it."

With visible reluctance, Morrissey turned to the want-generator. Then he shrugged, glanced at the list of settings, and got to work.

Hammell glanced at Roberts. "I wish they'd had something like this when *I* was in school."

Roberts nodded absently. He was starting to have doubts about this approach. "How long is this going to take? Education is great, but it's kind of a long-range proposition. We want to get off this planet some time in the foreseeable future."

"Well," said Hammell, "we worked up a small war in less than a day."

Morrissey straightened. "There we are. Now, what do we do? Shall we all watch it at once, or should we set up a system of watches?"

Hammell shrugged. "Why not let it work for an hour or so? 'A watched pot never boils.'"

"No," said Morrissey. "It doesn't boil *over*, either."

Roberts said, "I don't see how it could do any *quick* damage. Suppose Hammell and I work for a while on the game we caught yesterday? If you want, you can keep watch on the 3-V."

Morrissey nodded. "What happened yesterday makes me uneasy."

"Nothing bad," said Hammell positively, "can possibly come out of education."

Morrissey visibly readied a sharp reply.

Roberts poured oil on the waters. "Probably nothing will happen, but there's no harm being on the safe side. Let's go see if anything got in last night."

Hammell nodded, and went along with Roberts into the cargo compartment.

"Well," he said, "we should have fresh meat pretty soon. Nothing got in here last night."

They examined the game they'd caught the previous day, bled, gutted, and then hung up till they had time to skin it. Then they got out their knives.

An hour later, their knives were blunted, and their hands sore.

Hammell growled, "It couldn't be harder if it were frozen."

The stiff skin, held to the meat by tough membranes, gave way an inch at a time.

"*Whew*," said Roberts. "No wonder those technicians seemed so ugly. Probably everything they've got only came after a struggle."

Hammell nodded. "Or maybe they got that way from *eating the meat*."

"That's a thought." Roberts eyed the animal with calculating gaze. "We've got to figure it out somehow. Those emergency rations were meant for a whole crew, but they won't last forever."

"Yeah. Well, if we keep at it—"

From the other end of the tender came Morrissey's voice. "Ah, for the love of . . . Well, GREAT HOLY LEAPING . . ."

Without a word, Roberts and Hammell jumped up, and headed at a run for Morrissey and the 3-V set.

"Just listen to this," said Morrissey.

" . . . will be done," the communicator was saying, "in order to supply suitable study materials. We repeat, however, that books, films, spools, and exhibits on such subjects as shoplifting, explosives, safe-cracking, mental-suggestion, seduction, death rays, hypnotism, aphrodisiacs, sabotage, secret jujitsu blows, and undetectable murder methods are forbidden under a law which has just been enacted. However, if anyone wishes to learn about anything else, the necessary materials will be provided, following due and careful consideration of the request."

Hammell sagged against the bulkhead.

Roberts shook his head. *"Another* zero."

Morrissey had an odd smile on his face. "What next?"

"First," said Roberts, "we don't get discouraged. We've got to keep trying—"

"Sure," said Morrissey. "If once you don't succeed, try, try again. If twice you don't succeed, try, try again. If three times you don't succeed—"

Roberts said, "What do you say I take the next turn at this?"

"Anything so I don't have to watch any more of it. What are you going to try?"

Hammell said uneasily, "I know the last one didn't turn out, but I've got another idea."

Morrissey smiled. "Sure."

Hammell thrust out his chin.

Roberts said, "Try it. If we're going to get out of here, we've got to get *some* kind of improvement started. Just watch it."

"I'll watch it," said Hammell grimly. "You go ahead."

Morrissey said, "It's all yours. I'm going on vacation, starting now."

"Bring your knife with you," said Roberts. "I hope it's sharp."

⚜   ⚜   ⚜

Roberts and Morrissey had been wrestling with the local variety of antelope for the better part of two hours, when a stream of incredible profanity burst out on them from the other section of the ship. They sprinted for the air lock.

" . . . Miserable, brainless, incorrigible *cretins*," Hammell was snarling. He glanced around at Roberts. *"Look at this.* I set up 'desire to work.'"

Standing out from the screen, in realistic three-dimensional solidity, was a small crowd with hammers, pipes, and crowbars. As they moved back, it was possible to see that they were crowded around a half-disassembled police robot. Proudly, they took out gears, shafts, and small electric motors, and divided them up amongst themselves.

" . . . sort of activity," the communicator was saying, "will not be tolerated, nor will further removal of paving blocks, doors and window frames, or lengths of gas or water line. Your law-enforcement agency orders you to cease and desist from further demolition, remodeling, and private unauthorized construction. Strict penalties will be imposed . . ."

"That does it," said Hammell.

"Well," said Roberts, "we've only started—"

"O.K., *you* try it." Hammell went out the air lock. Morrissey lost no time following him.

Roberts found himself alone, eyeing first the want-generator, and then the sight of a weird structure, built of torn-up paving blocks, that was rising in the middle of a street, blocking the two center lanes.

"Whew," said Roberts. He went out into the control room, sat down in the control seat, tilted it back, and just let his mind drift. A few ideas came into his field of consciousness. How about 'desire to do right'? But that depended on what anyone thought was right. How about 'desire for progress'? Roberts didn't think he and Morrissey and Hammell had hit on that setting yet, but even if they did, what would that produce? Whose *idea* of progress? How about 'desire for religion'? His mind presented him with a picture of devotees hurling babies into the flaming idol.

Roberts groaned, lost the thread of his thoughts, fell into a kind of stupefied daze, and emerged thinking, "Obviously, one man can't figure this out. It will take *everyone* to do it."

He woke up abruptly to ask himself what this meant.

Then suddenly he sat up. He swung his legs over the edge of the tilted control seat, and balanced there, hanging tight to the idea.

Everyone has got to do it.

Do what?

Figure it out.

How can that be?

Everyone will have to want to think.

Without *wanting* to, they won't do it, and every other desire will lead to a mess.

Roberts got up, frowning, and walked out to look at the list tacked by the want-generator. Halfway down was the notation: "Desire to meditate, consider, think things through."

From the other part of the ship, he could hear heavy breathing as Hammell and Morrissey wrestled with the tough hide.

Roberts looked at the notation again, then studied the linked want-generators. Carefully, he disconnected one from the others, adjusted it to the proper setting, and turned it on, using low power.

At once, he had a strong insistent desire to think things over. What did life mean? Did what he was doing make sense? How—

Roberts carefully cut the power further.

"Hey," came Morrissey's voice. "What are we using *knives* for?"

"Agh!" said Hammell. "How could we be so stupid? What we need for this beast are hatchets. Wait a minute."

There were rapid footsteps, then a moment later, there was a *whack* and a grunt. "Ah, that's better. *Now* we've got a chance."

Roberts connected the want-generator back into the larger circuit, and considered it carefully.

What *was* the chief difference between men, anyway, except that some men thought more and deeper than others, and put the thoughts into action?

Carefully, Roberts adjusted the want-generator.

One hand on the switch, he asked himself, "Is 'desire to think' the cure-all? Anyway, it's one of the ingredients, and probably the one that's missing. They've got plenty of experience. But is it all such one-sided experience that they'll end up with the *wrong conclusions?* Then what?"

Exasperated, Roberts paused to set the power lower yet, and threw the switch.

Then he went out into the air lock, and called Morrissey.

Morrissey came over, entered the hatch, and followed Roberts through the air lock, to hastily glance at the 3-V. Nothing was visible save a few people wandering around with looks of vague disquiet, as if they had just remembered that they wanted to do something, but what was it?

Morrissey looked at the want-generator to see if it was on, blinked in surprise, and studied the setting.

" 'Desire to meditate, consider, think things through.' Why didn't I think of that?"

Roberts shook his head. "It won't work. Count on it. It looked great a minute ago. But it's not enough."

"At least, they aren't tearing the place to pieces."

"No, but we've got to work in some other wants and desires, or they aren't going to accomplish anything, either. Let's let 'desire to think' run for a while, then very carefully we can switch to another signal, maybe 'desire to improve,' and see what happens. If some kind of mess starts up, we can go back to 'desire to think' again."

Morrissey began to look excited. "That might work, at that."

"O.K., let's give them a vacation for a few hours, then start hitting them with 'desire for sleep.' They'll be in better shape to think straight tomorrow if they get plenty of sleep tonight."

"Good idea. Swell, we'll do that."

That night, the roboid police patrolled in vain. Not one crime was committed, anywhere in the city. All the humans were asleep.

The next morning, around 6:15, the people of the city began to wake up. Everything went along normally until around 9:00 a.m., when an insistent urge to think things over began to seize hold of them. The roboid police were now unemployed till noon, when the inhabitants stopped frowning in thought long enough to eat. Activity picked up to normal until 1:00 in the afternoon, when gradually everyone began feeling a progressively stronger urge to think

things over. This went on until 5:00 p.m., when the populace gradually began to lose interest, stretched, and felt a
desire for physical exercise. The roboid police, who had
wheeled vainly up and down the long empty streets all
afternoon, now suddenly got their whole day's workout in
twenty minutes. The populace chose to take their exercise
by bombarding the police with bottles, trash, and broken-
up chunks of paving. When the furious twenty minutes came
to an end, at precisely 5:20, the populace started to lose
interest, and drifted back into the buildings, where they
thought things over until around six-thirty. Then they began
to want something to eat and things came back to comparative normal until around 9:00 p.m. when everyone began
to yawn. By 9:30 the human part of the city was asleep.

All that night, the roboid police had nothing to do but
travel up and down the empty streets.

"Now," said Hammell, "this is more like it."

Morrissey beamed. "We're starting to get the hang of this
thing."

Roberts, conscious of having originated the idea, modestly
said nothing.

The next day went along the same way, until 6:00 p.m.,
when Roberts shut down operations till 9:00.

"It's working," said Hammell. "You can see an improvement in their appearance."

"That sleep helps," said Morrissey.

"Not only that, they *look* thoughtful."

"What we're doing ought to really uplift this place,"
Morrissey agreed.

Roberts basked, and remained silent.

There was a jarring buzz from the communicator.

Morrissey sat up. "Who might *that* be?"

"Probably the technicians," said Hammell.

"Leave the visual transmission off," said Roberts, sitting
up. Morrissey nodded. "How about visual *reception?*"

"O.K. by me."

Morrissey snapped on the communicator.

The three-dimensional image of Kelty, assistant-chief of
the City's law-enforcement department sprang into view. Kelty
looked exhausted.

"O.K., you win, Roberts."

Roberts looked blank.

"*Roberts,*" said Kelty. "Do you hear me?"

"I hear you."

"I'm throwing in the sponge. You'll have your repairs as soon as we can get the shop set up."

"You said that couldn't be done."

"The events of the last few days have given the computer some new data to work on. That uprising came within a hairbreadth of success. The computer now knows it can be destroyed. One of the computer's built-in directives is that it safeguard itself, so long as the resulting actions aren't inimical to the long-term welfare of the populace. That directive is now brought into operation."

"I see. But why call me?"

"I've been thinking things over for the last couple of days. Believe me, I haven't thought as much in most years as I've thought in the last couple days. The thing is perfectly obvious. First, there's the worst upheaval we've ever had on this planet. Following this, we have the most fantastic set of exasperating petty-sabotage operations, in turn followed by utter silence. Then, there is one concentrated burst of violence, followed again by silence. We have this two days in a row."

On the 3-V, Kelty shook his head. "By no stretch of the imagination could a thing like this come about by *accident.* This is a demonstration of control that stuns the mind. Control by whom? The most searching investigation, using surveillance devices all over the City, reveals not the slightest evidence of how it's done. So we're blocked there. But who *could* provide the leadership for a thing like this? Only the technicians, or complete outsiders. I happen to know that the technicians are in no position to do it. With them, in that wilderness, it's touch-and-go.

"Now then," said Kelty, "where does this leave us? We have the following events: You and your cargo-control officer present yourselves to the City government, requesting repairs. You are refused. A couple weeks go by, and someone masterminds an attack that all but destroys the entity that refused you help. Following this, there is a demonstration that someone is exercising nearly absolute control over the populace. All I can say is, I'm sorry I was so slow to catch on. I've put the problem to the computer in the light of these facts, and it is prepared to rebuild the Class II repair facility at once, especially if you'll hold down the destructiveness of the populace until the work is done."

Roberts waited until he was reasonably sure he had control of his voice. "Kelty, you understand that I don't admit interfering in the internal affairs of this planet?"

Kelty nodded glumly.

"However," said Roberts, "from what you've told me, and from what we've seen watching the 3-V, it does seem that this destructiveness you speak of ought to die down for long enough to get the repair facility completed."

Kelty sighed in relief. "Consider it done. Listen, Roberts—"

"Yes?"

"I don't know who you *really* are, or what are your intentions. With such power as you've demonstrated, obviously you're far more than the captain of a cargo ship. I don't ask you to admit that. All I say is this: If you decide to fit this planet into your plans, just *tell me what you want done.* Is that all right, Roberts?"

"I hear you," said Roberts, fighting to keep his voice even.

"That's all I ask," said Kelty. "I'm sorry it took me so long to catch on."

The three-dimensional image faded out.

Roberts turned off the communicator.

Morrissey said, in a surprised voice, "That's it. That's what we've been trying for."

Hammell said hesitantly, "You know, he's right. With this device, we could exercise enormous power." He paused. "But, of course, we wouldn't want to."

"Of course not," said Roberts, scowling.

"It would be selfish," said Morrissey.

They dropped the subject, but it hung in the air afterward.

The days till now, having been filled with trouble and danger, had crept past a minute at a time. The following days, filled with success, went by in a flash. Suddenly the repair facility was done, the special tools made, the repairs finished, and the three injured men were on their way back to the tender. Roberts, Hammell, and Morrissey disassembled the want-generator, and stood watching the city on the 3-V.

"Well," said Hammell, "believe me, we *earned* those repairs."

On the screen, the people had changed in a way that was hard to pin down, but that came across as a marked increase in self-respect and self-reliance.

Morrissey said exasperatedly, "The planet's still a mess, though. Look there."

A group of youths stalked past, four abreast, wearing armbands marked with triple thunderbolts. They were neat, trim, and confident; the rest of the citizens hastened to get off the sidewalk as they approached.

A roboid policeman cruised by, plainly uncertain just what to do about this phenomenon.

"Somewhere," said Morrissey, "there must be someone in that city who did a lot of thinking—about just how much power he could get, with the right organization."

Hammell nodded. "Kelty's going to have a great time when that outfit gets going."

Roberts was frowning at the screen. He could sense what was coming. Morrissey and Hammell both had a feeling of dissatisfaction. The job wasn't done yet.

Hammell said, "We've all got accumulated leave coming. I was wondering—"

Morrissey was frowning at the screen. "That's a thought. We ought to be able to *finish* this."

Hammell and Morrissey glanced questioningly at Roberts. Something told Roberts that they were not asking his opinion as to *whether* they should come back. They were asking if *he* wanted to come back with them.

Kelty's last comment occurred to Roberts. Kelty thought some gigantic cosmic plan was afoot. But Roberts and the others had merely been driven here by bad luck, and the want-generator was just a device they found handy to help them get away.

Roberts paused, as his memory played back this last thought, and then his perspective shifted.

The steam engine was once just a device that people found handy to pump water out of mines.

The airplane had been only a device that could hold a man off the ground for fifty-nine seconds, and in the process carry him not quite three hundred yards.

The spaceship was once just a device that could lift an experimental animal into orbit for a few days.

It was merely that kind of device that the three of them had stumbled on.

Why get excited about a thing like that?

Roberts was dizzy with a sudden vision that flashed into his mind, and as suddenly was gone. Morrissey and Hammell were still looking at him questioningly.

Roberts waited a moment, to be sure his voice would be natural.

Then he cleared his throat.

"O.K.," he said.

THE DUKES OF DESIRE

Vaughan Roberts glanced from the viewscreen to the landing display, and dropped the salvaged Interstellar Patrol ship into the clearing, between a gnarled tree with thorns as big as a man's forearm, and a battered space yacht whose big hatch was just swinging open.

Roberts pushed forward a toggle-switch on the left side of the control panel, and with a faint whir the stabilizer feet telescoped out, to steady the ship on its smoothly-curved underside. Roberts switched off the gravitors and unbuckled his safety harness, then slipped out of the control seat, ducked under the long shiny cylinder that ran the length of the ship, and went up several steps in the cramped aft section, to release the clamp on the small outer hatch. He spun the lockwheel counterclockwise, pulled the hatch-lever down and slammed it forward, and the hatch swung up and back. A shaft of sunlight shone in, casting shadows of large sharp thorns partly hidden by leaves.

Roberts looked warily all around, loosened his fusion gun in its holster, and pulled himself out the hatch. He sucked in a breath of fresh planetary air, glanced around at the rustling leaves and gently blowing grass, looked up at a white puffy cloud drifting across the clear blue sky, and abruptly snapped his gun out of its holster as brush moved in a rippling motion at the edge of the clearing.

A thing much bigger than a tiger, mottled gray in color, silently blurred out of the brush to bound straight for Roberts, forepaws outstretched.

Roberts fired, fired again, jumped down the hatchway, grabbed the lever and heaved.

Clang! The hatch slammed shut.

WHOOM! There was a noise like an enormous gas burner, gone almost as soon as it began. The ship quivered. Then there was a thud somewhere aft.

Roberts crouched in the cramped space under the hatch, gripping the fusion gun, and listened intently. He heard nothing more. Very cautiously, he opened the hatch.

In the slit of sunlight revealed, he could see, farther aft, the number two reaction-drive nozzle slowly settle back into position. A wisp of smoke was rising from a small gun turret a few feet from the hatch. A long shiny metal stalk, not quite as thick as a man's wrist, arced out from another turret forward, extruded a set of metal fingers, picked up a riddled and smoldering furry head and dropped it over the side. Roberts looked around, but if the rest of the body was anywhere nearby, he couldn't see it.

He thought a moment, went back and put on a bulky suit of battle armor, and decided to try again.

He shoved open the hatch, and climbed out to look at the ship. Wherever he turned, guns bristled. Small turrets, meant for short-range defense, dotted the smooth armored surface. Amidships, a movable belt of fusion turrets faced aft, so that he was looking down their muzzles. Further forward, two large turrets, one behind and above the other, mounted fusion cannon big enough for a man to put his arm into. The sight of all these gun turrets, and of the snap-beam transceptor head steadily rotating atop its mast, gave Roberts a warm pleasant sensation, far different from what he'd felt the last time he'd been on this planet.

From above, where to one side the big hatch of the battered space yacht was now wide open, a rough masculine voice called down.

"The place hasn't changed much, has it?"

Roberts looked up, to see a strongly built figure, somewhat foreshortened by his angle of vision, grinning down at him. This was Hammell, who'd been stranded here with him the last time.

"No," said Roberts, automatically glancing around the clearing, and taking a quick look overhead. "Not out here, at least. Where's Morrissey?"

"Up above. He just got through setting up the gear. Come on up, if you can stand to leave that flying fort of yours."

Roberts grunted, took another quick look around, studied the ground below the curve of the patrol-ship's hull, walked aft along one of the horizontal fins, and dropped off. The moment he was clear of the ship, there was a clang, and Roberts turned to see that the patrol-ship's hatch had shut.

From overhead, Hammell laughed, and called, "You've got that thing trained."

Roberts gave a second grunt, but no reply. The patrol ship was a sore point between them. Marooned on the planet earlier because of gravitor trouble, the three men had promised themselves to come back under better conditions, bringing with them an improved version of the device that had made their escape possible. One of the little details they hadn't settled beforehand was what they would come back in. Hammell and Morrissey wanted something roomy, comfortable—if possible luxurious. Roberts wanted plenty of firepower, and as much armor between himself and the planet as possible. Hammell and Morrissey duly selected a large roomy yacht with a solitary energy-cannon mounted in the bow, but otherwise equipped like a luxury hotel. Roberts selected the much smaller patrol ship, cramped and functional perhaps, but armed to the teeth, and fitted with a powerful drive-unit. Neither side had compromised, and the argument was still going on.

Roberts, climbing the ladderlike recessed holds up to the space yacht's big hatch, reminded himself that he, Hammell, and Morrissey were all equals in rank for the duration of their leave. At work, Roberts was captain of the fast interstellar transport *Orion*, Hammell was cargo-control officer, and Morrissey was communications officer. Possibly for this reason, there was a little extra friction now and then. Roberts was determined not to add to it if he could help it. But he didn't intend to lean over backwards so far that he fell on his head, either.

He reached the top of the ladder, and Hammell reached down to help him up.

"It would be better if we were all in the same ship," said Hammell. "You wouldn't have to go around looking like a gorilla in an iron suit every time we have to get together. It would be a *lot* more convenient."

"You take the convenience," said Roberts, "and I'll take the guns. Where's Morrissey?"

"Up on the sixth level."

Roberts thought a moment, and remembered that on the yacht, which set down upright on its tail, the horizontal levels started with the drive-unit and storage compartment at the base, below where they now stood. The sixth level would be the control room.

"Wouldn't there be more room down one level?"

Hammell nodded. "That's where he's got the spy screen set up. But right now I think he's back up in the control room checking the communicator again."

"Good," said Roberts. "We can get an idea whether things have changed much."

Hammell touched a button beside the hatch, and the hatch swung silently shut. He and Roberts walked towards a softly-glowing oval on the deck. The right half of this oval was green, and the left half red. Roberts stepped carefully on the green, and at once the walls of the ship dropped downward, and with a soft murmur an oval section of the next level overhead slid back. One-by-one, the levels dropped past, disclosing entrances to a succession of medium-sized rooms with curving walls, designed for entertainment, eating, sleeping, and then they passed the level where Morrissey had set up the equipment, and reached the control room, which seemed comparatively small because of the inward-curving sides near the nose of the ship. Roberts caught a polished silvery bar, and stepped out of the lift. He nodded to the lean sandy-haired individual who glanced up with worried electric-blue eyes from the communicator.

"Hello, Morrissey," said Roberts.

Morrissey blinked in momentary alarm at the battle armor.

"Sir," he said automatically, then added. "Something's changed since we were here before."

"What?"

"The screen no longer gives continuous news broadcasts from the city."

"That doesn't sound good."

"It sure doesn't. So we can see what's happening, I've

let go the spy-system pickups, set to tap into the city's surveillance network. I hope *that* works."

"Yes," said Roberts, remembering that this had been Morrissey's big worry. "When will we find out?"

"If nothing's wrong, we ought to be able to pick up the relayed signals any time now. I came back up here because I didn't want to sit down below chewing my nails."

"Let's go take a look now. If we can't get that spy screen to work, we're in a mess right at the beginning."

They dropped down to the next lower level, to see with relief that the big spy screen, though still unfocused, was already lit up. As Morrissey and Hammell dragged over some chairs, Roberts climbed out of the battle armor.

They sat down in the three chairs, in front of the wide improvised control panel, and Roberts, in the center, adjusted the focus of the spy screen. At once, he had a sharply-detailed view of a potholed street strewn with trash. To the left was a large building with the windows knocked out. To the right was a park where rats scurried amidst the leafless dead trees and smoldering heaps of garbage. Straight ahead, in the center of the street, two small boys stood menacingly with short lengths of iron pipe, their legs wide apart, their clothes ragged and dirty save for armbands marked with triple lightning-bolt insignia. Just rolling onto the screen were a pair of roboid policemen, their whip antennas swaying, the sunlight flashing on the spokes of their high bicycle-type wheels.

Morrissey, to Roberts' right, gave a surprised grunt.

Roberts said, "If this is typical, no wonder they aren't broadcasting."

Hammell nodded. "There's nothing like disorder and violence to get people worked up. And there's nothing like having people worked up to bring on disorder and violence."

"And this is just the spot for it," said Roberts. He was thinking of the gigantic slum-city, built by a beneficent foundation, and peopled from the slums of half-a-dozen older worlds. But it struck him suddenly that it applied to the whole planet as well.

He glanced out one of the space yacht's portholes at the small bristling Interstellar Patrol ship below. Roberts had located the patrol ship in a salvage cluster, and the salvage

operator had been only too happy to trade it for most of
Roberts' accumulated savings. There were quite a number
of special devices on the patrol ship, any one of which was
worth far more than the purchase price. But this didn't affect
the salvage operator's delight in getting rid of the ship.

In the first place, his sharpest tools and hottest torches
wouldn't cut the patrol ship's armor. In the second place,
the patrol ship's large and numerous weapons were controlled by a combat computer, which came on automatically whenever anyone tried anything that promised to blast
off a chunk of high-grade metal. In the third place, worst
of all, the ship was partially controlled by what was sometimes called a "symbiotic computer." This computer had
apparently existed in a special relationship with the former
crewmen, and now it passed judgment on prospective
purchasers, applying roughly the same standards that were
necessary to enlist in the Interstellar Patrol. If the prospective purchaser wasn't up to par—mentally, physically, or
morally—the computer disdained him. As a result, nothing on the ship would work for him.

Roberts had barely squeezed by the computer's forbidding
scrutiny. But that was all he needed to do. The ship flew
for him. Roberts soon found himself with a ship equipped
with an armament fit to dent a planet. The salvage operator, for his part, relievedly blew a kiss after the dwindling
speck in the distance, and resolved never again to touch
anything like that unless he had a private dreadnought to
break it up with.

Now, on the planet, Roberts looked out with pleasure at
the ship, but at the same time got a view of the trees that
surrounded the clearing. Just what was hidden back in those
trees, perhaps only fifty feet from the clearing, would have
been hard to say. But the space yacht, while coming down
to land, had run into some kind of monster with the bad
judgment to jump up and take a snap at one of the big
fins that would steady the yacht as it stood on its tail. The
fin, with the weight of the yacht behind it, crushed the
animal. The smell of blood having already apparently spread
the promise of a free meal, Roberts could see that other
creatures were now prospecting around. There was a flap
of big wings overhead, and the rustle of leaves at the edge
of the clearing. Just what would pop out was hard to say,

but Roberts took a quick glance at his suit of battle armor, fixing its location in mind so he could get into it with no wasted time if he had to. Then he reluctantly placed his trust in the space yacht's energy-cannon, and turned back to the spy screen.

Hammell was leaning forward tensely, "Something's getting ready to blow in that city. Otherwise the police just wouldn't be this heavily reinforced."

On the screen, two more roboid policemen had swung into view behind the first pair, and these were followed in turn by a flying wedge of roboid police.

Straight ahead, the two boys in the middle of the street stayed where they were and jeered.

Roberts glanced at the locator screen in front of Morrissey. This screen was marked off in city blocks, like a big elongated chessboard with oval edges. A strip of street, running through an intersection and about a fourth of a block farther in both directions, was lit up whitely, showing the section now in view on the spy screen.

As Roberts glanced from one screen to the other, suddenly the two boys snapped their arms forward, the lengths of pipe arced out to slam into the roboid police, and twin flashes of dazzling light outlined a tangle of ripped and torn metal housings, shredded insulation, bent tubing, and bare gears, shafts, and axles. The first pair of roboid police smashed to a stop.

The two boys were already sprinting toward opposite sides of the street.

The second pair of roboid police rolled unswervingly past the wreckage of the first.

Roberts, Hammell, and Morrissey stared at the screen, their expressions perfectly blank.

From behind a heap of garbage at the edge of the park, two more boys raced out, clutching short lengths of pipe.

As Morrissey snapped a switch, twin speakers to either side of the spy screen came on, relaying sounds from the scene. An amplified voice spoke out:

"Clear the street. This warning will not be repeated. Clear the street. Further violence against your Law-Enforcement Officers will be met with maximum force. Clear the street."

The two boys sprinted directly toward the approaching

roboid police. Their right arms swung back. Their faces twisted in hatred and contempt, and their arms swung sharply forward. The short lengths of pipe streaked out, slammed into the fronts of the pair of oncoming machines. There were two dazzling flashes.

The roar of the explosions drowned out all other sounds. The boys had already separated, to sprint, off-balance from the force of the explosions, toward opposite sides of the street.

Two more roboid policemen smashed to a stop in a whirl of flame, smoke, and showers of sparks.

Behind them, the V of the flying wedge rushed forward. Unlike the others, which had been light-blue, these roboid police were painted black with silver markings.

In the building to the left of the street, the doors now swung open, and small groups of boys sprinted out to form a line completely across the street. The ends of the line rushed forward, then the center, forming a rough inverted U that raced toward the oncoming V. The V opened briefly to pass the wrecked police machines, then closed again in precise alignment.

For a moment there was a silence, broken only by the hiss of tires on the pavement, the pound of feet, and the panting of breath. Then there was a concerted yell, *"Kill the mechs!"* The boys' arms swung back in unison.

At the fronts of the police machines, small doors snapped up and back. From behind each door came a bright spurting flash.

The boys' arms flew out, their knees buckled, and their lengths of pipe dropped free as they fell sprawling to the pavement amidst sudden dazzling flashes of light.

The flying wedge of roboid police swept forward with no change of speed or direction. Their narrow tires, heavily-loaded, crossed the torn inert bodies, cut, ground, and slashed them. The tires and rims turned red, to lay down narrow red strips in absolutely straight lines on the pavement.

Hammell, Roberts, and Morrissey, momentarily unable to move, sat with their hands gripping the edge of the control panel.

A pretty woman, a baby bundle in her arms, rushed from a door down the street, screaming, "My boys! My boys!"

and ran toward a pair of the inert, mangled bodies, herself coming into the path of the flying wedge.

In the fronts of the onrushing police robots, the little doors snapped open.

Hammell gave an inarticulate sound of horror.

Roberts, his mind a whirling maze of calculations, came to his feet. His patrol ship was heavily enough armed to handle any concentration of police robots. If he took the ship to the edge of this section of the city . . .

On the screen, directly in the path of the flying wedge, the woman screamed, and raised her bundle high overhead, as if to lift her baby out of danger.

From behind the little doors, bright flashes spurted out.

Roberts had already started to turn away, his hand reaching out for the battle armor he had to wear to cross the clearing.

On the screen there was a huge, brilliantly dazzling flash as the "baby" blew up.

Roberts, blank-faced, one hand on the battle armor, stared at the screen.

Beside him, Morrissey stood motionless with a perfectly blank expression.

Hammell grunted in disgust, and settled back into his seat.

Roberts tilted the battle armor back against the wall of the ship and sat down.

On the screen, the wedge of roboid police swept by, followed by two long columns of roboid police firing as they passed at the building and into the dump on opposite sides of the street.

Down the street at the end of the building, a flash of movement left Roberts with a brief afterimage of something vaguely shaped like a camera, that had apparently recorded what had happened so far, and was now pulled inside as the roboid police came dangerously close.

The long double column of roboid police was now slowing to a halt, the point of the wedge extending exactly to the center of the intersection beyond the far end of the building. From the left, a second wedge followed by another two columns appeared from behind the building, moving along the intersecting street, and joined up with the first wedge. The individual roboid police now had turned ninety degrees, to face the building and the adjoining parks, and the lines of police themselves moved farther apart, to open up a wide protected strip of avenue between the lines.

Down this protected roadway came something long, low, and broad, with jointed body sections running on many wheels, with turrets on top slowly swinging large muzzled uptilted guns toward the building.

From the building came shots and small bundles that arced out and down. Up and down the street, more small bundles flew out from the cellar windows. With bright flashes, gaps began to appear in the lines of roboid police.

The long many-wheeled device now slowed to a stop. Its upward-pointing barrels moved slowly, methodically. At the mouth of each barrel there was a blur, then another blur, then another blur.

From the windows of the building came a flash, then from the next window another flash, then from the next window another flash.

Another long low many-wheeled device rolled past the first and stopped farther down the street, to heave its explosive shells through the next section of windows.

The repeated short blast of a whistle cut through the roar of explosives. The tossing of bundles from the windows abruptly stopped.

Down the street came a chunky vehicle with several big hemispherical bulges at the top. It stopped at a thing in the street like a manhole cover, flipped the cover off with two pronged levers, eased forward and dropped something round and bellowslike over the hole. Wisps of yellow smoke began to escape around the edges.

"Sealing off the sewer system," said Hammell. "No one will get out of the building that way."

"They'd better get out *some* way pretty quick," said Morrissey, "or they aren't going to. Look there."

A low blocky object, like a huge metal brick, heavily mounted the sidewalk, and moved massively forward on concealed wheels or rollers. The door of the building snapped back before it like a matchstick, there was a bright flash from underneath, with no visible effect, then the device was inside. It backed up, taking half the doorframe and part of the adjoining wall with it, and rolled forward again. In the silence now that the shooting had died away, there was a dull heavy *crunch*. The massive device then reappeared, and rumbled down the sidewalk toward the next door. Behind it, there now moved forward a host of spidery devices, varying from about one to four feet tall, that moved methodically into the building, followed by low long broad things with many short legs, like metal centipedes. They crawled off of a steady procession of low broad-roofed carriers with open sides, that rolled up the street, discharged their cargo, and moved on to vanish around the corner.

Time passed, and spidery many-legged metal forms appeared on successively higher floors of the building, and finally on the roof. But only two humans were carried out, and both of them were plainly dead.

Meanwhile, a small crowd of people had gathered, apparently from neighboring buildings, to watch raptly from the far side of the double line of roboid police. As the metal devices appeared on successively higher floors, the people pointed and shouted in pleasure. As the dead bodies were carried out, they cheered.

Roberts sat back and looked blankly at Hammell. Hammell shook his head. Roberts glanced at Morrissey. Morrissey ran his hand over his face.

"Well," said Roberts finally, "before we can decide what to do this time, it looks like we're going to have to figure out what's developed out of what we did the last time."

Morrissey nodded. Hammell looked moodily out at the clearing.

From behind them came the bland voice of Holcombe, the life-like roboid butler that had come with the space yacht, and added a special touch of luxury that had enabled the manufacturers to charge what they had for this deluxe version of the ship when it was new.

Holcombe was saying deferentially: "A little light refreshment, my lords?"

Morrissey said wearily, "Just a pitcher of water, Holcombe. Plus three glasses and a large bottle of aspirin."

"Yes, my lord." Holcombe bowed and retired.

The three men stared moodily at the screen.

It took them most of the day, methodically working with the spy screen, to get a rough idea what was going on in the city. Once they had it, they sat back in exasperated bafflement.

From one end of the city to the other, barring only the region around the Planetary Control Center itself, a highly-organized gang of fanatics seemed to be at work, operating from a network of their own tunnels. These tunnels were independent of the city's network of steam lines, cables, pipes, and underground maintenance tunnels, though the two connected at a number of points. Except at these points, the city's surveillance devices showed nothing of what went on inside the newly-dug tunnels. Hence the spy screen, which operated from taps on the city's surveillance system, also showed nothing, except at these points. But from watching the movement of maintenance and combat devices inside the city's tunnels, it became obvious that a continuous skirmishing and probing was going on, with the computer trying to isolate and clean out sections of the fanatics' tunnels, while the fanatics calculatedly sabotaged water pipes, steam lines, and power cables, to keep the computer distracted with maintenance problems, and its tunnels clogged with maintenance devices. Meanwhile, above ground, gangs of fanatics, wearing triple lightning-bolt insignia, burst out to seize able-bodied protesting citizens for work in the shovel gangs. The general bulk of the populace, if anything, looked more run-down and put upon than before. Now they had two sets of rulers instead of one, and the rulers were at war with each other.

"This network of tunnels," said Hammell finally, "makes it a mess. How do we know what effect we're having on them if we can't see them?"

"We can try," said Morrissey, "to figure it out from what happens afterward."

"That's nice. We can figure out whether a bottle had nitroglycerine in it by 'what happened afterward' when we jarred the bottle."

Roberts studied the screen. "Suppose we bring them all to the surface, then?"

"How?"

"Have we got anything on that list that will serve the purpose of claustrophobia?"

Morrissey blinked. "That's a thought." He ran his finger down a paper tacked by the locator screen, flipped the paper up, and ran down a second list underneath.

"Here we are. 'Desire for light and air.' 'Desire to escape

confinement.' " He flipped up the next page. " 'Desire for room, space.' "

"Just what we need. How would you like to be down in a tunnel and suddenly start to feel one of *those* desires?"

"I wouldn't. But if I were a fanatic, maybe I'd be able to resist it."

"Could we work it so that a *blend* of all those desires would be generated? After all, with this synchronous rotor setup you worked out, we can hit different sections with different settings at the same time. Why not the same section with several settings at once?"

Morrissey blinked, and looked wary. "But not throughout the whole city?"

"*No*, of course not," said Roberts. "Who knows what would happen? No, just try one place at a time. A good spot to start might be near that building where all the fighting was earlier. There should still be some people in tunnels under there. Then we can see how this works."

Morrissey nodded. "Good idea. We'll try it."

They switched the spy screen back to a view of the building, and of the garbage-filled park beside the building. Morrissey set up the want-generator to hit just that section of the city with "desire for light and air," "desire to escape confinement," and "desire for room, space."

Then they watched the screen.

Somewhere underground, there should be some fanatical humans, lurking in tunnels, and suddenly stricken with an urgent desire for light, air, and unconfined space.

Very soon, these humans should come to the surface somewhere.

For a long time, they waited.

But for a long time, nothing happened.

Roberts, frowning, studied first the building, then the park, to make out finally, in the center of the park amidst the enormous heaps of garbage, the remains of what appeared to be a bandstand. He was frowning at this structure, when a wild-looking individual with improvised gun in one hand suddenly burst out a trapdoor in the center, and plunged out into the heaped-up garbage. Right behind him came two more, their faces frantic and chests pumping desperately for air. After the first three came a flood of humanity, each carrying a club, a length of pipe, a gun apparently taken from a wrecked roboid policeman, and fitted with a stock, or some other weapon. There was no room for them all on the bandstand, and in any case they didn't try to stay there, but immediately sprang off into the heaped garbage, to plunge and heave desperately, as if trying to climb up into the open air itself.

Last out of the hole came a man about five feet ten inches tall, strongly built, neatly-dressed in coveralls with triple lightning-bolt armband, carrying a rifle in his right hand, and plainly boiling mad. He gestured angrily toward the trapdoor, shook his fist, and threatened the others with his gun. His voice came out in a flow of words so rapid that all Roberts could make out was the sense of urgency, and the tone of command. Meanwhile, the scores of armed men ceased their struggles and lay flat, face-down in the garbage, or stared up dazedly at the open sky overhead, and tried to act as if they didn't hear.

At the same time, around the edges of the park, roboid police began to pour in from eight different directions, coming both ways along the four wide streets that intersected to form the boundaries of the park.

It dawned on Roberts that this scene must have appeared on some panel in the Planetary Control Center, or otherwise have come to the attention of the planetary computer. And the computer was losing no time in taking advantage of the windfall.

A new urgency came into the voice of the man on the bandstand.

Around the sides of the park, the rapidly accumulating roboid police milled, searching for some route through the heaps of garbage. Here and there, one or two eased in, went forward a little distance, lost headway, came to a stop, backed up, and slammed forward again, to bog down once more in towering piles of decaying trash and garbage.

Down one of the intersecting streets came a long snake-like wheeled carrier, that pulled alongside the edge of the dump and slowed to a stop. The arched armored roof tilted up and back in sections, the first sections swinging far back to brace the carrier from tipping off-balance, as successively, other heavy sections swung up and over. Out of the carrier crept a long device like a metal centipede, with flanged underside instead of legs. The device inched its way forward as successive waves of expansion and contraction moved along its length. The headlike appendage at the front, fitted with multiple visual receptors behind thick glass plates, and two groups of four large gun muzzles on a side, selected a low place between two heaps of garbage, and pushed forward steadily, thrust ahead by the metallic bulk following along behind in steady successive waves of expansion and contraction; the flanges lifting, tilting, flowing forward, dipping down and thrusting steadily back.

Now an amplified voice boomed out: "You are surrounded. Surrender peacefully and you will be remanded for psychiatric examination to the Central Medical Computer. You will not be harmed. Resist, and you will be destroyed at once. You have no choice. Surrender. Throw your weapons toward the—"

Atop the bandstand, the man who'd been arguing with the others had dropped to one knee, his gun resting on a half-rotted rail at the edge of the platform.

There was a solitary bang, and the voice demanding surrender went silent.

Morrissey said, "They aren't throwing their guns out, and they aren't fighting, either. That metal snake is going to get to them in about a minute-and-a-half and blow them to bits. Isn't there something we can—"

Roberts thought fast, and said, "Reset the generator. Hit them with 'Desire to obey the law.'"

Morrissey flipped quickly through the list, glancing nervously back at the screen as the enormous metal centipede crawled steadily through the piles of trash.

"Do we *have* 'Desire to obey the law'?"

Roberts tore his gaze from the screen. "It's halfway down the list. 'Obedience to authority' or something like that."

"That's it," said Morrissey. Quickly, he reset the want-generator.

On the screen, the leader of the humans, on the bandstand, was talking in a low urgent voice, lying flat on the stand as a metallic head started up over a mound of trash, and suddenly every other human stood up. Every single individual either threw a length of pipe, or threw a padded bundle, or fired a gun, or lunged right or left through the garbage to get a clean shot or throw around the side of the stand.

Everyone's aim was good.

In a terrific series of flashes, the head end of the huge metal centipede blew apart.

In one spontaneous surge, the humans then plunged through the garbage to the stand and in a line that moved like clockwork, dropped one-by-one through the trapdoor into the interior.

All save for the leader, who was now on his knees, hands clasped and head uplifted, lips moving, his expression earnest.

"Shut it off," said Roberts exasperatedly.

On the screen, the leader suddenly bowed his head, opened his eyes, and jumped down the hole. The trapdoor slammed shut.

A plume of dirty smoke climbed up from the wrecked front end of the metal centipede.

"*Now* what?" said Morrissey, glancing from the controls to the screen. "Did I somehow get the wrong setting?"

"No," said Roberts. "As usual, it was the right setting, but they just interpreted it their own way. To them, 'desire to obey authority' meant desire to *obey their leader.* And to the leader, it apparently meant desire *to obey God.* None of them had the slightest impulse to do what *we* intended, and obey the *city* authority—the computer and the roboid police."

"Well," said Morrissey, "all I have to say is, this little incident opens up sweeping vistas of trouble ahead. *Other* groups of people in that city *would* have obeyed the city authorities."

Roberts nodded. "Their reactions are more diverse than they were the last time. It's as if they were somehow splitting up into factions that respond differently to the same desire."

Hammell cleared his throat. "And there's one minor faction that apparently can resist the desire-field when it conflicts with his purpose—the leader of that gang. To hit *him* with the effects we want might take an intensity that would send the others into shock."

Roberts considered that in silence.

"You've got to admit we're getting nowhere." said Morrissey.

"We've just started," said Roberts stubbornly

Hammell said sourly. "Yeah. We're finding out the things that *don't* work."

Outside in the forest, where darkness was starting to gather, something gave a bellowing roar that the yacht's thin hull hardly seemed to muffle.

The roboid Holcombe appeared at the entrance to the gravity lift, and bowed.

"Dinner is served, my lords."

Dinner was a sumptuous meal, but halfway through the dessert the curving wall of the space yacht's dining saloon lit up in a reflected pinkish glow. There was a bellow of pain and rage from outside. From overhead came a metallic rattle, then a muffled booming voice:

"Your attention, please. This vessel is fully protected by appropriate devices of the Advanced Synodic Products Corporation. It will retaliate automatically against any aggressive or hostile action."

There was a second glare of pink light, the deck shook underfoot; there was a bellow that traveled around in a large circle outside; then abruptly there was a dazzling white glare, followed by a sizzle as if ten tons of meat had been dropped into a monster frying pan.

Roberts quickly understood that sound. It meant that some gigantic beast, singed by the space yacht, had galloped around and got too close to the patrol ship. Which of the patrol ship's big fusion guns had done the business was a good question, but it was all the same to whatever got in their way. Roberts finished his dessert quickly, anxious to get back to something with a hull that wouldn't fold up if some irritable monster took a crack at it.

Hammell said nervously, "The stinking fifth-rate computer on this tub must not be able to distinguish between dead behemoths lying around, and live ones sneaking in. Otherwise, how did *that* thing get so close?"

"Yes," said Roberts, getting up and reaching for his suit of battle armor. He tilted it off-base, lugged it over to the table, reached inside and turned a valve that relaxed the hydraulic columns inside. The suit slumped facedown on the table, which creaked under it, then Roberts heaved the back panel open and climbed in. Without a sling to hold the suit upright, getting into it was a fairly ridiculous procedure, but neither Hammell nor Morrissey had anything to say about that. They were too busy staring out into the dark clearing, and worrying about ways to get a little more protection out of the energy cannon and the pure-routine computer that operated it. Hammell finally shook his head, glanced absently toward Roberts, and suddenly jumped back.

Roberts had straightened up, and was just swinging the back panel shut. He grinned.

"What's the matter? Don't I look nice in this thing?"

Hammell's laugh came to him clearly, through the earphones of the suit. "I've already told you. You look like an overgrown gorilla. I was thinking about those animals outside, and for a second, I thought one had got in. Ye gods, that suit is big! Is it hard to work the arms?"

"A little," said Roberts. "Not too bad."

"Why's the helmet so big?"

"I don't know. It's not big inside."

"Well, it must be comforting to be inside that."

"You want one?" said Roberts. "There are three extras just like it on the patrol ship—for three other crew members. In fact, you could sleep there. There are four bunks. I could bring back a couple of extra suits for you to wear across the clearing, and—"

Hammell hesitated, then shook his head.

"No, thanks. Even at used-ship prices, we've got too much invested in this yacht to leave it to the mercies of these beasts, even overnight. And we couldn't work in armored suits, so—thanks anyway."

Reluctantly, Roberts nodded. "O.K. then."

The three men said good night, and Roberts went down the grav-drop, out the hatch and into the night.

Roberts was sound asleep when, sometime during the night, there was a banging noise somewhere outside. It reached him, well-muffled and distant, and he merely turned over and pulled the covers more tightly around him.

Several hours went by, broken by very distant bellows and screams, and booming far-off public-address-system noises.

Around four in the morning, there came a thundering crash.

Roberts woke up enough to wonder if he had heard something, but quickly fell asleep again.

About 0630, the symbiotic computer gradually turned up the lights, and then woke him with a buzz.

Roberts slid out of the bunk, performed a series of exercises to the computer's satisfaction, shaved, showered, dressed, ate an A-ration bar, drank two glasses of water, swung the suit of battle armor out on its sling, got into it, and headed for the hatch.

Roberts had the hatch up, and had already pulled himself halfway out, before he saw what was going on outside.

Three huge mottled-gray cats were working on the remains of several gigantic bony-snouted creatures, tearing the meat off the bones in chunks, and wrestling with sheets of tough fibrous membrane that apparently separated one huge bundle of muscle fiber from another.

Creeping in on the cats, apparently for a quick grab at a chunk of the meat, was a long many-legged segmented green creature with jaws about three feet long.

Overhead, light-blue against a sky that was a darker blue with drifting white clouds, huge birds circled, the dark green of their upper feathers showing from time to time as they dipped, eyeing a behemoth with a suggestively flicking sledgehammer tail, that was upright on two pillarlike hind legs beside the space yacht. The head and shoulders of this beast were inside the yacht, the big door of the space yacht being buckled outward, and the side inward, to make room.

Studying the other animals with cold calculating gaze from the foliage of a nearby thorn tree, was a large snaky head.

Roberts dropped back inside the patrol ship, and slammed the hatch.

The voice of the symbiotic computer spoke from the helmet's earphones.

"For an armored member of the Interstellar Patrol to retreat in the face of mere beasts, with onlookers watching from another ship, is unacceptable."

"To do anything else would be nuts. And as I've explained at least a dozen times, I'm *not* a member of the Interstellar Patrol."

"Evidently you've neglected to study your 'Model A-6 Battle-Suit Dynamics.' A demonstration is in order. Press down the chin-lever in the left side of the helmet."

Roberts, not wanting to pointlessly antagonize the computer, pressed down the lever. He immediately found himself walking toward the hatch. Before he knew what had happened, he'd thrown the hatch open, and was climbing out.

The three gigantic cats looked up from their meal and bared their teeth. The green many-legged creature swung its yard-long jaws around and hissed. In the thorn tree, the snaky eyes looked on with cold calculation.

Roberts dropped off the curving side of the ship, his feet sinking deeper into the soil at every step, as if the suit were acquiring mass as it moved forward. He was headed straight for the green many-legged creature.

After a moment's startled hesitation, this beast opened up its yard-long, four-foot-wide jaws, and lunged for Roberts.

Roberts' right foot came up in a kick that left a ten-inch-wide groove in the soil, hit the creature's lower jaw and shut it with a **CLACK!** that echoed around the clearing.

His right hand then reached out, seized the top of the creature's snout, and yanked it down, cracking its nose into the ground.

The three huge cats began edging back toward the forest.

All the many legs of the green creature now began to kick, but Roberts set his feet, turned the whole head over sidewise, pinned the upper swell of the head under the right arm of his suit, and gripping the forward curve of the snout with his left arm, heaved the head of the monster along with him as he started for the space yacht. Behind him, the rest of the beast lifted clear of the ground, like one cable of a suspension bridge, the far end anchored out of sight somewhere back in the forest.

Roberts kept going for the space yacht, his feet sinking as if he were in soft muck.

Behind him, there was a heavy rending, a loud creak, successive cracking, straining noises, then the rustling and swishing of uncounted leafy branches, followed by the ground-shaking crash of a big tree.

The far end of the many-legged creature suddenly was trotting along, stumbling and lurching as it crossed ground not selected by the head end, so that some of its feet went down into holes while others banged into rotting logs and low hillocks, but the creature did its best, and stopped instantaneously when Roberts stopped, beside the gray pillarlike leg of the behemoth that had its shoulders and snout inside the space yacht, and its huge sledgehammer-like tail swishing threateningly behind it.

Roberts unhesitatingly reached up, gripped one of the tail's muscular cords, that stood out like tree roots, and yanked on it.

The upper end of the creature froze. There was a menacing rumble. The tail wrenched, twisted, and couldn't get free. The head and shoulders of the behemoth jerked back and out of the space yacht. Roberts gripped the tail. The animal tried without success to step back to get its balance, but Roberts held the tail while his body blocked the right rear leg.

Ponderously, stamping hard with its left leg to try to right itself, the creature tipped over, to land full-length with a shock that jarred the earth.

Overhead, in the thorn tree, a little flutter of leaves marked the departure of the snake.

The behemoth lay still for a moment, in shock, then sucked in a huge breath of air, let out a ringing high-pitched bellow, rolled over, twisting its tail loose at the expense of a large chunk of skin, and staggered to its feet.

Roberts took a few steps, bent, shoved his armored left hand through the dirt under the behemoth's left hind foot, and heaved it up.

Roberts himself sank into the soil as if it were quicksand, but the behemoth's left hind leg shot high up into the air, and the whole creature went up and over on its back with a jar that made the trees sway.

The many-legged creature again had its nose pinned to the earth, this time because Roberts was down inside a form-fitting foxhole in the soil, but was still absently holding onto the many-legged creature with his right hand. For its part, it kept its eyes shut, its mouth closed, and just waited to see what Roberts wanted it to do next.

Roberts pulled himself up out of the ground.

The behemoth staggered to its feet, gave a pitiful bleat, and bolted for the forest.

Roberts let go the head of the many-legged creature, its

eyes came warily half-open, and with steadily gathering speed, it headed for the forest.

Roberts looked around, saw the clearing was deserted, and climbed up the handholds into the space yacht.

Inside, Hammell and Morrissey stared at him as he climbed out of the battle armor. The suit having done practically all the work, Roberts was just slightly damp with perspiration.

Hammell and Morrissey, on the other hand, looked like they'd spent the night being bounced around in an oversize tin can. Which, Roberts thought, was probably exactly what had happened.

"Well," he said, "are you guys *sure* you don't want to come over to the patrol ship?"

Hammell stared at the armor, and said hesitantly, "Ah— No offense, but—Look, was it *your* idea to just go out there and kick those monsters around?"

"No," said Roberts frankly, "the symbiotic computer on the patrol ship got the idea, and it . . . well . . . made the initial suggestion."

"Ah. And so you—"

"Naturally," said Roberts, standing the battle armor against a bulkhead, "when the symbiotic computer is unhappy, the ship isn't worth living in. I have to extend myself a little now and then to keep the symbiotic computer happy."

Morrissey glanced out into the clearing where the huge dead carcasses were lying around, swallowed hard, and said nothing.

"We'll stay here," said Hammell firmly.

Roberts shrugged exasperatedly. "Suit yourself."

They went over to the spy screen, and as they turned it on, a dazzling flash loomed out through an unfocused scene of grayness and glowing smoke, and when Roberts adjusted the focus, a nightmarish barren landscape came into view, with running figures briefly glimpsed in the distance.

Roberts glanced at the locator screen, and realized that he had a view of the dump they'd watched earlier. He frowned at it for a moment, then said, "Let's see the streets adjoining this."

Morrissey changed the setting, and in quick succession

Roberts saw views of four different streets. On all of them, there were overturned roboid policemen, being taken apart by humans using tools apparently improvised from the axles, shafts, and cover plates of other roboid policemen.

On the streets, leading toward the center of the city, little groups of men and boys went past, alternately running and walking, carrying guns, short lengths of pipe, and heavy axles sharpened on one end to a needle point. Other groups of men carried buckets and still others carried garbage cans slung on pairs of long pipes.

"Ye gods," said Hammell. "It looks like that first time we tried to do something, and they had a revolution going before the day was over."

Roberts said, "The want-generator hasn't been on overnight, has it?"

Morrissey shook his head. "We couldn't even have started to figure out what to do. We left it turned off."

"Then we don't have that to worry about, at least. Let's follow one of these avenues toward the center of the city."

The scene shifted, up one of the long avenues, to show, at first, scattered gangs of men moving forward out in the open, then men moving single file next to the buildings, then men sprinting across intersections to file through narrow lanes through the trash-filled parks, to emerge opposite the center of the next block, cross the street at a run and disappear through doorways guarded by armed men who stayed flat against the wall and peered warily toward the nearest intersection.

As the scene shifted still farther forward, the alternating checkerboard pattern of buildings and garbage-dump-filled parks was suddenly interrupted. Two-thirds of the way down the next block, the buildings were smashed to rubble, and the dumps were burnt black. A tangled confusion of barbed wire and tetrahedral clusters of razor-sharp needle-pointed blades was shrouded in a foamy mass of solidified translucent bubbles, through which could be dimly seen the glitter of other, finer wires, of narrow sharp-edged metal strips, and the looming shapes of dark spheres, ovoids, and platelike objects, suggestive of explosive mines.

In the street bordering this barrier, armored turrets mounting four guns apiece, in two opposite pairs, were thrust up out of manhole-like openings in the street. Mobile guns were clustered at the corners of the parks. In the avenues farther back long, low, many-wheeled devices waited.

With growing amazement, Roberts, Hammell, and Morrissey watched as they shifted the scene, and the length of this barrier became clear. It stretched on far across the city from west to east, then swung far to the south, then finally west again, with massively fortified squares at the corner.

Hammell said in astonishment, "Two-thirds of the city is outside that barrier."

"At least," said Roberts. As the scene changed, they could see, at the high windows of the smashed buildings outside the barrier, triple lightning-bolt banners hung out. In the dumps, pipes torn out of buildings were thrust deep in the heaps of garbage, with triple lightning-bolt flags flying from them. Along the edges of the barrier itself, there were flashes of occasional explosions as small parties of men tried to force their way through. Then, apparently, some new command was given. Along the whole length of the enormous barrier, the attempt to break through gradually died out.

After a lengthy silence, Hammell said, "Trying to make something out of this place is like trying to build a house out of hand grenades."

Morrissey nodded. "It was easy to see what they needed before: They were too sunk in the backwash of all the slums they'd been taken from before they were put here. But what do they need *now*?"

Roberts stared off into the distance.

Hammell shook his head. "Where do we even start? Last time, we had an inert mass to work with. This time, we've got something that explodes from one crisis to the next. How did this mess ever come about anyway? I thought we'd improved things—not set up a powder keg!"

Roberts, who at least had been sleeping at night, began to dimly see a possible cause of the trouble.

After a moment, he said tentatively, "Every time we've used the want-generator, except at very low power on just the three of us, there's been an *inertia*. Once started, the effect seems to go on, even though we turn off the want-generator itself. We've accepted this as a fact, but we haven't tried to find any mechanism to explain it. What if each individual has, in effect, a slight *want-generator capacity*

himself? Suppose that once his desire is aroused, it ener-
gizes a *field,* similar to an electric field around a wire. This
hypothetical desire-field, once energized, would create, in
effect, a force tending to maintain the desire, because any
lessening of the desire would cause a flow of energy from
the collapsing field to reinforce the desire. The result would
be an *inertia of the desire,* once created."

Morrissey blinked. "In that case, there should be induc-
tion effects. Once a strong desire is created, it will tend to
induce a corresponding desire in others, and there will be
something similar to attraction and repulsion, based on these
interacting desire-fields."

There was a moment's silence as they thought it over,
then Roberts said, "To begin with, to all intents and purposes, these people were *desireless,* or rather, their desires
were comparatively few, simple, and predictable. It follows
that there would be comparatively few of the interacting
desire-fields. What *we* apparently did was to *set up more
of these interacting fields."*

Hammell said, "Of course, this is just a theory."

"Sure," said Roberts. "But are you under the impression
that we were operating without a theory before? We *had*
a theory. The theory was that the city, and the people in
it, were *passive subjects for the operation of the want-
generator.* Granted that when the effect was concentrated
on just the three of us, here, it seemed to work that way.
But then, the city is much larger, the effect is more widespread and there are far more of what you might call 'natural
want-generator units' in the city. Well, we've been acting
on the theory that the want-generator operated on a passive object, and the passive object is now running away with
the experiment. It looks like time to reconsider the theory."

Hammell thought it over. "You figure we've set up these
'desire-fields' with the want-generator, and now they're in
operation, whether we run the want-generator or not?"

"How else do you explain what's going on? It's exactly
as if such fields were in operation. If so, where do they
come from?"

"But look, remember how we hit the whole city with
'desire for achievement?' And how then we discovered that
their idea of achievement was to 'kill mechs'? And to stop
that, we had to give them a stiff jolt of 'desire to give up'?

Then there was an uncontrollable panic, and we gave them
a shot of 'desire to fight' to break the panic? That incidentally
started a mess of fist fights, and we had to use 'desire to
sleep' to end that? Remember?"

"Yes," said Roberts. "I wouldn't be likely to forget that."

"Well, if 'desire to give up' knocked out 'desire for achievement,' and if 'desire to fight' knocked out 'desire to give
up,' and so on, these hypothetical fields have all been
discharged except the last one, which, as I remember, was
'desire to think.' Where's the problem? Where did this mess
come from?"

"It depends on what you mean when you say the desires
were 'knocked out,'" said Roberts. "Maybe 'desire to fight'
eliminates 'desire to give up.' They're directly opposed to
each other. But how does 'desire to think' eliminate 'desire
for achievement'? And how do either of them eliminate the
'desire to kill mechs' which these people had to start with?"

Hammell was silent for a moment, then his eyes narrowed
in thought. "Yes, I see. One desire may just be *set aside*
for a while, as when you tune a receiver to pick up one
signal instead of another."

Roberts nodded. "And it seems to me that we've added
quite a few signals to those that can be picked up in that
city. 'Desire to achieve' seems to be operating, and in practice
it's still interpreted the same way: 'Kill mechs.' This affects
'desire to learn,' which is interpreted as 'desire to learn how
to kill mechs.' And then, 'desire to work' seems to be in
operation, since, for instance, the improvised tools and
weapons take work. But that desire manifests as 'desire to
work at killing mechs.' And it's obvious that for all this to
happen so fast, 'desire to think' must have been operating,
no doubt in the form of 'desire to think how to kill mechs.'
Every desire we've added has apparently been brought to
serve that one dominating desire that they had before we
started, namely, 'Kill the lousy mechs.' Thanks to that,
they've got a fair chance to blow up the planetary computer and smash every machine that serves it."

"Yes," said Hammell. "And once they succeed in that,
there'll be mass starvation here, because the computer and
a few technicians run the mechanized farms through roboid
machinery. Once they destroy the computer they land right
back in a bare subsistence, dog-eat-dog setup."

"Speaking of technicians," said Roberts, frowning, "have you noticed these different kinds of specialized machines that weren't here before? Did that computer program itself to make them. Or—"

Morrissey had been experimentally changing the view on the screen, and now cleared his throat. "While you theoreticians have been groping for conclusions by pure deduction, I've got hold of some facts. Take a look at this."

Roberts and Hammell glanced at the screen, to see a tall gray-haired man wearing dark-blue clothing of good material and narrow cut, who was standing before a wall-size screen showing a roughly rectangular section of fortified city, with square bastions at the corners.

Beside him stood a burly giant with bristling red beard, who said angrily, "Damn it, Kelty, they'll tunnel. Right this minute, a dozen teams of shovel-gangs are digging under your fortified line."

Hammell stared at the red-bearded giant. "*That's* one of the technicians!"

Roberts ran his hand over his face. The last time they'd been here, Kelty, second-in-command of the city's huge police force, had told Roberts that the bulk of the technicians had left the city. Moreover, Kelty said, there was an implacable enmity between the bulk of the technicians and the computer, and hence no chance of the technicians returning to the city. So, how—

From somewhere in the ship came an odd creaking gritting noise, but Roberts was too preoccupied to pay any attention to it.

Morrissey said, "I suppose if anything could make that planetary computer give concessions to get the technicians back, this is it."

On the spy screen, Kelty was now saying, " . . . Very true. Right this minute, they're tunneling. But eventually, they'll have to come up, or come out in another tunnel that we control. And when they do—"

"No, they *won't* have to come out. That's the point. They can dig from that fortified line of yours, right under one of the power mains, all the way to Center, and with a little luck they can then blow the computer itself right off the map."

"*If,*" said Kelty, "they don't lose their following first."

"How?"

"This tunnel will take a long time to dig. A lot of food will be consumed in that time. They don't have it *to* consume. The stores outside the line have only so much, and no more is going to them. Without food, the fanatics will lose their grip on the populace. They'll be forced to give up."

The red-bearded giant shook his head. "Maybe we can starve the *other* eighty or ninety percent of the populace into submission, but not that crew. They're a bunch of fanatics, led by a fanatic to end all fanatics. They'll dig till they don't have the strength to lift a pick. And all they need to do to maintain their strength is to take the lion's share of the food for themselves."

"The point," said Kelty, "is in this other eighty or ninety percent of the populace you speak of. What will they do *when they don't get food!*"

The giant snorted. "Raid the remaining food stores, steal from each other, run around screaming till they're out of strength. Don't kid yourself that they'll attack the fanatics' Leader. *He's* got ninety percent of the men with weapons. The best the rest of them will do is to knock off a few stragglers and isolated guards here and there to relieve their feelings. Meanwhile, the fanatics and their work-gangs will tunnel. When the computer blows up, you and I and the rest of us will have no choice but to get out somewhere beyond the forest, and I can tell you from experience that that's no fun. But it's better than starving, which is what will happen to us if we're back here once the computer is gone."

Kelty's face had the look of a man forcing himself to consider unwelcome facts. He turned away, then suddenly turned back again.

"What's your idea?"

"We're producing some items of machinery I haven't mentioned before."

"Namely?"

"I've got three oversize trenchers in process, and the largest is almost finished. These are step-trenchers. The first makes a trench big enough for a canal. The second rides in the bottom of that and sends its dirt up on a conveyer. The third rides in the bottom of *that* trench and makes a deep cleft like a glacial crevasse. Let the fanatics try to tunnel across *that*. For good insurance, we can drop projectors of some good heavy gas in there, and when their tunnel comes through the wall of the trench down below, the gas will go to work on them."

Kelty looked horrified. "That's too hor . . ."

"It will *work*."

Kelty shook his head. "A trench like that would cut every power and water main from Center out."

"We can stop the flow from the cut mains. We've . . ."

"I don't mean that. This will cut off their water supply."

"Let it. We'll still be alive afterward, and we'll have the wherewithal to put the whole place back together again.

"Do you have some way to put millions of dead men back together? The minute you cut those mains, you sign the death-warrant for three-quarters of the human population of this planet."

"The minute you let the Great Leader blow up the computer, you sign the death-warrant for ninety-nine percent of the human population of this planet."

Kelty hesitated. "Suppose we cut off the water in the mains from here? Just shut the main valves?"

"Now you're grasping at straws. Their leader thought of that before we did. He's already got gangs of men doing nothing but carrying up buckets and cans filled with water. A deep trench is what we need, to cut their tunnels. Shutting off the water from here won't do it."

Kelty shook his head wearily. "These trenches of yours *will* cut through the mains. Won't they break down?"

"They'll chew right through them. *That* part's no problem. What we need is your approval, so we don't waste any time. When you're dealing with fanatics, you can't afford to give them any advantage, and we don't want them to get a minute's lead on us."

"But it's my job in a situation like this to *restore order with a minimum loss of life.*"

"That's exactly what I'm talking about. You spend a winter out with us in that forest, and you'll run into situations that make this seem easy by contrast. All *you* have to do is *stop those fanatics,* and the best-skilled, most cooperative section of the populace *lives.* This is horrible in its way"—the giant shrugged—"but what do you expect? This way, you get to save the sources of power, the skills, and the organization, to hold back what you might call the wild forces of this planet. Do you know what it's like to fight the elements and the beasts and insects of this so-called Paradise *with no technology? That's* the problem, Kelty. To save *humanity plus technology.*"

Kelty, his face pale and shaken, said, "How long before this first big trencher of yours is ready?"

"Not long. About three hours."

"I'll think it over."

"The sooner we get started with it, the better."

"All right. I'll think it over."

Roberts glanced at Morrissey. "Is there any way we can possibly find the chief fanatic they call the Great Leader?"

Morrissey shook his head. "So far as I can see, only by pure luck. He's almost sure to be in one of those tunnels, and since the city's surveillance system doesn't cover the tunnels, the screen won't either. How do we find him?"

"Yes. That's no solution."

From somewhere in the ship came a creaking noise that momentarily caught Roberts' attention, but then he saw what was happening on the screen. The red-bearded technician had left the room, and Kelty had crossed to a kind of typewriter keyboard set out from the wall. His hands flashed over it in a blur. After only a moment's delay, the wall lit up in several lines of green letters:

**PLAN FEASIBLE
LONG-RANGE COST ACCEPTABLE.
PLAN IS APPROVED.**

Now that it was too late, it suddenly came to Roberts that the crisis might have been delayed by using the want-generator on Kelty. But now the computer had accepted the plan, and the want-generator could no more influence the computer than a bee could intimidate a sledgehammer.

Hammell said, "Wait—Why not hit the whole city with an overpowering jolt of 'desire for peace'? Just pour it on, and *end* this!"

Morrissey's face cleared. "Why didn't we think of that

sooner?" He set up "desire for peace" on the want-generator, and turned it on.

Roberts, Hammell, and Morrissey waited tensely to see what would happen.

Somewhere, there was a grinding crunching nose.

Roberts looked around curiously, then a flash of movement on the screen caught his attention.

A number of hard-looking individuals were walking out of doorways and climbing out of trenches in the garbage dumps. They tossed their guns aside, and waving their hands over their head, shouted "Let's be friends!" and walked out toward the burnt bare no-man's-land and its wire barrier.

The roboid police devices waited until the men were well out in the open. Then they opened fire, and shot the men down.

More men came forward behind them, shouting, "We want peace!"

The roboid devices cut them down with automatic efficiency.

Still more came forward.

"Shut it off!" said Roberts.

The roboid devices waited for a better shot, and suddenly the target vanished in flying dives into the nearest gutter, through cellar windows, and behind heaps of trash.

The three men stared at the screen and the unmoving bodies.

"Well," said Morrissey in a dull voice, "*that* sure didn't work."

Hammell said shakily, "Suppose we hit Kelty with an extra-strong dose of 'desire for peace'? He could call off the police, couldn't he?"

Roberts through a moment, then shook his head. "If the computer is in its right mind, so to speak, it will sack Kelty if he tries that. The fanatics have apparently booby-trapped the roboid police so many times that any call for peace will ring false to it—like the woman with her 'baby,' but on a larger scale.

"Damn it," said Hammell, "we can't influence the *computer*. The thing has no emotions *to* influence."

Roberts was frowning. "There's a thought."

"What do you mean?" said Hammell.

Roberts glanced out the porthole, which was nearer

Hammell than himself, at the patrol ship. "It just occurred to me that if the want-generator won't influence the computer, maybe we've got something else here that *will*."

"We have?" Hammell turned around, looked out, and froze.

"There are advantages," said Roberts, "to having something a little stronger than a space yacht. We . . . what's the matter?"

Hammell drew in a slow deep breath.

"Have you been hearing a funny gritting noise lately?"

"Now that you mention it," said Roberts, "I have. But every time I've heard it, something else has come up. Why?"

"Ease over here a little, and look outside from a different angle. Don't make any fast move, or the thing may jerk back and hurt the ship."

Frowning, Roberts carefully eased over toward Hammell— to look directly into the cold calculating gaze of a pair of snaky eyes as big as his fists. The thing had a pointed head large enough at the thickest to wrap both arms around and just clasp hands. Roberts at once recognized the creature. This was the thing that had been looking down at him earlier from the trees. Apparently it had coiled itself around the ship to climb up this high, and the pressure of its coils had created the creaking noise.

Roberts carefully glanced aside at his battle armor. Probably the best thing to do was to get into that, go out, and—

Hammell sitting as if paralyzed, murmured. "Oh, oh. Look—"

CRACK!

The porthole, transparent plate, frame, gasket, rims, and all, smashed inward and clattered and bounced on the deck.

The big head was right there in the ship beside them, looking at them and the want-generator coldly.

Somewhere there was a creaking grating noise. The head flowed in farther on its dark-green muscular neck.

Roberts, half-paralyzed, began to have the illusion that he was dreaming. This *couldn't* be real. With an effort, he forced his mind to face the facts.

For him to try to quickly reach the battle armor now would only get the snake's attention. *Any* sudden motion was a form of suicide. Yet, to stay still promised the same result after a slight delay.

Very gradually, he began to ease toward the armor. Then he began to wonder, how was he going to go through the awkward process of getting into the armor with the snake looking on?

Meanwhile, the snake was feeding another length of coil in steadily; but abruptly it froze, looking back past Roberts.

It dawned on Roberts that the snake had just spotted the battle armor standing against the wall. Its attention intensely riveted, the snake hung motionless.

Roberts barely murmured.

"Morrissey."

"Sir?"

"Turn on 'desire for peace.' Focus it on the yacht here."

Morrissey, moving with slow careful motions, focused the want-generator.

Roberts warily turned, very slowly, to look around.

A sleepy film suddenly seemed to come down over the snake's eyes.

At the same moment, Roberts felt an intense yearning for peace and quiet. *Enough* of conflict. "For heaven's sake," the thought went through his mind, "why can't everyone get along together?"

The snake was moving carefully, its huge head lowered and somehow suggestive of a dog expecting a kick. With increasing speed, the length of neck went out the hole in the ship, followed by the head.

There was a grating, grinding, scraping noise, and Roberts cautiously put his head out, to see the creature drop free at the base of the ship and rapidly head for cover.

Roberts sucked in a deep breath, and glanced around.

"Morrissey?"

"Sir?"

"Is there a timer in that circuit?"

"Yes, sir."

"Set it for a minute, and give us a stiff jolt of 'desire for sleep.'"

Morrissey bent briefly at the controls.

Roberts suddenly realized that he was worn out, dazed. The room spun around him, and he sat down, cradled his head on his arms, sagged against the control panel . . .

. . . Somewhere, tinnily, a bell was ringing, and Roberts

dazedly sat up. He felt as if he had been dredged up from a hundred fathoms down, but he was amazed at the way his desire for sleep evaporated. Now he felt rested, refreshed, and—

Suddenly he remembered something, and sprang to the porthole.

Outside, the huge snake lay motionless, half in and half out of the forest.

Hammell and Morrissey were both face down on the control panel. As the timer's bell rang on, only Morrissey was even beginning to stir.

The alarm kept ringing, and now Morrissey groped around dazedly but couldn't seem to connect with it.

Naturally, Roberts thought. He glanced around sourly. After a night spent in this bucket, who *wouldn't* be worn out? Every time you turned around, some monster was coming in after you. Why not just live in a cheesecloth tent, and get it over with quick?

Morrissey finally found the timer, shut it off, and passed out again.

So far, Hammell hadn't even moved.

Roberts grunted in disgust, looked back out into the clearing, and decided the snake mustn't have spent a very restful night, either. It lay on the ground like a felled tree.

Roberts leaned out farther, to see what damage it might have done to the yacht in climbing up it, and at once he heard a rustle overhead, and felt the heat of the sun, shining down on his neck, abruptly cut off.

There was a dazzle of light.

WHAP!

Roberts was inside so fast that he knocked Hammell half out of his chair, and himself landed in a sprawl over the edge of the want-generator's control panel.

The air outside the porthole was suddenly filled with huge blue and green feathers. There was a sizzling noise, a smell of cooked meat and burnt pinfeathers, a kind of low popping sound, and a burnt-paint smell.

Cautiously, Roberts looked out, to see one of the smaller turrets on the patrol ship swinging back into position.

Just what caused it, Roberts didn't know, but there was something about the patrol ship as he looked at it that suggested reproach.

Roberts eased farther back and looked around. Morrissey and Hammell—despite the fact that he'd almost been knocked flat—were still asleep. Roberts glanced at the patrol ship. How had it—

That thought was drowned out as it began by a crackling noise, and the boom of a loudspeaker close by:

"YOUR FULL ATTENTION, PLEASE. THIS VESSEL IS FULLY PROTECTED BY APPROPRIATE DEVICES OF THE ADVANCED SYNODICS PRODUCTS CORPORATION. IT WILL RETALIATE AUTOMATICALLY AGAINST ANY AGGRESSIVE OR HOSTILE ACTION."

Hammell was immediately on his feet. Morrissey lurched out of his chair and looked stuporously around.

"The *snake!*" said Hammell. "Where—"

"It's right down below," said Roberts, "and it's just started to move. This warning system you've got here just *woke it up.*"

Morrissey looked blankly at the want-generator.

"Then—"

"Then," said Roberts, "it follows that the snake, at least, is affected by the want-generator. The last time we were here, we used a 'desire to help out' field to persuade the technicians to trade with us on a fair basis. The instant that field was shut off, there was an uproar out in the forest. It occurred to me at the time that there might be a bunch of predators out there being obliging to their prey."

Hammell glanced at the hole in the side of the ship. "That knowledge may just get us some sleep tonight. But we're *still* stuck with the problem of what to do about this city. The want-generator may affect the wild animals, but it still doesn't affect that computer."

"No," said Roberts, "but something we can do *may* affect the computer. I was thinking of doing it with the patrol ship alone, but this snake suggests new possibilities."

Hammell glanced uneasily out into the clearing. "What were you thinking of?"

"Well," said Roberts, "the immediate problem here is that the fanatics and the computer are opposed. Either one, if successful, can destroy the other. The enmity has to be gotten around somehow inside of three hours or so, or we are right on the edge of a crisis that can mean the death of millions of people."

"Yes," said Hammell, "I see the *problem*. But where's the *solution?*"

Roberts said, "Why do we get unexpected reactions from the people in the city when we beam desires at them? Isn't it because *their thought processes are different?*"

"Sure," said Hammell exasperatedly. "But how do we—"

"We have to affect, not only the emotions, but the thought processes, too. The want-generator affects only the emotions. *We've got to reach their minds.*"

Morrissey looked puzzled.

Hammell said, "I can see, with the guns on that patrol ship of yours, that you can reach their *bodies*. But how you get at their *minds*—"

"When you and your brother," said Roberts, "are about to shoot each other, it really breaks up the family quarrel fast if you find some outsider waiting around to shoot the survivor."

"Yeah," said Hammell, frowning, "that's a point. You mean, we make ourselves the villains, in order to unite them?"

"Once we're the villains, will they listen to us?"

Hammell looked momentarily foolish. "Then how *do* we do it?"

"Obviously, somebody *else* has to be the villain."

"*Who?* There are only the three of us."

Roberts thought a moment. "How's 'Oggbad' sound?"

Morrissey said blankly, "Who in space is Oggbad?"

"If we're going to have a villain," said Roberts, "I fail to see why any of *us* has to be stuck with the job. Let Oggbad do it."

"Who's Oggbad?" said Morrissey.

"Do *what?*" said Hammell.

Roberts said, "Amongst other things, attack the city. Can you think of any better way to get our advice listened to than by a demonstration of what the fiend Oggbad is up to?"

Morrissey looked at Hammell. "Have we missed this much sleep?"

Hammell shook his head. "We can follow it this far: a) The city is divided into two warring factions. b) We've got to unite them to straighten out the mess. c) An outside menace is the best way to unite them. d) *We* don't want to play the part of this outside menace ourselves, because that would debar us from taking any direct part in the situation. e) Therefore, somebody *else* should do it—I suppose Oggbad is as good as anybody; but, in the first place, where do we get Oggbad? And how do we provide Oggbad with an army to attack the city? And, just incidentally, that computer may be stupid in dealing with people, but that doesn't mean it can't check facts. We've got to convince *both* sides. How do we outwit the computer? And best of all, how do we do all this in three hours or less?"

Roberts said patiently, "With a decent night's sleep, all this should be obvious. Who says we've got to have a *real* villain? A real villain is likely to get out of hand and complicate the situation when you want to simplify it. Oggbad is strictly a fiction of our imaginations."

"*Your* imagination," said Hammell.

"But," said Roberts, "Oggbad is to *appear* real, to the city. This he will accomplish by attacking the city."

Morrissey said earnestly, "How does a figment of your imagination attack the city?"

"Take a look out that porthole," said Roberts. "As we should know, there are beasts out in that forest that can create chaos in nothing flat. Do you mean to tell me you don't see how Oggbad can attack the city?

"But," said Hammell, "to lead the animals—How does he—"

Morrissey gave a sudden start. "Ye gods. We *must* need sleep. We've already seen that the want-generator affects the animals. If that holds true, *we* can control the animals!"

"I don't *mean* that," said Hammell. "How do we *explain*, so it convinces the computer, among others, that this *Oggbad* can influence the animals?"

"Obviously," said Roberts, "the only conceivable ways are for Oggbad to be either a great animal trainer, a great biologist, or a great sorcerer. And if the story is going to have to stand the computer's scrutiny, I'm in favor of putting in broad claims right at the beginning, so if the computer is going to choke on it, we find it out immediately."

"Hm-m-m," said Morrissey. "How is the computer, based on science, going to judge a *sorcerer*?"

Hammell said thoughtfully, "There *are* rumors of planets run by . . . ah . . . if not sorcery, something just as good."

"Exactly," said Roberts. "That's what I want to take advantage of."

Morrissey shook his head. "This part starts to make sense to me, but there's a catch. Kelty saw you and Hammell when we were here before. So did the computer's surveillance system. The technicians have seen all three of us. How do we explain that a cargo-ship captain, his cargo-control officer, and his communications officer, are tangled up in a fight with this Oggbad?"

"Frankly," said Roberts, "I'm a little sick of being a cargo-ship captain. I don't think a cargo-ship captain is going to have much impact on them, anyway. If we're going to deal with the city, let's deal with them on nothing less than an equal basis. I'm not interested in going through another dose of what we got the last time."

Hammell nodded, but Morrissey still shook his head. "They've got records of our last visit."

"That won't do them much good," said Roberts, "if every time they see us, we're *inside a suit of battle armor.*"

For the first time, Morrissey smiled. "Yes, that's a point. But how do we explain—"

"If we get things on the right basis to start with, I don't think they're going to *ask* for too many explanations."

Hammell said, "Are you going to say we're investigative officers of some kind?"

"No, because then we have to say what bureau we're working for, and so on. I'm in favor of our appropriating so much rank, right at the start, that it jars them back on their heels, makes them listen when we talk, and makes them hesitate before asking *any* questions. If we're going to get them out of this mess, I fail to see why we have to do it on bended knee. The last time we were here, the animals tried to eat us, the plants tried to smother us, the people threw bottles and chunks of cement at us, and the roboids slapped us in prison. This time, let *them* accommodate themselves to *us.* I don't know what you guys intend to be, but as far as I'm concerned, I aim to get a little satisfaction out of this mess. I'm going to be Vaughan the Terrible, Duke of Trasimere, and I'm on the trail of the evil prince and sorcerer Oggbad the Foul, and if anyone disbelieves or doubts my word, I'll punish his impertinence with a couple of blasts from my fusion guns, *which are real.*"

Hammell grinned. "Between the fantastic story, and the real power, it would be possible for the computer to get tied in knots."

Morrissey said, "And there's nothing to prevent our beaming 'desire to believe' at the people. The computer won't be affected, but we should be able to so tie up that computer that it doesn't know what to accept and what to reject."

"That's it," said Roberts.

Hammell said, "Time's passing. This seems to hang together. Let's try it and see what happens."

Morrissey nodded. "Let's get started."

"O.K.," said Roberts.

He got into the battle armor to go back to the patrol ship.

Roberts had intended to make a few slapdash preparations, such as smearing some fresh paint over the Interstellar Patrol identification of the ship—which always showed through any covering he put over it, but the symbiotic computer immediately took a hand.

"Effacing the patrol ship designation without good reason is prohibited."

"I *have* good reason," said Roberts promptly.

"What?" demanded the computer.

Roberts, stupefied at this last-minute delay, gave a quick explanation, and waited angrily for the next piece of obstruction.

"Excellent," said the symbiotic computer. "The plan shows admirable insight into the nature of the problem. However, you evidently have neglected to study your 'Patrol Ship Special Board Number Three—Typical Ship and Equipment Disguises and Physical Aspects of Stratagems.' A demonstration is in order. Press down the blue lever numbered '3' at the left of the control panel."

Roberts hesitated. Beads of sweat popped out on his brow. Then he took control of himself, stopped thinking what the last demonstration had been like, and pushed down blue lever number "3" at the left of the control panel.

At once, there was a hum, and a clank from the weapons lockers where, among other things, the suits of battle armor were stored. From outside came a low whirring noise and a faint sliding sound. Then there was a continuous low rumble, followed by an odd noise Roberts couldn't place. Then the ship lifted.

Roberts waited a moment, then snapped on the outside viewscreen, to see in astonishment that the space yacht was already painted jet black with silver markings, and was now acquiring a set of weird symbols—oddly distorted silver cats, skulls with one red and one blue eye, silver snakes with their gold-colored insides apparently pulled out through their mouths. The sight gave Roberts a nauseous sensation, but he watched as the slender arms with their batteries of nozzles moved over the space yacht while the patrol ship circled it.

There was a clank and rumble from inside the weapons lockers, then the patrol ship set down again.

Roberts quickly climbed out the hatch, and was startled to see that the patrol ship was now gold with a kind of platinum trim. Some kind of dark purple marking was evident farther forward, and Roberts glanced around, walked aft along a horizontal fin, dropped off, and took a look at the ship.

From a short, distance, the impression of wealth and power set Roberts back on his heels. No detail of trim had been overlooked, and on the sides of the ship were three complete coats of arms, the center one placed slightly higher than the other two, and surrounded by a kind of bright golden sunburst.

Roberts shook his head, and glanced up at the big hatch of the space yacht, where Hammell was leaning out to stare at the lurid designs on the space yacht.

The two men looked at each other blankly, then Roberts grinned, and called, "Ready?"

Hammell nodded. "How many passes?"

"Two should do it, especially if there's some time in between."

"O.K."

They got back in their ships, lifted off, flew low and fast away from the direction of the city, and then rose high into the sky on the far side of the planet. From very high up, Hammell and Morrissey dove on the city, the speed of their passage creating a crack and rumble that brought people into the streets on both sides of the barrier. A few moments later, Roberts flashed low over the city, the sound of his passage creating an even sharper crack and louder rumble.

The communicator buzzed, and there was a faint click, as if someone had just snapped it on. An authoritative voice said, "Planetary Control Center, Paradise City, Paradise. No flights are authorized, and no landings permit—"

A harsh voice snarled, "Be damned with your authorization. This is the Imperial light cruiser *Droit de Main*, flagship of Search Force IX. Vice Admiral Sir Ian Cudleigh is aboard this ship, in direct service to their Imperial Highnesses, the Dukes of Malafont and Greme, who accompany His Royal and Imperial Highness, Vaughan, Duke of Trasimere, surnamed The Terrible, Prince Contestant to the Throne. You seek to bar our way at your own immediate and deadly peril. Submit at once, or we destroy you and every inhabitant of this place. We are on a business of holy vengeance, and you stand warned. Master of the Ordnance! Give them a taste of our steel!"

Roberts sat wide-eyed and half-paralyzed. As thick as he had intended to lay it on, this beat anything he'd had in mind.

There was a faint clicking from somewhere forward, and on the outside viewscreen, two buildings, one inside and one outside the foam-covered barrier of wire and mines, erupted in sheets of flame and smoke.

The harsh voice wasted scarcely a second. "Enough. Stand ready if this place lies servile to the fiend . . . All right, which is it? Oggbad, or Vaughan?"

There was a brief buzz from the receiver, then "Vaughan."

"So be it. Now, know you that their Imperial Highnesses are locked in mortal combat with Oggbad the Traitor. Know you that Oggbad, though shorn of his material power, still sways mighty forces in the realms of sorcery. Only if his soul be cleaved from his body, and chained for its million years of punishment in the nether regions, will the blight be ended. Know, then, that as this condition is as yet unmet, and as you serve the Duke Vaughan, Oggbad may seek to smite you. Now, listen closely. If, under fear of the traitor's evil power, you recant to Oggbad, Duke Vaughan with fire and sword will smite you to the death. If, mayhap, under influence of the fiend's sorcery, you are bound over mindless into his evil cause, Duke Vaughan will then faithfully seek to cleanse your soul by agony here, before sending you to your reward. These are—*There goes the fiend! Give chase!*"

The scene on the viewscreen flashed backwards, whirled, and for the second time, the patrol ship streaked after the space yacht.

The communicator clicked off. The voice of the symbiotic computer said, "The instruments in the city are now picking up all the signs and indications of a formidable fleet passing the planet."

"Good."

Roberts, streaking along the curve of the planet after the space yacht, was starting to wonder what a patrol ship with fully trained crew would be like. What had happened so far was apparently mere routine, as far as the symbiotic computer was concerned.

Then he was swinging the patrol ship low over the forest, and following the space yacht in a wide curve to a landing in the clearing. He extended the stabilizer feet, snapped off the gravitors, and got up.

He yanked open the weapons locker, to get out the battle armor, and a glittering suit of armor with helmet curving up into a slender spire came out on its sling. The breastplate of this suit was covered with a dazzling coat of arms. The big fusion gun that hung on the right side was matched on the left by a broadsword. Tied to the top of the helmet's spire was a thing like a pink silk handkerchief.

Looking closely, Roberts could see that his armor was essentially the same as what he'd been wearing before. But the effect was very different.

He wasted a moment asking himself how that had been done. Was there some kind of metal-working equipment recessed into the hull behind the weapons locker? How—"

The voice of the symbiotic computer spoke dryly: "In a crisis, each minute is a precious jewel."

Roberts swore, got into the armor hurriedly, and started for the hatch. On the way, the sword banged around and got crosswise of his legs. He'd barely recovered his balance when he straightened up and rammed the helmet's spire into the ceiling. There was a sarcastic throat-clearing noise in the earphones, but the symbiotic computer didn't actually say anything; the cause of this trouble was its own fault.

Roberts finally managed to get the hatch open despite the spire, heaved himself out, and crossed to the space yacht, where Morrissey and Hammell looked up from the spy screen to stare at him in amazement.

"Not my idea," said Roberts, getting out of the armor. "This idea belongs to the computer. What's going on in the city?"

Morrissey said, "I've been watching this screen since we started, and as nearly as I can tell, the people generally are scared, and subject to all kinds of rumors. The general impression seems to be that the planetary computer got a spaceship up, and the Great Leader is up there fighting it with one of his own. As for the fanatics themselves, the more rank they have, the more uncertain they seem to be; but again, so far as I've been able to find out, the top ones are still out of sight."

"That makes it nice," said Roberts, trying to tilt the armor against the wall. The needlelike tip of the spire, even though it rested at a shallow angle against the wall, looked as if it just might push a hole through the hull. Exasperated, Roberts tilted the armor away from the wall, and tried to ease it down on the deck. At the last moment, it got away from him, and hit with a heavy thud.

Hammell and Morrissey jumped and looked around. Roberts straightened up carefully, "This thing sure isn't made of feathers. And watch out for the spike on the helmet. I don't know what kind of metal it is, but it doesn't give, and it's got a point like a needle." Hammell and Morrissey acknowledged the warning with bare grunts and immediately turned back to the screen. Roberts, uneasily conscious what ship he was in, looked around at the porthole to find it temporarily repaired with an airtight double plate-and-gasket screwtight seal. Satisfied that nothing was going to come in there, Roberts slid into his chair, and immediately saw, on the screen, Kelty and the red-bearded technician.

"Nuts," the technician was saying. "There isn't any such place. You've been sold a bill of goods. The whole—"

"Shut up for a minute," said Kelty, "and see for yourself. We got the whole thing down as it happened. Look at this." He tapped one of several buttons on the edge of his desk, and the far wall of the room suddenly was like blue sky, across which a black-and-silver ship, weirdly decorated, streaked erratically into view, followed a moment later by a dazzling golden ship that unleashed searing bolts of energy that missed the black-and-silver ship by the narrowest of margins. The golden ship was suddenly enormously magnified, to fill the wall. The details of its trim and armament stood out clearly, the coats of arms thoroughly detailed and distinct, the center coat of arms raised above the others and set off in a blaze of bright gold trim.

Kelty said, "A bill of goods, huh? Are you going to tell me the Great Leader dreamed this up?"

The technician looked dazzled. "Still, I never heard of—"

"Wait," said Kelty. "The computer's air-traffic-control circuit ordered the ship off. Here's what happened." He touched a second button. The wall blanked.

A voice said authoritatively, "Planetary Control Center, Paradise City, Paradise. No flights are authorized, and no landing permit—"

The wall flared with color, and a hard face, eyes narrowed, scarred below the left eye and across the bridge of the nose, appeared against an unfocused background, to snarl, "Be damned with your authorization. This is the Imperial light cruiser *Droit de Main,* flagship of Search Force IX. Vice Admiral Sir Ian Cudleigh is aboard this ship . . ."

The red-bearded technician stared at the screen, where the tough figure suddenly turned aside:

"Master of the Ordnance! Give them a taste of our steel!"

Kelty hit another button, and the wall lit with a view of buildings exploding in sheets of flame and smoke.

At the end, Kelty turned to the technician. "Then the first ship showed again, and the two ships went out of view, and the long-range pickups started feeding in more data. *There's a fleet out there.*"

The technician, obviously shaken, stared at the blank wall. "Where does this leave us?"

"You tell me. The computer had to make a quick choice which side to be on, and it must have only taken one-tenth of one percent of its circuits to decide that. There wasn't much choice, if you know what I mean."

"But where in space did these—"

There was a jarring buzz. A voice said urgently, "Now receiving."

The wall lit up again. A very pale face, marked by dissipation but with intense dark eyes, looked out under a narrow golden crown.

"I see you not. To whom do I speak?"

"This is the Planetary Control Center, Paradise City, Para—"

"Listen closely. It is I, Oggbad, Prince of the Empire, Premier Peer of the Kingdom, High Master of the Unseen Realms. I require your immediate aid to repulse the treasonous assaults of the low villains, Vaughan, Percy, and Ewald. Yield at once to my command or come under ban of the most hideous punishment. How say you?"

There were several buzzing sounds of varying pitch, then the words, "Owing to a lack of sufficient data—"

"Bah! These are the words of poltroons, or traitors! I am Oggbad! *Yield!*"

There was a total silence, then, "Very well! You think the material power of the traitor Vaughan will protect you. I say it will not! Nay, if the fools hound me throughout the length of the universe, and drive me from sun to sun, and destroy the last remnant of my worldly power, still, I am Oggbad! In the unseen realms, guns count for nought. All is unchanged, and I am still High Master of the Unseen Realms. As an earnest of my intent, and a warning to those who believe matter can of a right rule the universe, I shall inspirit the very animals with a hate of your treason, and hurl the might of the forest against you. Nay, I say, yield, or face the most dread powers of the Unseen Realms!"

The computer could manage nothing but a buzz.

"So be it," said the pale dissipated face looking at them from the wall, its dark eyes blazing. "You anger me. And though I be shorn of material power you will soon learn the might of my dominion. I *will* regain a footing for my power! And as I am here, *you* will serve, or I will destroy you. Bear my words closely in mind."

The wall went blank. Kelty stared at it dazedly. The technician passed a hand across his eyes.

Finally, Kelty said, "All right. But we're on the right side, at least. That last business was lunacy. That's—"

There was another jarring buzz. "Now receiving."

Kelty and the technician winced and turned back toward the wall. The wall lit up with a view of the same scarred tough face they'd seen first. This face now had a thoughtful exasperated look.

"The fiend has slipped away. No cloak of invisibility could hide so large a ship from our instruments, but there it is. He is gone. Trouble is on foot again. But he'll not leave this world alive. Well, so be it. I speak now to the Earldom-Designate of Paradise, so-called. *Answer!*"

The computer gave another buzz. "We are listening."

"Why have you a voice but no face?"

"Owing to technical difficulties."

"Be damned with technical difficulties! On all we know, Oggbad is still alive! Listen closely. As you have yielded to His Royal and Imperial Highness, Vaughan, Duke of Trasimere, Prince Contestant to the Throne, on the truth of whose cause the light of Heaven shines, so are you in duty bound to obey him. You are now a part of the Empire, in immediate fiefdom to Duke Vaughan himself. Whosoever denies this, does so on instantaneous peril of his life. Now then, the cursed Oggbad is loose on the planet. You must set your defenses in order. Mischief is afoot, and on such a scale as you may never have seen before. But fear not. Duke Vaughan is here. His material power is no small weight against the invisible might of Oggbad. Oggbad must first ensheathe his strength in material form to act in the visible realms. The Duke Vaughan's power is already on rein to act. And we are quick, ready, and hold our minds to the task—we will come through the storm. Oggbad's first onset is the worst. Prepare to meet the Duke Vaughan himself within the hour. There is no time to waste."

The wall went blank.

Like two punchdrunk fighters, Kelty and the red-bearded technician stared at the wall.

Roberts, himself half-dazed, suddenly realized that Kelty and the technician, probably the two most important humans in the computer-run part of the city, were now stuck on dead center. The slightest push would move them in either direction.

"Quick!" said Roberts. "Hit Kelty with 'desire to inform,

explain, and expound!' Easy at first, then if he does what he should, step it up. We want the rest of the city to know what's going on."

On the screen, Kelty was saying dazedly, "Are we dreaming? How do we *handle* a thing like this?" The red-bearded technician was starting to grin. "They don't waste any time, do they? Well, well. What does the computer say to *this?*"

"That's a point," said Kelty. He crossed to the keyboard set out from the wall. Almost immediately, the wall lit up in yellow letters:

INSUFFICIENT DATA

Kelty stepped back as if he'd been struck.

The technician nodded. "That's about all we can expect from it. After the crisis is over, *then* it will have the data and the answers."

"Damn it," said Kelty, "we've got to do *something!*" His face cleared. "Yes, we'll let the people know what's going on!"

"What good will that do?"

"Maybe it will give that collection of fanatics something to think about besides blowing up the computer."

"Yes. That's an idea."

Roberts glanced at Morrissey. "O.K. So far so good. But now we have the little problem of providing Oggbad with an army."

Morrissey said, "I've been thinking about that. It strikes me we're making big promises, and don't know whether we can actually come through with any results."

"If not, they're no worse off in that city than before. And as for us, we can always explain it away by 'capturing' Oggbad, and then having him escape by sorcery as soon as we figure out what to do next. After all, when you've only got three hours to save the lives of millions of people, you can't expect perfection."

"Well, no—" said Morrissey.

"What *might* work," said Roberts, "is to make a kind of large U-shaped pattern of 'desire to escape', and move it slowly forward, from the forest across the cultivated belt toward the city. Can we do that?"

Morrissey nodded. "That's about what I'd planned. What I don't know is whether it will *work.*"

"Let's try it. If we can get those behemoths really moving, they should be able to cover that distance pretty fast. Then there's the problem of the city. Unless that symbiotic computer puts its oar in again, what I think we ought to do is for Hammell and me to land near the border, between the two parts of the city, while you move the animals along . . ."

"If they move," said Morrissey.

" . . . And also pour 'desire to cooperate' at the city's populace. Once we get them in the right frame of mind, we'll wait till the animals arrive, and then there'll be a common enemy. After that, any time the people start to break into factions, Oggbad will bash them over the head. Meanwhile, we can use the want-generator to pour the right desires at the city, while the situation itself tends to make it certain that these desires are *interpreted the right way.* Once we really get that setup going, we can probably shut off the want-generator entirely, except for emergencies."

"We don't know yet," said Morrissey stubbornly, "if those animals will *move.* I'm going to have to use different intensities of U-shaped regions of 'desire to escape,' one region inside the other, to create a kind of fear-gradient, if you know what I mean. The desire to escape has to be strongest at the outermost region, so that the animals will move forward in the right direction, toward the center-line of the U."

"Good." Roberts glanced at Hammell. "Now, unless this Duke Vaughan is going to turn up all alone, probably you'd better come with me."

Hammell nodded without enthusiasm. "I guess so."

"Great," said Morrissey. "And what happens if some tree-sized animal with eight-foot jaws goes after the ship? What do I do then? It takes concentration to work this want-generator and watch the screen to be sure things aren't getting out of hand. I can't do that and fight off a horde of monsters, too."

"Hm-m-m," said Roberts. "Why not hit them with 'desire to sleep'? It certainly worked on that snake."

Morrissey called: *"Holcombe!"*

"Yes, my lord?"

"The tranquilizers."

"At once, my lord."

"O.K." said Roberts, heaving the battle armor over on its face so he could get the back plate open, "then *that's* settled. Watch out for the point on the helmet when I get up."

"Listen" said Morrissey, "I keep trying to tell you, these animals *may not move.* Or they may mill around, fight each other, and generally be slow as mud."

"Use 'desire to cooperate' on them in the center of the U. Do the best you can. Just pour on the power and hope for the best. It will be quite a coup for Oggbad if you *can* manage it."

Morrissey said something Roberts didn't quite catch, but then he was inside the armor, and the rest of the comment came across clearly in the earphones: " . . . to be quite an experience. Who got this bright idea, anyway?"

Hammell's voice, somewhat hollow, replied, *"We did."*

"Yeah. Then I guess we're stuck with it. Well, stay healthy."

"I'll try. Watch out for the gangbats. Don't let Oggbad get you."

Roberts, inside the armor, swung shut the back plate, listened critically to the multiple click of the latch, and shoved home the lock lever.

"O.K., let's go. Stick close to me crossing the clearing."

"I sure will," said Hammell.

"And look out for the spike on this helmet."

A few minutes later, Roberts and Hammell were aboard the ship.

And a few minutes after that, they were sweeping out in a wide curve, in order to come back toward the city high up, and from a different direction.

Kelty was apparently acting fast under the influence of "desire to inform, explain, and expound." The patrol ship's symbiotic computer, in the guise of a tough no-nonsense Imperial officer, made arrangements to land, and immediately the buildings nearby were crowded with nervous onlookers.

Roberts and Hammell, taking care not to run each other through with their helmet-spikes, squeezed out the patrol ship's hatch, to face an uneasy-looking Kelty, who was accompanied by a nondescript individual with triple lightning-bolts on his armband, on the sash across his chest, and on the visor of his floppy cap. The place was surrounded with roboid police, who with apparent uneasiness faced the gap blasted in the barrier that last time Roberts had gone by. Through this gap, a number of armed toughs were seeping forward, but the roboid police hesitated to stop them lest they provoke an uproar in the midst of the ceremonies.

Roberts decided there was no point fooling around. His voice came out amplified into a close resemblance to thunder:

"I am Vaughan of Trasimere. Let all who would serve me kneel. Let all who would serve the traitor Oggbad stand."

Kelty wasted no time kneeling. About fifty percent of the toughs with armbands took a quick glance at the guns on the patrol ship, and either kneeled or dove for cover. The remaining fifty percent remained upright. The nearest tough, with the largest number of lightning-bolt insignia, gave a peculiar laugh, and a sidewise flick of his right hand. His followers snapped up their guns. One heaved a sharpened axle straight at Roberts.

There was a brief crisscrossing dazzle of white lines from the patrol ship's fusion cannon.

The wind blew away a few puffs of smoke, and all that was left of the immediate opposition was a smoldering armband here, a red-hot piece of metal there, and a scattering of grisly trophies that Roberts tried not to look at.

Giving no time for the stunned silence to turn into a new show of opposition, this time from under cover, Roberts demanded in a voice of thunder, "Who else serves Oggbad the fiend? Know you not that each man of this city will serve his true liege-lord or die? What manner of treachery is this?"

To give emphasis to his words, and because he sensed he might look silly just standing there after this speech, Roberts whipped out his sword. The sword came out with a menacing hiss that carried a long way in the silence. Then, since it would have been ridiculous to threaten the whole city, he took a quick step toward Kelty.

A roboid policeman immediately blocked his way.

Roberts' sword flashed out, sliced the machine in two with one blow, and a hard kick of his right foot knocked the pieces twenty feet away. He gripped Kelty by the shirt front.

"Serve you Oggbad?"

"No! But this has all been so fast. And we have a . . . ah . . . a *rebellion* going on here—"

"A rebellion? *Against me?*"

"No. No. Against the machines." Hastily, Kelty gave an explanation of the situation in the city, at the end of which Roberts shrugged.

"This is no matter. It is of the past. What concerns us now is Oggbad. I accept the submission of the part of the city ruled by the thinking-machine. And by the grace of the power invested in me as suzerain create the thinking-machine a Baron of the Duchy of Trasimere. So, too, do I create you, Kelty, a Baron of the Duchy of Trasimere. Let no man raise his hand against your joint authority in the Inner City, by which I so designate that portion of land within this barrier of fanged wire and subtle entrapments, upwards to the limits of the aery realm, and downwards to the center of the world. Now, so much for that. We have still this Outer City to deal with. Who rules there? Every minute the power of Oggbad ensheathes itself in matter, and we waste time on this foolery? *Who rules?* Come forward now, or I destroy your power root and branch, thorn, twig, seed, and fruit! Come forth, I say!"

Roberts was becoming aware of an urgent desire to cooperate. If everyone else was feeling it as strongly as he was, the factions in the city wouldn't last long. But how could he cooperate with somebody who didn't show up?

Just then, as he was wondering what to do next, and wishing the symbiotic computer was handling this instead of him, a strongly built figure about five-feet ten, carrying a rifle in his left hand, strode forward, handed the rifle to one of a small group of followers, and walked toward Roberts unarmed. This man had a look of intelligence and intense self-discipline. When he was directly in front of Roberts, he dropped on one knee.

Roberts said, "You rule in the Outer City?"

"I have five to ten percent of the people behind me. My men are armed. The others aren't."

"Good enough. Do you yield to me, Vaughan of Trasimere—or would you serve the foul traitor Oggbad?"

"I'm for you."

"Then by grace of the power vested in me as suzerain, I create you a Baron of the Duchy of Trasimere, and ruler of the Outer City, by which I designate that portion of the presently-existing city outside this barrier of entrapments and fanged wire, upwards to the limits of the aery realm, and downwards to the center of the world. Let no man raise his hand against you in the Outer City. Rise, Baron. Now, we have no time for the pleasures which should attend these ceremonies, or for their proper form. Each minute spent here the foul cause of Oggbad advances that much further. Dissension within our ranks must be healed at once, as it serves Oggbad's cause. Now then, you, Baron Kelty, and you, the thinking-machine with rank of Baron, and you, Baron of the Outer City, listen close.

"What Oggbad will do, we know not. But he vanished to the west, and from the west will his attack almost certainly come. Therefore, so far as is possible, post your main strength to the west, with but light forces toward the other quarters. And your strength permit it, hold strong reserves in hand. Fight by craft and cunning, from hidden places. Oppose stone walls and empty space to Oggbad's attack, so far as it be possible. Fight him not by main strength. That I will do, as my strength surpasses his. Seek to pin him, entangle him. Chisel at his power. When confronted, run, hide, and appear again at his flank. Let his arms fight stone and air, while your sword seeks his belly.

"Oggbad fights by—"

Hammell's voice interrupted. "Your Grace! Look overhead!"

Roberts looked up to see three huge birds, their feathers blue underneath, winging past. He glanced at Kelty. "Do these birds often fly over the city?"

"Sometimes one alone. I never saw three together before."

Roberts turned toward the ship. "Master of the Ordnance! Bring down those birds!" Roberts turned to his two wide-eyed human Barons. "Their form is but a physical envelope for Oggbad's purpose. Now it begins."

From the ship, a voice called, "Your Highness, this planet must have crystal on it, and Oggbad has found it! The guns are enwrangled!"

Roberts grappled blankly with the word "enwrangled," then turned around, to see the big fusion guns aimed generally toward the birds, but apparently unable to aim precisely.

The guns were moving in small circles around their true point of aim, and not one pointed directly at any of the birds.

"Then," said Roberts, thinking fast, "it *is* Oggbad! Well, gentlemen, get your men quickly in hand. Remember, Oggbad's first onset is the worst. I will shield you as best I may, and in the end we will win, because our cause is just. Now, get to cover! *Quick!*"

A terrific desire to fight was building up in Roberts, and, no doubt, in everyone else around. But only Roberts and Hammell knew that the same angry desire they felt was, in all likelihood, shared by the huge birds.

Suddenly, there was a fierce scream from overhead. Roberts looked up, to see the birds draw in their wings. At that same instant, he realized that their camouflage was far better than it seemed. He had seen three birds. But when they began to dive, their green upper feathers came into view, and there were nearly a dozen of them. At once a voice, so like Roberts' own amplified voice that he thought it must be his, roared:

"*Guards!* We'll fight on foot!"

This sounded valiant. It sounded heroic. It just suited the situation, except for one little detail:

There was no one left in the patrol ship.

Hammell already had his sword in one hand and his gun in the other. The patrol ship was already letting off futile bolts at the birds, its "enwrangled" guns doing no damage. So far as Roberts knew, there was nothing left in the ship but a couple of empty suits of battle armor. Meanwhile, from windows and doors, people were looking at him, the birds, and the patrol ship to see what would happen next.

Roberts, cursing himself, turned back toward the patrol ship, and braced himself to shout another order.

The patrol ship, somehow sunk deeply as if it were digging its way into the cracking concrete, disgorged from its hatch an armed man-sized figure in silver armor. Then another, and another, until there were half-a-dozen of them outside. Since they couldn't be human, they must be roboid, controlled by the symbiotic computer. But where in the cramped interior, with so much space already taken up by guns and missile storage, was there room for the fabricating machinery and the stocks of materials? Was the ship so much more advanced than it seemed? Roberts looked around, hastily gave up trying to find the answer, and roared, *"Have at the fiend!"*

A huge shadow was sweeping over the ground, and now gigantic claws shot toward him. Roberts fired his fusion gun, sheared off one of the clawed feet with a savage stroke of his sword, was grappled and knocked backwards by the other, beheaded the bird, and landed in a tangled bloody mass of bone, sinew, and feathers. He pulled himself free, to find the air suddenly thick with birds of every description, fighting the people and each other. A moment later, carnivorous bats began to arrive, to dive at Roberts' faceplate, bounce off, then cling to his armor, and squeak their teeth grittily over every bump and joint, in the hope of getting through into the flesh underneath.

The city's loudspeaker system was booming, "Take cover! Get to the tunnels! The city is under attack! Get to the tunnels!"

Flying insects were all over the place now. The air was like fog. The screams of the people told of the attacks of every kind of flying pest known to the planet. It dawned on Roberts that Morrissey had been successful beyond their wildest dreams. If they weren't careful, they might exterminate the very population they were trying to save.

Then the onslaught of another gigantic bird knocked Roberts back into the foam-covered entanglement of wires, mines, and sharp-edged strips of metal. Something seemed to snap inside him, and in a terrific outburst of anger, he sliced the bird in half, cut the entangling wires, and settled grimly to the work of slaughter.

He had killed half-a-dozen giant birds, and uncounted numbers of smaller birds and carnivorous gangbats, when Oggbad's main force arrived on the scene.

Huge gray cats, ordinarily day-time creatures, loomed at him out of the gathering dusk. The computer's roboid police, firing from windows and doorways, were suddenly confronted with gigantic beasts with armored bony snouts and tails like giant sledgehammers. Many-legged segmented creatures crawled up the sides of buildings, groped around out in the air, vanished within, and reappeared in the tunnels. Enormous snakes grappled with equally enormous armored metal caterpillars, and, as often as not, the snakes crushed or

smashed some vital part before the guns of the metal caterpillars could kill the snakes. The street lights came on to
light a scene out of a nightmare, a war amongst animals
and machines, with no humans in sight but Roberts and
Hammell, dripping blood, the golden coating of their armor
chipped and dented, but swords and guns in hand and
hewing to the task with such savage energy they seemed
to be everywhere at once.

Toward dawn, a powerful amplified voice boomed out:
"The power of the fiend yields to the Duke! The usurper
weakens!"

As daylight shone down on the bloody shambles, the same
voice roared: "By command of the Duke, clear the tunnels
of the enemy! The worst is over!"

By noon, dented roboid maintenance machines were
dragging off the bodies of huge creatures in one direction,
while towing disabled machines away in the other direction.

Kelty, covered with large and small bandages, beside an
equally-bandaged figure with tattered lightning-bolts armband,
was in a building along the boundary between the two parts
of the city, listening attentively to Roberts, whose armor
looked as if it had spent the last thousand years grinding
along under a glacier. Roberts wasted no time finishing up
the conference with his two subordinates.

"That's how it is," he said. "Now you've experienced it.
Oggbad inspirited those beasts, using the arts of the Unseen
Realms, and had he been able to calm their mutual distrust,
it would have gone ill with us. Next time, he may have
learned that lesson. By that time, our strength must encom-
pass a portion of the forest itself, and all of the fields, lest
he destroy the food supply. No man can rest easy while
the fiend's soul still cleaves to his body. Now, then. My
duties do not allow me to oversee the details. Great affairs
are afoot in the Empire, and I must see to them. But count
on me to come back, to reward the diligent, destroy the
faithless, cleanse by agony the souls of those ensnared by
Oggbad—and, if possible, surprise the fiend himself when
he expects it least."

Kelty glanced at the fanatics' leader, who looked back with
the expression of someone tangled up in a legal matter that

threatens to go on forever, but who is determined to find a way to somehow warp it around to his own advantage. This fit right in with the atmosphere of the Baron's Council Hall, which was what Roberts had named the building. In this building, there was a mild, but nevertheless noticeable urge to *think*. Since Roberts had been in here, several patrolling guards had turned away uneasily, while others had briefly stepped in with an air of interest. Other parts of the city had other faint, but noticeable, suggestions of a desire to work, a desire to study, to relax, to worship, or to rest. For each place, a slight but definite atmosphere had been created, and was being maintained, by the want-generator. But that didn't mean that it couldn't readily get out of hand, if a person seriously misinterpreted the *purpose* of the desire.

"I *hope*," said Roberts, noting the intensely-calculating look on the faces of his two human companions, "that there will be *no warring among my vassals*. In the Empire, it is our custom to submit such affairs to heavenly judgment. This we do by sending both disputants into the next world. We can get them there, but so far have found no way to get them back again. Now, gentlemen, I must leave for a time. Would that Oggbad were destroyed, but at least his material power and the strength of his coalition are broken. While you hold him here, we must smash the last of his confederates." Roberts stood up. "Good-bye for now, gentlemen. I am sorry to be in such haste. But I'll be back."

Roberts went out to the ship just outside, and, worn-out and half-dazed, and not knowing if he were the Duke Vaughan, or whether Oggbad was real, or *what* was going on, Roberts got back into the patrol ship, managed to get out of his armor without spearing Hammell with the tapering helmet-spike, and lifted off.

The viewscreen showed him that, down below, battered and bandaged tens of thousands were cheering the rising patrol ship. "Well," said Roberts, sucking in a deep breath, "either they're cheering us, or our departure."

"Our *apparent* departure," said Hammell.

"Correct," said Roberts, starting to feel like himself again.

He swung the ship in a fast steep climb, taking it apparently toward outer space. When he'd gotten up high enough, the symbiotic computer told him that that was enough to enable it to fool the planetary computer into thinking they'd left the planet. Then Roberts came back from a different direction, and headed for the clearing.

"Well," he said, "that gets us past the first crisis, anyway. Now they've got an urgent reason to stick together. The next thing we want to do is to lay down an overall 'desire for order' field in the city, and a 'desire for adventure' field outside. It seems to me there's an interaction between a person's natural desires, and the field impressed by the want-generator. People can only be comfortable when the two are compatible. What we want is for the workers to be in the city, and the warriors and hunters to be in the forest. This business of trying to cram different types into the same mold in the same place won't work. Let's have it so that if a man wants out, he can *get* out. But, after he does get out, survival is his problem."

"What you figure," said Hammell, "is that the ones that want to learn will find it possible to study; the ones that want to fight, to conquer something, will be able to do that; the ones that want to work will be able to. And the desire-fields will keep the warriors from raiding the workers, and the teachers from trying to drag the warriors into the classrooms; while the *individual*, if he outlives one desire, is free to settle in another place with a different outlook, so long as his own desire doesn't so conflict with the desire-field there as to make him acutely uncomfortable?"

"That's the general idea," said Roberts. "And if we can do it, it ought to eliminate a lot of need for external controls, allow a good deal of freedom, and bring this place closer to being a paradise than it would ever be with a computer monotonously doling out food, clothing, lodging, and everything else on a ration system, and then insisting that now everyone should be happy. The computer is great for rationalizing the production and distribution of the necessities of life. But it just naturally gets stuck when it leaves *desire* out of its calculations."

"Which," said Hammell, "it naturally does. Human leaders do it themselves. There's nothing quite like desire to wreck *anyone's* calculations. Maybe even ours."

Roberts nodded soberly. "Very possible. Well—We'll see."

Their accumulated leave was almost up when the three men took a final look at the city on the spy screen. The change in the place was noticeable not only in the glazed windows and painted buildings, but in the walk of the people who remained in the city. They no longer had to fear being knocked over the head and robbed for daring to do anything. Those of them who best loved a good knock-down drag-out fight, an ambush, or a raid for plunder, were out beyond the roboid-manned barrier line fighting Oggbad's army. Either they had what it took, and came back with a heavy leather sack of fangs and claws which the computer—on Duke Vaughan's order, relayed from a distance—would redeem at an impressive price in whatever merchandise or service the victorious warriors might choose—or else they lacked what it took and "went to Oggbad." Those that tended to be warriors mostly with their mouths were in a worse spot yet. The workers invariably asked to see their trophies, while the warriors were becoming adept at spotting them on sight, and would lug them off to the forest just for the fun of it.

"Boy," said Hammell, "what a place! And yet, if anyone should go around there now demanding a revolution, he'd get brained."

Roberts nodded. "They don't want to revolt, because their *real* desires have a legitimate outlet. Not just the desires they *ought* to have, but the desires they *do* have. A man who wants steak can get awfully sick of a steady diet of ice cream—even if it's the best ice cream made, and he can't find any fault with it."

Morrissey said moodily, "I hate to leave this place. And I *still* don't trust the head of those fanatics."

Hammell said, "Just among the three of us, it's going to be a little hard to go back to being a cargo-control officer after being His Imperial Highness, Duke Ewald of Greme."

Roberts said, "The first chance we get, after we stock up on more parts for the want-generator, I think we'd better come back here."

Hammell and Morrissey at once looked up with enthusiasm.

"After all," said Roberts, "from the way things are going, poor Oggbad is going to need help."

THE KING'S LEGIONS

Vaughan Roberts, in the control seat of the salvaged Interstellar Patrol ship that had cost most of his life savings, glanced briefly at the battle screen, which showed his two friends' second-hand space yacht being hauled around in a gravitor beam. Then he looked back at the auxiliary screen, where an exaggeratedly military-looking individual, with the insignia of a lieutenant colonel, spoke in brisk authoritative tones:

"By order of the Commanding Officer, Squadron R, 876th Interstellar Combat Wing, Space Fleet XII, you are hereby commanded to halt for inspection re Exotic Drugs Act, Section 16 . . ."

Roberts, who had spent some time in the Space Force himself, had never before seen such a combination of meticulously close-cropped iron-gray hair, stiff face, and ramrod-straight posture, with uniform pressed into dentproof, knife-edged creases. Over the left shirt pocket of this uniform were three rows of ribbons, and while Roberts did not recognize half of them, there was one that he knew to be the Cross of Space, with three stars. The Cross of Space was awarded sparingly—to win it required proof of heroism in the face of such danger that it was rare for the hero to come back alive. Try as he might, Roberts could not visualize the miracle that would enable the same man to win this award four times and live.

" . . . Paragraph E," the stiffly-erect figure went on. "You will not resist the beam. You will not attempt to parley. You will open outer hatches to admit boarding parties without delay . . ."

Roberts glanced around.

The patrol ship, the purchase of which Roberts considered an unusual stroke of luck, was equipped with devices he could never have afforded to buy new. One of these could extrude a set of metal arms, to spin a shell of camouflage around the ship, hide its formidable armament, and create the appearance of a harmless rebuilt derelict. Other devices could make fast precise measurements of shape, size, mass, and other characteristics, passing them to computers which searched almost instantaneously through hosts of reference standards to determine what the data might mean. On this information, presented to the pilot in symbols on the battle screen, the patrol ship's battle computer could act at once, bringing the ship's weapons to bear on changing targets, and altering speed, course, and attitude to meet the situation. Presiding over the weapons, sensing elements, computers, and various special devices, and acting toward the pilot as a combination conscience and subconscious mind, was what was known as the "symbiotic computer." At this moment, the symbiotic computer, in its own way, was doubtless considering the rasping, authoritative voice:

"You will at all times obey the instructions of the inspecting personnel. You will cooperate fully in exposing your ship to thorough search for contraband. Resistance, or procrastination, will be dealt with severely . . ."

But the many symbols now appearing on the battle screen were what riveted attention.

It gave Roberts pause to consider who would want such things as:

a) A large salvaged cruiser stripped for ultrafast acceleration.

b) An irregular rocky object some four hundred feet in diameter, hollowed out inside, with several large masses of undetermined nature floating around the interior.

c) A simulated Space Force dreadnought mocked up on a girder-ship frame.

d) An irregular metallic object eighty feet across, with fusion guns sunk in hidden wells.

Roberts fingered the curved surface of a small glowing ball recessed into the control console. As he turned the ball, a corresponding white circle on the battle screen moved from one symbol to the next, and each in turn was enlarged, to show fine detail. Roberts now saw such things as a big cargo section with what looked like severe damage; hidden inside were grapples to seize any ship that came close enough to give help.

Now it was clear why the "colonel" on the screen looked so exceptionally military. Real military men had work to do, and doing this work was their job. But this fellow's job was to look military. Where the fake-wreck artist collected his victims by drifting along a traveled route looking helpless; and where the trap-miner made his profit by maneuvering his chunk of "ore" into position to catch prospectors unaware; and where the slugger prospered by sudden attack—for the same purpose, the two-day wonder mimicked the Space Force.

Now the "colonel" was looking at Roberts with hard authority.

"Is that clearly understood?"

Roberts' course display now showed its line of big dashes drifting off to the right. The track display showed a curving line that wove past the asteroid belt to the stylized image of the blue-green world optimistically called Paradise—with the little image of the ship slipping well off the line. The battle screen showed the patrol ship caught in a wavy blur, representing another gravitor beam.

Roberts asked himself what all these commerce raiders were doing here. Two previous trips told him there wasn't enough commerce past this system to make a living for a tenth of them. If they weren't here to prey on commerce, what *were* they here for?

He considered one possible reason.

When he, Hammell, and Morrissey had been on Paradise before, Morrissey had invented a device to influence desires, and had developed it so it could be focused on a given place from a distance. Suppose someone had been shrewd enough to deduce, from what had happened, the existence of a want-generator?

What would a gang of commerce raiders do to get hold of a device that could influence desires from a distance?

But then, Roberts realized, if such a person had been on Paradise, he would have learned still more.

The last time Roberts, Hammell and Morrissey had been here, the only way they'd found to keep two of the planet's factions from slaughtering each other had been to use, not only the want-generator, but also Roberts' patrol ship, to create the myth of two *outside* factions fighting for control of the planet.

Now, Roberts asked himself, suppose the commerce raiders had learned of this myth, and of the formidable personages who were part of it. Would the commerce raiders care to tangle with such a crew? What if it should turn out that the creatures were real? What if Oggbad, the sorcerer, and the three Dukes *were* fighting for mastery of an Empire? Then what? The want-generator was worth taking on whoever had it, even if he was an armored Duke with an Empire behind him—but the risk should be spread by gathering a strong force, in case of trouble. That was how the commerce raiders would think.

While Roberts considered this, the imitation colonel gave signs of impatience.

"Let's have your attention here, Mister!"

The only way out Roberts could see was to convince the raiders the situation was too dangerous for them to handle. Yet, a simple calculation showed more firepower on their side.

It followed that Roberts would have to run a bluff.

On the screen, the two-day wonder's fuse burned short again, and he turned away, as if to rasp some order to an unseen subordinate.

Roberts spoke first: "This is a King's ship."

The "colonel" swung around. "What's that?"

Roberts looked the two-day wonder directly in the eye. "Sobeit you wish death, there is no surer way than this."

The two-day wonder stared at him.

Roberts spoke grimly: "A King's ship will not stand inspection by any mortal power in or out of space. He who attempts it, will face the full might of the Empire. You are warned."

The figure on the screen momentarily congealed into a living statue. Then he leaned completely back out of focus of the screen.

There was a garbled noise from the speaker, then the automatic descramblers went to work, the garble seemed to distort itself into new shapes and forms, and suddenly it came across, rough and low-pitched, but understandable: "Quick! Where's Maury?"

"Holed up with Parks and the lawyer. Why?"

"Get him on this screen!"

"Are you nuts? He'll—"

"I said, get him!"

The "colonel" reappeared, his manner conciliatory: "We certainly don't want to . . . er . . . detain a foreign ship against its will, Mr . . . ah . . . ?"

In a chill voice, Roberts said, "My name is not at issue. Neither is it at issue whether you will hold this ship against its will. You lack the power to hold this ship against its will. You will release this ship or die. *That* is what is at issue."

In the silence that followed, Roberts became aware that, around him, there were a great many quiet noises. There was a hum, and a low clank from the weapons locker. From outside came grating and whirring sounds, and from somewhere forward there was a continuous murmuring rumble. The patrol ship, though it lacked room, had a trait that endeared it to Roberts: When trouble was coming, the patrol ship got ready. Its captain didn't have to concern himself with the little details any more than a man on the brink of a fist fight had to consciously raise his own blood pressure.

On the screen, the "colonel" glanced around. "Yes! Put him on!"

The screen divided vertically, to show an additional face. This new face took a cool glance at Roberts, and turned very slightly toward the imitation colonel. "What's all this about?"

"It's like that stuff down on Three! I grabbed this guy on a beam, and—"

"Are you wasting my time over a reel-in on some spacer punk? We'll talk about this lat—"

"No! Hold it, Maury! This is that Empire stuff!"

"Nuts. That's a rebuilt dogship. Look at your long-range screen and read the lines. Grow up."

"But, this guy—"

Roberts flipped a switch on the control panel.

There was a slight jar, and the outside viewscreen showed torn camouflage drifting past.

"You hold a King's ship at your peril."

Roberts reached for the firing console, but the symbiotic computer got there first, and the switches moved of their own accord. A large white beam sprang out from the patrol ship toward the asteroid belt.

In the asteroid belt, there was a dazzling explosion.

From a previously-unused speaker to the left of the instrument panel came a clear questioning voice: "Imperial Dreadnought *Coeur de Lion* to masked Imperial Ship *Nom de Guerre*. Do you need help?"

On another auxiliary screen appeared the image of a tough officer in glittering helmet and breastplate, with eyes of a blue so pale that they resembled ice.

It took Roberts an instant to realize that the symbiotic computer was filling in the details. Then he answered: "Imperial Ship *Nom de Guerre* to Imperial Dreadnought *Coeur de Lion*. We are detained by outspacers, who claim the right to halt and board us, in search for contraband."

"Outspacers? In what strength?"

"Fleet strength, of varying type and quality."

"Do the dogs know they hold a King's ship?"

"They do."

"Inform them that if they wish a fleet action, they shall have it."

"I have already told them. They doubt my word."

"Demand if the scum be leagued with Oggbad."

Roberts glanced back at the communications screen. The two-day wonder looked ready to shut his eyes and slide under the table anytime. The other individual, Maury, had a look of intense awareness.

Roberts looked him in the eye, and spoke in a tone suggesting the crack of a whip: "Serve you Oggbad the Fiend?"

Maury's brow wrinkled. His face took on the look of a rocket specialist grappling with his first gravitor. He opened his mouth, shut it, then opened it again. "No."

Roberts glanced at the auxiliary screen. "He denies allegiance to Oggbad."

"It is the policy of the Empire to avoid clashes with the outspacers till our present wounds be bound up. Warn this dog to stand clear of the Earldom-Designate of Paradise. Demand that he let loose his hold on you and the bomb ship. If he does so, take your departure. If not, run the iron down his throat."

"Have I leave to slam home the bomb ship?"

"Do that first. Then the rest will go quicker."

Roberts glanced back at Maury. Robert's voice was brisk and businesslike: "I propose to you that you let loose my ships, and further that you agree to stand clear of the Earldom-Designate of Paradise, which is the third planet of this star, counting from the star outward. Do you agree?"

Maury, his expression baffled, said, "I agree."

Roberts turned back to the auxiliary screen. "He agrees."

The figure on the screen looked faintly disappointed. "If he does as promised, you have no choice but to break off. At some future time, we may settle these old accounts."

Roberts watched the battle screen. The wavy blurs vanished. The patrol ship and the space yacht were free.

Roberts nodded coldly to Maury.

Maury, his expression that of a person thinking very hard, nodded back.

Roberts broke the connection.

So far, so good. But one careless slip would unravel the whole illusion.

Roberts made certain the communicator was off, thought a moment, then tapped a button beside the glowing amber lens marked "Smb Cmp."

"Any fishnet pickups between us and the space yacht?"

The voice of the symbiotic computer replied, "Two. They were drifted out on narrow pressor elements of a compound beam. They're in position between here and the yacht."

"Fishnet pickups are expensive. If we don't hurt them, our friends in the asteroid belt will pull them back *in* again when we leave. If—"

The symbiotic computer spoke complacently. "The parasite circuits are already in place."

"Good. Let's see these fishnets on the screen."

The outside viewscreen promptly showed, outlined in red, two large fuzzy networks of fine lines, between the space yacht and the patrol ship.

"O.K." said Roberts, and carefully guided the patrol ship away from them, as if he were moving off on his own. When he reached an angle that would avoid the pickups, he switched on the communicator, and called the yacht on a tight beam.

Hammell and Morrissey appeared on the screen, their faces tense.

Roberts said, "Don't talk. Just follow me."

Hammell nodded, and Roberts snapped off the screen.

The patrol ship moved slowly off, and the space yacht swung slowly after it.

Carefully, Roberts watched the battle screen for any sign of trouble. When nothing developed, he glanced down at the course display, and sent the little symbol of the ship gradually angling back toward the line of red dashes. As he moved, Roberts gathered speed, so that not long after the symbol of the ship was again centered on the display's dashes, the dashes themselves faded to pale pink, then white. The ship was now back on course, and moving at the correct speed.

The asteroid belt by now was far behind.

But all the way down to the planet, Roberts could see Maury's face—thinking, weighing, calculating.

The landing itself was no problem. The two ships slid down through heavy clouds, moved low over dense forest, and came to rest a little before sunset in the same clearing where they'd set down before.

Roberts ran the stabilizer feet out, switched off the gravitors, and unbuckled the safety harness. He ducked under the three-foot-thick shiny cylinder that ran down the axis of the ship, and went up several steps in the cramped aft section. He released the clamp on the outer hatch, spun the lockwheel counterclockwise, pulled the hatch lever down cautiously, and peered out a one-inch slit. Past experience told him that to actually *go* outside, without battle armor, might be to wind up instantaneously in some creature's digestive tract. But after all the time he'd spent in the ship, he wanted a breath of fresh air.

As the hatch eased open, he peered out into the clearing, sniffed the cool fresh air, inhaled deeply, sighed with pleasure, raised the hatch further, felt the breeze on his face—

There was the faint tick of an automatic turret.

WHAP!

A blur of yellow fur and claws blew apart in mid air.

Roberts shook his head, shut the hatch, and went to the nearest weapons locker to get battle armor. He opened the locker, and out on its sling came a glittering metal suit with a tall tapering spire on the helmet, a gauzy pink cloth on the spire, and a dazzling coat of arms on the breastplate.

Again, to fit the part Roberts was playing, the patrol ship had "improved" the armor.

Roberts looked at it irritatedly, and tried another locker. Out came a more dazzling suit, with spire plus flashing crown on the helmet, and a larger broadsword in a lavishly jeweled scabbard.

Roberts tried the other two lockers—which stubbornly refused to open.

The voice of the symbiotic computer said dryly, "When playing a part, little inconsistencies add up to a big loss of belief."

"Exactly who," said Roberts, "is going to watch me go this short distance?"

"Those who are not seers should avoid predicting the future."

"Nuts." Roberts climbed into the armor, and made his way to the hatch. He turned backwards, head bent, and managed to get the hatch open without ramming anything with the spire. He crouched, turned around, aimed the spire out the opening, followed it through, and dropped to the ground. The hatch clanged shut behind him, and Roberts started for the space yacht.

About halfway there, he became conscious of a face back in the shadows, watching him with awe. Roberts corrected himself—watching the *armor* with awe.

That the symbiotic computer had been right again did nothing to improve Roberts' frame of mind—especially since he could now see that it was obvious. The accumulated effects of the want-generator had led thousands from the city to venture deeper into the forest, seeking adventure and trophies, and the most capable survivors might by now be on an almost equal footing with the creatures that naturally lived there.

Roberts climbed up the handholds of the yacht, and banged on the big cargo door. At once it swung open. Roberts used the spire to keep Hammell back, and as soon as he was inside, jabbed the button that swung the door shut.

"Ye gods," said Hammell, staring at the armor, "let's not bother with *that* until we need it. Incidentally, you almost stabbed me with that helmet spike when you came in."

Roberts said shortly, "There's somebody watching from the edge of the clearing. Don't forget, we've got a lot of these people interested in going into the forest. That's what they're doing."

Hammell momentarily had the foolish expression of one caught overlooking the obvious.

"Moreover," said Roberts, "I was using the spike to keep you away from the hatch. You don't look too much like Duke Ewald of Greme right now." He hesitated, then cleared his throat. "When you're playing a part, little inconsistencies add up to a big loss of belief. You want to remember that."

Hammell looked groggy. "I should have thought of it, but for some reason, I forgot."

Roberts said cheerfully, "Where's Morrissey?"

"Up on the fifth level, checking the gear."

"You'd better go up first. We don't want him to get speared with this helmet spike."

"O.K."

Hammell stepped onto the green half of the glowing oval on the deck, and drifted up the grav-lift. The doors overhead slid open and shut, and he was gone from sight.

Roberts allowed time to warn Morrissey, then followed. The doors slid open one after another, then the fifth level dropped into view, and Roberts gripped the handhold and pulled himself out.

Hammell and Morrissey were standing by a wide improvised control panel. Roberts said hello to Morrissey, got out of the armor, and glanced around.

"How are things in the city?"

"That's a good question," said Morrissey. "There's no broadcast from the city, and the spy screen doesn't work."

Roberts glanced at the blank gray screen. "Can you fix it?"

"If it was something wrong with the screen *itself*, maybe. But I tried a test transmission, and the screen's O.K. The trouble is, there's no transmission from the city."

"What would cause that?"

Morrissey shrugged. "If we had our own spy devices in the city, I might be in a position to say. But this setup is tapped onto the city's own surveillance system. Now, how does that system work? If the city's general power supply fails, does the system fail? If so, it could be that they've had a power failure. Or, it could be that the power supply is O.K., but that somebody has knocked out the surveillance system itself. Not knowing how the system works, I don't know what's possible."

"Could the technicians have found out someone had tapped the surveillance system?"

Morrissey nodded. "Among other things. It could even be that there's a gentleman's agreement that the system will only be used during certain hours. All I *know* is the screen doesn't show us anything, because there's no transmission to pick up."

Roberts shook his head. "What we're here for is to use the want-generator to straighten out the mess in that city. But how can we use it, when there's no way to watch the effect? Moreover, we've got this fleet of commerce raiders. How do we concentrate on what we're doing with a troop of baboons ready to drop in anytime?"

Hammell said, "It's worse than that. The odds are, they've got at least one agent already *on* the planet. Any time we make a public move, this guy will report it."

Morrissey frowned. "Come to think of it, they'll be able to use their instruments to follow the movements of our ships here. Then they can compare what we *say*, as reported by their agent, with what we *do*, as shown by their instruments. We can't say we're going off to fight Oggbad, for instance, and then just land our ships out of sight while we decide what to do next."

"No," said Hammell, "They'd know we were faking."

"And we can't afford *that*," said Roberts.

Morrissey said, "The wonder is that we ever got away from them at all. How did you work it?"

Roberts described what had happened, adding, "I'd think it was a pretty good bluff if we were far away by now. But since we aren't, our safety depends on keeping them afraid to try anything, for fear the mighty Empire will blow them to bits."

"Which," Hammell growled, "means every move we make not only has to make sense for our purposes, but also has got to be convincing to the commerce raiders."

"Correct," said Roberts.

Morrissey, scowling, said, "This is going to complicate things."

"When you consider the likely situation on this planet," said Roberts, "it's going to pile up complications to the point where it's a question whether we can move at all. Just think of the factions here. There's the planetary computer with its roboid devices and built-in directives. As a sort of semi-independent extension, there's Kelty and his army of roboid police. There's the technicians, and the machines and devices the technicians have made. Then there's the Great Leader and his fanatics—plus the general bulk of the populace itself. On top of all this is the effect of the measures *we* took while we were here the last time. And, of course, the whole thing is bound to have developed since then, even though we won't know *how* until we get the spy screen to work."

Morrissey nodded moodily. "And since the trouble is on the other end, there isn't much we can do."

There was a moody silence.

Out in the clearing, it was getting dim, and Roberts absently tapped the switch to opaque the portholes, lest they be watched from outside. Then the silence stretched out again.

Finally Hammell said, "There ought to be *some* way to simplify this."

Morrissey nodded. "Sure. What?"

Roberts was about to suggest, yet again, that they move into the patrol ship, where, at least, their skins would be safe. But just then—

BAM!

The ship jumped underfoot.

Roberts instantaneously dove for his battle armor.

There was a rapid series of jolts and heavy crashes. Something clattered on the deck, hissed, spun, and bounced, in a blur of escaping mist.

Roberts heaved open the backplate.

Hammell and Morrissey, caught in the mist, stumbled toward the grav-lift, and were lost in swirling grayness.

Roberts squirmed into the armor, his eyes shut, and holding his breath. But even though he was now inside, so was a certain amount of gas. He staggered to his feet, swung shut the backplate, groped for the emergency-breathing chin-lever, couldn't find it, and suddenly, despite himself, his straining lungs sucked in a little breath of air that smelled sweetish and strange.

Roberts' thoughts vanished like startled fish. There was a gap when he was aware of nothing at all, and then he was standing, stuporous and empty-minded, as there appeared through the fog, from the direction of the grav-lift, a heavily-armed figure wearing an armored suit with wide transparent faceplate, flexible air hose looped over the left shoulder, and speaking diaphragm in the side of the mouthpiece.

From somewhere down in the clearing, an amplified voice boomed out:

"YOU ARE UNDER ARREST! BY ORDER OF THE PLAN-ETARY DEVELOPMENT AUTHORITY, YOU MUST EVACUATE THESE SHIPS AND COME OUT DISARMED AND WITH YOUR HANDS CLASPED BEHIND YOUR HEADS! YOU HAVE FIFTEEN SECONDS TO COMPLY WITH THIS ORDER!"

A second armored figure loomed through the fog. The two figures bent, and carried Hammell and Morrissey below.

A third figure came in, peered around, stepped forward, looked straight toward Roberts, and froze.

Another armored figure, and another, came in the grav-shaft, peered through the fog toward Roberts, and suddenly stood motionless.

Roberts, aware of an urgent need to act, at the same time was unable to remember who or where he was. All he really knew was that he was standing still, breathing in air that smelled slightly less sweet at every breath. Then, dimly, he caught the tail end of a train of thought, struggled to hold it, sucked in a great breath of air, and in a blinding flash the situation was clear to him.

He fought off a host of other thoughts and kept his mind riveted on that one thought that clarified the whole situation:

I am Vaughan, Duke of Trasimere, Prince Contestant to the Throne. This planet is the Earldom-Designate of Paradise. Its every inhabitant is rightly subject to my command, save only Oggbad, the sorcerer.

That was straightforward.

Once Roberts knew who he was, everything simplified itself wonderfully.

Alertly, he studied the armored figures edging toward him.

The expressions of fear and awe visible through their face-plates suggested that they were not ill-intentioned. What had happened, then?

In a kindly voice, with the natural overturns of power and authority that followed from a knowledge of who he was, Roberts said quietly: "Kneel to your liege lord."

The armored figures, wide-eyed, dropped to one knee.

This told Roberts that the men were not from off the planet, but from the city, and were acquainted with what had happened on his last visit, when the sorcerer Oggbad had escaped into the wilderness, and the leaders and population of the city, after a little unseemly wavering, had rallied to the true cause. Their allegiance once pledged, and his power to reward and punish once established, they would not readily turn against him.

With a tinge of regret and a hint of sternness in his voice, Roberts said quietly, "What brings you here?"

Nobody dared to speak, and now Roberts said, "I must have an answer. Rise. Was it Oggbad?"

They stumbled to their feet. But still no one could bring himself to speak.

Roberts now noticed that the armored suits bore the words, "Citizens' Defense Force." One of the armored suits bore the chevrons of a sergeant.

Roberts' voice became sharper. "Before this evil can be destroyed, I must know its source. Let whoever is of highest rank among you answer my questions. Did Oggbad send you here?"

The sergeant looked around, but there was no one else to do it. He said, "No, your . . . your highness. A man landed in a . . . ah . . . official Planetary Development Authority ship, and announced that we'd been tricked, and he was taking over the planet. He had an army of . . . 'administrators' . . . with him. They're all over the Inner City. He gives the orders. We didn't know *you* were here."

"This fellow is an outspacer?"

"He . . . ah—?"

"He does not belong to the Empire?"

"No."

"Then he is an outspacer and has no right here. Did this fellow come with you?"

"Yes, he—"

"Is he in this ship?"

"He's outside, at the loudspeaker. There he goes now."

The amplified voice boomed out:

" . . . AT ONCE, OR WE WILL DESTROY BOTH OF THESE SHIPS AND . . ."

Roberts nodded. "Go below, and warn your companions that I shall be down to settle this shortly."

The men went out.

Roberts, breathing air that the suit had now cleared almost entirely of the fumes, was having more and more trouble fighting off a throng of distracting thoughts that conflicted with his new-found clarity of mind. He took a few moments to shove these thoughts out of his consciousness. There would be time enough for all that later. The main thing *now* was to take care of this officious usurper.

With this purpose clearly in mind, Roberts checked sword and gun, and stepped into the grav-shaft.

A throng of armored men moved back respectfully as Roberts walked to the cargo door to look down into the clearing.

Below, some eighty to a hundred heavily armed men nervously ringed the patrol ship. Closer to the patrol ship, redly-glowing fragments lay like driftwood marking high water at a beach. The larger turrets of the ship aimed straight ahead, as if disdaining such petty opponents, but the smaller turrets made little adjustments that served as warnings to come no closer.

Floodlights, mounted on dish-shaped grav-skimmers, lit the scene, which was given an inferno aspect by a thin mist blowing across the clearing from a ring of generators around the edge. Through the upper reaches of this mist, hosts of bats with glistening teeth dove at the clearing, but then with desperate twists and turns flitted away again.

Between the patrol ship and the space yacht stood a little cluster of figures beside a loudspeaker aimed at the patrol ship. One of these armored men spoke into a microphone, and his words boomed out:

" . . . AND I *REPEAT*—YOU WILL SURRENDER AT ONCE OR BE DECLARED OUTLAWS, SUBJECT TO ATTACK ON SIGHT, FORFEITURE OF ALL PROPERTY AND ASSETS, AND DENIAL OF RIGHT OF ENTRY AT ALL CIVILIZED . . ."

His tone of voice spoke of close familiarity with rules and regulations, accompanied by a dim understanding of human nature. It came to Roberts that even if the fellow had any power over him, his conclusion would be the same:

Better dead than that man's prisoner.

The loudspeaker was now blaring the words:

" . . . THEREFORE, BY THE AUTHORITY VESTED IN ME, I HEREBY . . ."

Roberts suddenly had enough. The suit amplified his words into a voice of thunder:

"MASTER OF THE ORDNANCE! SILENCE THAT DOG!"

From the patrol ship, a bright line of light reached out to the loudspeaker. There was a brief display of sparks, then a pleasant quiet.

Beside the loudspeaker, the man with the microphone swung around. "Take *that* man prisoner!"

Roberts rested his hand on his sword hilt.

No one moved.

Roberts studied the usurper coldly. "What false illusion of power emboldens a fool to challenge the true liege-lord of this world?"

The only sound was the murmur of wind and the hiss of the generators spaced around the clearing.

Then the armed men in the clearing were grinning at the little group by the loudspeaker.

The individual in the center, firmly gripping the useless microphone, spoke in a determined voice. "I am P. W. Glinderen, Chief of Planet. Owing to the . . . spectacular irregularities . . . which have taken place on this planet, the Planetary Development Authority has regressed the planet to pre-provisional status. I have duly and officially been appointed Chief. You are evidently the cause of the irregularities. I, therefore, place you under arrest, and instruct you to strip yourself at once of all weapons and armor, open this other ship to immediate inspection, and instruct those within to come out at once, disarm themselves, and surrender. If you carry out these instructions promptly, I believe I can endorse a plea for clemency in your case."

Roberts replied irritatedly: "No one can enforce his will where he lacks both right and power. The rulers of this world have yielded to me. Your vaunted authority is either fraudulent or void."

P. W. Glinderen opened his mouth, shut it, and then spoke determinedly:

"In other words, you admit to planetary piracy? You state that you have seized this planet by force?"

Roberts spoke as if to a child: "Is the authority of lord over vassal based on force alone? Better to die, than to yield to such a claim, and better never to seize such a perilous allegiance. None need yield to a foul or empty cause. Against such, there is the appeal to Heaven, which will grant victory or apportion vengeance."

P. W. Glinderen began to speak, looked thoughtful, and tried again:

"May I ask if your name is not—" he leaned over to another of his party, listened, nodded, and said, "—Vaughan N. Roberts, and if not, what *is* your exact identity?"

The question caused Roberts a moment of uneasiness. But one who has lost his identity, and then recovered it, is none too eager to let it go a second time. Roberts' voice came out with anger and conviction:

"To question another in this manner assumes a superiority dangerous to one who is, in fact, a trespasser, without right or power, and with his life in the hands of him he seeks to question. You ask my name. I am Vaughan, Duke of Trasimere. Seek you any *further* answers?"

The Planetary Development official stared at Roberts, then again gathered himself to speak.

A loud ticking sounded from the patrol ship.

Someone in Glinderen's party looked around, then urgently grabbed Glinderen.

The patrol ship's big fusion cannon aimed directly at him.

Glinderen opened his mouth, and tried to speak, but was unable to get any words out.

Roberts turned to the men who had surrounded the patrol ship and were now gathered between the patrol ship and the space yacht.

"Take this man and his fellows prisoner, and return them to the city. Give warning that I shall soon be there to set straight whatever folly these people have brought about."

The armored men below enthusiastically seized Glinderen and his companions, and hustled them onto the grav-skimmers. Then the men on the space yacht asked for orders, and Roberts sent them off with the rest. The whole outfit roared away with impressive efficiency, taking prisoners, loudspeakers, floodlights, and mist-generators with them.

Roberts, with the feeling of having satisfactorily completed an unpleasant task, turned to see Hammell and Morrissey, holding pressure-bottles and masks to their faces, watching him wide-eyed.

At that instant, with the tension relaxed and Roberts himself off guard, suddenly the thoughts he'd held off burst into consciousness.

Vaughan, Duke of Trasimere, Prince Contestant to the Throne, suddenly realized with a shock what was myth and what reality.

Morrissey held the mask away for a moment.

"Was that PDA Chief a fake—I hope?"

Hammell added nervously, "The whole Space Force will come out on a planetary-piracy charge." He sucked in a fresh breath through the mask. "You know that, don't you?"

Now Roberts knew it. Now that he had, in effect, challenged the whole human-occupied universe to war.

Then something more immediately urgent occurred to him.

"Once the fumes from the generators blow away, those gangbats will be down here, and no one knows what else. The yacht's hull is riddled. You'd better be in the patrol ship before it's too late."

For once, Hammell and Morrissey made no objection, but hastily followed him down the handholds and across the clearing. The instant they were inside, Roberts slammed shut the hatch and locked it tight.

Now, he thought, he would have to answer some awkward questions.

But already, the two weapons lockers, that Roberts had been unable to open, were swinging wide. Glittering suits of battle armor traveled out on their slings.

"The new recruits," said the symbiotic computer, "will suit up at once, and return to the yacht to gather necessary goods and equipment."

Hammell and Morrissey stared at the two glittering suits of battle armor.

"New recruits?" said Morrissey.

Roberts said reassuringly, "Don't worry about that. That's just how it talks. But you'd better go along with it; otherwise you don't get any food or water, and the bunk stays locked in place and you wind up having to sleep on the deck. But never mind that. We've got to get the want-generator over here anyway. Not only could animals damage it, but conceivably somebody might get at it while we're away."

"Away?" said Hammell. "Where are we going?"

"Where do you think?" said Roberts. "There's only one place to straighten out this mess, and that's the city."

Hammell and Morrissey got into the battle armor without a word. But they looked as if they were doing a good deal of thinking.

Transferring the want-generator and spy screen to the patrol ship took the better part of two hours, but things didn't stand still while they did it. At intervals they could hear, on the patrol's ship communicator, the voice of Kelty, in charge of the city's roboid police; the voice of the redbearded spokesman for the technicians; and the voice used by the planetary computer itself. On the other side was a harsh demanding voice that wrung the facts from stammering humans and toneless computer, and made it plain that everyone on the planet would obey his liege-lord the Duke, or his liege-lord the Duke would smash the place into smoldering rubble.

Once the want-generator and spy screen were set up, the three men got out of their armor and considered the restricted space in the patrol ship.

Standing near the hatch looking forward, the most prominent feature was the glistening three-foot-thick cylinder that ran down the axis of the ship, creating a shimmer of reflections exactly where anyone would naturally walk. Hammell and Morrissey had already banged into it, and now moved more warily. To the left of this cylinder was the control seat and console, forward of which was a blank wall. To the right of the cylinder, the space was now cluttered with the spy screen and want-generator, while straight ahead the deck itself warped sharply upward over the missile bay.

Aft of where Roberts stood, everything was constricted. Between the cylinder and the various drive and fuel-storage units, there was little but a set of claustrophobic crawl spaces so tight that it was necessary to exhale to get in.

Beside Roberts, however, was one of the patrol ship's better features. Whatever might be said about other details, the

final maddening touch—cramped sleeping arrangements—
had been left out. The bunks were large and comfortable,
and once in his bunk, a man could stretch out for a full
night's rest. But there was no denying, most of the ship
lacked space.

Hammell and Morrissey, after looking around, glanced at
each other, and then Hammell turned to Roberts accusingly.

"It's even smaller on the inside than on the outside."

Roberts was listening to the symbiotic computer warn Kelty
that Glinderen's party shouldn't be allowed to use a communicator. Roberts replied absently. "It's a thick hull."

"Maybe so, but . . . what's behind that?" Hammell pointed
to the wall that took up the space in front of the control
console.

Roberts frowned. "At first, I thought it was some kind of
a storeroom. But I've never been able to find any way into
it."

Hammell said, "That looks like the edge of a sliding door,
in front of the control console."

"When you're at the controls during an attack, that door
slides shut. If the ship out here is holed, you can still
function."

Morrissey looked around. "What's under the deck here?"

Roberts bent, and heaved back a section. Underneath was
a tangle of tubes, cables, and freely-curving pipes, of various sizes and colors, smoothly branching and reconnecting,
some sinking out of sight beneath the others, and the whole
works set into a pinkish jellylike insulation or sealant of
some kind. As they watched, a translucent pipe about the
size of a man's forearm began to dilate. In a series of waves
of contraction and dilation, ball-like lumps of something with
a golden glint traveled along, to vanish under the next section
of deck.

Roberts lowered the panel, and glanced at Morrissey. "Any
more questions?"

Morrissey scratched his head, but said nothing.

Hammell looked around in puzzlement. "This seems to
be pretty advanced." He stepped forward and glanced up
through an opening overhead.

"Is there another deck up there?"

"No. That's the upper fusion turret."

"What's that . . . ah . . . thing like a wheel, with a handle?"

"The handwheel for elevating the gun."

Hammell blinked. "You aim the gun by hand?"

"There's a multiple control system. The gun can be operated by the battle computer or the symbiotic computer, with no one on board. Or, you can operate it yourself from the control console. But if you have to, you can also do it completely by hand."

"Which has precedence, the manual control, or the automatic?"

"So far as the guns are concerned, I think the manual. Where the flying of the ship is concerned, the computers can lock you out anytime. It's not that the manual controls are disconnected, or don't work, but that they take a setting and you can't move them. If a man were strong enough, I don't know what would happen."

Morrissey said, "What about the communicator?"

"Same thing as the flying controls, except that if you're around, at least you know what's going on. You can hear what the symbiotic computer is saying. The computer can *take off* in the ship, and unless you happen to hear the slide and click of the levers and switches, you won't know what happened."

Hammell looked around, and squinted at the bulkhead, or reinforced section of hull, or whatever it was, in front of the control console.

"I'll bet that symbiotic computer is in there. It's the logical place. You're on one side of the controls. It's on the other."

Morrissey shook his head. "Too vulnerable. The same hit might knock out pilot and computer both."

"Where is it then?"

Morrissey pointed at the deck.

Hammell shook his head. "There's a symmetry about having it on the other side of the control console. If it's heavily enough protected, that business about the same hit wouldn't count. And it would make it easier to—"

Just then, Roberts heard the communicator say, " . . . Preparations had best be complete to receive His Royal and Imperial Highness, the Duke Vaughan, at the Barons Council Hall within the quarter hour. Your own head will answer for it if aught traceable to you goes wrong. His Highness is in no sweet mood after what happened here a few hours ago . . ."

"O.K.," said Roberts. "Here we go."

Hammell and Morrissey, tied up in their argument, looked surprised.

"Wait a minute," said Hammell, "what are we going to *do?*"

Roberts pulled his battle armor out on its sling. "The only place we can straighten the mess out—or even find out what's going on—is in the city. So, we have to go to the city."

"Yes, but what do we *do* there?"

"We've got to simplify the situation. There are too many factions. It's like trying to go somewhere with half a dozen different pilots, each backing his own flight plan. We've got to simplify it. The only way I can see is for us to get control of the major factions ourselves."

Hammell shook his head. "That would have been fine— before Glinderen showed up. He's the Chief of Planet."

Roberts frowned. "I don't think Glinderen, or anyone else who approaches this planet on a routine basis, can ever hope to straighten things out. I don't see any way to unite these factions unless *we* do it."

Morrissey said, "Suppose we *do* unite the factions? Suppose we throw out Glinderen? Suppose we end this fighting? Suppose we scare off Maury and his fleet of commerce raiders? Suppose we even get halfway started on the job of straightening out this place? Then what? P. W. Glinderen merely goes off-planet, and signals his report to PDA Sector Headquarters; PDA Sector HQ then notifies Space Force Sector HQ and the Colonization Council; Space Force Sector HQ says it's overburdened and calls for reinforcements; that call gets to Space Force GHQ at the same time as an urgent recommendation from the Colonization Council; Space Force GHQ sends out the orders for a reserve fleet to come in here; meanwhile Glinderen brushes his teeth, takes a shower, slides in between the cool sheets, and sleeps the sleep of the just; down here, so far as any court in the known universe is concerned, *we* are planetary pirates. One fine day, the Space Force sets down, and we either give up or get blasted into molten slag. Glinderen comes back down here, and methodically undoes everything we've done, and puts it back together *his* way. Where's the gain?"

Hammell nodded. "That's what I mean."

Roberts silently got into his armor, then glanced at the instrument panel.

"Here's an example of what I mean. While we've been talking, the ship has taken off. We're almost there."

Morrissey said urgently, "Look, Glinderen has us on the horns of a dilemma. If we *don't* give up, the Space Force kills us. If we *do* give up, *he* imprisons us. I don't want to get gored. But if I have to, I'll pick the shorter horn."

Roberts checked fusion gun and sword. "You say the Space Force can finish us off. That's provided Glinderen notifies them. What if he gets no chance to do it? That horn breaks off."

Morrissey blinked, and, frowning, started getting into his armor; but Hammell looked worried.

"Let's not get out of a *false* charge of piracy by carrying out actual piracy. Glinderen is lawfully in charge here."

A sliding sound from the direction of the control console, and a quiet alteration in the tone of the gravitors, told them that they were starting down.

Roberts said quietly, "You're overlooking something."

Hammell said, with considerable strain in his voice, "I don't know what. Glinderen's authority is real. I don't like to do it, but this has gone far enough. I'll have to go to Glinderen, and—"

The voice of the symbiotic computer said, "We are now landing at Paradise City." The voice added, with the rasp of a drill instructor, "If the recruit standing with one hand on his armor will kindly put it on, this operation will proceed. If not, we will carry out disciplinary action now, and the recruit will spend the next five days aft cleaning out the maintenance tunnels."

Roberts said, "*That's* what you've overlooked. This is an Interstellar Patrol ship. The Interstellar Patrol is famous for its justice and incorruptibility. The symbiotic computer wouldn't even let the ship be sold until it was satisfied the buyer had the right moral standards. Would it let us do this if we were doing wrong?"

Even as he spoke, Roberts saw the flaw in his argument.

But Hammell, with an expression of profound relief, got into the battle armor.

The Barons Council Hall, near which the patrol ship landed, was floodlit and surrounded by roboid police and heavily-armed members of the Citizens Defense Force. More roboid police rolled up to form a double line, with narrow lane between, from the ship to the Council Hall.

The patrol ship promptly blew up the nearest roboid police, and blasted to bits those that tried to take their place.

Roberts, coming out the hatch, decided that what looked fishy to the patrol ship looked fishy to him. He drew his sword.

As Hammell and Morrissey came out, he called: "Be on your guard. This has a look I like not."

The two men, in glittering armor, whipped out their fusion guns.

The roboid police eased a trifle further apart.

Roberts, studying the Citizens Defense Force, observed that no one was faced *out*, to guard the site. They were all faced *in*.

Roberts strolled into the narrow lane between the roboid police. "Draw these lines apart!"

The roboid police backed up an inch.

With one violent blow of his sword, Roberts sliced the nearest roboid policeman in half. He chopped the next one apart, hewed his way through the third—

Suddenly there was room around him.

He strode between the lines toward the Council Hall, then abruptly came to a halt. Ahead and a little to his left, where he would have had to step if he had gone between the original lines, was what *looked* like a repaired place in the concrete.

Roberts drew his fusion gun, aimed deliberately, and fired.

A geyser of flame roared up. Chunks of concrete shot skyward like the discharge of a volcano.

From the patrol ship, searing shafts of energy reached out. There was a sizzling multiple *Crack!* like a dozen thunder-bolts striking at once.

The roboid police were two lines of glowing wreckage.

Roberts jumped the smoking crater, and headed for the building. On the way, he shot down a large sign that pro-claimed, "Municipal Detention Center," uncovering the more solidly anchored plaque bearing the words, "Barons Coun-cil Hall." Roberts kicked the fallen sign out of his way, and opened the door.

At the near end of a big table, two men came to their

feet. They were Kelty, the lean, well-dressed assistant chief of the planetary computer's roboid police, and the redbearded giant who was spokesman for the technicians. At the foot of the table sat P. W. Glinderen, and to his right a knowing cynical individual who looked at Roberts with a smirk. Beside this individual was a bored-looking man with broad shoulders and a detectable bulge in his armpit. To Glinderen's left were seated several neatly-dressed smooth-shaven men who apparently were administrators of some kind.

Roberts stepped to the empty place at the head of the table, and pulled out the chair.

Hammell and Morrissey took their places to Roberts' right, but as he remained standing, they, too, stayed on their feet. At the far end, Glinderen and the officials to his left methodically glanced over papers, while to Glinderen's right, the shrewd-looking individual eyed Roberts, Hammell and Morrissey with a knowing smile.

Hammell's voice remarked, "Your Grace, I like not the air of this rabble at the foot of the table. They should stand till you are seated."

Glinderen looked up.

"*You* are at the foot of the table. And let me warn you, before you try any theatrical display, that I have notified the Space Force, and the three of you will be in prison before the week is out." His voice changed to a whiplike crack. "Now, sit *down*."

Roberts, aware of the orders he had earlier heard the symbiotic computer give, knew that Glinderen was not to have been allowed the use of a communicator.

Roberts glanced at Kelty. "Is this true?"

Kelty nodded unhappily. "I tried to stop him. But Glinderen convinced the planetary computer, and it blocked me."

Roberts said coldly, "Then this means war. Their so-called Space Force is in the asteroid belt. If it attempts to interfere with this world, I shall summon the battle fleets of the Empire."

At the other end of the table, the crafty individual to Glinderen's right laughed silently.

As Roberts contemplated this low point in his plans, Hammell's voice reached him:

"Your Grace, I know that these outspacers have customs different from ours. But their bearing is an insult. Not alone to Trasimere and the Empire, but to Malafont and Greme as well."

Roberts looked at the individuals at the far end of the table. Glinderen and his officials were ignoring everyone else. To Glinderen's right, the crafty individual sat back and grinned, while to *his* right, the tough was studying Hammell as if he were a peculiar kind of insect. No one at the far end of the table was taking Roberts and his party seriously. Moreover, they now controlled the planetary computer, and they had already called the Space Force.

Hammell's voice was courteous but firm:

"I know, Your Grace, of your desire to avoid conflict with the outspacers while our own struggles are yet unsettled. Nevertheless, Your Grace, I respectfully call to your attention that this world is yours, and that I am your *guest* upon it."

The shrewd individual rocked back in his chair, grinning.

Roberts said politely, "If the gentlemen to Mr. Glinderen's right belongs to Mr. Glinderen's party, I trust that Mr. Glinderen will call him to order while there is yet time for Mr. Glinderen to call him to order."

Glinderen glanced up, frowning. "Mr. Peen is a commercial representative for Krojac Enterprises. He is entirely—"

"I see," said Roberts.

Mr. Peen went into a fresh fit of silent laughter.

Through no volition of his own, the fusion gun jumped to Roberts' hand. A dazzling lance of energy reached across the table.

Glinderen and his aides sprang to their feet as Peen went over backwards.

Roberts heard his own voice say coolly, "I apologize to their Graces of Malafont and Greme for this incivility."

Hammell's voice said, "The stain is wiped away, Your Grace."

Morrissey's voice added coolly, "Say no more of it, Your Grace. However, that other fellow, also to the right of Glinderen, hath a look which I care not for."

Roberts' voice inquired politely, "That second gentleman, Mr. Glinderen, is of your party?"

Glinderen said, "No, no! He's Mr. Peen's—"

Crack!

The second gentleman, springing to his feet and yanking

a short-barreled weapon from his armpit, collapsed on the floor.

Roberts' voice said coolly, "I apologize to His Grace of Malafont, for this unpleasantness."

Morrissey's voice said cheerfully, "The unpleasantness is transmuted to pleasure, Your Grace."

As a matter of fact, the sudden departure of the grinning pair was a relief to Roberts. But the way they had departed was something else again. To see whether he now had control, or whether the battle armor was just going to operate on its own from now on, Roberts said experimentally, "Let us be seated."

The words were dutifully reproduced by the armor. He sat down, and Hammell, Morrissey, Kelty, and the redbearded giant, smiling cheerfully, followed his example.

At the far end of the table, Glinderen stared from the pair on the floor to Roberts.

"This is murder!"

Roberts was inclined to think Glinderen had a point. But, before he could open his mouth, a duplicate of his voice said coldly, "Had they been of your party, Mr. Glinderen, they might yet be alive, but you might not. The great houses of the Empire are not filled by hereditary lackwits or degenerate scions forty generations removed from greatness. Neither are they filled by those of such eager humility that they may at will be trodden underfoot by rats in human form. He who insults a Great Lord of the Empire, Mr. Glinderen, lives at the mercy of that Great Lord, out of religious motives, or as an exercise in self-command, not out of an innate right to insult his betters. You, Mr. Glinderen, are yourself deeply in my debt, and in the debt of their Graces of Malafont and Greme. Thus far I have used against you less than my full strength, out of recognition that you believe you do right. This is past. One wrong move on your part, and you go the way of the two on the floor. Seat yourself and let your men seat themselves. Let them keep silent, on peril of their lives. Let you answer my questions and ask none of your own. Your actions have already strung the bow of patience so tight that just a little more will break it."

Glinderen sat down, wide-eyed. His subordinates swallowed, sat down, and kept their mouths shut.

✤ ✤ ✤

Roberts waited an instant, but the battle armor had apparently said all it—or the symbiotic computer speaking through it—intended to say. It was up to Roberts to fill the growing uncomfortable silence.

Roberts leaned forward. "Where is the Baron of the Outer City, Mr. Glinderen?"

Glinderen swallowed hard. "He was carrying on a brutal policy. I—deposed him. He is in prison."

Roberts glanced at Kelty. "Is this true?"

Kelty said, "From Glinderen's viewpoint, it's true. There was a lot of bloodshed in the Outer City—mostly in the attempt to straighten the place out in a hurry. I didn't have any authority there any more. The roboid police couldn't go in. That meant order had to be kept some other way. The way it was being kept was rough, all right. The general idea was that the first time a man was caught stealing, for instance, they beat him up. The second time, he lost a hand. The third time, they killed him. That was pretty tough, but it was creating a sense of property rights. Without that, they couldn't get anywhere, because if someone did do a good job, and got rewarded for it, the reward could be robbed or stolen anytime, so it was meaningless. Well, it was working, and then Mr. Glinderen came down, and convinced the computer, which placed the roboid police at his command, and the next time the Baron of the Outer City came in here, Glinderen imprisoned him. Glinderen then tried to take over all the rest of the city with the roboid police, but by now it was too tough a proposition. Then he tried to pacify the populace by being very lenient. In the process, crime skyrocketed. We have crimes now that we never dreamed of before."

At the other end of the table, Glinderen was beginning to show an impatient urge to speak.

Roberts deliberately laid his fusion gun on the table, the muzzle pointed at Glinderen.

The planetary administrator stopped fidgeting.

Roberts said to Kelty, "Release the Baron. Have him brought up here, with all the respect due his rank and duty."

"I don't know if the computer will cooperate."

"The computer will cooperate—or cease to exist."

Kelty got up, and left the room.

Roberts looked at Glinderen. "What was Mr. Peen's business here?"

"He was a . . . commercial representative for Krojac Enterprises."

"Why was he here?"

"To arrange for an emergency repair and salvage facility here. A new colonization route is being established. This will mean a sizable flow of traffic past this solar system. Krojac Enterprises is contractor for a rest-and-refit center farther along the route, and naturally they want to increase their business. The traffic past here should be sufficiently large that a repair-and-salvage facility would serve a useful purpose, and be profitable."

Roberts sat back. Suddenly the reason for the gathering of commerce raiders was clear. The looting of a colonization convoy offered enormous profits in captured ships.

He said, "Do these colonization routes of yours suffer from the attacks of brigands?"

Glinderen nodded. "Occasionally. These are usually very brutal affairs. Why do you—" He paused, looking at the fusion gun.

Roberts said easily, "This explains why your Space Force should set up a watch in the asteroid belt of this sun. It is a convenient place to protect against such attacks."

Glinderen's face cleared. "Yes," he said.

Just then, the door opened, and Kelty came in. "The computer has released him. He's on the way up."

"Good." Roberts glanced back at Glinderen. "Now, Mr. Glinderen, I am curious to know how you could seek to wrest a world of mine from my grip without fear of what would follow. I also wonder at your effort to name me as someone other than Vaughan of Trasimere. I want a short clear rendering, and it had best be courteous."

Glinderen's face took on the look of one asked, in all seriousness, why he thinks planets are curved and not flat.

"Well—" said Glinderen, his voice betraying his emotions, and then he glanced at the gun lying on the table. He started over again, in the voice of one humoring a dangerous lunatic: "Your . . . er . . . Grace may be aware—"

Hammell said, with a flat note in his voice, "None of lesser rank and station may so address His Royal and Imperial

Highness. From you, though you intend it not, this is a familiarity."

Morrissey added, less graciously, "A complete foreigner,
unfamiliar with the proper code, had best avoid such bungling meticulosity—lest he put his foot in the wrong place
and be dead before he know it."

Roberts said courteously, "There is no need, Mr. Glinderen,
to try to speak as one who belongs to the Empire. Just
answer the question in plain words."

Glinderen was now perspiring freely. "Yes," he said. "First,
I never heard of this Empire before. Second, there was
an . . . an incredible reference to a certain 'Oggbad the
Wizard.' Third, you and your men invariably appeared in
battle armor of a type that offers little view of the face;
this was an obvious . . . a . . . ah . . . apparent attempt at
disguise. Fourth, only two of your ships ever appear at close
range. That suggests that there are no more. Fifth, Vaughan
N. Roberts and a number of companions were on this planet
some time ago, and the records show that very strange things
happened at that time also.

"It seemed to me that the conclusion was perfectly clear.
To disprove it, you have only to remove your armor, one
at a time if you wish, and show that your appearance is
not that of the people who were on this planet before, and
who were known to Mr. Kelty and others here. Also, if you
will bring in, to close range, some more ships of your . . .
ah . . . Imperial Fleet—it might do a good deal to convince
me. That such an Empire should exist, and be unknown,
seems to me frankly incredible."

Glinderen snapped his jaw shut and sat silent, trembling
slightly. Roberts studied him, well aware that Glinderen had,
in a few well-chosen words, exposed the whole masquerade. Kelty and the red-bearded technician were glancing at
Roberts, as if to try to read his concealed facial expression.
At the door, the Great Leader, the fanatic known as the Baron
of the Outer City, stood listening attentively. If these people
should be persuaded by Glinderen, Roberts' only support
would be the patrol ship's weapons.

To Roberts' right, Morrissey shoved his chair back. "This
fellow hath a tongue that—"

Roberts put his hand on Morrissey's arm. "It is true he
is frank-spoken, but it is at my request."

Morrissey settled reluctantly into his seat. Roberts looked at Glinderen. "First, you say you never heard of the Empire. Space is large, Mr. Glinderen. The Empire knows of the outspace worlds, if the outspace worlds know not of it. This planet is out of our way. We would never have come here save for an attempt on the part of Oggbad to seize the throne by intrigue and the use of his magical powers. That you know not of such things is proof of your ignorance, nothing more. Possibly you suppose that Oggbad is a harmless fellow, who with vacant mind recites some empty formula, traces a wandering sign in the air, and with palsied hand shakes a wand the while he gibbers his insanity at the yawning moon. If so, you judge not by the thing itself, but by your image of the thing. You hear the echo of a distant explosion, and smile that people feared it where it tore the earth open. You charge us that we do not expose our persons and faces, and yet Oggbad with all his powers is on this world! What would you have us do, hand ourselves over to him bound and gagged?

"You say that only two of our ships have appeared at close range, and it would perhaps convince you if there were more of them here. I have but to give the word, and this planet is ringed with them. But to bring them to the surface of this world were a source of grave danger. How, then, could we know that Oggbad, using arts that are the none less real for your disbelief, had not escaped aboard one of these ships? With Oggbad, one must keep a firm grip, lest a seeming illusion turn out real, and what was thought reality dissolve into mist. Next, you say a man with a name like mine passed this way before, and strange things took place. That this should convince *you* is not odd. My wonderment is greater yet, as I see here the design of Oggbad, forehanded to prepare a trap for the future, if it be needed.

"What you know not, Mr. Glinderen, is that at this time, the mere rumor of the escape of Oggbad would work great evil in the Empire. At this moment, the Electors are met in solemn conclave to weigh the might and worth of the contestants to the throne. None of the contestants may remain on hand, lest by threat or subtle blandishments they seek to weight the scales of judgment. All are retired from the lists, some to prepare their minds for the outcome, others to repair the neglect of their domains occasioned by the struggle for primacy. Just so am I here. But if word were now given that Oggbad were loose, no one knew just where, who could trust the deliberations of the Electors? Who would accept their decision, and who claim that the influence of Oggbad had weighed invisibly in the balance? The trouble we have had from this sorcerer beggars a man's powers of recollection. To risk that he be let loose on us again is too much. Only after the Electors' choice is made dare we think to risk it. His power for mischief shrinks once the choice is made. Then the Empire draws together, no longer split, but one solid whole."

Roberts paused, noting that Kelty, the redbearded technician, and even the fanatical leader of the Outer City, were all nodding with the satisfied expressions of those who hear their leader successfully defeat an attack that threatens them as well as him.

What surprised Roberts was the wavering expression on the face of Glinderen.

"Yes," said Glinderen, wonderingly, "this certainly does answer many of my objections. However—"

Roberts spoke very gently, "Remember, Mr. Glinderen, I am not on trial here. Have a care. Where I have explained to you, many would have said, 'The actions of this outspace dog, and the wreck he has made, offend me. Dismember the fool.'"

To Roberts' right, Hammell started, like one whose attention has wandered.

"Your Grace?" He glanced from Roberts to Glinderen, and there was a click as he gripped his sword.

"Not yet," said Roberts. "It was only a thought."

"Your Grace has but to give the word—"

"I know, but it is not yet given." Roberts glanced at the redbearded technician. "As we talk here, has Glinderen some hidden device to record our actions?"

"Not Glinderen, but that pair on the floor are wired from head to foot."

"We may wish to speak privately later. Let us take care of this now."

The technician called in some guards, who carried the bodies outside.

Roberts, considering what to do next, now heard a perfect reproduction of his voice say calmly, "This business is about complete. The authority of Glinderen here is at an end. The laws he has enacted exist now on the sufferance of you, my barons, who may do as you wish to right the damage as quickly as possible. I like not what I have heard here. This fellow Glinderen could not doubt Oggbad if Oggbad had acted full-force against him. Has Oggbad been quiet of late?"

Kelty nodded. "No attempt to break through since Glinderen has been here."

Roberts settled back to let the armor do the work—whereupon the armor quit talking.

Roberts said, "By holding back, Oggbad recuperates his strength, convinces Glinderen the tales of his prowess are naught but wild imaginings, and allows Glinderen free reign to turn our arrangements into chaos at no cost to Oggbad. The next move may be an attack by Oggbad in full strength. Are we prepared?"

Kelty said, "If the Baron of the Outer City will take over control of his territory, I can put back in line all the roboids we've pulled in to keep order."

The Baron nodded. "O.K. Provided you deliver to me that lot of special prisoners, and let go everybody jailed under the no-defense law."

"Done," said Kelty. He glanced at Roberts. "We'll have a far stronger setup than we had when Oggbad made that first big attack. I doubt that a similar attack would get by the walls, except for some coming in by air."

"Unfortunately," said Roberts, "Oggbad is not likely to attack the same way a second time. What if he ravages the crops?"

Kelty hesitated. "We have gas generators, an airborne corps of the defense force, and a few very fast gas-laying vehicles. We'd have more but our production program was cut back by Glinderen."

Roberts turned to the redbearded technician.

"How is your production of special devices?"

"Derailed. We're back on the old maintenance routine. Somebody in KQL block smashes a light bulb, so we put in another one, and he smashes that, and so on, until everyone who feels like smashing a light bulb gets bored, and they decide to let us put one there. It's PDA order that all kinds of stuff must be maintained. Well, you can see what level we're operating on."

Kelty said, "But the best of it is that whoever gets caught gets his picture and an account of his exploits in the *Paradise Star*. Some PDA administrator claims this 'gives the offender a sense of identity and beingness.' The lack of that was supposed to be the cause of the trouble, so this is to cure it." Kelty glanced at the technician. "Did you bring that—"

The redbearded giant smiled ironically, and handed over a folded glossy sheet, which Kelty opened out and turned around. "Yes, here we are. We wanted you to see this." He handed the sheet to Roberts.

Roberts flattened the sheet on the table. It was nicely printed, with the words "Paradise Star" in large flowing letters at the top, over the picture of a small angel carrying a harp and flying toward a stylized star. Under this was a banner headline:

DULGER SLAYS SIXTEEN!

LRP Block. Citizen Surl Dulger today killed sixteen women and children using as weapon a knife he made from a New Venusian wine bottle that he stole himself.

Asked if he did not feel sorry for the victims, Surl Dulger said, "They had it coming." When officers asked what they had done to have it coming, Dulger replied: "Grermer only got fifteen. This is a record, right? I got the record?"

Officers assured him that indeed he had.

This is a new homicidal record for LRP block. Surl Dulger, the new record holder, was born in a neat white room in the Heavenly Bliss Hospital just seventeen short years ago. Strange to say, seventeen is just one more than the number of women and children Dulger slew this morning.

Whether he . . .

Roberts looked up. "What manner of joke is this?"

"Oh," said Kelty, "that's no joke. That's *news*. That paper is turned out by the millions of copies."

The technician said, "Right this minute, we've got between six and seven hundred of these guys undergoing rehabilitation downstairs, and we've got sixty more second-guessing after making new records."

Kelty nodded, "And at the present rate, it won't be long before they're coming around the third time. What gets me is that we have to arrest citizens if they try to defend themselves. If you protect yourself, you're denying the murderer his 'right to an identity,' and only a trained psychologist is competent to decide whether this will interfere with the murderer's later treatment."

Roberts looked at Glinderen. "This was *your* idea?"

"No," said Glinderen. "It was recommended by my Chief of Psychology."

"But you approved it?"

"I lack the specialized knowledge to evaluate the program. Therefore it received automatic approval."

"Where's your Chief of Psychology?"

"Probably in his office. I can—"

"Did you have any *doubts* about this procedure?"

"Well . . . I asked some questions. I was reassured, however, that this was a valuable therapeutic method."

The technician nodded. "I happened to be watching that conversation on the surveillance screen. That was before Glinderen ordered us to stop using the surveillance system. What happened was that the psychology chief said this method would 'create a sense of real importance and meaningful existence' in the criminal. Glinderen hesitantly asked, 'What about the victims?' The psychology chief said, 'Unfortunately, they are dead, and we can do nothing for them. *Our* duty is to rehabilitate the living.' Glinderen nodded, and that was it."

Hammell growled, "If I might have directions where to find this Chief of Psychology—"

"No," said Roberts, "that's too good for him." Roberts glanced at the fanatical leader of the Outer City. "Baron, have you considered this problem?"

"Yes, but I can't think of anything slow enough."

"Hm-m-m," said Roberts, forgetting he was in armor, and absently putting thumb and forefinger to the faceplate of the suit. "There must be some—"

Glinderen said, "He is a PDA—"

"But," said Roberts, "if he should *volunteer* to take up residence in Paradise—in order to give the planet the benefit of his vast experience—"

The Baron of the Outer City nodded agreeably. Kelty

smiled. The redbearded giant absently flexed his large muscular hands.

"If he should volunteer," said Roberts, "then perhaps the best place for his services would be in whatever block has the most vigorous competition for a new homicide record. Possibly he can contribute to 'a sense of real importance and meaningful existence' in someone there."

"Yes," said the Baron of the Outer City, with a beautiful smile.

Glinderen burst out, "What if he should be *killed?*"

Roberts said regretfully, "Unfortunately, he would then be dead, and we could do nothing for him. *Our* duty is to rehabilitate the living."

Glinderen nodded, blinked, and stared at the wall.

Roberts said, "Then *that* is taken care of. Gentlemen, these matters must be settled, but the longer we dwell on them, the greater the danger that Oggbad may make some determined move—"

Kelty said suddenly, "*If* he's still here. I don't know why I didn't think of this. Glinderen's PDA ships have come down here and taken off again. He could have sneaked away on any of them."

Everyone looked at Roberts. Once again, the whole structure of his argument threatened to collapse.

Roberts thought fast, then shrugged. "*Outspace* ships. Yes, he could leave the planet, but what then? Oggbad's ambition is to seize the throne of the Empire. Luckily, to pass from here to the Empire requires special navigating devices which outspace ships lack, and which Oggbad himself does not understand and cannot build. His own ship, he has lost. Yet, if he escapes, it *must* be on a ship of the Empire, with such a navigating device installed, unless Oggbad wishes to carve out a new domain in the outspace realms. If so, why, we are well rid of him. *I* believe he is here."

Once again, everyone looked convinced. Roberts himself *felt* convinced. Oggbad and the Empire were taking on such reality that Roberts had to remind himself to do nothing that would commit him to produce proof.

Noticing this, Roberts felt a sudden suspicion. But there was no time to check on that. He turned to Glinderen. "If you are given the opportunity to leave this planet, how long will it take you?"

"Several weeks, to get everything in order."

"You may as well start now."

Glinderen and his party obediently left the room.

"Now, gentlemen," said Roberts, "there remains one problem. Glinderen has called for help from the outspace fleets. Of course, the Imperial battle fleets"—Roberts found himself believing this as he said it—"will defend the planet, but there is still the problem that our ships dare not come so close that Oggbad can use his powers upon them. This means that close defense must be handled by the city itself." Roberts glanced at the redbearded technician. "We need multiple rapid-fire guns and missile launchers. Have you plans for them, and can you make them?"

The technician nodded. "We were working on those, as a defense against Oggbad, when Mr. Glinderen landed. With this maintenance headache off our necks, we can get back to it."

"Good," said Roberts. "The city must quickly be put in order, and its defenses made strong."

His three principal human lieutenants expressed eagerness to get to work, and the planetary computer made no objection, so Roberts stood up, and everyone else at the table followed suit.

Just then, with the tricky meeting completed, with the major factions on the planet unified, and with Glinderen safely sidetracked, the outside door opened up and, one-by-one, there walked in to the quiet tap of a drum, six man-sized figures in silver armor.

Roberts watched speechlessly as they approached. The armored figures themselves he recognized as the type of roboid the patrol ship had put forth once before. Where they came from in the cramped ship was a good question. But even more pressing was the question why the patrol ship had chosen this instant, when everything seemed momentarily straightened out, to toss in a new complication.

The six silver-armored figures, meanwhile, crossed the room, directly toward Roberts. The first, with drawn sword, stopped to Roberts' right. The second, stopped to his left. The third, with a golden tray, halted directly before Roberts, and kneeled. The other three, heavily-armed, halted and stood guard.

Roberts did the obvious, lifted up a large glittering jewel, took the sealed envelope lying underneath on a silver cushion, and spent a few precious seconds futilely turning the envelope. The battle armor, strong enough to toss gigantic creatures around like kittens, had nothing corresponding to fingernails.

Roberts exasperatedly tore off an end, worked the message out, and read past a set of figures, dates, and code words, to the sentence:

. . . ELECTORS CHOSE THIS DAY HIS ROYAL AND IMPERIAL HIGHNESS, VAUGHAN, DUKE OF TRASIMERE AND EARL OF AURIZONT, TO BE KING AND EMPEROR . . .

What good this did, Roberts didn't know. But he was now stuck with it.

"The Electors have chosen," he said, and handed the paper to Hammell and Morrissey, who at once dropped to one knee, heads bowed, to murmur, "Your Majesty—"

Cursing inwardly, Roberts considered the problem of Kelty, the technician, and the fanatical leader of the Outer City. He held the message out to them, and said, "For the immediate future, this changes nothing. Oggbad in his rage may still lash out. All preparations must go forward without delay. But"—his voice took on a harder tone—"the day of faction in the Empire is gone. Outsiders now interfere at their peril. 'Tis customary to kneel, my lords and gentlemen, as a sign of fealty." The three men, with varied expressions, dropped to one knee.

Roberts considered how to quickly bring the thing to an end.

"Rise," he said, "we must be about our duties without delay. No one knows when Oggbad will attack, or what the outspace vermin will do next. Good evening, gentlemen."

With the silver-armored figures serving as guards, Roberts, Hammell, and Morrissey left the hall.

Once inside the ship, they watched the armored figures disappear through an opening forward of the control console. Once the figures disappeared, the opening disappeared. The three men got out of their armor, and looked at each other.

Hammell said, "When there's time—"

Morrissey nodded. "We'll have to go over this ship. There's more to it than I realized."

Roberts locked the hatch, and said, "What that business about the Electors did to improve things *I* don't know. But we've got Glinderen off our necks, and the chief factions on the planet are now united."

Hammell shoved his armor into the locker on its sling. "I had my doubts in there whether we were doing the right thing, but that business about Glinderen's Chief of Psychology did it for me. If we don't get anything done here but to deliver that guy to the wolves, we've accomplished something."

Morrissey shoved his armor into his locker, and glanced at the spy screen. "The screen's working. I don't like to say anything, but I left the want-generator set for 'desire to sleep' and it's now set for 'desire to believe, to accept on faith.'"

"Stands to reason," said Hammell dryly. "Where's it focused?"

"On the Barons Council Hall."

Roberts had already put his armor away and now stripped and jabbed a button in the wall. A cramped shower cubicle popped open. "The only thing that bothers me," he said, "is the Space Force expedition headed for the planet. But there must be a way to straighten *that* out, too—if we can just work it out."

The following weeks went by like a pleasant interlude between hurricanes. Glinderen was too busy getting ready to leave to make trouble. His Chief of Psychology, having made the mistake of walking alone past the wrong doorway, "volunteered" to become a citizen of Paradise, and was now cozily bedded down in the most murderous section of the city. Every authority in the city was working day and night to prepare against attack. Roberts, Hammell, and Morrissey devoted most of their time to the want-generator and spy screen. By now, they had a formidable total of partly-trained soldiers who could put up a fight in fixed defenses. The Citizens' Defense Force, and the fanatics of the Outer City, promised far worse trouble for an invader. The roboid police, so long as they were on solid footing, had the advantages of speed, uncanny coordination, and an impressive lack of fear.

The city's technicians, meanwhile, relieved of endless

maintenance, put back in shape all the devices they had hidden on the arrival of Glinderen. These devices, combined with the rapid-fire guns the computer's automatic factories were now turning out, promised that the city would be able to put up a tough fight.

However, one little problem remained to be solved.

The day following the departure of Glinderen and his administrators, Hammell remarked, "So far, so good. Now, what do we do when the Space Force shows up?"

Morrissey suggested, "There's no love lost between the Space Force and the Planetary Development Administration. And Glinderen belongs to PDA. Can we make anything out of that?"

Roberts shook his head. "If we make PDA look silly, the Space Force will be secretly delighted. But it's still their duty to physically back up Glinderen. We'll be just as dead afterward, no matter *how* they chortle at his expense."

"One thing I wonder about," said Morrissey, "is why you told Glinderen the Space Force had a detachment in the asteroid belt?"

"Because Glinderen is almost sure to go straight to them. I'm eager to see what happens."

"How will we see what happens?"

"When Maury and his boys had us in their gravitor beam, they sent up some fishnet pickups to listen in on any tight-beam messages passed between our ships. The symbiotic computer planted parasite circuits in the fish-net pickups. Those pickups are expensive. They've long since been pulled back in, and stored where Maury can see that no subordinate appropriates them. Many of the parasite circuits—which outwardly are little more than electrically-charged dust particles—have floated off into the atmosphere of Maury's base, to stick to walls and view-ports, and get carried out to other places on people's clothing. Every time Maury checks his pickups, more parasite circuits float out. Each of these circuits will relay signals from other circuits. And on the way from the asteroid belt to the planet, here, the patrol ship sowed microrelays at intervals to pass along the signals. That's how we'll know what happens."

Later that day, Glinderen's ships arrived off the asteroid belt, and were stopped by the two-day wonder. Glinderen immediately reported the situation on Paradise. The two-day wonder got hold of Maury. Maury appeared, dressed as a general, speedily dug out all the information he wanted, and gave orders to let Glinderen proceed. Glinderen refused, and demanded action.

The two-day wonder now exhausted his stock of military poses trying to get Glinderen to move on. Glinderen angrily accused the two-day wonder of trying to evade his responsibilities, and threatened to report him to Sector Headquarters. The two-day wonder called Maury. Maury, determined not to saddle himself with a horde of administrators who were worthless for ransom, but sure to bring on a crusade if he killed them, promised immediate action, and sent some followers disguised as Space Force men, who methodically smashed the infuriated Glinderen's transmitters, but otherwise left the ships undamaged.

Having got rid of Glinderen, Maury remarked to one of his chief lieutenants, "The more I hear of it the better this Empire looks."

"Tricky stuff to fool with," said his lieutenant uneasily.

Roberts listened alertly.

"Yes," said Maury, "but they'd ransom that king."

"Get our head in a sling if—" Maury's lieutenant paused. "But if they made trouble, we'd kill the king, right?"

"Right. And he's down there with just two ships. Get the latest on that convoy. It's already had a five-day delay at R&R XII-C. If we stick around waiting for it, we'll be here when the Space Force comes through after this king. If *we* grab him first, then if he's real, we get the ransom. If he's fake, we take over his racket, whatever it is."

Hammell said shakily, "Boy, that's all we need."

Morrissey, at the want-generator, said "Now what?"

"Maury," said Hammell, "is coming down here with his fleet of commerce raiders to grab 'the king' for ransom."

Roberts smiled the smile of the angler when the fish takes the worm. "Yes, and *that* gives us our chance."

"How?" demanded Hammell. "Maury may not be as tough as the Space Force, but he's next best."

"Yes, but if this preliminary bout with Maury turns out right, maybe the main event with the Space Force will get canceled."

"How do you figure that?"

"If we aren't here, there isn't much the Space Force can do to us."

"Meaning, if we run for it—"

"No. In *that* case, the situation is open-and-shut. We're guilty, and our story is a fake."

"Then, how—"

"If we disappear—If Maury *is seen to capture us*—"

"Then Maury's got us! How does that help?"

"Suppose the sequence of events goes like this: Maury attacks. After a stiff fight, he is seen to haul us into his ship on a gravitor beam. He leaves. The Space Force arrives. Beforehand, naturally, we've destroyed any identifying marks on the yacht. All the Space Force has to go on is that Maury swallowed us up, and then Maury vanished. Now, on that basis, who can prove anything about anything?"

Morrissey was nodding enthusiastically. "It's not foolproof, of course, but—"

"Not foolproof!" said Hammell. "Ye gods! Look, Maury captures us and then disappears. How do we get away from Maury?"

Roberts said irritatedly, "Obviously, he never captured us in the first place."

"You just said—"

"He is *seen* to haul our ship in on a gravitor beam. That's how it *looks*. Our ship disappears into his larger ship, and his ship, and his fleet, then leave. That's the *appearance*. But what actually happens is *we* capture *him*."

Hammell's eyes widened.

"We use *our* gravitor beam," said Roberts, "and once in Maury's ship, you and I get out, in battle armor, while Morrissey beams 'desire for peace' at Maury and his crew. We'll be drugged against the effect of the want-generator. We put it to Maury, do as we say or else. Then, if necessary, Morrissey beams 'desire to obey' at the rest of Maury's fleet as Maury orders them to leave. Bear in mind, Maury is out to *capture* us. He won't attack to kill."

"Hm-m-m," said Hammell. "That does seem to provide a natural explanation for everything. What Maury thinks, of course, won't match what everyone else thinks—but he won't be in any position to do anything about that."

Morrissey nodded. "It's risky. But it *does* give us a chance."

"I'm for it," said Hammell.

"Now," said Roberts, "it's just a question of working out the important details—"

Maury's commerce raiders came out of the asteroid belt like no Space Force fleet ever flown, each separate chief keeping his own ships of whatever size and class together.

The two-day wonder went to work at once:

"By order Space Force Sector H.Q., Lieutenant General Bryan L. Bender Commanding, this Force is directed to proceed to the planet Boschock III, and there establish formal relations with the representatives of the political entity known as The Empire."

The patrol ship was prompt to reply: "By command of His Royal and Imperial Majesty, Vaughan the First, surnamed The Terrible, this planet is inviolate soil, bounden into the fiefdom of His Majesty as Duke of Trasimere, and thereby into the Empire. You enter here at your own instant and deadly peril."

The two-day wonder lifted his chin heroically: "The Space Force has its orders. We can do no less than our duty."

The patrol ship headed directly for the onrushing fleet.

Hammell uneasily watched the battle screen. "That's a lot of ships."

"Yes," said Roberts, "but dead kings don't bring much ransom."

Maury's fleet closed in, and a new, more oily voice spoke up: "Certainly we of the Space Force do not have the slightest desire to do any harm to the most sacred person of your king. We are prepared to do whatever we can to accommodate these differences and smooth relations between our separate nations and viewpoints. We suggest that a meeting be held immediately following the landing—"

The patrol ship interrupted: "Following the landing, nothing will remain for you but penance in hell."

In quick succession, two gravitor beams reached out to grip the patrol ship.

In instantaneous reply, dazzling shafts of energy reached out from the patrol ship, to leave bright explosions in the distance.

An "asteroid" towed by two massive high-thrust ships, was now cut loose, and reached out with a narrow penetrating beam aimed at the patrol ship's reaction-drive nozzles.

The patrol ship deflected that, and two searing bolts of

energy struck the massive asteroid, which was not visibly affected. There was a faint rumble as a missile dropped free from the patrol ship. There was another rumble, and another.

More of Maury's ships methodically lanced out with fusion beams aimed at the reaction-drive nozzles. While the patrol ship could frustrate each attempt, the response was taken account of in the next try, the individual blows woven together to create a net in which the patrol ship's efforts grew rapidly more constricted. This was happening so fast that to Roberts it appeared to be a blur of dazzling lines on the battle screen, leading to one obvious result, until suddenly the patrol ship was caught, its own fusion beams deflected harmlessly by the combined space-distorters of the commerce raiders—

—And then, in rapid succession, dazzling bursts of light sheared an enormous chunk from the asteroid, while others knocked out four of Maury's ships.

Roberts blinked.

The patrol ship's missiles had somehow gotten through, completely undetected.

The auxiliary screen, still transmitting the scene in Maury's headquarters on an ultrafast rebuilt cruiser, showed the commerce raiders' consternation. But then the patrol ship swerved crazily, and swerved again.

"*Got* it!" growled Maury, mopping his brow.

From the patrol ship, fusion bolts lanced out in all directions, striking two of Maury's ships apparently by sheer chance. A missile blew up short of the mark, shot-holing another of his ships with flying bits and fragments.

Cursing, Maury's gunners reported that neither they nor their battle computers could keep up with the patrol ship's movements. They couldn't predict whether a hit would be crippling or deadly.

"Aim to miss," snarled Maury. "As long as they don't know we're doing it, it won't matter."

Firing furiously, with an inferno of attack around it, the patrol ship withdrew toward Paradise, spun down through the atmosphere, and by a remarkable last-minute feat of piloting, set down in only a moderately hard landing outside the Barons Council Hall.

A roboid policeman immediately rushed out, to guard the

ship. From all directions in the Inner City, roboid police began racing to the scene.

"O.K.," said Maury. "Lay smoke."

A series of missiles streaked through the atmosphere, landed within several hundred yards of the downed patrol ship, and exploded in enormous clouds of dirty gray smoke.

The inrushing roboid police slowed abruptly.

"Landing ships down," said Maury.

Four big ships dropped fast through the planet's atmosphere, to disappear in the boiling uprush of smoke.

"Landing teams out," said Maury.

Roberts depressed a communicator switch. "Kelty—open fire!"

The roar reached Roberts only faintly through the patrol ship's hull, but listening critically, Roberts was grateful not to be on the receiving end of the city's rapid-fire guns at short range. He gripped the controls. "Cease fire five seconds."

The firing died away.

The patrol ship burst up through the smoke. "Morrissey—"

"Ready."

"Coordinates—"

As Roberts flashed toward the ultrafast cruiser that was Maury's headquarters, suddenly the symbols on the battle screen seemed to multiply. At the same instant, Maury's fleet broke into individual squadrons racing in all directions. Maury's headquarters ship exploded, and out of the fragments shot a streak that dwindled to a speck before Roberts realized what had happened.

Then the outside viewscreen changed its scale, and showed the whole scene shrunk down to small size.

From the distance, a sizable fleet approached, its ships precisely positioned for mutual support. Before this fleet, like startled fish, the commerce raiders dispersed in all directions. Already moving off the edge of the screen was the chief commerce raider of them all, his escape ship pouring on acceleration as it streaked for the nearest breakpoint to some quiet hideout far from trouble.

Roberts swore, whipped the patrol ship around, and shot after the fleeing commerce raiders, laying down a ruinous fire, and under its cover dropping inflatable deception packs among the widening clouds of debris.

Hammell, waiting in his battle armor to go into Maury's ship, called, "What's wrong?"

"The Space Force has showed up!"

Roberts spun the ship after another fleeing commerce raider, succeeded in laying a few more packs, and gave it up in disgust.

On the outside viewscreen, the approaching fleet was decelerating fast.

Morrissey said nervously, *"Now* what do we do?"

"Well, I've sowed a lot of deception packs—"

"What for?"

Roberts exhaled carefully. "The idea was that we could inflate them to dummy ships, beam 'desire to believe' at that fleet, and—"

Hammell said incredulously, "What, the Space Force?"

Roberts could now see just what likelihood there was of that working. "It's a *chance*," he said stubbornly, "and we're in no spot to ignore a chance."

"Then" said Morrissey, "let's get out of here! This ship is fast, isn't it?"

"That's an admission of guilt," said Roberts, inwardly kicking himself for not "chasing" the commerce raiders at top speed.

Hammell had the same idea. "Why didn't you go after Maury? Nobody would have known whether you were chasing him, running away, or what."

"It would have been out of character," said Roberts lamely, "for the king to leave with a larger force approaching."

"Nuts!" said Hammell. "His screen could have been damaged. He could have been wounded or knocked out."

The communicator buzzed imperatively.

Moodily, Roberts reached out to snap it on. Before he could reach the switch, there was a *click*, and a cold voice said, "What interstellar force is this? Stand warned! This is a King's ship, on the King's business, and you have no right to patrol here."

An auxiliary screen lit up, to show a frowning officer in the uniform of a Space Force lieutenant general.

"What ship is this?"

"Imperial ship *Nom de Guerre*. Who asks?"

"Lieutenant General Nils Larssen. What Empire?"

"The Empire."

"Who commands that ship?"

There was a silence, and Roberts, fearing that the symbiotic computer had run out of words, snapped on the sound transmission.

"*I* command this ship!"

Roberts suddenly found himself at the parting of the ways. He could meekly identify himself. Or he could carry the bluff to the ridiculous point where he challenged the Space Force.

Abruptly he discovered that he couldn't back down.

He said coldly, "You come too late to save your comrades. They are dead, or fled like cowards. Now I wait to test *your* steel."

Larssen looked blank. He pursed his lips, turned away, then turned back, apparently to rephrase the question.

Roberts waited, grimly aware of the cracking ice he stood on.

At this delicate juncture, the symbiotic computer put its oar in. With icy hauteur, using Roberts voice, it said: "I have spoken."

Larssen opened his mouth, and shut it. His face reddened. "Listen—I don't give a damn *who* you are! You'll answer my questions, and you'll answer them straight!"

Roberts groped for some way out.

Then he heard his own voice speak coldly from the communicator, as if to someone nearby, "The bark of this interstellar dog hath a petulant note."

Hammell's voice, though Hammell was standing by in silent paralysis, said coolly, "We know ways to train the surly cur, if he intrudes too far."

Morrissey was sitting at the want-generator, looking from Roberts to Hammell as if they'd gone insane, and now he had the added treat of hearing his own voice contribute, though his mouth was tightly shut.

"We'll send this rabble to the Earl of Hell, and let them mount patrol on the fiery march."

On the screen, Larssen paused, an odd listening expression on his face.

Roberts' own voice called, "Master of the Ordnance!"

"Ready, Sire!"

"Master of the Helm!"

"Ready, Sire!"

"Then we'll put it to the test! Master of the Helm, brace your engines! Master of the Ordnance, pick your targets!"

A roar and a howling whine sounded together as the gravitors counteracted the reaction drive, in a prelude to a furious burst of acceleration.

On the control console, a switch snapped forward, to activate the deception packs and create the appearance of a formidable squadron—though the Space Force detectors should quickly spot the trick.

Larssen, suddenly perspiring, called, *"Wait!"* Then he whirled and shouted an order.

On the screen, the hurtling formation of ships began slowly to turn, swinging away from Paradise.

Roberts, startled, saw Larssen turn back to the screen, his expression intent and wary.

"I didn't mean to intrude on a region you patrol."

An elaborately courteous voice replied, "To do so were an incivility bordering on the interstellar."

"Then *patrol* it if you want it so damned much!" snarled Larssen.

"The interstellar regions subject to the rule of His Royal and Imperial Majesty, Vaughan the First, we will patrol, surely."

Larssen shut his mouth with a click of the teeth.

The screen abruptly went blank, but a silent burst of profanity seemed to radiate from it after it was off.

Roberts, drenched in sweat, groped in his pocket for a handkerchief, but couldn't find one.

Hammell got out of his armor, looking like a ghost.

Morrissey staggered to his feet, and promptly banged his head on the shiny cylinder.

Roberts finally located the handkerchief, and wiped the sweat out of his eyes. He took another look at the outside viewscreen.

Larssen's fleet traveled past in formidable array.

Roberts glanced at the battle screen. On his side there was only the patrol ship, and the imitation ships blown up out of—Roberts blinked, and adjusted the outside viewscreen—

There amongst the seeming patrol ships and cruisers lay a gigantic ship—a dreadnought fit to take on whole fleets all by itself. The sunlit side was toward Roberts, and the name was clearly visible: *Coeur de Lion.*

The deception pack out of which a thing like that might be blown up would take a battleship to carry it.

Roberts took a deep breath. "Well, men, we're still alive. And here's one big reason."

Hammell ducked under the glittering cylinder, and looked at the screen.

Morrissey warily slid one hand along the cylinder and ducked under to stand beside Hammell.

"Great space!" said Hammell, suddenly seeing what Roberts was looking at.

Morrissey murmured, *"Coeur de Lion.* Isn't that the ship you said called you—when Maury stopped us at the asteroid belt?"

"Yes," said Roberts. "But I thought it was just a clever gambit of the symbiotic computer. Now there it is."

Hammell said uneasily, "It's friendly?"

"I hope so. But where did it come from?"

Hammell said hesitantly, "Apparently the Space Force didn't see it till the last minute. They were going to chop us into mincemeat, then all of a sudden, they changed their minds."

"It must have been *undetectable*—they've got some kind of device that blanks them out to radar, gravitor, and all the other standard detection systems!" said Roberts. "Wait, now. What—" Suddenly what he was trying to think of came to him: "Listen, our missiles got to Maury's ships *undetected.*"

Morrissey said wonderingly, "They were the missiles originally supplied with this ship?"

"*I* haven't bought any."

Morrissey stared at the screen. "Listen, this may sound nuts, but when I look at that ship, it looks to me a lot like *this one we're on.* That one is a whole lot bigger, and the proportions aren't identical, but there's a kind of similarity of plan that . . ."

Hammell said nervously, "That dreadnought was undetectable. This ship's missiles were undetectable. That dreadnought looks like this ship, owing to a kind of similarity of plan. This ship is an Interstellar Patrol ship. It follows that that dreadnought—"

Roberts' throat felt dry.

Morrissey said, "What happens to unauthorized individuals who get caught using Interstellar Patrol ships?"

Hammell sucked in his breath. "The Interstellar Patrol is even worse to tangle with than the Space Force. They don't operate by the book. Setups nobody else can handle go to the Interstellar Patrol."

Roberts uneasily considered the bargain he had gotten— even though it had cost the better part of his life's savings— when he bought the patrol ship at the salvage cluster. Now he wondered if, through some piece of treachery, the original crew had been slaughtered, and now the dreadnought was waiting patiently for Roberts to identify himself, and if he didn't—

"Nuts," said Roberts. He snapped on the communicator.

"Imperial Ship *Nom de Guerre*, His Royal and Imperial Majesty Vaughan the First commanding, to Imperial Dreadnought *Coeur de Lion*. How many of that first batch of outspace dogs got away with their skins?"

Immediately, a tough-looking individual appeared on an auxiliary screen. His gaze drilled into Roberts' eyes.

Roberts saw no virtue in pussyfooting around. If the dreadnought was going to blow him up, well, then *let* it blow him up. He looked directly into the eyes of the face on the screen, and growled, "The Empire does not maintain these ships at heavy cost that her captains may use them for toys. Speak up! Hast swallowed thy tongue? Didst accomplish anything, besides to look pretty?"

The tough scarred face on the screen broke into a momentary grin. "Your Majesty, forgive my witless hesitation. We feared you dead from these verminous outspacers. We cleaned out the lot, save for one that broke into sub-space even as we poised thumb and forefinger to pop him like a grape."

"That one was the worst," said Roberts, as Hammell and Morrissey stared. "There went the brain and guiding will of the evil band."

"Some other time, he may run afoul of us, and have a slower ship, or we a faster."

"Hasten the day," said Roberts, smiling. He was beginning to think he had worked out the combination.

The face on the screen changed expression slightly.

"If Your Majesty please, the Empire anxiously awaits your

return, to heal its wounds in the pomps and pleasures of the coronation. The Great Lords and Nobles count the days, till they may reaffirm their loyalty to the Crown, and swear allegiance to Vaughan the First. If we may accompany you— lest other outspace dogs pop up out of nowhere—'Tis daring greatly, I know, to suggest it, but *Coeur de Lion* has spacious accommodation—We may take aboard *Nom de Guerre* and all, if you like—'Twould speed the day of your return. I crave forgiveness if I presume—"

"And it were freely granted, but your offer is welcome. We shall come aboard at once."

The man on the screen bowed his head respectfully. "Your Majesty doth greatly honor us."

"'Tis an honor to honor such loyal subjects."

The tough face looked humbly appreciative. Then the screen went blank.

Hammell and Morrissey stood speechless as Roberts headed the patrol ship toward the dreadnought.

Hammell took a deep breath. "Look—no offense if I just call you 'sir'? Is this an Interstellar Patrol ship? You must know a lot more about this than *we* do. Or is it a . . . ah . . . an *Imperial* ship?"

Morrissey swallowed and listened alertly.

Roberts said cheerfully, "We weren't talking on tight-beam, and there are plenty of technological ears on that planet, now that the technicians have had time to go to work. The more wide-awake among them will put together the number of times 'interstellar' and 'patrol' occurred in the conversation with Larssen, and then they will realize in whose tender hands their fate rests. But they can't prove a thing."

"Then," said Hammell, thinking hard, "this last conversation was a blind?"

"No, it just takes a certain piece of key knowledge to figure it out."

"What might *that* be?"

"Anyone listening to that conversation would be justified in thinking I was the boss. And because of the fact people might be listening, that's how it *had* to be. But what do *you* think?"

Hammell smote his forehead. "You were *ordered* to come on board?"

"That's right," Roberts said.

Morrissey said, "Why not just have the conversation on tight beam?"

"Because I wanted to put them on the spot, to see what they'd do."

Morrissey glanced at the gigantic dreadnought on the outside viewscreen. "Anyone who'd do a thing like that ought to *be* in the Interstellar Patrol."

Roberts nodded. "As Hammell says, they don't operate by the book."

Morrissey stared at him. Hammell said, "Holy—"

Roberts pressed the button to the left of the instrument panel, near the glowing lens lettered "SMB CMP," and said, "How does the Interstellar Patrol recruit new members?"

The symbiotic computer replied, "By whatever method works." It then described several reasonably conventional methods, and added, "*Ships* are sometimes used to obtain recruits, as nearly every independent individual actively operating in space, and hence basically qualified as a recruit, at one time or another needs a ship. The patrol ship is always modestly priced for its value, as the salvage operator finds it hard to dispose of, and impossible to break up. The ship attracts only a certain basic type. Those who want it must have the proper mental, physical, and moral equipment, and the right basic style of self-respect, or the ship's symbiotic computer won't accept them. Those accepted are next tested by the use to which they put the power of the patrol ship's equipment. Those who successfully pass the built-in obstacles become members of the Interstellar Patrol, captains of their own ships, and, in due time, they often recruit their own crew at no expense to the Patrol—sometimes before they really accept that they are members—"

"Oh, my God—" said Hammell.

Morrissey looked thunderstruck. "I *knew* we should have stayed on the yacht!"

"—Or before the prospective crew," the symbiotic computer went on, "expresses a truly sincere desire to enlist. However, just as the judgment of the symbiotic computer is accepted in the selection of the ship's captain, so is the judgment of the captain accepted in the selection of the ship's crew. This method has proved highly satisfactory and inexpensive." The symbiotic computer paused a moment, then added, "Moreover, the procedure is in accord with the highest traditions of the Interstellar Patrol."

Hammell nodded. "It would be."

"Well," said Roberts, "don't complain. It's not everyone who escapes from a routine space-transport to be a king or a duke—or a member of the Interstellar Patrol."

Roberts saw the look of puzzled surprise, a brief glint of pride, and the glow of interest light the faces of Hammell and Morrissey. They weren't going aboard the gigantic ship as *prisoners*, to be interrogated. They were actually going as members of the legendary Interstellar Patrol.

Roberts saw the brief outthrust of jaw that told of determination to make good. That was how *he* felt, too.

It occurred to him that neither he, nor Hammell, nor Morrissey, would have voluntarily tried to enlist in the Patrol. The thing was too much. They might not make it. Their qualifications might not meet the standards. They might not like it if they did make it. So the Interstellar Patrol, with deep-laid craft, so arranged matters that none of them had the faintest idea what was going on until the thing was accomplished.

An organization run on that basis must be no lover of red tape and stuffed shirts. In an organization so capable of understanding human nature, it might be possible to get things done.

Roberts guided the patrol ship on its course, and gradually, the gigantic curve of the dreadnought loomed closer, to fill the viewscreen.

Before them, the big hatch slowly swung wide, to reveal the brightly-lighted interior. Spacesuited figures stepped into view, to wave them forward.

Carefully, Roberts guided the patrol ship through the hatchway into the gigantic spaceship.

Part II: *Boot Camp*

A QUESTION OF ATTITUDE

Dan Bergen lay motionless on his narrow limb amongst the big green leaves, and wished he had never heard of the Interstellar Patrol.

A yard from Bergen's nose, the constrictor glided ahead, then stopped. A small bump on its back bulged up and an eye looked out. The eye swiveled around like a rotating radar antenna, then came to a stop with its gaze fixed on Bergen.

Bergen didn't move. He looked at the eye. The eye looked at him.

A long moment passed.

The eye swung away again. Bergen instantly looked away. The eye swung back, its gaze again fixed on Bergen. Bergen didn't move. The eye swung around, then pulled inside. The bulge on the constrictor's back diminished to a small bump. The snake glided ahead.

Bergen allowed himself the luxury of a breath of air. He relaxed.

The snake continued to glide ahead.

Before, the constrictor had moved, at most, a few feet at a time. Now, yards of it were sliding past.

Frowning, Bergen looked around.

About three feet above the level of his head, and perhaps eight feet away, the big leaves thrust aside. A pair of large opaque green eyes looked at Bergen over a blunt green-and-brown snout.

Bergen for a split-second balanced the question whether he should roll off the limb. That would send him in a headlong plunge through wide-spaced branches toward the forest floor a hundred and eight feet below. Or should he—

The snake's head blurred. Its jaws clamped, in a burst of pain, on his left shoulder.

Bergen struck at it with his right fist.

The head twisted and wrenched, sinking its fangs deep into his shoulder. There was a steady hiss as the rest of the snake slid forward. A thick coil looped around him.

Bergen sucked in a deep breath, and stabbed at the snake's eyes with his extended forefingers.

A thick skin blurred down over its eyes. Another loop passed over Bergen's body. The muscular coils tightened. There was a crushing pressure at his ribs.

Through a red haze, Bergen's right hand found the snake's eyes. The head moved, something gripped his hand, mashed and snapped and ground it, then crushed it at the wrist.

Somewhere within Bergen, a cool sense of calculation told him the fight was all over. But at the same time, he knew he *had* to get free.

For one white-hot instant, this urgent need took control of his body. For this instant, the contractions of the constrictor's huge muscles were blocked, and Bergen struck savagely at its head with his mangled right arm. His left hand, caught in the loops of the snake's body, nevertheless contracted in a grip that tore a section of tough hide from the underlying muscles.

A savage yell of defiance burst from Bergen, and for just a fleeting instant the snake's gaze held a look of blankness— such as might appear in the eyes of a constrictor in the jungles of Earth, when the victim it has selected turns out to be an adult male gorilla.

The instant passed. The energy was gone, and in place of defiance, Bergen felt a wave of exhaustion. There was a final, horrible, increasingly distant sense of crushing pressure, and then dizziness. For an instant something took place that Bergen could not quite recall afterward.

And then he was lying on his back, looking at a gray ceiling overhead.

Very cautiously, Bergen drew up his right hand and looked at it. It was unharmed. He felt of his left shoulder. His left shoulder was unharmed. He sat up. A slight dizziness passed as he swung his feet to the floor.

The memory of the past few instants came back, and Bergen could vividly see the head of the constrictor twist and wrench as the big loops settled around him—

Bergen sprang to his feet and swore savagely. Full consciousness had now returned.

"*Damn* it," he said, forcing the mental picture of the constrictor out of his mind by focusing his attention on the immediate cause of the trouble—the people who gave these tests.

A buzzer sounded its peremptory warning. Bergen again became conscious of his surroundings. He noted the gray bulkheads, gray steel deck, and gray ceiling overhead. There were three short rows of steel cots in the room, and above each cot was a long wide bulge in the ceiling. With a sense of relief, Bergen noted that the other cots were empty—had been empty when he'd gained consciousness. That meant that, though he had failed at the end, he had at least outlasted the other candidates.

A small speaker nearby said, "Bergen to Evaluation. Candidate Daniel Bergen report to Test Evaluation Office."

"Coming," said Bergen. He braced himself for the walk through the Special Effects storeroom. He drew a deep breath, opened the air-tight hatch, and stepped into a shadowy space jammed with apes, alligators, imitation dead trees, grizzly bears, hollow lichened boulders, simulated rotten logs covered with moss, rolled-up bolts of spider web with spiders attached, one dozen wharf rats packed head-to-tail in a crate, and other unattractive odds and ends that loomed, half-recognizable, through the gloom. Bergen was grumbling to himself as he reached the hatch leading to the corridor. Then he straightened up, assumed an alert, resolute look, and stepped out into the corridor.

A brisk walk brought Bergen to a hatch marked: "Test Evaluation, Colonel Sanders." Bergen knocked, heard the colonel's crisp "Come in," and stepped inside. He was in a small compartment lined with filing cabinets and electronic equipment, and with wires and odd headsets dangling from the ceiling. A spare athletic individual with colonel's leaves, a shock of crew-cut hair and a look of cool objectivity eyed Bergen from behind a bare-topped desk. Bergen reported his presence. The colonel motioned him to an olive-colored drum that doubled as a chair.

Bergen thoughtfully eyed the drum, which was labeled: "RATTLESNAKES, 1 doz. (assorted)." He made sure the lid was on tight, and gingerly sat down. He looked at the colonel. The colonel looked back coolly. A period of time passed. Bergen forced himself to wait.

The colonel cleared his throat, clasped his hands behind the back of his neck and leaned back in his chair. His eyes came to a sharp focus. He said accusingly, "That was a stupid stunt, Bergen."

"Sir?" said Bergen, pathetically uncertain which particular stunt the colonel had in mind.

"Why didn't you just put both hands out in front and dive straight down his throat?"

Bergen cast around mentally, then said, "Oh, you mean the constrictor, sir?"

The colonel snorted, and Bergen felt an overpowering sense of stupidity. Whenever he entered this room his I.Q. seemed to drop off twenty or thirty points. He would recover his lost intelligence when he returned to the corridor, and then he would *really* see how dull he had been.

"Well?" snapped the colonel.

"Sir?"

"*'Sir?'*" mimicked the colonel. His face reddened, and he roared, *"Answer the question!"*

Bergen looked at him blankly.

The colonel sat up and leaned forward on the desk. "Why," he said, "didn't you just put your hands over your head and jump down the constrictor's throat? You'd have accomplished exactly the same thing, and with a great saving of energy." The colonel had the air of a person putting forth a reasonable suggestion.

"Well," said Bergen, trying dully to synchronize his reactions with those of the colonel, "my purpose, sir, wasn't to get killed."

The colonel nodded, and leaned back. "But so far as the simulation was concerned, that's exactly what you accomplished, isn't it?"

Bergen could now see he had walked into a trap. Gloomily he said, "Yes, sir."

"Why?"

"Sir?"

"Tell me, *why* did you get killed?"

"I guess I did the wrong thing."

"*What* wrong thing?"

Bergen hesitated.

The colonel waited.

Bergen shook his head. "If I'd dropped off that limb, sir, I'd have smashed right to the bottom of the forest floor. That was certain death. I don't see that I had much choice."

The colonel shook his head. "You made a series of mistakes. To begin with, you looked directly into the constrictor's dorsal eye. That was the first error, and a serious one. When you stand at attention during an inspection, do you look *into* the eyes of the inspecting officer?"

"No, sir."

"What do you do?"

"I look straight ahead."

"Why?"

"Well . . . it's regulations."

The colonel nodded. "It's regulations. But there's a reason *why* it's regulations. If you look *into* the eyes of the inspecting officer, you make, as it were, personal contact with him. He will notice it, and of necessity he will have to respond. An inspection is an impersonal matter, and he will reprimand you. And yet, you had no hesitancy about looking into the dorsal eye of that constrictor. Did you think that because the constrictor came from another planet, it wouldn't sense you were looking at it?"

"Well, I—" Bergen paused.

"Yes?" prompted the colonel.

Bergen finished lamely, "I guess I just didn't think about it at the time, sir."

The colonel nodded. "That was your basic error, underlying all the other errors. You didn't think about it. The next thing you didn't think about was looking *away*. The constrictor looked away, *you* looked away, then the constrictor looked back, and promptly noticed the change in the position of your eyes. Next, you didn't think about the snake's *motion*. You saw it glide forward, knew it was moving a lot farther than it had before, knew it had seen you, and yet *you didn't change your position.*"

Bergen stared at him, blinked, and shook his head in weary disgust. "Yes. Now I see it."

"You've been talking," said the colonel, "as if your only alternative was to jump off the limb. Not so. The snake *had to get into position to strike.* While it was doing that, you could have moved, and at least gained time."

"I see it now, sir."

"But you didn't see it when it counted."

"No, sir. I didn't."

"All right. You made a number of mistakes. First, you stared the snake in the eye, then when it looked away, you looked away; both of these things the snake noticed and correctly interpreted. Next, you stayed where you were till it was all set to get you. Then, in addition, you *still* stayed where you were when there was an instant left to act."

"Well, sir, I admit I was wrong before. But there was still *some* chance the snake wouldn't do anything. Whereas, if I dropped off the limb—"

"You'd have caught a vine about nine feet below," said the colonel.

Bergen slowly brought his jaw shut.

"Pretty stupid, wasn't it?" said the colonel.

Bergen drew a deep breath. "Yes, sir, I guess it was, at that."

The colonel sat back. "Most of us are accustomed to think of ourselves as intelligent people. We move through life in our accustomed orbits, expect things always to remain basically as they are now, have repeated opportunities to rehearse our behavior patterns for the few standard situations we meet, and nevertheless we fall into one mess after another—because we don't really think. If things turn out badly for us, our reaction is to complain that the situation *wasn't set up right in the first place.*"

The colonel looked at Bergen intently, and Bergen sensed that this comment had a personal application. "Yes, sir," he said.

The colonel leaned back and said thoughtfully, "There are two basic attitudes, or ways of looking at things. The human race uses these two attitudes to move forward, much as a man uses his legs to walk. And it's just as catastrophic for a member of the human race to misplace these two attitudes as it is for him to cross his left leg in front of his right leg, and then try to take a step with his right leg.

"The first attitude is that of recognizing the defect. In one form, this is pure gripe, the attitude of 'headquarters is too stupid to get their head out of their boot.' But it's also the attitude of the man who looks around, and asks himself if things couldn't be improved. From this attitude arises a lot of noise, but, properly used, it's also one of the main driving forces for progress. If men had always been satisfied, who would ever have tried anything new?

"So, you see, it's useful to see imperfections. But it's useless to *keep our minds focused on imperfections*. Having seen the imperfections, next we shift our attention to look for some means of improvement. We see the obstacle, then look for the way through or around. And that is what you *didn't* do. Right?"

"Yes, sir," said Bergen miserably.

"Don't worry about it," said the colonel. "It takes time to develop the right attitude. But you have to show strong enough signs of it or you can't pass this last test. You've got to be alert. Never be dismayed at the most stunning examples of basically unfair mechanisms and situations. Assume that somewhere in the mess there is something you can use, an opening you can get through, and set yourself to find it. Remember, mountain climbers regularly go up vertical rock faces that the average man wouldn't think a fly could climb. It is obviously *unfair* to expect a man to climb a thing like that. And yet, the holds are there, if you can find them, and if you have the few pieces of fairly simple equipment that will help you get a grip."

"And if you slip," said Bergen drily, "you're finished."

The colonel shrugged. "You could also say, 'Why climb?' That's beside the point. The object is to show what people *can* accomplish if they look for the handholds, instead of deciding at a glance that the slope is too steep, so it's impossible."

This was a longer lecture than Bergen had gotten any of the other times, and he was starting to feel uneasy. The colonel was watching him intently, and seemed to be waiting for the significance to sink in.

"Yes, sir," said Bergen dutifully.

"Now," said the colonel, "I wouldn't bother to say all this

if you hadn't gotten up into a respectable category for a candidate. You started off with a class of fifty, distributed to various testing facilities. This fifty has so far been given a total of four tests. About half of you flunked the first test, and roughly the same proportion have flunked each test since. One candidate died of heart failure. One candidate blew up and quit. That leaves exactly three of you coming up for the fifth test."

Bergen blinked. "Forty-seven out of fifty are washed out already?"

"That's right."

"How many more tests after this one?"

"The fifth test is the last, unless there are special circumstances."

"And only one of us can pass this test?"

"No. All or none of you may pass the fifth test. We've had both things happen."

"Suppose I flunk it? Is there any second chance?"

The colonel shrugged. "You can take the tests as often as we offer them. Moreover, taking these tests isn't the only way to get in. But it's the only way open to you right now, and even if we should offer them again, you have to take the full series each time. We'd advise you to put everything you've got into passing this one test you've still got in front of you."

Bergen thought of the miserable spot he'd been in and to which he'd return if he failed this test. Bergen, a natural hater of authority, had had the poor luck, when called up for military training, to find himself under a natural martinet. The fellow tore beds open to inspect the mattresses, then sent the recruits on K.P. because their beds were unmade. Accompanied by a few toadies, he would snap on the barracks lights at 2:00 on stormy nights, and order everyone outside into the rain, while he and his sycophants searched the barracks for concealed liquor. Returning to the outside steps of the barracks he would note angrily that these men were up after taps, and would order them marched through the soaking downpour all night for punishment. On the following day, he would harass them for their sluggish unsoldierly bearing, and, to correct their attitude, would give them close order drill till they were dead on their feet.

One day, following a lengthy lecture on soldierly behavior, some worn strand of Bergen's self-control snapped.

The officer and an admiring toady strolled past in front of Bergen as he stood in ranks. Bergen's right hand reached out as if of its own accord, gripped the officer by the uniform jacket and jerked him around. The hand released him, then came up again, to strike him full in the face. As Bergen stepped out of ranks, several companions came to life and grabbed him. Bergen was about to bash the officer's head against a post when they finally got him stopped. In the resulting court-martial, the officer's numerous and flagrant misdeeds came to light. But Bergen nevertheless was still in the stockade when Sergeant Hale of the Interstellar Patrol came through searching for recruits, with his talk of good pay, forgiveness of past sins, and a splendid future—*if* he could pass the tests.

"Now," said the colonel, his cool voice snapping Bergen back to the present, "we might as well get on with this final test."

Bergen once again found himself lying flat on his back. This time, the cots to either side were empty, as no other candidate on the ship had gotten this far. Bergen closed his eyes, and was conscious of a drifting sensation such as he had felt before the previous tests. Then a voice was speaking to him, saying, "You have passed each of the first four tests. Each was designed to test certain elements of your physical or mental make-up, and of your basic character. The test which follows is intended to examine one particular personal trait. This trait has been tested only incidentally in previous tests. But it is a trait especially important to a member of the Interstellar Patrol.

"History shows that in any given situation, certain individuals tend to survive. In a group of gunfighters, for instance, certain men stand out over a period of time. Is this a matter only of reflexive speed, or is there also *something else?* Amongst politicians, some rise rapidly to prominence, then fade into insignificance. Others remain steadily in office. Some businessmen maintain a high position while others rise and sink around them. Why? Is it a matter only of luck, friends, special skills, or inherited wealth? Men have had all of these and failed. Others have begun with none of them, and succeeded. Why? Is there some special skill— or perhaps some higher skill—that enables a man to use other skills and advantages, combining them to gain his ends?

If there is, you will need it badly as a member of the Interstellar Patrol. You have already been given some idea of what we consider this special skill or attitude to be. We will give you just one more hint:

"Julius Caesar, like many other great leaders of the past, had this quality in good measure. Caesar was once confronted by a walled town on a steep rocky hill. To attack it, he must advance uphill. The enemy could hurl their missile weapons down at him, while his troops had to throw theirs uphill. The enemy was sheltered. Caesar's troops were exposed. The walls were strong. The enemy had an abundance of food stored inside, and, for water, had built close to the site of a spring. To besiege the place would be a long, slow, time-consuming process. To try to overwhelm it suddenly was likely to result in heavy losses.

"What should Caesar do? Should he attack with all his troops? Or should he carry out a slow, methodical siege?

"Answer: Caesar cut the underground channel that fed the enemy's spring. With the spring dried up, there was no water, and the enemy quickly surrendered.

"The test will now begin."

The drifting, floating sensation ended. Bergen opened his eyes to find himself lying on a sloppily made-up cot. He was in one corner of a cabin, with a window opening sawed through the log wall near the head of the cot. The log at the bottom of this window had been smoothed to form a rough sill, and on this sill sat a crude earthenware jug with a corncob in it for a cork. As Bergen watched, a dirty hand reached up from outside, and took the jug off the sill. There was a *pop!* followed by a gurgling sound. Then there was a long sigh. The jug reappeared on the sill.

Bergen frowned, and looked around. The situation seemed to make no sense. But the apparent senselessness might itself be part of the test.

Bergen carefully sat up and looked around the room. A double-bitted ax with broken handle lay on the rough plank floor across the room. A long-barreled gun had been slammed against a corner of the stone fireplace with enough force to chip the stone and knock the gun barrel out of line. The gun lay on the floor near the ax. A number of smashed handmade tables, chairs and benches made several heaps of wreckage that cluttered the room. Large chunks had been chopped out of the log wall, and chips were strewn around on the floor amidst the wrecked furniture, ax, and gun. The general effect was as if someone had gone into a maniacal rage, and wrecked everything in sight. As Bergen's eyes adjusted to the gloom, he could see the remains of a smashed earthenware bowl, and bits and pieces of what had evidently once been a rough window glazed with a cheap transparent plastic.

Evidently, he was on a colony planet of the most primitive kind. And, somewhere nearby, was whoever had been driven half-crazy by the conditions that just naturally existed on such a colony planet.

Bergen cautiously put one hand on the foot of the cot, and leaned on it to step across a pile of debris. The cot teetered and collapsed. Bergen was struggling to regain his balance when a billet of wood came through the open window and struck him in the back of the neck, knocking him into a pile of broken furniture with jutting legs and braces. One of these caught him in the middle of the forehead. He saw a dazzling burst of sparks.

Outside, someone spat.

Bergen dizzily picked himself up. His head was throbbing painfully. In the previous tests, he'd at least had a definite purpose. Now, he was told to manifest some obscure quality that was supposed to distinguish successful gunmen, politicians, businessmen, and generals. Bergen snorted. He wasn't even sure there *was* any such quality.

From outside came a deep male voice. "Coming out? Or do I *drag* you out?"

A burst of laughter followed, as if two or more men were outside, enjoying the situation.

Bergen was now sure that he must be on a colony planet in an early stage of development. Only on such a planet would he be likely to find a roughly-built log cabin, with ax and gun used as tools, and with a light plastic, flown in by the supply ship, to serve the function of glass.

As he was thinking this, the cabin door flew open, and an individual whose shoulders spanned the doorframe came in, glanced around and slung a billet of wood at him.

Bergen ducked. His opponent sprang across a pile of trash, gripped him by the shirt and slammed him against the log wall. There was a burst of lights, then blackness and dizziness.

The colonel's voice was saying, "You're very close to failing this test, Bergen. If your total score had been a little lower in the other tests, we'd flunk you now. Do you hear me?"

"Yes, sir."

"Anyone with a brain in his head could have made better use of his time than you have. The room was filled with potential weapons. You had more than enough time to collect one. Instead, you did your meditating on the situation before you were armed, even though that block of wood in the back of the neck should have shown you had enemies. When your opponent came in, his vision was momentarily dim because of the bright light outside. But he found you in full view and empty-handed. Your performance so far is pathetic."

"Yes, sir."

"Thanks to this pitiful start, the simulator has you on a track where you'll find yourself completely at the mercy of petty opponents. This is going to be an unpleasant experience. If your performance is no better than it's been so far, you'd be better off to stop now. If you want, we'll end the test."

"No, sir. I want to go on."

"You're warned, Bergen."

"Yes, sir. Thank you."

"All right."

Bergen felt dizzy.

A voice was saying, "Tickle him again, Con."

"Happy to, Milt."

A white-hot pincers took hold of the calf of Bergen's right leg and tore out a piece of flesh.

The pain snapped Bergen wide-awake. He found himself sitting up, his back toward the outer edge of the cabin's porch, with two men bent over him, one of them holding in a leather glove what looked like a large insect. Bergen tried to spring to his feet, but his hands, tied behind his back, jerked him off balance, so that his head banged back against a badly weathered post that supported the porch roof.

A familiar voice said, "Let him see how they *taste*, Con."

The nearer man leaned toward him, forced open Bergen's mouth and shoved something in. A multitude of sharp claws scraped at his tongue, teeth, and the inside of his mouth.

Bergen was wide-awake again. For an instant, he felt an uprush of rage. But then a sense of cold calculation told him that, in this spot, the rage wouldn't work. Bergen concentrated on this cool inner thought, nearly lost it, then brought it into full awareness, and suddenly he was perfectly cool himself, his mind concentrated on finding some opening. After a moment's intense thought, he saw one possibility—then an instant later he saw another. And then his thoughts moved from point to point like a lightning bolt seeking the line of least resistance, and suddenly he had a plan.

Bergen shifted his position to test his wrists and ankles. He wrists were tightly tied. His legs were free. No one was in sight save the two men bent over him. One of these was the broad-shouldered man, apparently named Milt, who had knocked him out. The other was an older man, called "Con," who now jammed the large struggling many-clawed insect further into Bergen's mouth.

Bergen turned slightly, his left foot hooking behind the left ankle of the broad-shouldered Milt, his right leg drawing back as if he would try to roll to his left to get up. At the same time, he expelled the air in his mouth, closing his lips without clenching his teeth.

He slammed his right foot forward, to hit the broad-shouldered Milt at the left knee. Bergen's left foot was already hooked behind Milt's left ankle. Milt slammed back against the wall of the cabin.

But this was only one part of his problem. Meanwhile, the big insect squirmed violently in his mouth, its light and air cut off. Bergen opened his mouth slightly. The insect urgently thrust out into the light and Bergen spat it towards the other of the two men, who sprang back out of the way.

Bergen got his feet under him and stood up, his hands, still tied together behind him, around the post of the porch. The post felt about five inches thick, was smooth to the touch, and soft enough so that his fingernails could dig into the surface.

Meanwhile, the older of the two men, Con, was just reaching to pick up a billet of wood from a stack at the corner of the cabin. His large friend, Milt, was starting to get to his feet, a savage light in his eyes. To either side were tumbled-down cabins, with no one else in sight but a woman who now leaned against the front wall of the nearest cabin, impassively watching the fight. Bergen cast a glance over his shoulder. Behind him was a large furrowed weedy field dotted with mounds from three to fifteen feet across, and from two to ten feet high. The whole place had a desolate, deserted look.

At the corner of the porch, Con had now selected his bolt of wood, and Milt was on his feet.

Bergen was facing Milt, with the post at the center of his back. He glanced at Con. "What's the matter? Milt too yellow to fight his own fight?"

Con glanced at Milt. Milt hurled himself at Bergen. Bergen dropped.

Milt hit the post solidly.

With a splintering crack, the post gave way.

Bergen, twisting as he fell, landed heavily on his side, his hands still tied around the post, the dazed Milt on top of him.

Bergen wormed his way along the post, and got his still-tied hands over the end.

Con was now coming toward him, holding a billet of wood ready to throw. Bergen rolled to his feet, and jumped onto the porch.

The earthenware jug with the corncob cork still sat there on the windowsill. Bergen remembered the sigh of pleasure he'd heard earlier.

"Throw that, and I smash the jug."

Con hesitated. Bergen climbed in the window, twisted, and closed his fingers around the neck of the jug. "Start trouble and I smash it."

Milt now struggled to his feet. Con spoke to him in a low voice. Bergen picked his way over the wreckage to the corner of the room, dropped to a sitting position, let go of the jug, and found the broken double-bitted ax.

His eyes were becoming accustomed to the relative dimness of the cabin. Holding the ax head by the remnant of its splintered handle, he crossed the room to a still dimmer corner behind a clutter of wreckage. He crouched behind an overturned table, took a fresh grip on the ax head, and carefully worked it back and forth as the blade cut through the rope.

At the window, Milt, swaying slightly, looked into the room. Bergen massaged his wrists, quietly picked up a solid round table leg.

The door opened, and Con eased in, blinking and holding a billet of wood in either hand.

Bergen tossed a small broken stool across the room at the jug. The jug smashed. Con slung a billet of wood toward the noise. Bergen sprang past the pile of wreckage, and rammed the end of the table leg into Con's stomach. The rush carried him out the door. He caught a glimpse of Milt climbing in the window, smashed him on the back of the neck, knocking him all the way in, followed him inside, hit him over the head, and looked around.

Con was stretched out by the door. Milt was stretched out by the window. Bergen glanced outside. The woman was leaning against the porch post of the next cabin, watching him.

From one of the tall circular mounds in the field, a column of marching insects was winding out across the field, its far end nowhere in sight. Bergen stepped out on the porch, and looked all around.

When he glanced back, the woman was standing about six feet away, smiling. Her eyes had a glazed look.

"Honey," she breathed, and swayed toward him.

Bergen uneasily stepped back.

From somewhere came a peculiar rustling. He looked around, to see that the ribbon of insects issuing from the mound in the field had changed direction, and was approaching the cabins in a wide lane. As he watched, the insects burst out of the grass onto the porch.

The woman looked around, screamed, and fainted.

Bergen swore, heaved her onto his shoulder, and stumbled toward the next cabin. The rustling continued, apparently all around him, and he saw another wide line of insects pour onto the porch of the cabin in front of him.

A faint shadow swung across the side of the cabin in front of him.

Bergen whirled and strode toward the edge of the field. For a moment, his thinking processes were almost blotted out by the realization of what must be happening to the unconscious men in the cabin. But there was nothing he could do about it.

Meanwhile, as his thoughts dwelt on this, the shadow he'd briefly noticed streaked fast across the field, there was a rush of wind, sharp talons sank in at the base of his neck and left shoulder, there was an agonizing wrench, and then the ground was falling away, the woman lying on the ground looking blankly up at him, huge leathery wings creaking around him, and he was carried up, and up, to hover high over a large stained boulder, and then he was let go.

There was a terrific concussion.

Bergen dazedly opened his eyes.

The colonel was standing by the cot. He beamed. "I had my doubts for a while there. But you made it."

Bergen sat up dizzily. He took a deep breath. "Your mind has to be always on the problem, doesn't it? You have to keep looking for a chance, an opening, and be poised to take advantage of it."

"Let's say," said the colonel, "that there's a certain hard-to-define attitude you have to attain, a certain frame of mind. In the other tests, it was incidental, though lack of it would finish you in time. In this test, it was central. Self-pity, complaining, prolonged indecision, fear, dread, any of a number of distractions would finish you in short order. The test was programmed to keep the crises coming at you faster and faster. You bungled the first part, but once you straightened out you did well. We're proud of you."

Bergen felt the heady flush of victory. He had succeeded. He had outwitted the stockade.

The colonel gripped his hand, then turned toward the hatch. "Follow me, my boy, and we'll get you your outfit. Then you can begin training immediately." He led the way out through a storeroom filled with temporarily paralyzed gorillas, alligators, grizzly bears, and other assorted tools-of-the-trade.

To make conversation as he passed through this place, Bergen remarked, "It'll be a relief to get to work. That's the roughest entrance exam I've ever heard of."

"Oh, sure," said the colonel, brushing aside a sack full of coral snakes. "But we have to make the process of selection tough, so you can survive the training." He gave Bergen a look of fatherly pride. "The time will come, my boy, when you'll look back on these admission tests and *smile.*"

The colonel stepped out into the corridor.

A chill passed through Bergen as he followed.

As he trailed the colonel down the hall, now a full-fledged recruit in the Interstellar Patrol, a little question occurred to Bergen:

"Just what was so bad about the stockade?"

THE ROYAL ROAD

Colonel Valentine Sanders of the Interstellar Patrol had just emerged from a session with the simulator when the call came. Against this opponent, the colonel always lost. Scarcely anyone was able to hold the simulator to a draw until the preset time was up. Nearly always, sooner or later, it found some weakness in the man, and by means of the weakness, beat him. This time, the colonel had wasted a precious fraction of a second congratulating himself on his performance, and that fraction of a second, once wasted, was the margin by which he lost. Now, seeing it all clearly, the colonel was in an angry frame of mind as the call buzzer sounded.

"Code number," demanded the colonel.

On the gray bulkhead opposite, the numeral "4" appeared. The colonel frowned. "Go ahead."

The gray bulkhead vanished, to show a strongly built man with piercing blue eyes, seated at a desk facing him.

"We have a little problem, Val."

The colonel's expression was alert. "This business with the Space Force?"

"No, that will work out however it works out. If they open fire, we'll fuse a few turrets, to get it across that Imperial Trasimere will stand for no nonsense. Right this minute, we're beaming our recognition signal at them, and this new recruit's ship is giving Larssen enough hints so that even a Space Force general ought to catch on."

"Larssen has high-grade steel between the ears."

"Can't be helped. He's Space Force."

"How did we get in this spot?"

"As nearly as I can figure it out, it started when the main gravitor went haywire on one of Interstellar Rapid Transport's fast freights. The nearest repair facility seemed to be on Boschock III, so they headed there for help."

"Ouch," said the colonel.

"Exactly. They discovered that the settled part of the planet was nothing but a gigantic slum, run by a computer."

"What did they do?"

"We'd like to know. Whatever they did led the planetary computer to divert effort from maintenance and *rebuild the repair facility to help them.*"

"Quite a feat."

"Wasn't it? Since, at that time, we had nothing but a set of out-phased watch satellites observing the planet, we don't know just what they did. But of course, after they left, we watched them, and the watch quickly boiled down to a surveillance of three men—Roberts, the captain; Hammell, the cargo-control officer; and Morrissey, the communications officer. These three took their accumulated leave, and started looking around for a ship to go back to Boschock III."

"So they could perfect what they'd used there before?"

"Why else would anyone go back to that place?"

"Hm-m-m. So then we found out what they were using before they got back?"

"We did not. We sent an 'I'-class crew after them. As usual, we were short-handed, but that should have been enough. However, these three men are tough, and secretive. There wasn't anything to be found. Then Roberts, the captain, latched onto a 'J'-class ship planted in a salvage cluster. It rejected the other two men, but accepted him."

"Complicates the issue."

"Yes. Now we were up against our own stuff. SymComp was perfectly happy, of course, since it could follow what was happening through this J-ship's own symbiotic computer. But where did that leave *us?* Roberts, of course, merely thought he'd bought a good ship at a comparative bargain price. We couldn't contact *him* because that would wreck his trial period. Meanwhile, on this end, SymComp was perfectly bland and uninformative. Doubtless Link knew what was going on, but we weren't informed from there, either."

The colonel said curiously, "What happened when these three men got back to Boschock—or Paradise, as they call the miserable hole?"

"What happened? Well, while they'd been gone, the inhabitants had split up into warring factions. When they came back, Roberts presented himself as their liege-lord, Vaughan, Duke of Trasimere—*and they accepted him.*"

The colonel looked startled.

"And that's the ultimate cause for this masquerade we're carrying out right now?"

"That's just the barest suggestion of it. Next, there was a war between Duke Vaughan, and a sorcerer called 'Oggbad.' Where Oggbad came from, we have no idea. But there's some ferocious wild life on that planet, and the wild life *cooperated by attacking the city in support of Oggbad.*"

"Holy—"

"Naturally, the inhabitants suspended their differences to protect themselves against Oggbad. That temporarily ended the factional strife amongst the inhabitants. But you see the significance of all this?"

"Sure. Roberts and the others must have developed an emotional-field generator and learned to use it. It must be big and powerful, too."

"Exactly. And with that, if they choose, they could carve out quite an empire. But they don't seem to be doing that. Instead, as nearly as we can judge, they're trying to straighten out the mess on Boschock III. Now, in brief, that's what brings us here, and if Larssen doesn't run wild on us, we should have them on board shortly, and start to figure this business out."

"Wait, now. With their own E-G, aren't we taking a certain risk in bringing them aboard?"

"*If* they had with them one of the power that they used on the planet, sure. But Ahrens tells me that's impossible. Anything they've got on their ship, we can beat down. He'll pour on the power as soon as they're in range, and reel them in so dewy-eyed and overcome to be members of the Interstellar Patrol that they'll hand their plans over voluntarily, and be grateful to do it, at that."

The colonel frowned, then shrugged. "Well, that gives a clearer picture of that part anyway. But, that's not what you called about, is it?"

"No. We're already doing about all we can there. This other business is unrelated, except that it adds to the strain. It's nothing of *our* choosing."

The colonel smiled. "You don't mean the Space Force is calling on us for 'interservice cooperation'?"

"Not the Space Force—PDA."

The colonel's smile faded. "When Planetary Development admits it needs help, it *is* in a mess. What's got them by the throat this time?"

"Nothing serious. Just two dozen petty kings and princes."

The colonel frowned. "Two dozen petty—"

"You see, PDA is opening up new regions for colonization. Since travel by colonization ship is not the best possible preparation for the rigors of life on a new planet, PDA likes to give the colonists a chance to recover, and to finish their fitting out, at a Rest & Refit Center, before the final stage to the colony planet. It generally works out that if the R & R Center is on an Earth-type planet, it simplifies things for everyone. PDA has found exactly one Earth-type planet that's ideally situated as a site for an R & R Center. This planet is already settled by an intelligent life form so human in appearance that, for all practical purposes, you might as well say there's no difference."

"So PDA has to get the approval of these people before they can put their Rest & Refit Center on the planet."

"Exactly. And that's where the fun starts. This place is backward. Each pipsqueak nation on the planet is run by a petty monarch of some kind. A few of these local princes do their jobs. But the bulk of them spend their time popping grapes into their mouths, spurring on the recruiting teams for the harem, and figuring out how to wring more taxes out of their subjects."

The colonel thought a moment, then shrugged.

"Then the people should happily vote the princes out of office. Let PDA run the Space Force in there, to cover them while they explain the principle of the vote, and, in no time at all, they'll have the approval of the populace." The colonel leaned back, and clasped his hands around his knee. "That solves the problem."

The figure on the screen smiled sourly, and held up between finger and thumb a small message spool. "This is a record of the story as I got it from PDA. What's on this spool explained the thing to me, and it will explain it to you just as well. Then you can figure out the solution for yourself."

The colonel sat up. "Wait a minute. Then *I* can—"

"Obviously *someone* has to handle this mess. And SymComp has made its choice. The problem is all yours."

The wall screen faded out.

Across the room, the "incoming message" lid of a pneumatic chute snapped open. A shiny metal cylinder popped part way out, opened up, and dumped its cargo.

With a clang, the message spool dropped into the tray.

II

The colonel stared at the spool for a moment, then gave a short bark of a laugh, scooped the spool up, and went out the hatch-type door. A brisk walk down a corridor brought him to an unmarked hatch that gave way at the pressure of his hand. He stepped into a small neat room, one wall of which was lined with books, while another wall bristled with a formidable array of weapons. A small viewer sat on a stand by the desk at the foot of his cot. The colonel shut and locked the hatch, then snapped the spool into the viewer, spun the chair around, and sat down.

He was at once presented with a view of a desk, behind which was seated a fussy-looking individual in a state of considerable nervous tension. On the desk was a nameplate reading, "R. Halstead, Senior Administrator." On the desk were three viewers, several racks of spools, and a pile of reports. A small side table held an ash tray heaped with cigarette butts, a half-empty glass of water, and a small pill bottle with the cap off.

The administrator cleared his throat self-consciously.

"Ah . . . I have been assured by my superiors that it will be within the normal canons of proper procedure to apply through channels to determine the availability of . . . ah . . . interservice assistance regarding a matter of some consequence to the . . . the fullest settlement by humanity of the available interstellar territory consonant with equitable treatment of less-favored inhabitants of the planets in question."

The colonel listened intently. With all this jargon, the administrator must have something to hide. He went on:

"The situation is of more than normal urgency, having been the subject of many exhaustive studies by the foremost authorities in the relevant fields of supply factors and trans-solar jurisprudence . . ."

The colonel waited out a lengthy statement designed to show how much work PDA had done. Then came a complex justification of PDA procedures, which the colonel listened to closely, since he had no idea what esoteric point they might be hung up on now.

In due time there emerged the sentence, " . . . Since, of course, due consideration must be assured for the established customs of the indigenous sentient populace, it would obviously be intrusive and autocratic to force upon them our conception of representative government; a more enlightened policy requires that no such intrusion be tolerated; the existing allocation of administrative authority must be regarded as uniquely suited to the conditions obtaining at the moment amongst the populace; and hence their leaders, whatever the outward apparent form of their government, must be regarded as the *duly-chosen representatives of the people* . . ."

The colonel hit the replay button. He went over this section until he was satisfied that he knew what it meant: Regardless of circumstances, whoever was in charge when PDA got there, *that* was who PDA dealt with. In this case, that meant two dozen wrangling petty princes.

The administrator went on, "We find it most unfortunate that these Planetary Representatives, by a vote of eighteen to six, have chosen to reject the building of a Rest & Refit Center on the planet. There is no other suitable planet *for* this facility. Obviously, we can't send colonists into this region without proper preparation; and yet, to be true to our own principles, we can't *force* the local princes to accept the R & R Center. Any administrator who did choose to do that would be removed by higher authority. We can't permit any outsider to use force against them, either. They are our responsibility. We must *lead* them, not *force* them. Yet we must have this Rest & Refit Center. Hence we've had no choice but to put the Center out to contract, on the assumption that the contractor will persuade the People's

Representatives of the advantages of accepting the Center. Unfortunately, no contractor has felt confident enough to submit a bid."

The administrator now projected three-dimensional views of the planet's location, and its single inhabited continent, showing the rocky, reef-bound coastline, primitive cities, loosely connected by the wandering network of local roads, and fertile river valleys given over to a checkerboard of tiny plots. Then came a view of the people in one of the cities, wrapped in white robes and jostling one another as they streamed across the baked-mud plaza, to hastily jump back as a gilded coach drawn by four weasel-headed animals rushed around the corner. Through the open windows of this coach could be seen an immensely fat individual wrapped in gold and orange cloth. The people, taken by surprise, were a little slow to get out of the way, and a petulant face bellowed orders out the window. The coachman lashed out right and left with a long whip. After the coach passed, the people fell on the ground to kiss the dirt where it had gone by.

The scene vanished, and the administrator said, "We've done our best to find some solution, but unfortunately we haven't succeeded. There seems to be no way to proceed, but the R & R Center is vital. Any assistance you can give us will be deeply appreciated. The remainder of the spool contains a statistical summary of conditions on the planet, for your information."

The colonel skimmed through the summary, then turned to a dial on the blank wall against which his desk rested. He tapped out a call number, then his own identification code. A moment later, the wall seemed to vanish, and he was looking at the same strongly built, sharp-eyed man who had given him the assignment, and who now smiled at his expression.

"How do you like it?"

"It's an interesting problem," said the colonel. "As I understand it, it boils down to the fact that PDA has *got* to have a rest center on this planet, can't get it without interfering locally, and yet its own rules forbid it to interfere locally, since there's a sentient race on the planet."

"Worse yet, PDA can't let anyone *else* go down there and use force, bribery, or any of the obvious ways to get these princes to change their minds. If it weren't for that, some contractor would have turned the planetary politics inside out, and the R & R Center would be built by now. But the rules are ironclad, even if the result is stupid. And there are watchdog committees to look for any break in observance of the rules. What unavoidably has to be done here is to get results that are just, but possibly—considering only the letter of the law—illegal. PDA isn't set up for that. That's in *our* department."

"How much help can I count on for this?"

"Anything you want . . . in the line of full departmental aid, equipment, supplies, any free ship you'd like—"

"I was thinking of personnel."

"Well—You know what *that* situation's like."

"Yeah."

"We're recruiting by every means we can think of, and we're still short-handed. There isn't much we can do about it. Lowering standards certainly won't help." He shook his head. "You can have anyone available. But there are none too many available."

The colonel thought a moment. "Anyone not already assigned, I can use? *Anyone?*"

"Right."

"O.K. I'll get right at it."

"Good luck."

As the scene faded from the wall, the colonel sat back, his eyes narrowed, and then he sat up and his fingers flashed over the dial. The wall remained blank, but a voice said briskly, "Personnel Monitor."

"The day before yesterday, I administered the oath to a Candidate Dan Bergen, inducting him as a Recruit. I then sent him for routine orientation, and clothing and equipment issue. Where is he now?"

"One moment . . . Recruit Bergen is at this moment arguing with the Quartermaster Assistant regarding the fit of a pair of uniform trousers."

"Then no one has claimed him for any assignment?"

"No. He is only a recruit."

"O.K. Thanks." Rapidly, he punched out a new call. A voice replied, "Project Monitor."

"Any current project with the designation, 'Operation New Vote'?"

"Spell this, please."

The colonel spelled it.

"One moment . . . No. Additionally, we find no past such designation recorded."

"Thanks. Put me through direct to the project controller."

The wall lit up to show a tough-looking individual with sandy hair and an alert watchful expression. "Hello, Val. What can I do for you?"

"I want to register the project-designation, 'Operation New Vote.' I've already checked with monitor."

"O.K. That part's easy."

"For personnel, I'm assigning, first, Recruit Dan Bergen—"

The project controller squinted. "Wait a minute, now. I know what the personnel situation is, of course, but—a *recruit?*"

"This one we got out of a Space Force guardhouse. The boy is rugged, did splendidly on his physical and attitude tests, is smart and mentally alert—very fine material, and I believe this operation, while not subjecting him to any particular danger, will give him a splendid opportunity to gain an insight into how we operate, and should . . . hm-m-m . . . motivate him excellently for his more formal training when he returns."

"We just want to be sure he *does* return. Every qualified man we can lay our hands on is worth a basket of diamonds. What *is* this excursion you're taking him on?"

The colonel briefly described the situation on the planet.

"Hm-m-m," said the project controller. "Why not take a battery of emotional-field generators, and wrench these princes around to the right viewpoint?"

"PDA is duty-bound to watch this planet like a hawk. What happens when all these petty despots suddenly get cooperative? Sure, we've solved the problem for PDA; but we've also presented them a piece of information that's none of their business."

"Yes—They might deduce the existence of the E-G. Hm-m-m . . . and if you provide some logical reason for the princes' change of heart, that logical reason will doubtless fall under the heading of 'bribery,' 'compulsion,' or something else PDA can't allow."

"Right," the colonel said bluntly.

"You're going to have to be kind of subtle on this one."

"Yes."

"All right. I'm going to recommend that this recruit be assigned to Operation New Vote. I'll put him on the personnel list provisionally, until we see whether Personnel melts its coils over this one. Who else do you want?"

"Recruits Roberts, Hammell, and Morrissey."

The project controller shook his head. "I suppose if this isn't too dangerous for one recruit, then in theory, it's not too dangerous for four. But you need some sprinkling of trained men. *One* recruit is one thing. Four of them is something else again. I'm afraid I'll have to—"

The colonel spoke quickly. "Well, I agree, if these were *ordinary* recruits, but these are very exceptional men, who—"

"All our recruits are exceptional men. They're hard to get. That's why we can't have them shot to pieces because they weren't trained in the first place."

"I mean, seasoned men. These are all . . . that is, the captain—"

"What captain?"

The colonel realized that he had come close to letting the cat out of the bag. He started over. "I mean, these men have their own J-ship."

"Ah? You mean, they're all ship-selected?"

There was the catch. If he admitted to the project controller that two of these men had failed to pass the scrutiny of the J-class ship, and had apparently been admitted only on Roberts' say-so, the project controller would naturally decline to let them go along. The colonel said, "What I mean to say is that the captain of the J-ship was formerly captain of a fast transport, which involves plenty of responsibility. He's not likely to be green or rash."

The project controller looked impressed. "What about the other two?"

"They were his cargo-control officer, and his communications officer, on board the transport. His personal selections, apparently. Too bad we can't get more recruits to bring in recruits. It might solve our problem, or ease it anyway."

"Yes—Well, I'm sure Personnel has thought of—"

While the project controller was momentarily distracted with this line of thought, the colonel added, "Anyway, it seems as if they should be reasonably stable men."

"True enough." The tough face frowned, as if in partial awareness of something wrong. Then the controller shrugged. "The main point is, we don't have four unseasoned or suggestible recruits. O.K., who else are you taking?"

"I'll have to check with Personnel to see who's available. I wanted to get these men assigned before anyone grabbed them."

"What about ship and equipment?"

"I'm going to have to study this information to get a preliminary plan. *First* I wanted to be sure that when I had a plan, I would have somebody to carry it out."

"O.K. I'm definitely assigning the J-crew as a unit. I'm tentatively assigning Recruit Bergen. How's that?"

"Fine. That's a load off my mind."

"I hope this personnel shortage eases up pretty soon. Well, let me know when you have your ship and equipment lined up."

"I will. Thanks."

The wall went blank, and the colonel wiped a fine beading of perspiration from his brow and punched another call number. A voice promptly replied, "Personnel Monitor."

"I'd like to know what personnel are available for assignment."

"One moment . . . No personnel below the equivalent grade of colonel are currently on the Available List. There is a Colonel Valentine—"

"I'm Colonel Valentine."

"Then this is of no assistance."

"Correct. What about new recruits?"

"Only one new recruit is available at this location. One moment . . . This recruit has already been assigned, provisionally, to Operation New Vote."

"How about . . . ah . . . recruits expected to arrive here in the near future?"

"I will check . . . Only three recruits are expected to arrive here in the near future. They are already assigned to Operation New Vote. If you wish to contact the operation commander—"

"Thanks. I'm in charge of that operation."

"Ah. Then that is no help. In summary then, these are the total personnel at this location currently available and unassigned: zero."

"O.K.," said the colonel. "Thanks."

He rapped out another call signal. A new voice replied.

"Ship Operations Monitor."

"Give me a report, please, on the current confrontation between ourselves and the Space Force fleet commanded by General Larssen."

The wall immediately lit, to show, hurtling past against a brilliant backdrop of stars, the rigidly-spaced array of a formidable fleet.

"General Larssen," said the monitor, "has accepted the situation with an ill grace, and is withdrawing under imminent threat of attack by His Royal and Imperial Majesty, Vaughan the First, backed by the massed power of Imperial Trasimere, as symbolized by this dreadnought."

"Mm-m-m," said the colonel, scowling. It was all right to go along with this masquerade, so far as the outside was concerned. But to dish it out to their own people seemed like too much. "And when," said the colonel dryly, "is His Royal and Imperial Majesty due to get here?"

"At any moment."

The colonel came to his feet. "What bay?"

"Center Main Number One."

"Thanks."

He was out the hatch and running up the corridor in an instant. If he delayed, Intelligence would grab his men for a prolonged interrogation. It would be all he could do anyway to get Intelligence to settle for a memory simulation. And to do that, he had better be right on the spot when they got here.

He stopped at a door marked in glowing green letters, "Express," pulled it open, jumped into the empty gray shaft within. "Center Main Bay Number One! Emergency! The Chief's business!"

The walls blurred around him.

A cool voice spoke from a slim strip grille running along the length of the shaft.

"Relax your muscles. Physical resistance may create severe pain and bodily injury."

The colonel relaxed, and closed his eyes to shut out the dizzying blur as the walls flashed past. More and more rapidly, his limp body bent and twisted at each curve of the shaft, his movements progressively more forced and violent, as if against his will he were being put through a course of strenuous calisthenics. And then the rapidity and force of these movements mounted until he felt as if he were being shoved through a winding twisting maze at top speed. Yet he felt no sense of forward motion at all. He concentrated on staying relaxed, his attention focused first on the muscles of this limb, then of that, as his body bowed and jerked like a marionette run by a madman.

Then the motions began to slow, and he allowed himself to open his eyes. He had time to remind himself not to use that phrase, "The Chief's business" quite so lightheartedly the next time.

Then the door of the grav shaft opened up and spat him out, the words from the grille reaching him, "Center Main Bay Number One is straight ahead."

He strode swiftly down the broad corridor, through a wide thick double door, and then there stretched out before him a space huge in itself, though small in relation to the size of the ship, in which rows of racks of various sizes stood nearly empty. Here and there a ship, itself of respectable size, nestled in a rack exactly fitted to it, a rack equally well-fitted holding it from above, so that no sudden acceleration or shift in gravitic field could tear the moored ship loose.

All this was familiar to the colonel, and he had also expected the score or so of men, some of them with Intelligence insignia, who stood a little back from the near end of the entrance, waiting. Nevertheless, something unusual in the air led him to look around uneasily.

To his right, in the surveillance shell projecting out beyond the near end of the membrane, half-a-dozen men operated big E-G machines. The men leaned back in their raised seats, guiding the snouts of the machines according to the image of a battered J-class ship on the wall before them, visible almost as clearly as if seen though a sheet of glass. These machines, no doubt, were only a part of Ahrens' overpowering battery of emotional-field generators. The colonel frowned. Just as long as they *were* overpowering. He wasn't eager to find himself in a battle of E-G machines, however weak the other side might be by comparison. Just let Ahrens pop them out of their ship in a wave of devotion and awe, and the colonel would have them

on his team before there was time to say "Yes," "No," or
"But," and while Intelligence was still choked on its own
outrage.

Alertly, he watched the image of the ship move forward,
and then, from his viewpoint, it vanished. The E-G operators, receiving slightly different patterns of light from their
viewpoints, raised the snouts of their machines an instant
later, and threw the main switches to "Off" lest they unin-
tentionally affect their own people. The nearest E-G operator now raised a fluorescent yellow-and-black paddle
overhead. An answering wave from behind the rack told of
the E-G machines concealed there, taking up the slack.

And that gave the colonel's uneasiness a focus.

Had there been a gap between the coverage of one set
of machines and the turning on of the others? And if so,
why?

Then the nose of the J-ship appeared through the thick
membrane, the membrane close against it at all points, so
that no slightest detectable loss of air took place. The gradually appearing J-ship, though obviously battle-worn, blazed
in gold and platinum, and now a dazzling set of three coats
of arms flashed into view.

The colonel felt an unaccountable sense of awe.

He heard an indrawing of breath from the men waiting
in the bay.

The glittering J-ship was now fully inside.

. . . And now the colonel was stricken with an urge to
drop reverently to his knees.

III

Inside the J-Class Interstellar Patrol ship, Roberts, Hammell,
and Morrissey had spent the last hour in that state of nerves
induced by having their fate in the hands of others.

First, there had been the question whether Larssen would
call their bluff and wipe them out, and then there had been
the agonizing question in their minds about this huge
dreadnought. But the voice of the symbiotic computer had
answered their questions, and the reply from the dreadnought
had seemed reassuring, and they had been content enough
during the first part of the approach to the dreadnought.

More than content, they had been proud. Proud to serve with the legendary Interstellar Patrol. And more than proud, they had been humble. Humble because they really did not feel that they deserved the honor. And not only had they felt proud, and humble, but also determined. Determined to make the best of their good fortune, and do their best to deserve to be in the Interstellar Patrol. And so far, it was all right. So much emotion might naturally follow from what they had experienced. But then, not only did they feel proud, and humble, and determined, but as they entered the huge port of the dreadnought, they also felt awed, and impressed, and worshipful, and unworthy, and submissive, and obedient, and earnest, and loyal, and apologetic—and when the thing reached a certain pitch, there was an instant of sanity, and Roberts glanced at Hammell, and both men looked at Morrissey, who turned to look at the want-generator, and said, "It's turned off."

Roberts said, "Maybe *ours* is, but there's one somewhere that isn't."

And before he fell blubbering on the deck in his humility, he managed to shake a supertranquilizer pill out of a small can, crumble it to bits, and swallow some.

A plate of thick glass seemed to descend, cutting him off from the rest of the universe. Outside this plate of thick glass, there was a sense as of mighty forces beating in vain against an unyielding barrier.

Hammell also ate several bits of the pill, and so did Morrissey. Then they looked at each other like so many vegetables nodding in the hot sun, and for a little while they were so stupefied that no ideas at all came. Then Roberts glanced at the outside viewscreen. "We're almost inside the dreadnought."

Hammell said dully, "Not that it matters, but we're in kind of a hole. It's all come about step by step; but how we're going to get out of it—"

Roberts groped for something to say, and then, possibly because he had taken very little of the supertranquilizer, he felt a sudden flare of defiance and spirit.

Moving swiftly, for someone under the influence of the drug, he slipped out of the control seat, ducked under the shiny cylinder that ran down the axis of the ship, and bent to set the want-generator.

IV

The colonel, watching the J-class patrol ship glide fully through the membrane, felt the sense of awe strengthen unbearably. The glittering ship seemed to blaze in glory. His mind, groping for some explanation, was overloaded with sensations. Dazedly, he heard a clear, deep, faintly ironical voice say, "On your knees, gentlemen. It is His Royal and Imperial Majesty, Vaughan the First, our Most Just and Fearless Sovereign."

The colonel knelt, his first thought being wonder at his own hesitation. His second thought comprised a clicking together of these last words and what he had heard before about this ship and its crew. The logical answer sprang into his mind:

They're taking over the dreadnought!

Holding his mind locked on what he had to do, the colonel staggered to his feet.

Directly in front of him, forty feet away beside the glittering J-ship, stood a crowned figure in blazing golden armor.

The wave of awe was almost too much for the colonel, but he managed to stay upright on his feet.

Then he heard a cool voice say dryly, "You shut yours off, and we'll shut ours off."

The meaning came through to him. He sucked in a deep breath and roared, *"All E-G batteries! Cut to zero and stand by!"*

To the colonel's right, the men staggered to their feet and pulled themselves up into their control seats, their hands near the levers and switches. Their machines were already shut off, but they must obey the order to "Stand by."

A judicious voice called from the J-ship. "It just let up. Shall we shut it off?"

"Shut it off. But stay right with it."

The sudden relaxation of the sense of psychic pressure staggered the colonel. But his mind and body were well exercised, and he recovered his equilibrium quickly, thinking, "So that's what a battle of emotional-field generators is like!" But it seemed obvious which side had the heavier guns, and they obviously had the will to use them, so it looked like a good idea to get this business settled quickly.

Brusquely, he said, "We'd appreciate it, Recruit, if you'd get out of that monkey suit on the double and report for assignment."

A chilly voice replied, "We don't much care to have our emotions tampered with. If this is your standard practice, you can look elsewhere for recruits."

The colonel's original uneasiness at the way this was to be handled returned, and he said in a conciliatory voice, "Whether you realize it or not, people who have just used an emotional-field generator to take over a planet, for whatever reason, and whatever motives, are not so harmless that they can be welcomed into a ship without precautions."

There was a brief silence, then the armored figure turned away.

"We'll be right out."

The colonel appeared to have won. But there was no "sir" at the end of the sentence, and it was evident that the new recruits had suffered an early disenchantment.

Still, they *were* recruits. And recruits were desperately needed.

Impatiently, the colonel waited for them to come out.

V

Inside the patrol ship, Roberts, Hammell, and Morrissey glanced at each other doubtfully, then shrugged. They might conceivably fight their way *out* of the huge ship, but then what? Once outside, the gigantic weapons of the dreadnought could squash them with ease. And, assuming they were able to use the want-generator to immobilize the whole gigantic ship, then make good their escape, which seemed doubtful, they would then be in the position of having acquired for an enemy the Interstellar Patrol. Anyone with any faint experience in the matter would rather be hunted by the Space Force. The Space Force at least had strictly-defined limits on its sphere of action. Possibly the Interstellar Patrol had such limitations, but, if so, no one seemed to know what they were.

Roberts ducked under the shiny cylinder that ran down the axis of the ship, leaned across the control panel, and tapped a button marked "SymComp."

"This dreadnought we're inside of *is* an Interstellar Patrol ship?"

SymComp replied: "It is."

"And it's still under the control of the Interstellar Patrol?"

"Yes."

"Those people waiting for us outside are members of the Interstellar Patrol?"

"They are."

Roberts straightened up, and glanced at Hammell and Morrissey.

"We might just as well go on out."

"O.K."

The three men got out of their battle armor, made themselves as presentable as they could, and climbed out.

They found themselves at one end of an enormous spaceship hangar, with a spare, strongly built colonel facing them with a look of genuine welcome.

Roberts, keenly aware of everything about him, saw the ships, of various sizes but roughly the same overall shape, held tightly in their cradles. He noticed a large, peculiarly-shaped device at the edge of the door they'd apparently come through; in an upraised control seat, the operator of this device, a faintly punch-drunk expression on his face, was glancing down ruefully toward Roberts. That same punch-drunk expression was on the faces of several other men standing around with various insignia on their uniforms.

The insignia and the uniforms themselves caught Roberts' attention. The colonel's insignia of rank was the usual Space Force eagle, its wings spread and claws clasped about a slender rocket. But the uniform itself was unusual. At first glance, it appeared to be made of a fine leather of some kind. It was hard to say its exact color, though Roberts at first was certain it was dark-green. An instant later, he thought it was a very dark brown. Then he became aware of a gray tone, like the bark of maples transplanted from Earth, and seen in shadow. The uniforms were cut to allow ease of motion but they appeared tailored to a near-perfect fit, just loose enough not to hamper movement. At the waist was a moderately wide belt, apparently of some dark leather, that held a holstered pistol on the right side, and what appeared to be a hunting knife on the left side. There were also several small leather cases fitted to the belt. Roberts was reasonably certain that these belts would be awkward and uncomfortable to wear, yet everyone he could see was wearing them. Possibly, he thought, they'd only put them on to be inconspicuously armed, in case there was trouble.

In the short space of time that they stood silent, before the colonel spoke, a great many forms, colors, sounds and barely perceptible odors flashed in upon Roberts' consciousness. The sum total of these, and perhaps of something else that wasn't so easily pinned down, combined to ease his wary sense of restraint.

The colonel smiled. "Well, Captain, does the Patrol pass inspection?"

" 'Captain'? A few minutes ago, sir, I was a recruit."

"You're still a recruit. But you've passed the inspection of the symbiotic computer, a patrol ship has accepted you, and you've passed your trial run without disqualifying yourself. Whoever does that has the rank of captain automatically. But there's obviously a great deal you don't know, so necessarily you're still a recruit. This may seem strange to you, but it will make sense when you think about it. There are many things about the Patrol which may seem strange at first, but will make sense when you think them over. For instance, we sometimes take recruits along on our milder operations, even before they're thoroughly trained. This, you see, gives the recruits a chance to see the Patrol in action. I don't imagine any of you would object to that, would you?"

The three men, without bothering to think about it, automatically shook their heads.

The colonel then added casually, "Then, men, you're assigned to Operation New Vote. How's that?"

They all looked more or less surprised, but said "Fine, thank you, sir," and tried to look alert and happy, though Operation New Vote could be a trip through the nearest sun, for all they knew.

"Good, good, gentlemen," said the colonel, friendliness and approval shining all over his face as he thrust out his hand. "I'm in charge of Operation New Vote. Now, of course, you'll be Roberts?"

"Yes, sir," said Roberts, shaking hands. He introduced Hammell and Morrissey, and the colonel was just turning to lead them off, all one tight little group now, when three men standing to one side suddenly gave themselves a shake, and stepped forward.

"Hold it," said one, wearing at his left lapel a small golden plow and still tinier letters that appeared to read "Tiens et" followed by something totally undecipherable. A second man, his branch of service indicated by a robed female figure holding a large ax, said angrily, "What's this? You're not trying to assign these men, are you?"

The third man, crossed spear and arrow at his lapel, said exasperatedly, "Listen, Val, we've got to question them. You can have them about two weeks from now."

"Sorry, gentlemen," said the colonel. "Why didn't you mention this sooner?"

"Sooner? We were right here when they got out of the ship!"

"I can't help that. They're already in Operation New Vote."

"Sorry. We're assigning them to quarters on call for the next three weeks."

"They've already freely agreed to go with me on Operation New Vote."

"That's preliminary, not final. Ted, get the project controller."

The colonel said with icy politeness, "The project controller has already assigned them to Operation New Vote."

"It's not final till published in the Assigned List."

"Oh, I imagine by now that's taken care of."

"Check it, Ted."

The officer with the small golden plow at his lapel had slipped a little green and orange striped device from a belt case, and now held it to his lips. His lips moved, apparently without sound, and a moment later he glanced around. "Recruits Roberts, Hammell, and Morrissey are on the Assigned List for Operation New Vote."

The officer with crossed spear and arrow at his lapel eyed the colonel as if he would like to cut him into small pieces and throw the pieces in a fish pond. The colonel smiled back cheerfully, glanced aside at his three recruits, and said, "Stay right with me, men." He tossed back, over his shoulder, "You can take a memory simulation, if you want."

"We *will* want. Listen, the Chief will—"

"The Chief has given me permission to draft anyone not

already assigned. I'd avoid pointless antagonisms if I were you."

The colonel moved away. After a moment, he turned to Roberts with a smile. "A shame, the way some officers will try to chain-gang new recruits into three weeks of interrogation and virtual house arrest, without anyone's permission."

"Yes, sir," said Roberts blankly.

The colonel pulled open a door marked "Express" in glowing green letters, said "Operations Branch," and motioned Roberts and the others to precede him.

Roberts stepped into the empty shaft, the gray walls blurred around him, seemed to wind, twist and bend, more and more rapidly, and then finally to change shape more slowly, until they came to a door marked with several numerals, and lettered "Operations." This door came open, and they landed in a wide corridor.

The colonel said, "These men are recruits Roberts, Hammell, and Morrissey. They are to be allowed access to this floor, but for the time being can leave only with my permission."

Roberts looked around, but there was no one there save themselves, the colonel, and the door. The door swung shut behind them, and as the colonel strode off, Roberts tried the door. The door wouldn't budge.

Roberts glanced at Hammell and Morrissey, and the three men, frowning, followed the colonel up the corridor. The colonel stopped at a door numbered "14," and opened it, to show a room with two sets of double bunks, one above the other, with four desks in pairs, back-to-back, their sides against the wall, and with four lockers against the wall. There were two more doors; one opened into a tiled lavatory, while the other held a round heavy glass porthole, through which shone what appeared to be bright sunlight.

The colonel said, "Captain Roberts, Recruits Hammell, Morrissey, and Bergen."

Roberts glanced around. There was no one there but the colonel, standing in the doorway, making notes on a small pad. "All right, gentlemen," said the colonel, "You're free until 1800. At that time you will eat, in your room. At 1830 you will put on your uniforms, which you'll find in your lockers. Don't worry about the fit; they'll be all right. You will then report to Room 18, just down the hall. There you will receive about an eight-hour orientation course; this will acquaint you with our methods, generally, and also with the specifics of Operation New Vote. You will then return here. Lights out at 2200."

He nodded to them, stepped out, and shut the door.

Roberts, Hammell, and Morrissey stared after him.

VI

Hammell said exasperatedly, "Am *I* confused?"

Roberts tried the door, and it opened readily enough. The colonel was already out of sight. But now that Roberts had the door open, he noticed the list of names on the outside of the door, below the number "14":

Captain Roberts
Recruit Hammell
Recruit Morrissey
Recruit Bergen

Morrissey was saying, in a wondering voice, "At a little after 1830, we report to Room 18. There we get an *eight-hour* orientation course. Then we come back here, and put our lights out by 2200. But, eight hours, starting at 1830, brings it to 0230 tomorrow."

Hammell said exasperatedly, "Either he meant we'd get back after lights out, or else we've gotten into the Interstellar Patrol's private Institution for Mentally Disadvantaged Persons."

Roberts ran his hand lightly across the lettering on the door. It felt perfectly dry, and smooth, as if the lettering had been put on with a very thin quick-drying paint—or as if the letters were inset flush with the door.

Roberts cleared his throat. "Before we jump to conclusions, what was on this door when we walked into the room?"

"Just a number," said Hammell. "The number 14, I think."

"Take a look at it now."

Hammell and Morrissey came over, looked at the door, felt of it, and glanced around wonderingly.

"There's more to this place than meets the eye."

Roberts walked to the far door, where sunlight appeared to shine through. He was looking out on a broad sandy beach. To his far right, blue water sparkled, while, close by, white foaming surf rushed far up the beach. To his left was a kind of open park, with occasional tall spreading trees, and roughly-cut grass. As he watched, a mower went by, floating perhaps three inches above the ground, the cut grass pouring out in a green fountain, to be dispersed by a brisk wind.

Hammell shut the corridor door and came over. "That's an effective illusion."

Morrissey said, "Why put it in a *door?* In a larger window-type frame, it would be refreshing. This is just tantalizing. You don't see enough to enjoy it, yet you can't actually go out, either."

Roberts glanced around, and spotted a small clock on the wall. This told him that ship time was a little after two in the afternoon, or 1400. That left almost four hours until 1800. The colonel had said they were "free" until 1800. Free to do what? He glanced back at the door, then reached out.

"Brace yourselves," he said. "When I pull the handle, that will probably work some switch that will show us a snow scene, or a waterfall, or a beautiful girl sitting on a rock with spray splashing around her."

Hammell shrugged. "Go ahead. Obviously, there's nothing there. We know they don't have a beach and half an ocean inside the ship."

Roberts snapped the handle back, and pulled sharply.

The door swung open.

Bright sunlight and sea air filled the room.

Just beyond the threshold was a very short open passage, a second high threshold, and dazzling sand.

They simultaneously started forward, and then simultaneously gripped each other. "Wait a minute. *Maybe* this is alsens. But if it's some kind of 6-V, we don't want to smash into the projector heads."

Morrissey said, "If it's alsens, the whole room must be part of it. We could see it from across the room."

"With the door *shut*," said Hammell. "That could be 3-V. Then the alsens goes on when you open it."

Roberts glanced around, saw no warning sign, and felt

his way forward. He stepped over the second threshold, groped around in the air, felt nothing but sunlight and a fresh breeze, stooped, felt the hot sand, and glanced back.

"Morrissey, get back out of range of this. How does it look?"

Morrissey backed until he was across the room. "It still looks the same."

Roberts shook his head. "One way to find out." He scooped up a handful of the hot sand, and stepped back inside.

The sand, red grains and yellow grains with separate flecks of black, was still there in his hand.

They looked at each other in astonishment.

Roberts tossed the sand back on the beach, looked around exasperatedly, and said, "Well, *you* know it isn't real, and *I* know it isn't real, but can you think of any better way to spend the time from now till 1800?"

"No. Let's try it." They went back inside to toss shirts and trousers on the various bunks, then started out.

The water, when they dove in, turned out to be not quite ice-cold. They plunged and swam, were buffeted and rolled over and over by the breakers, staggered to their feet, sinking slightly in the soft sand, and dove in again. The sun blazed steadily down from above, and the white-capped breakers crashed endlessly in. Before an hour was up, feeling refreshed and yet tired out, they sprinted back across the blazing sand, showered in hot spray, and then stretched out on their bunks, to fall asleep at once.

Roberts became aware of the distant clanging of a gong. He fought his way up some kind of dark tunnel, and sat up dizzily, to find that he was lying on a bunk in a room where three other men were stretched out insensible, the covers over their heads. Roberts, overtired and feeling irritated, dropped off his bunk, and at once the clanging stopped. He looked out the door to the "beach," and it was just starting to get dark out there. Then he became aware of a smell of freshly-grilled steak. It hadn't occurred to him until then that he was hungry. He looked around, to see a tray of steak and French fries on each of the small desks in the room. He took hold of the metal uprights of the bunks, and shook them. Hammell and Morrissey staggered out, stupefied and muttering incoherently. From the last bunk, a lean face about twenty years old looked out. This face was pink complexioned, with angry light-blue eyes, close-cropped blond hair so light that it was almost white, and an out-thrust chin with a slight cleft or dimple that seemed to set the seal of stubbornness and pugnacity on the face.

Roberts sensed a tough material that something useful might possibly be made out of. "You're Dan Bergen?"

"Yes," said Dan Bergen roughly, putting a thin muscular arm threateningly over the edge of the bunk, "And who do you think *you* are?"

Hammell and Morrissey glanced at each other, picked up their trays, and abruptly started for the "outside."

Roberts' irritation heightened for an instant, then transmuted itself into pure pleasure. He yanked Bergen off the cot—mattress, mattress cover, sheets, blankets, and all, so that he landed with a solid thump on top of the mattress with the covers strewn all over him.

"Conceivably, I am your commanding officer," said Roberts, "but don't let that bother us. Stop hiding under the sheets, unless you've got a broken arm, and let's hear you use that tone again."

Morrissey opened the door, and carried his tray outside.

Hammell followed close behind.

Bergen erupted out of the tangle of covers like a jaguar out of a brush patch, and slammed Roberts back against the corridor door.

Roberts struck Bergen an open-handed blow to the side of the head, that gave a crack like a fusion gun. He pinned Bergen's legs with one arm, heaved him over his shoulder, and dumped him on the other upper bunk.

"Now, friend, we begin again. The alarm has rung, knocking one of your fellow roommates out of bed. Time is passing, and we all have to get to Room 18 in thirty minutes. It would be easier to let you sleep but duty calls. With gentle blandishments, we bid you cast off the blinkers of Morpheus."

Roberts gripped the bunk, and shook it till Bergen was flung around like a boat in a hurricane. "Please decide," said Roberts, "whether you wish to get up or stay in bed. The choice is entirely yours, of course."

Bergen stared out dazedly as the room danced around him. "O.K. I'll get up."

"There's a little word," said Roberts, stepping back politely as Bergen dizzily swung his feet over the edge, "that soothes the egos of those who hunger and thirst after rank. It's only a short word, but what self-respecting man can say it without its catching in his throat and gagging him? His stomach turns over, he feels nauseous and cheapened, but—"

Bergen stared at him. "Sir."

"That's it," said Roberts, smiling. "How it soothes my soul to hear it. Drop it into the conversation now and then, when you have time. It will cement our friendship."

Bergen dropped off the edge of the bunk, steadied himself with one hand, and said, "I'm sorry, sir. I always wake up in a bad mood when I'm tired, and I was worn out. I—"

"Say no more about it. I understand. Count on me to waken you with the softest whisperings from this time forward. But meanwhile, time's passing. Take a tray."

"Yes, sir," Bergen sat down beside the nearest tray. He looked up at Roberts, who waved his hand beside his head, and called out to Hammell and Morrissey. "Better come back in. That alsens is so real I've got illusions of gnats flying around my head."

They came inside and shut the door. "It would be nice if we could figure the thing out."

"Better save our strength for Room 18," said Roberts.

They all sat down with their trays, and ate hurriedly.

On the wall, the second hand of the clock swung steadily around.

The uniforms the colonel had said they needn't worry about turned out to be a poor fit: Tight at the shoulders, loose at the waist, the sleeves binding their muscles when they bent their arms. Roberts, Hammell, and Morrissey angrily expressed their opinion of these sack-like uniforms, in words of few syllables. Then Bergen said, "My uniform fit the same at first. I don't understand it, but it's looser where it used to bind, and tighter where it sagged, and now is a decent fit."

"Another puzzle," said Roberts. "Come on, it's almost 1830."

They went out and down the corridor to Room 18. They shoved the door open and went in, to experience a peculiar blur that caused them to pause just inside, then step on through the doorway, pull the door shut behind them, glance up and down the now extremely dim corridor, then turn to look back blankly at the closed door, marked "18," behind them.

For a second, they stood frozen, then Roberts shoved hard on the door. The door didn't move.

"What in—"

"We just went *in* there!"

Roberts shook his head. "Wait." Mentally, he retraced his steps, down the corridor at 1830, through the door, and, with no memory of turning, back out to pull the same door shut behind him, and find himself in this dimly-lit corridor.

"Hold on," said Roberts. "There was a *blur* back there. What did the colonel say we were going there for?"

"To get an eight-hour orientation course, that would acquaint us with their methods, and also with the details of Operation New Vote."

And then they all stood there in silence.

Operation New Vote, they now knew, without any memory of being told, was the problem of getting a Rest & Refit Center accepted on that planet run by a collection of petty humanoid princes. Roberts could see the planet in his mind, could see the inhabited continent's rocky coast, the small farms, the haughty princes, and the enduring trudging people. And, with all of this vivid information, there was the reservation, "This is the information as received from Planetary Developmental Authority. Reserve final judgment until we see it ourselves at first hand."

Hammell said, in a peculiar tone, *"Daira go nasht?"*

The meaning came across to Roberts clearly: "And this that transpires here—It is what?"

Morrissey said dazedly, "We've even got the languages!"

Dan Bergen said, "And—We're all members of Garoujik Construction Corporation!"

That was right there in their minds, too. PDA wanted *someone* to bid on a contract to put up the R & R Center. This had now happened. The Garoujik Construction Corporation had bid on the contract.

And what was the Garoujik Construction Corporation?

PDA didn't know it, but Garoujik Construction Corporation was the Interstellar Patrol.

VII

When they got back to their room, they got another shock. That the clock should stand at 2156 was no surprise. They had already deduced the passage of time, and made allowance for it in their minds. What they hadn't suspected in the darkened corridor looked at them now out of the mirror in the tiled washroom. When they stood before the mirror, not a one of them could recognize his own features. Four strangers looked back at them with expressions of amazement.

They washed, and got ready for bed. "What was it the colonel said this would do—acquaint us with their methods?"

"Yeah," growled Hammell.

Morrissey said, "*I* can't think of anything having to do with their methods."

Roberts growled, "The *whole thing* acquaints us with their methods—indirectly."

Overhead, the inconspicuous lights of the room suddenly dimmed. The slightly-glowing clock face showed that it was one minute before 2200.

Irked and disgruntled, their thoughts a whirl of information about the planet they were headed for, and their duties as members of "Garoujik Construction," they climbed into their bunks.

The second hand of the clock swung to the vertical, and the lights went out completely.

The only glow in the room now came from the softly-lighted clock face, and moonlight shining on the "beach."

That scene outside, with the water washing in long white streamers up the sand, should have been restful, even romantic.

With growls of exasperation, they turned their backs to it, pulled the covers around them, buried their heads in their pillows, and fell asleep.

Down the hall, the colonel was on his feet facing the screen above his desk, where the same strongly built man who had given him the assignment in the first place now looked out with a puzzled frown.

"Tomorrow morning? Sure. You can leave yesterday, as far as I'm concerned. As long as Intelligence has its memory simulation, the sooner you get out of here, the better. They're sure to find something about the simulation that isn't clear. They'll want to question your men, and on top of this damned super E-G, the last thing I want is to referee a fight between you and I-branch."

"Fine. There are just a few more details, and I can get started."

"O.K., then. Good luck."

The screen went blank.

The colonel gave a satisfied grunt, hung up his uniform shirt, sat down at the desk, got pad and pencil, and jotted down the few things that still had to be done. Then he sat back and looked at the list critically.

Unless he had overlooked something, he was in good shape to get out of here early tomorrow.

But he always *did* overlook *something*.

It would occur to him tomorrow, as they were ready to leave. Or, worse yet, after they had left, and then he would have to come back, and bully everyone in reach, or else they would catch on to the silly oversight he'd made, and he would look and feel like a complete boob.

He sat back, and imagined himself ready to leave. It was tomorrow, and the ship was ready, the cargo on board, the men climbing in, and now he told them to shut the hatch, and—

He sat up abruptly. How had he forgotten *that*?

He reached out to impatiently tap the dial near his desk.

Roberts, Hammell, Morrissey, and Bergen were awakened by a clanging, bonging noise so loud and rude as to bring them all out of their bunks in a nasty frame of mind.

The colonel's voice, brisk and cheerful, reached them from a speaker they were too sleep-drugged to try to locate.

"Good morning, gentlemen! As you see, it's a fine day outside. I've gotten you up half-an-hour early, so you'll have time for a little fresh air before we start. Anyone who wants to crawl back in his bunk is free to do it. But, believe me, it's nice outside. A horn will tell you when it's time to get back. You'll eat in your quarters, and we'll be ready to start immediately afterward. You need bring only yourselves, the uniforms you received yesterday, and your hand-weapons belts. Meanwhile, have a good time."

The four men looked around stuporously, made spasmodic motions toward getting back in their bunks, then turned to look at the sunlight flooding through the thick round window of the door. Bright blue sky showed overhead, and a gentle wash of the sea on the sand could be faintly heard. Roberts growled under his breath, and walked over. Outside, the sea was far calmer than the day before, and the sky was a deep blue, with just a small white cloud moving slowly past high above. He glanced at the disguised stranger who was Hammell. Hammell nodded exasperatedly, and Roberts pulled open the door.

Outside, the air was fresh and cool, the sun hot, and the bright sand sizzling underfoot. They sprinted down the beach to the cool dark sand washed by the surf, then waded out in the cold water. Half-freezing, they ducked underwater, swam furiously out from the beach, and now the water seemed pleasantly mild. After a while, Roberts methodically swam far out, to look back at a sweep of sandy shore that stretched, gently curving, out of sight in both directions. Far off to his left, he could see the hazy outline of a kind of tower, and what appeared to be a thin rail stretching out into the sea. What might *that* be?

There was a quiet splash, and Hammell surfaced beside him.

"Some illusion," said Hammell, looking around.

"And yet," said Roberts, "as you said yesterday, they obviously don't have a beach, and half an ocean, inside the ship."

"I know it."

They considered the situation in silence, then Hammell said, "What do you think of this outfit, so far?"

"Well—They're exasperating. And they aren't infallible, as you can see from what we did to them yesterday. But they don't fool around, either. I get the impression there's a high ratio of brains to mass in this outfit."

Hammell nodded. "And we've only begun to get a look at it. It's like an iceberg. Seven-eighths underwater. Maybe more of it will come to the surface when we tangle with this Operation New Vote. Boy, there's an impossibility if I ever saw one. You can't hit them, and they're unpersuadable. Where do you take a grip on a thing like that?"

"There's one hopeful sign."

"What's that?"

"According to the information we got last night, five or six of these two dozen petty kings are *sensible.*"

"Yeah, but the vote has to give a big majority, or the R & R Center is no go."

"Well, it's an opening, anyway. But we don't have to figure it out now. Come on, I'll race you to shore—that is, if you know anything besides the dog paddle."

Hammell, born on a planet named "Poseidon," smiled faintly, sucked in a deep breath, and ducked underwater.

Roberts started a fast crawl toward the shore. As he'd been Hammell's captain on the fast freighter *Orion,* he was familiar with Hammell's record, and knew what he was taking on. Roberts went through the water in a streak of foam. But Hammell was waiting when Roberts reached the shore.

An instant later, there was the loud blare of a horn.

VIII

The trip to the planet began with a series of shocks that made successively weaker impacts until the four men nearly reached the stage where nothing would surprise them.

To begin with, well before their ship was to leave the dreadnought, Roberts, standing beside the big hatch as he adjusted his unfamiliar weapons belt, somehow dropped the belt. It didn't *fall* to the deck outside. It *floated.* Roberts climbed down the handholds of the space-yacht-type ship, stepped out to pick up the belt, and the ship was gone. As he stood staring around stupidly, a voice from above irritably directed him to put out his hand. He touched the side of the ship, and immediately could see it again. When he climbed back in through the big hatch, he happened to notice the total thickness of the beveled edge of the hatchway. It was at the very least six times thicker than any space yacht Roberts had seen before.

Bemused by these preliminaries, the men started for the grav shaft up to the next level, and banged head-on into a thick highly-polished column that ran vertically up the axis of the ship. When they did go up the shaft, they discovered that it stopped short of the sixth level, which usually contained the control room, but now had no visible entrance at all. The fifth level consisted merely of a space seven feet high, three feet wide, by two feet deep, the walls of which were fitted with a screen showing the detailed *illusion* of the usual fifth level. The control room turned out to be on the fourth level, along with five different weapons lockers, and the control seat and the controls themselves were unlike anything Roberts had ever seen on a space yacht. They were a lot closer to what he'd found in his salvaged patrol ship. The sleeping quarters were on the third level, along with highly functional kitchen and washroom sections.

Hammell said ironically, "This space yacht is sure luxurious—like a barracks."

Morrissey smiled. "And flimsy—like a fortress."

Roberts said, "It doesn't seem possible, but I know what this ship *looks* like."

"What's that?"

"A large Interstellar Patrol ship, *in disguise as a space yacht.*"

"It *does*, at that."

Their speculations were ended abruptly by the appearance of an impressive-looking individual who radiated financial know-how and business acumen. When this tycoon opened his mouth, the colonel's voice came out:

"If I remember correctly, Roberts, you are supposed to be the pilot of this ship. Suppose you jar yourself off the mark and get in there and do some piloting."

After this, Roberts was in something of a state of shock until they reached the planet.

The planet drifted up toward them like an old acquaintance that they knew well from some previous visit. Their first sight of the green and tan continent, its forbidding coastline lit in hard-shadowed relief by the early-morning sun, was like a familiar face. They stared down at half-lighted valleys, swift-flowing rivers, and numerous patchworks of small farms, many of them far removed from any sizable cities.

"That orientation," growled Hammell, "was pretty effective."

Roberts frowned at the screen and drifted down toward what looked at first like a collection of small towns inside a strong wall on a bluff above a wide swift-flowing river, with a granite palace near the center, and a number of large rectangular buildings in many separate walled enclosures throughout the city. Near the palace, on the other side of a wide stone wall, was an open square that Roberts knew to be the "Visitor's Campground."

As Roberts headed toward it, the colonel stepped into the control room.

"When we set down, gentlemen, I am going to need the services of my 'lawyer' and my 'financial advisor.' My 'crew,' however, is free to see the sights, and you'd better go through the city, and get as good a sense of the general atmosphere as you can. Are the people content, or miserable? Is the place well run? Are the people reasonably well fed? Take a look at the food-storage warehouses. Look over the roads. Watch for one particular phenomenon—If you've learned something in your orientation, and it's contradicted by the facts here, there will be an instant of surprise and disorientation, and then the incorrect fact will vanish like the memory of a dream. The instant you feel that disorientation, hang on to the memory of the misleading 'fact' and tell me the first chance you get. If PDA is trying to run our head into a noose, we want to know it."

Roberts set the ship down, and they looked out at the capital city of Mardukash, one of the larger of the planet's two dozen kingdoms.

As the colonel conferred with the disguised Morrissey and Bergen, Roberts and Hammell put on native-style loose blouse and trousers, under long white robes, and set out through the city.

Their knowledge of the general layout proved accurate, and they found themselves walking down wide cobbled streets that sloped toward gutters in the center, with shops to either side whose owners were putting up their shutters to display earthenware jars, baskets woven of reeds, brightly-colored cloth, cheap jewelry, woven hats with wide down-curving brims, and a variety of handmade iron tools. Here and there, they passed more strongly built places, with iron grilles in front. These were spice shops and the business places of goldsmiths.

Everyone Roberts and Hammell saw seemed brisk and cheerful.

"O.K. so far," said Hammell. "Isn't one of their food-storage warehouses around here?"

"If we take that street to the left up ahead, it ought to bring us to it."

They turned left, and gradually a massive gray stone wall came into view. Armed men, spears and bows ready, patrolled the walls. Beyond loomed the tops of buildings, long and with steeply-sloping roofs, that they wanted to look at. But they soon found that the outer wall blocked their view of the inside.

A long walk, past a part of the city devoted to stables for beasts that looked like a kind of big slender otter, and past a section devoted to the sale of seeds, and plows made of hard wood or iron, brought them to the city's east gate. The gate was open, and beyond it, heavily braced from below, a bridge reached out across a wide ravine, turned ninety degrees toward the north, then swung ninety degrees east again to reach the opposite bank. The bridge was wide, but had only a flimsy rail at the edge. Just as Roberts and Hammell came up to it, a gaily-dressed rider, approaching at a gallop along the dirt road to the east, was desperately slowing his mount. After almost plunging into the ravine, he called out to the guards, "I come to purchase spice from far Iandul. May I enter?"

"Yes, friend, and we have the spice," said the guard atop the wall. "For once, the cursed reefs let a ship through unhurt. But enter at a walk. No one rushes the Iatulon's capital at a gallop."

"So I see. Your roads are so good, compared to our own rutted bogholes, that I was careless. I will be more alert."

The guard smiled. "I observe you are a noble, so let me warn you. If you use your lash on a commoner here, the Iatulon's guards will have you in a flash, and you will spend the night in poor accommodations, and go out in the morning with a lighter pocket. On the other hand, if any commoner attempts to provoke you, report it to the first guard you see, and the nuisance will be ended. Go through with a plain, cheerful manner, and all will be well. Try haughty airs, and you will have your foot in a hole from now till you leave. The Iatulon doesn't use the grand manner, and no one else can."

"Ah? No one? And what then of the Iatulon's queen?"

"Of that, friend, say no more. In any case, no one knocks a woman's head off for pride, but *you* are a man."

Smiling, the nobleman came through the gate, nodded to Roberts and Hammell, and trotted into the city.

Roberts called up to the guards, "We are strangers here, and want to go up into those hills to look at the city from a distance. Is it all right?"

"It is permitted, but if you go beyond the open pastureland into the forest, it is dangerous. There are beasts there that forage for nuts and the root bark of certain favored trees. They have an evil disposition, and worse yet, they are armed with a horn like a dagger in the center of their foreheads. If you come upon them amongst those trees, they will rip you open from groin to gizzard. The only safety is to climb a tree, and then you are stuck there till they decide to move on. Owing to their disposition, they will starve a while in the hope that thirst will bring you down. Best keep to the open. If they come at you there, yell at the top of your lungs, and run for your lives, downhill and away from the forest. They cannot catch you, and will fear that your screams will bring mounted men, who will attack them in the open. After a short run and much snorting, which will increase your speed, they will give up."

Roberts laughed and thanked the guard.

The guard smiled and waved, and they walked on up the dirt road into the open grassy hills.

When they were high enough, but still well below the trees, they looked back. From here, they could see over the walls around the storehouses.

Each storehouse was white, made of a native concrete, and raised ten to fifteen feet off the ground on massive arches. The storehouses were rectangular, with steep roofs that had a wide overhang on all sides, and screened ventilators at the ends. Each was set apart from the others by a smooth, out-curving cement wall some eight feet high, with a tightly-fitted metal gate at either end.

Roberts and Hammell, studying the scene through binoculars, noticed men coming out of the warehouses with the critical look of inspectors, as others checked the walls and grounds. Wagons went in through the metal gates, and the gates closed tightly behind them. The wagons pulled out of sight under the storehouses, as other wagons reappeared heaped with yellow grain, to leave by the opposite gates. Within and between the separate walled warehouses, there roamed animals that Roberts at first though were the local form of rats. But a little more watching showed that they had no fear of the men, who in turn paid little attention to them. It followed that they were roughly the equivalent of barn cats.

After watching an hour or so the two men glanced at each other.

Everything they had seen spoke of foresight and good order. Without a word, they got up and started back.

On the way, the city seemed more familiar than ever, until they reached the Visitor's Campground. Here, the ship was practically lost from sight, in the center of a host of tent makers and their poles, cords, and gorgeous rolls of purple, gold, and yellow cloth, with wagons hastily unloading chests and boxes, then rattling off at a fast trot, to bring in yet more merchandise.

When they finally located the colonel, he was examining a large ruby, while a beaming jeweler poured out a selection of flashing stones from a purple velvet bag. The colonel excused himself, listened to Roberts' report, then smiled.

"I think this place will be all right. We ought to be able to do it."

The following days saw the colonel's fame spread. He was soon known as Yel Den Garoujik—the Star Prince Garoujik—and when the rumors of his wealth and impressive dominion amongst the stars had spread widely enough, the Iatulon, consumed with curiosity, had one of his court functionaries drop a hint that His Highness might be willing to grace the Yel Den's table. The Yel Den promptly sent an invitation engraved on a silver plate, with an emerald at each corner for decoration.

The colonel was in the control room, his robes slung over the back of the control seat, when Bergen popped in to tell him the Iatulon had accepted the invitation. The colonel nodded, and glanced back at a small auxiliary screen, where the signal degarbler showed a member of the Interstellar Patrol's legal staff.

"It's O.K., Val," the staff member was saying. "The local PDA consul on the planet isn't likely to interfere until later, if at all. PDA is so desperate to get this job done that they won't want to wreck it unless you should blossom out with bribery, or coercion. They'll *watch* intently, though only an expert in spy devices would know it. But they'll be watching only for any interference in local affairs. Any effective interference is illegal."

The colonel smiled. "All I intend to do is talk—starting with the Iatulon."

"I don't see how words will straighten this mess out."

"They're just the first link in a chain of events."

"Well, good luck with the Iatulon, anyway. He's got a double-edge three-foot sword, remember."

"Sure," said the colonel, smiling, "but he only uses it on people who don't do their jobs."

That evening, the Iatulon, a tall impressive figure in flowing robes, showed up with a small but businesslike escort, ate moderately of the feast spread out before him, and cheerfully accepted a magnificent ruby put at his place with the dessert, according to local custom when entertaining royalty.

He retired in a benevolent mood to the flowered terrace beside Yel Den Garoujik's pool, where the stars were mirrored, as magical musicians played softly, rendered invisible by the power of the Yel Den's wizards.

After a lengthy but companionable silence, the Iatulon glanced thoughtfully around. "An entertainment to dwell upon in pleasant memory, Yel Den Garoujik. I thank you."

The colonel bowed his head, and settled himself to the customary flowery exchange of compliments. "And I thank you, Great Iatulon, for your presence here."

"I have done nothing."

"This is but a setting for the jewel of your presence. What is the setting without the jewel?"

The Iatulon looked at him with a smile. "Jewels are expensive, Yel Den Garoujik. One does not spend of his substance to place a jewel in a setting unless he has a purpose."

The colonel, slightly off-balance, said courteously, "That is true, Great Iatulon."

The Iatulon leaned forward. "Then let us to the business, Yel Den. I am hung about the ears with those who are too frightened of my sword to think, and with those who would not think if they could think, because of the pain that would come with their first thinking. Around my borders dwell rulers who neither think nor work save when dire need rouses their hunger. I would sweep away these triflers, but long thought shows me the task outweighs my resources. Thus I am condemned to a circumscribed sphere, amongst fools and would-be idlers. What has brought the jewel to this setting, Yel Den, is not the thought of food and drink, or sweet music, though such things are pleasant, but the prospect of *discourse amongst equals*. You are here for a purpose. Let us now to the purpose."

The colonel promptly discarded some carefully-prepared flowery phrases.

"In the future, many star ships will travel near this world. Whoever can induce the rulers to accept the landing of the people from these ships, will add much to his treasury."

The Iatulon looked puzzled. "I have heard of this plan. But I tell you, Yel Den Garoujik, that no one, unless he employs sorcerers of the highest degree, will persuade the rulers of this world to agree to such a thing. *I* will agree to it. Therefore, without thought, my neighbors will disagree. They will not judge a matter on its merits. They will not *think*. Hence they will not agree."

"And yet, I believe there is one condition in which all the rulers *would* agree."

The Iatulon shrugged.

"Have you a magic potion which will make them think, Yel Den Garoujik?"

"Unfortunately, only a few will think."

"But if only a few will think, and only those who think will agree, how can you say *all* will agree?"

"I say only, 'There is one condition in which *all the rulers* would agree.' "

"*If* all think."

"Yes."

"We travel in circles, and arrive nowhere. They are fools, and will *not* think."

"Fools may not think, yet all the *rulers* might."

The Iatulon began to speak, and suddenly stopped. He turned to stare at the colonel, who looked back quietly.

The Iatulon cleared his throat. "Forgive my slowness, Yel Den. I realize now, there is some reason why you would have the thought arise in my own mind with but a hint from you. I follow the trail thus far. My ears are attuned, and my attention prepared, to grasp the idea when you set it free."

"You have roads here, Great Iatulon. What do you think of them?"

"I would not poison your air with my thoughts of them. The streets are cobbled and bearable. In this season, the roads, though most are narrow and winding, are not bad. In very early spring and in late fall, most of them, because of mud, are good only as obstacles to an intruder. Man or beast will sink to his hips in the worst of these roads. Wagons disappear in them to the axles, and sometimes to the bed. Such are our roads, and yet they are good enough for our needs. If we travel far, we come to the border, where the enemy has soldiers to put an arrow through us if we cross. Your mention of roads carries me nowhere, Yel Den Garoujik."

"Then let your thought travel upon a finer road, Great Iatulon—a road such as can be made by choosing the route with care, sending men ahead to clear the way, while others bring stone from the place where the road has already passed, and gravel and dirt, and pack it into place to make way for the wagons that bring yet more dirt, stones, and gravel, from the places where this road has already gone, and that have been leveled to make it smooth. Such a road could carry a big idea, amongst other things—Such things as spice, gold, fine tools, and works of craftsmanship, which now must come by sea and upriver, with many shipwrecks and at great cost."

The Iatulon stroked his chin. "That *is* a big idea. But Yel Den, ideas of any size founder upon the rocks of stupidity, as a spice ship on the coastal reefs. The kings will not agree to *that*, either."

"Even if they are paid the tolls?

The Iatulon looked blank.

"*Tolls?* What word is that?"

"What merchants would not gladly pay a small fee to trade by land with far places? This payment, or *toll*, would go direct to the king's treasury. This would be a *royal* road, Great Iatulon, and each length of it would be the personal property of the king through whose territory it passed. The king need only set up a strong guardhouse by the road, and a gate on the road, and collect payment from every merchant who passes through."

The Iatulon sat back. "This appears to be a practical idea. Whoever refused to cooperate would rouse the anger of those who wished to have the tolls, and hence he would risk his throne. If I understand this, the royal treasuries would be paid much of that money now lost to rocks and storms, along the whole length of the miserable coast."

"True. And since the merchants need no longer fear these things, they should be willing to pay the tolls. If all those princes who *do* think should start work on such a road—"

"Yes, but wait. There is a problem. My kingdom, although far from perfect, is at least better ordered than those of my neighbors. While I have a Master of the Roads, they leave it to the peasants to repair the roads on threat of a beating. Yet the peasants are already busy in the fields, tending the crops, and repairing the damage done by the feuds and hunts of the boisterous nobility of these countries. What with the local robbers, the nobility, and the lack of vermin-proof storehouses, there is little excess from one year to the next to carry them if they *did* work on the roads. Everything is ill-ordered. With no Master of the Roads, no work chiefs, no men accustomed to earn extra coppers each year on the road, and no stored surplus of food, how *can* they build? The only system and method in such countries is applied to the army, the tax collector, and recruitment for the harem."

The colonel nodded, his face expressionless. "And yet, such a road would be of great benefit."

"They will *wish* to build it. But they will be unable. As the carouser wishes to mount the steps, but his limbs will not function."

"And yet, if *your* work chiefs had *their* peasants to do the work—"

"Their peasants would not do it for my men, even if my

men had permission to cross the border. Their peasants leave their crops only on threat of the lash. There is no profit for them in it."

The colonel said, in a thoughtful voice, "What would happen if they *were* offered pay?"

"Their kings will not deprive themselves, and their treasuries are as disordered as everything else."

"What if *you* paid them?"

The Iatulon looked at him flatly.

"You suggest that *I* pay out of *my* treasury to build *their* road?"

The colonel said courteously, "It would be presumptuous of me to make such a suggestion. But it occurs to me to wonder *what would happen if you did?*"

The Iatulon stared, started to get up, then paused. He gave a low exclamation. Finally he looked at the colonel in astonished respect.

"Truly, Yel Den Garoujik, the man who thinks of such a plan thinks deep thoughts."

Courteously, the colonel said, "It merely seemed to me that such a road might be a benefit to the planet. I thought you would appreciate its virtues."

"You need say no more, Yel Den Garoujik. And when the time comes to vote, count on me to favor the rest camp for the Star Men."

IX

From Mardukash, the colonel moved on to Sil, then Yarum, then Garanzol, and in each of these places, good order reigned, and the colonel was listened to respectfully by rulers whose trend of thought followed the same pattern as the Iatulon's. Each was in turn angered, then wide-eyed, at the thought of subsidizing a road for his neighbors.

In each of these petty kingdoms, Roberts and Hammell found the people content, the troops loyal and alert, and the storehouses full.

Roberts, when not out gathering firsthand information, spent some time wondering about the colonel's plan. The basic idea seemed plain enough: The colonel intended that the best-organized kingdoms should combine in building a great Royal Road that would benefit all the kingdoms by providing a better route than the hazardous sea journey.

But why should the richer kings suddenly turn into philanthropists? And what good did all this do for Garoujik Construction and PDA? Roberts, puzzled, watched to see what would happen next.

When the well-organized kingdoms had been visited, the colonel had Roberts land at yet another Visitors' Campground, and this time Roberts reported that while the people seemed reasonably content, there were signs everywhere of inefficiency.

"Be specific," said the colonel.

"Well, sir," said Roberts, "first, you've got to give the guards at the gate a little something extra to 'oil the hinges,' in order to get in or out. Second, under the usual robes, the people wear the usual loose blouse and long loose trousers. But in this place, they sell a flat leather pouch you wear on a harness under the rest of your clothes. That's on account of pickpockets. When we asked one of the merchants, 'What about the guards?' he looked at us as if we were crazy, and said, 'The pickpockets divide with them.' Third, the public storehouses in the city are alive with rats. It seems that the Great Zaragol pays a bounty on every hundred rat tails that are brought in from the royal warehouses. The people in charge of the royal warehouses don't get any salary; they're supposed to live on the bonuses, and the more diligent they are, they more they get. It sounds good, but they can't trap rats in the warehouses unless there *are* rats in the warehouses, and we saw one of these people toss a piece of meat to a cat, take a quick look around, then bash the cat's head in and flip it over the wall."

"What do the people think of these things?"

Roberts shrugged. " 'So it has always been. So it will always be.' "

"Where do they get their food when the royal storehouses run out?"

"There are private storehouses that seem better managed, but they're always low by the end of the year. Then the Great Zaragol puts the squeeze on the farmers for 'trying to starve the people.' He can generally wring something out of them so everyone gets through to the next harvest. If not, there's a famine, and that lowers the population, so the next year's food supply will feed the remainder."

The colonel said somberly, "What about the army?"

"What soldiers we saw seemed tough and good-natured. It's hard to judge without knowing more, but it looked as if the men were probably good fighters, but not well organized."

"This fits with what PDA told us," said the colonel. "Well, the thing is now in motion. We'll just have to keep an eye on it, and see how it goes."

Roberts said politely, "Speaking as just a new recruit, sir, who doesn't know much, *what* are we supposed to keep an eye on?"

The colonel smiled. "Since we are inside this ship, Roberts, where PDAs receptors are being fed a thoroughly falsified picture, I suppose we can be frank."

"Yes, sir," said Roberts.

"When a clandestine organization can't hope to get its goal achieved directly, what do you suppose it does?"

Roberts groped mentally. "Apparently, it will have to go about it indirectly."

"For instance?"

"Well, ambush the opposition, tie up his communications, create diversions, wear him out with false alarms—"

The colonel nodded. "That's an armed *military* opposition. Suppose we consider the case of a *few* men who wish to reorganize a planet, and are forbidden to use force or large-scale bribery?"

"That's exactly what I don't see."

"They may be able to do it with an *idea*."

"Sir, that sounds good, but—"

"An idea that offers the locals a visible real or apparent gain, but that has as an inescapable by-product the starting of a chain of events that the majority of the locals do not realize. Those who do realize it may attempt to block it, but they will be silenced by the majority, who see only the immediate gain. The resulting chain of events is like a chemical reaction, Roberts, and although exact details are impossible to predict, the overall 'reaction' proceeds inexorably, to the final products—unless a new 'reaction'—a different chain of events—is started by the intervention of some new factor."

Roberts said hesitantly, "Sir . . . isn't that pretty theoretical?"

"Very. In practice, the problem, of course, is to find some idea that will appeal to the locals for their own reasons, and that incidentally will start the desired chain of events."

"Such a chain of events has been started here?"

"Of course."

"I don't see it."

"You will."

Roberts said wryly, "The Interstellar Patrol doesn't give information away, does it?"

The colonel smiled. "The Interstellar Patrol gives practically *nothing* away."

Roberts nodded.

"However," said the colonel, "when you've learned a little more about it, you will also see that the Patrol places very few restrictions on what you can *earn*."

Roberts said exasperatedly, "Sir, what *is* the Interstellar Patrol?"

"That is a piece of information that you will have to earn."

"And just how do I earn it?"

"By discovering the way to find the answer."

Roberts smiled. "And I suppose if I wanted to get rich, I could achieve that, too, if I could first figure out what mysterious thing to do to achieve it."

The colonel shrugged. "You don't have to achieve that. As far as that's concerned, you, Hammell, and Morrissey, *are* rich."

"You mean, rich in companionship, or some such thing?"

"No," said the colonel, "I mean rich in money."

"This is news to me."

"Then you don't understand how the Patrol works. When we take something, we pay for it. When you three men came on board, you brought along a gadget far in advance of anything we had in that line, and that promises to be extremely useful—if something of a headache. But, if someone else had discovered this and used it against us, it would have been much more than a headache; hence, you have brought us something extremely valuable. In return, you are given a large money reward. This is only fair."

Roberts said dazedly, "This can be drawn on?"

"Whenever you want, when you're not on assignment to a specific duty."

"It was Morrissey who actually worked out the device—"

"In apportioning the amount of the payment, all facts available to us and to SymComp were carefully considered. But bear in mind, you brought the device into the Patrol, intentionally or not, and this weighs heavily with us."

Roberts turned away, then paused, the colonel's words playing themselves over in his mind. " 'SymComp?' What's that?"

"One of those things you can learn about if you can discover how to find out what you want to know."

Roberts told himself he had assimilated enough for now, anyway. "I'll try to figure it out, sir, when I accumulate the strength. Thanks very much for what you've told me."

"Perfectly all right, Roberts. You were entitled to it. Otherwise, I wouldn't have told you."

As the days passed, the results of their efforts began to show up. Going out into town, they could not help but hear word of the "Great Road," as the people called it. Soon, they saw a more tangible sign—peasants who rode into town on weekends, money jingling in their pockets. Business picked up and became brisk. A boom developed, and merchants and artisans labored overtime to supply goods to meet the demand. Then, as the road came closer, the laborers began to come into town on weekday evenings.

Watching the cheerful throngs buy necessities, and later watching them buy the worthless trinkets that increasingly appeared in the shops, Roberts began to feel uneasy. Approaching a peasant laden with several dozen strings of glass beads, three stuffed dolls, a large bolt of cheap cloth, and fifteen pairs of sandals slung over his shoulder on a woven grass cord, Roberts spoke apologetically.

"Pardon me, sir, but I am a stranger here. If you will excuse my ignorance, I would wish to ask a question."

The peasant looked at him with shrewd good humor. "Ask away. But speak quickly, as I must return on the Great Road tonight with these goods." A glint of pride showed in his eye.

Roberts said apologetically, "I mean no offense . . . perhaps it is just that I am a stranger here . . . but I seem to notice a spending of good money for what, where I come from, some might think to be goods more for pleasure than for use. I mean no offense, but only wonder at such freely-spent wealth."

The peasant smiled and nodded. "We are all become like nobles, and spend money as they do. It is that the Neighbor King, who builds the Great Road, spends lavishly of his substance, for labor that is no worse than a man must do in his own fields for half the sum or less. Thus we have quickly supplied our needs, and that done, to what use shall we put the money? True, some of the silver can be put in the floor, and the spot smoothed over, but to earn much money and spend little is to tempt robbers, and that is not wise. Why should not my wife have that which will please her eye, and my children have that which will enliven their play, and keep sharp stones from their feet—especially when these are things that will be seen by those who steal, and these things will say to them, 'No money here. That fool Ayok has thrown it all away on his family.' Eh?" The peasant jabbed Roberts lightly with his elbow. "Are we, then, such fools?"

Roberts smiled. "Not now that I understand it. Your words have cleared up the mystery."

"Come work on the road. The silver flood cannot last forever, but while it lasts, it is better than to break your back in the fields. Nearly all who farm, and can reach the Great Road, will have a welcome rest this summer. You can share in the wealth."

Roberts smiled. "Perhaps I will. Thank you."

The friendly peasant moved away.

And then, like a blow to the back of the head, suddenly the next link in the colonel's chain of events came across to Roberts.

Here, all around him, spending cheerfully the money earned on the road, were a large proportion of the farmers of the country.

Across the road, under the sign "Logash and Brothers," grain and dried vegetables were being weighed out to a line of children who handed over their coppers, and hurried home with the food they'd been sent to pick up.

As, across the street, last year's grain was weighed out from the storehouses, over here the peasants laughed and joked, and then headed home to rest up for another day's work—*on the road.*

"My God," said Roberts.

He walked across the street, uncertain exactly what he had in mind, and nodded to a smiling man who stood in the storehouse, a little back from the wide doorway, watching the money rattle into his till.

"Sir?" said the man, half-bowing. "Will you have *dar*, *qadron*, or perhaps a measure of *nerbash*? We have dried *rashids*, *pinths*, and still some ground-nuts, though we are completely out of *tekkary*. I believe Gashar, across town, has some, but beware his *qadron*. It is said the rats have been in it, though do not say I said it."

Roberts said hesitantly, "I am a stranger here—"

The man said warily, "Do you have money?"

"Yes."

"Ah, but you do not know our delicacies? Well, our *rashids* and ground-nuts are very good this year. The *rashids* are three coppers the bunch, and the ground-nuts are a small silver-piece for one hand of them. It is high, but this is the last of the season's. Will you buy?"

"Yes."

"I will serve you myself. Ah, this Road is a great thing, is it not? When it is done, we will have spice from far Iandul, and not at the price of two hands of silver wheels to the half-leaf of spice, either."

Roberts said hesitantly. "But the Road takes many farmers from their work, does it not?"

"Yes, but how else? Who would not work at double the wage for less labor? Everyone prospers. Look at the money flow! Even those who do not work on the Road are rich, because of what they sell to the road workers!"

Roberts tried again. "How will the harvest be this year, do you think?"

"Who can say? There is something no man knows. But we'll get through. There are those who say that this prosperity will go on forever. And why not? If there is much silver, men can buy. And if they buy, other men have the silver and they can buy. Thus is everyone become prosperous. Here you are, sir. Thank you. If you find my goods to your liking, come back, and I think you cannot do better. You will find no rat tails and offal weighed out to you from my scales, even with the scrapings before harvest."

Dumbfounded, Roberts nodded and started back to the ship. On the way, he stopped, and gave his purchase to a little girl, who accepted it smilingly, and looked wonderingly after the somber stranger before running in to hand the food to her mother.

X

The Road approached the city, at first as a sound of crashing trees, and the shouted orders of men urging on beasts of burden. Then the crews clearing away the forest and bridging the streams actually came into view. Then came the bulwark of yellowish-brown dirt, rocks, and gravel, more dirt, rocks and gravel, endlessly cascading down as double files of wagons unloaded and went back, and endless lines of men, carrying wicker baskets between them, filled the gaps between the wagons, then walked back single file to let the unloaded and now faster wagons go ahead. To either side of the Road, swarms of men cleared away the under-growth, and made tangled barriers of felled trees as a dis-couragement to robbers when the road should be put into use.

The city, by now, was in the grip of delirious prosper-ity, the men working overtime to fill the unheard-of demand for goods, and the women and children coming out in crowds, to observe the steady advance of the cause of all this wealth. Silver and copper changed hands in a magi-cal flow, but Roberts and Hammell, going out into the countryside to look at the farms, saw only kitchen gardens, tended by the women of the families, and weedy fields, with occasional boys, too young for heavy work, out pulling up thorny vines, lest they grow big and interfere with the next year's harvest. At rare intervals, there was a good field, tended by an old man, who preferred to stay home, and do work he was used to, rather than make the trip to work on the road. But, with rare exceptions, the food-producing regions within reach of the Road were a wasteland.

"Will you have enough," Roberts asked a road worker in town, "when the stored food is gone?"

"Oh, Shachrim and Fazir have many good farmers, and when the Road crosses the border, we can buy from them. This Road will solve many problems. We never could buy from them before until after the ground froze, because the roads were so bad. Now all will be different. Excuse me, now, good sir, I am a moneyed person, and have many important purchases to attend to."

At last, there was nothing more for Roberts and Hammell to report to the colonel. The colonel, who each day lifted off with Morrissey and Bergen to observe the progress of the different sections of the Road, suggested that Roberts and Hammell go to work on the Road. Then they could report to him the mood of the road workers on the job.

Carrying a large wicker basket between them, Roberts and Hammell reported for work the next day, and by noon were exhausted, though the peasants around them trudged sturdily on without complaint. Angered at this unexpected weakness, Roberts and Hammell were grimly persisting in the middle of the afternoon when a shout went up somewhere ahead. Lost in the rhythm of the work, they set down the basket, tilted its load down the face of the advancing head of the Road, and were starting back when a murmur of dismay went up around them. They came to sufficiently to look around, and there in the distance was another tongue of dirt, gravel, and stone—the head end of a road advancing toward them from the direction of Shachrim and Fazir.

As the men and wagons milled, a work chief's voice rose angrily.

"Let the work go on! Fools! It is only another part of the Great Road! Did you think we would build it all ourselves?"

"But if they, too, are all at work on the Road—"

"Will you have your pay docked? *Work*, I say! Out of the way of the wagons, there!' A large, strong hand roughly seized Roberts by the arm, and shoved him ahead of Hammell. "Keep moving! When you are back with the next load, you can take another look. All of you, *keep moving!*"

By the end of the day, when the gong sounded that signaled the end of the work, the two roads were close enough together so that the men from both work parties mingled. Roberts and Hammell could hear the same exclamations from both sides, with just slightly different accents:

"How are your crops over there?"

"What crops? We know you will have a great surplus in such a year as this, and with the Road, we can buy from you!"

"But *we* planned to buy from *you!*"

Before their eyes, the confident cheerful faces grew frightened.

"There is nothing to do, then, but to buy from the hill people and the backlanders. But the hill people have such poor land, there will be little to sell us. And to get over the river and swamp from the backlands to here with a decent load of grain will be impossible until the ground freezes."

Roberts and Hammell looked at each other.

Another link in the chain of cause and effect had come into view.

XI

The two ends of the Great Road were joined, and abruptly the flood of money ceased. Men at once set out into the hill country, and along the back roads, to find out if conditions were as bad as they seemed. Already, the price of food was climbing, as hoards of silver earned on the Road were used to buy what was worth still more— food.

And then the men who had gone into the hills began to straggle back with the bad news: Here and there were those who had food enough for themselves, and would not sell it at any price, because then *they* would starve. The backlanders had some extra food and were willing to sell it. But after the harvest was in, the fall rains were sure to begin. Then the streams would fill, the rivers overflow, and the long winding roads would be more impassable than ever. Nothing would get through until the ground froze. That meant famine.

Already, Roberts and Hammell, serving as scouts for the colonel, could notice that people looked thinner.

Roberts said, "They're rationing themselves."

Hammell nodded. "They've been through scarcity before. But probably never like this."

As the days slid into weeks, they realized it was no longer a question of "rationing."

Now, as the price of food climbed, other prices began to fall, the proprietors of shops hoping to sell something, anything, so they could pay the ever-rising cost of food.

As Roberts and Hammell, during a brief hot break in the rainy weather, passed the barred front of a silver-smith's shop, a voice called, "This copper tray, good sirs. I will let you have it for nearly nothing. One hand of small silver coins, good sirs! See the workmanship!"

An old woman, passing in the dusty street with her gray robes tightly wrapped around her, hissed, "Don't do it. You will starve without silver."

The voice came again from the barred shop front.

"Or will you have this burnished bowl? Of good solid workmanship, and it shines like gold! Four silver coins, good sirs—the small ones. That is all!"

A cloud of dust whipped down the street, and with a dry rattle a flurry of leaves whirled from the trees.

The old woman was gone around a corner, but the silversmith's voice still followed them.

"Three silver coins, good sirs! I mistook the price! Three small silver coins! I have sold them for more than twenty. Come look. Look at it! It is a fine bowl."

They passed open shops, where people sat listlessly, then there was a sudden scurry of dust and leaves, and a small hand clasped Roberts' robes.

He looked down to see a thin face with neatly-combed brown hair, and large beseeching eyes. The face was vaguely familiar, and after a moment, Roberts remembered her. This was the little girl he'd given food to, the night that he'd first realized the famine was coming. He looked at her, and her gaze never wavered. The large eyes in the thin face held a steady look of faith.

Roberts took from his pocket a large silver coin, one of the kind locally called "wheels," because of their size and the design on the back.

The little girl took it, stepped back and bowed low. Then she ran unsteadily down the street toward the food store-house.

The wind whipped another flurry of leaves from the trees, and they rattled on the shop roofs, then blew across the roofs into the streets, to be caught up in whirling clouds of dust, and then rushed along, end-over-end, down the street.

Something gripped Roberts by the trouser leg.

A thin-faced boy said in a sing-song voice, "Please, good sir, give me silver. Or my mother dies."

Hammell said harshly, "A woman across the street just sent him out to beg."

The boy repeated, in the same singsong tone, "Please, good sir, give me silver. Or my mother dies."

The boy's eyes blurred, and he clung to Roberts' trouser leg, his hand clasping the white robe on top, and the trouser beneath, as if he were clinging to life itself.

He began again, in a singsong tone, "Please, good sir, give me silver. Or my mother dies."

Roberts took out eight to ten small and medium silver coins, and handed them to him.

The boy shut his eyes, swallowed painfully, and then stepped back and bowed.

"Come on," said Hammell.

From a pottery shop up the road, a little girl, her face and hands painfully thin and her belly swollen out with gas, teetered into the road, looked around listlessly, then started toward the two men. Hammell angrily threw a few small silver coins in the dust before her, and strode past, his hand on Roberts' arm propelling him at a fast pace.

"All that this giving to beggars does," growled Hammell, "is to shift the starvation from one mouth to another. Look."

They'd reached a private food warehouse, where a woman stood by a barred window, under a sign, "Silver Only."

From this warehouse, the little girl was walking very soberly back toward her home, carrying, hugged to her body, a small coarsely-woven bag. Seeing Roberts, she paused and bowed, then went on, walking a few steps unsteadily, then breaking into a tottering run.

Roberts turned and looked back, and for a moment, he saw the little girl at the corner, her bag of food clutched tightly to her. Then she vanished down the street.

With a moan, the wind picked up, and the air filled with dried leaves, and clouds of brown dust rushed down the street.

Roberts drew a careful breath, and looked at the food warehouse.

The woman there was holding a bundle in one arm, and in the other, outstretched, several medium-sized silver coins.

"But I *have* the money."

From the barred window came a patient voice.

"But *we* do not have the food. We have no grain at all, and will have no more roots and groundnuts till the hillmen come in again to sell to us. We have just sold the last."

"But I *have* the money, and my child must eat."

"Then go and try another storehouse. It may be that they have some. We have only enough for ourselves, and we live only from week to week. We cannot sell you what we do not have."

"I will pay you twice the price."

"Ten times the price will not buy it. It is gone."

The woman turned away, then hesitated.

"Will you sell me a little of your food? Just a little—"

The voice from the grilled window was pitying.

"No one will sell you their own food. What good is silver to a corpse?"

The woman turned, and walked slowly away, passing close by Roberts and Hammell as if not seeing them. Roberts had his hand in his pocket, and if the woman had even looked at him, he would have given her all the local money he had left. But she looked neither to the right nor the left as she walked by.

After she'd passed, Hammell shook his head. "It would have done no good anyway. The trouble here is, there *isn't enough food*. When you give money, you merely shift the food from one mouth to another.

Roberts felt sick and weary.

"Let's go on back. We've seen enough."

On the way back to the ship, they passed a small group of men and women beside a felled tree, The men were methodically stripping away the bark, while the women with sharp knives clipped off the ends of the twigs, dropping them into large baskets. They worked methodically and steadily, only looking up fearfully from time to time, as if afraid someone might come and take away what they had.

Back at the ship, Roberts and Hammell discovered a visitor in the form of a smaller ship marked with a string of numbers, and the letters, PDA. The colonel was just coming out, shaking his head.

"There is nothing I can do. It's a question of time and freight capacity. Let's say a pound of food per person per day will barely sustain their lives. How many people do you say are involved?"

An earnest-looking man appeared in the hatchway of the PDA ship.

"We don't know. We lack the facilities to say accurately, but on the whole continent—it could be anywhere from ten million to one hundred million persons."

The colonel shook his head. "If it's one hundred million, it will require a shipping capacity of fifty thousand tons per day. Where will we get the shipping? The food itself is problem enough. I know of no stocks in frontier regions on any such scale as that. And we're well out at the edge of the frontier. Now, this food will have to be brought from a great distance, and that will take *time*. When we get it here, it will have to be *distributed*. Can you begin to conceive of the organization this will require? I'm not equipped to begin to do this. Possibly PDA has the organization to handle it."

"I . . . I've received word we *cannot* handle it. I'd hoped you—"

"It's entirely beyond me. I realized, of course, when I suggested this road as a means to facilitate surface transport and . . . ah . . . cultural interchange, that some slight dislocation might result, but I didn't realize—You know, in a way I feel responsible—"

"Not at all, sir. We at Planetary Development have all been most impressed with the humanitarian selflessness of this project."

"Well . . . thank you. That means a great deal to me. All I can say is, we *did* urge that a sufficient proportion of the population be retained in essential occupations—"

The colonel paused, and glanced around at a jangling, clattering noise.

A glittering carriage, driven by a well-fed coachman and drawn by four sleek beasts of burden, came to a stop in a cloud of dust. A footman riding in back sprang off and pulled open the door. A second footman leaped off the back, ran around, and swung down a heavily-braced step. An immensely fat man in gold and scarlet robes, glittering rings on every finger, lunged out of the carriage, his face purple with rage, and faced the PDA representative.

"It is a trick . . . a swindle! I demand aid of the Star Men! You are their consul—you must help me!"

The PDA official said considerately, "We are right now trying to find some means to assist your people, Your Supremacy. But—"

"Assist my *people*? Why worry about *them*? Enough of them will live over to breed back to normal. We've had famines before. It's this Iatulon of Mardukash—*He's* the one who makes the trouble!"

The PDA consul's head drew back at the words, "Enough of them will live over to breed back to normal." He stared at the local king, started to speak, and then his jaw snapped shut.

"Now," said the enormous scarlet-robed figure, "You will see how crafty this fellow is. I have just had word, by messenger on my Road, that he will sell me 'enough grain to feed your people, at only a hand of coppers the half-measure,' *but I have to buy in bulk, and pay for it myself in big lots*. And I must send word back *at once!*"

The consul stared, then suddenly became excited. "Your hereditary enemy offers food? Then you must take it!"

"*Take* it? Not so fast. This is a high price!"

"But food is *bound* to be high. There is a famine!"

"Not in Mardukash, there isn't. The low born vermin keep their storehouses better than the palace. It is a *high* price. If I buy this food, my treasury will run out, I will not be able to pay my own army. That means ruin. But I *have* to buy, because word of this offer is being spread amongst the people. I will have a revolt if I do not buy! It's all this cursed Road! If it were not for that, the peasants would have raised their crops, and—even if we had a famine—no one could have got food in over the roads, so no outsider could have interfered." He shook his fist. "I demand that you destroy the Road!"

The consul looked staggered, then outraged. With an effort, he unclenched his fists.

"I am afraid I cannot associate myself with such an attitude, Your Supremacy."

"You, too, eh?" The local king whirled around, and lunged

back into the carriage, which sagged and swayed with loud creaks from the springs. *"Back to the palace!"*

The footmen snapped up the step, shut the door, and sprang on in back. The driver cracked his whip. The carriage whirled around in a cloud of dust, and shot out of sight down the road.

The consul stared at the dwindling cloud of dust.

"Incredible! A pure paranoid reaction!"

The colonel shook his head sadly, "In view of his attitude, possibly a change to a . . . er . . . more stable executive . . . might actually be a blessing in disguise."

"Yes. It certainly would. If the Iatulon actually brings food from his storehouses, he, at least, is showing the right attitude!"

The colonel nodded approvingly.

The PDA consul slowly passed his hand over his face. "If only they were *all* like the Iatulon!"

Three days later, his offer having been refused, the Iatulon's army came down the Royal Road like an avalanche, brushed aside a small force sent out to guard the border, clashed in a savage fight with the main body of the defending army, and was just entering the capital when the local king, surrounded by his mounted elite guard, shot out of the palace in a war chariot studded with double-edged knives, with a heavy oblong chest strapped into the chariot, gained the Road, and headed for the neighboring kingdom of Fazir. The Road offering excellent speed, he was steadily approaching the border of Fazir when a fast moving body of troops appeared in the distance ahead. This developed into the slitted and loopholed armored coach and household guard of the Arawak of Fazir, who was himself seeking sanctuary from the Ribar of Zaroom, the Ribar having fomented an uprising by offering food to the starving populace of Fazir.

As the two kings conferred, there appeared from each direction the rapidly-advancing cavalry of the Iatulon and the Ribar.

The two trapped kings briefly gripped each other by the arms. They whipped out their swords, and sprang back into their vehicles.

The chariot and the armored coach whirled around, pointed toward the enemy, and two angry voices rang out together.

"Charge!"

The household cavalry leveled their lances. The war vehicles thundered ahead of them down the road. The cavalry of the Iatulon and the Ribar went from a trot to a gallop.

As the antagonists met in a final bloody clash, already from Mardukash and Zaroom the grain wagons were creaking, heavily-laden, down the Royal Road from the swollen storehouses toward their famine-stricken neighbors.

XII

The colonel, looking like himself again, sat back at his desk, and looked over his four promising new recruits, once more recognizable as Roberts, Hammell, Morrissey, and Bergen.

"You see, gentlemen, a chain of events, if properly made, appears, one link after the other, very logically and inescapably. And here"—he picked up a yellow message form—"is the final link we're interested in, so far as this chain of events is concerned."

Roberts glanced at the paper, to read, " . . . In new vote, the surviving rulers have approved building of a Rest & Refit Center. Garoujik Corporation has subcontracted the actual construction work to Krojac Enterprises, and work is expected to begin at once . . ."

Roberts said, "The Iatulon, the Ribar, and the other efficient kings were able to end the famine?"

"Out of their accumulated stocks, they were able to ease it greatly, until the ground froze, and it became possible to also get food in quantity from the producing regions still cut off by bad roads. Then, between them, they built up stocks to get through the rest of the year on a reasonably normal basis."

"Why didn't anybody foresee this? To try to even suggest it to them was enough to drive you mad."

The colonel nodded. "There were only so many people here *to* see it, and they were all too busy seeing something else. The peasants saw the money they were offered. Overall allocation of effort wasn't *their* job. *That* job belonged to the kings. Their attention was on the money they'd get when the Royal Road was finished. If there was a famine—Well, they'd gotten through famines before. The consul, of course, should have seen it, but he is highly-educated, in economics that comes out of books written on highly developed worlds. 'Subsistence economy' is a pair of words that doesn't mean much on highly developed worlds. What counts there is capital accumulation and technological development. But wherever, for whatever reason, you're just able to produce enough food—or anything else you've got to have to exist—*any diversion of effort from that work is fatal.*

"The consul," said the colonel, "may have known it mentally, but it was about as real to him as the words 'cave bear,' when he reads about the experiences of humanity's remote ancestors. To people who've experienced the thing, the word 'famine' means a whole lot more."

Roberts involuntarily shivered as the colonel spoke the word "famine."

"Sir, does the Interstellar Patrol get involved like this very often?"

The colonel nodded soberly. "It has to. The universe isn't made out of cotton candy. Our job is to get things done. And often there is *no other way.*"

Hammell said, "Sir, how many people had to die to get that R & R Center in?"

"Very few," said the colonel. "Because the situation was thought out carefully."

Roberts said, "If there'd been an error?"

"Millions of people could have died."

"That's a big responsibility."

"It is. It requires thorough and determined training to be able to bear the responsibility. It's a help if you enter on your initial training with some idea what's in front of you. A man is less likely to throw away something if he knows he will desperately need it later."

Roberts said, "We are about to start our training?"

"You are," the colonel answered.

The four recruits looked at each other grimly.

The colonel said, "That will be all, gentlemen. You have tomorrow off. Then you begin training."

Roberts, Hammell, Morrissey, and Bergen filed from the room. The last man out closed the door gently.

The colonel glanced at the wall above his desk, where

gradually the strongly built keen-eyed man who had given him the problem came into view, smiling.

The colonel said, "What do you think?"

"I think you made the point. And it's an important point. Without it, half the training could be wasted."

The colonel nodded.

"I *think* they're motivated," he said.

THE NITROCELLULOSE DOORMAT

Colonel Valentine Sanders of the Interstellar Patrol tightened the restraining web as, around him, the globular screen showed the recorded scene of jungle and Space Force combat infantry.

Just ahead, beyond a thin screen of leaves, water poured in a wide sheet over a rock ledge, to foam and roar amongst the tumbled stone blocks below. On all sides, the blue-green trunks of giant trees twisted up through green twilight toward a sky that could be seen only as occasional patches high overhead. Through one of these rare openings, a shifting oblong of light shone down on the tangle of intertwined mossy roots on the jungle floor.

The air, hot, rank, and damp, with only a faint suggestion of a breeze, added the final touch to an illusion of reality that was almost complete.

The colonel glanced back. Through the trees, men darted forward, obviously well-trained, in good condition and alert, but very lightly armed. A little upstream of the waterfall, a lightly armed infantryman crawled out behind a mossy log, to peer through straggling weeds at the far bank of the stream.

The stream, about eight inches deep, and roughly forty feet across, was flowing swiftly over a bed of rock, strewn with occasional logs and flat stone slabs. The far bank rose steeply about eight feet high, topped by gently waving leafy branches.

What was atop the bank, behind the leaves, was anyone's guess.

247

Frowning, the colonel glanced at the Space Force infantryman lying behind the log. The colonel could think of a number of devices for solving the problem of that bank, but the infantryman's only weapon seemed to be a slug-throwing rifle, and his only protection appeared to be a helmet. The usual equipment of the Space Force combat infantry was such that one man armed as usual would have been more formidable than a thousand men armed like this.

Behind the log, the infantryman now bunched himself, as if to cross the stream in a rush. But then he paused and looked again. First, he would have to drop down the bank on the near side of the stream. Then there would be the splashing rush across forty feet of water, flowing over an uneven rock bottom that was probably coated with slime. Then there was the problem of getting up the bank on the far side.

The infantryman gave a slight shake of the head, and crouched lower. Without his usual equipment, his special skills would be a burden. He would constantly feel the need to use this or that piece of equipment—which he didn't have.

Scowling, the colonel looked around. In this situation, a band of aborigines could slaughter the best troops in existence.

Now a second infantryman, in a mottled green-and-gray camouflage suit, crawled forward and tugged at the first man's ankle. The two talked in low murmurs, then the second man crawled forward to take a look. He shrugged, scrambled out from behind the log, and slid over the bank. As he splashed out into the stream, the first man shoved his rifle forward and watched the far bank.

A third infantryman eased forward behind a tree as, halfway across the stream, the second slipped and fell. A fourth man crawled up behind a low pile of mossy rocks, and peered out at the far bank. The second, his wet uniform clinging to him, limped through the rushing water. A fifth and a sixth infantryman, as lightly armed as the rest, slipped forward through the trees.

In his mind's eye, the colonel could see the whole near bank filling up with men stopped by that stream. He stared out across it, to see the second man find a handhold, and start to haul himself up the far bank, where the leaves moved gently in the breeze.

From behind the delicately waving leaves, brilliant lines
sprang horizontally across the stream, to slice through brush,
trees, and men like knives of light. Dazzling puffs of lumi-
nous vapor reached across the stream, and on the near bank
blazing fireballs burst in explosions of bright droplets that
left criss-crossing tracks like a thousand fiery spiderwebs.
On all sides, the ground lifted in eruptions of flying dirt
and rock.

The edges of the restraining web bit in hard as the colonel
forgot himself and sought cover. With an effort, he relaxed
and looked around at the recorded chaos of blurs as the
viewing head left the site of the ambush. The record abruptly
came to an end, and the screen around him went blank.

The colonel took a deep breath, and unlatched the
restraining web. The globular screen divided into sections
and swung up, to nest itself out of sight overhead.

The colonel glanced across the room, where the strongly
built Section Chief, his penetrating blue eyes alight with
anger, looked up from a viewer, snapped out the record
spool, and said, "What do you think of it, Val?"

"Those were Space Force *combat infantry?*"

"Correct. Their best."

"If we used men like that, we'd be finished in a month."

"The circumstances were peculiar. Take a look at this."
The Chief tossed across the little spool, and the colonel bent
to snap it into a viewer on a stand nearby.

A Space Force brigadier general, spare, trim, and frowning, appeared.

"The scene you've just witnessed was the beginning of
an action that destroyed the 1866th Combat Infantry Regi-
ment. This was one of our crack units—every man was first-
rate. Four days earlier, the 1728th Combat Infantry was wiped
out in a similar action. By 'wiped out,' I mean destroyed
as a unit. Both regiments suffered over eighty percent killed.
Most of the remainder were seriously wounded. Only a total
of thirty-one men remained fit for service from these two
actions.

"These defeats were inflicted on us on the planet Terex,
an earthlike world with people like ourselves. Although their
technology was not very advanced, Planetary Development
considered them so far advanced in other respects that they
granted the planet provisional status. About two years ago,

a series of petty revolts broke out on Terex. The local government appealed for help. Planetary Development Authority is sympathetic to the locals, and regards the planet as a showcase of 'interplanetary cooperation.' PDA, therefore, put this request for help through in record time, and we were ordered in to straighten out the situation. We were also ordered, in the strictest terms, not to offend local sensibilities. The locals, while not very advanced technologically, have a powerfully developed set of priestly hierarchies, and we were *not* to interfere in religious matters.

"Unfortunately, little by little it developed that the local gods are allergic to modern technology. They don't like air transportation, or mechanized ground transport, or computers, satellites, or any of a very large variety of our weapons. The high priests explained that our equipment creates 'bad vibrations.' A reconnaissance satellite is a 'new star,' which disrupts all kinds of astrological considerations. Gravitors are anathema—they 'warp the lines of destinic action.' Aircraft are 'solid objects which unnaturally cut the rays of influence of the stars.' Ground transport is all right, provided it doesn't get its motive power from 'unnatural heat,' which 'disturbs the solar influence.' For similar reasons, all manner of our weapons can't be tolerated. All these things become *religious* matters. If we didn't obey these injunctions, we would be irreligious. This would offend local sensibilities in the worst way, and that is exactly what we were ordered not to do.

"Now, this situation didn't present itself in a clear-cut way. It developed piecemeal. At first, the locals enthusiastically welcomed our troops. Next, the priests insisted that it would be necessary not to use this or that device or weapon. Gradually, bit by bit, the situation changed. The final result was that our men wound up practically disarmed.

"To begin with, too, the guerrilla problem didn't look too bad, and the local transportation system, that we were going to have to rely on if we didn't use mechanized transport, seemed reasonably reliable.

"Unfortunately, we ran into a local religious sect called the Skaga cult. This gang operates on the theory that 'good can be made out of evil.' The Skagas do evil to others in confidence that the 'balance wheel of fate' will return good to the victim, evening up the score with no effort on the

Skagas' part. The Skagas evidently decided the Space Force was ripe for a lot of good done by their special methods. Without our even knowing there was such a cult, they infiltrated the loading stations where our supplies are transferred to the local transportation system, set up a black market, and began selling our weapons to all comers—including the guerrillas.

"Meanwhile, we were trying to prevail on the local priesthood to reconsider the ban on our weapons. They finally agreed to let certain banned weapons be used, tentatively. We rushed them down to the planet, and, thanks to the Skagas, the guerrillas got the weapons first. By torture, they forced our captured troops to explain the weapons.

"The guerrillas, incidentally, had the advantage by now. Our men weren't properly armed, didn't know local conditions, and were fighting in a way they weren't used to. The guerrillas dealt out a rough series of partial defeats, and then, using our own recently shipped weapons, wiped out two of our best regiments.

"Our local commander found himself with a series of defeats, a well-organized black market draining off supplies from the transportation network, a powerful guerrilla movement well supplied with our own weapons, and worst of all, a large proportion of the people who suddenly regard the Space Force, and humans generally, as inferior beings. 'See,' the argument goes, 'the Skagas are smarter, and the guerrillas are better warriors. The spacemen are weaklings. They cannot manage their own affairs. They are unfit to lead others.' The result of this attitude is every kind of obstruction and irritation, with the prospect of much worse in the near future.

"To straighten out this mess, our commander on the planet could see only one thing to do—use stronger weapons. But, by now, even this won't work, unless we carry out a general slaughter. Too large a part of the populace is now sympathetic to the guerrillas. And we are still hamstrung by our orders. To get them changed, through channels, is proving a very slow process. Well—when the final casualty lists from the two big ambushes came in, our commander shot himself. The mess has now been turned over to me."

The Space Force general drew a deep breath.

"This situation is now so hopelessly confused that I will be frank and say that I am out of my depth. I hereby respectfully request interservice assistance."

The colonel snapped the spool out of the viewer, walked over, and handed it back. The Chief, sitting back flipping through a bulky set of printed sheets, took the spool without looking up, and shoved a thick sheaf of reports across the desk. "Here."

The colonel took them and scowled.

"Are we supposed to *read* that stuff?"

"That's the general idea."

"By the time we get through, half the combat infantry in the Space Force could be buried on Terex."

"Just skim it. We aren't going to be able to prepare as thoroughly for this job as I'd like."

"Why not put it through the mill, and make it into an orientation?"

"Too realistic. This way, the misinformation has to go through a fine-mesh sieve before it gets into our minds."

The colonel frowned, and opened up the topmost report, to skim rapidly:

The Gr'zaen Religion:
Sun-Worship on Terex
by
J. K. Fardel, Ph.D.

While Terexian sun-worshipers, like those of other religions, on this planet . . . gladly welcome converts to their religion . . . they, too, have the regrettable habit of decapitating those who seek to observe their rites . . . A further obstruction to objective research . . . arises out of the fact that those who seek to question the true believers regarding religious details are soon shunned, while a true believer who reveals details of the rites and practices is . . . likely to be punished by hideous torture. Therefore, despite the use of . . . spy devices . . . a strictly accurate and complete description of the Gr'zaen religion is . . . somewhat hard to come by. Nevertheless, it is possible to make a few . . . reasonable approximations. On Earth, the sun-worshipers of ancient times—

The colonel looked up exasperatedly.

"At least, let's run this stuff through a condenser."

"No. That loses the unique flavor some of these reports convey. But, as a matter of fact, I think the basic situation is clear enough so we won't have to absorb all of this misinformation."

"I'm glad to hear that."

The colonel flipped through the sheaf, and came upon a report headed: "The Terexian Transportation Network." He skimmed this rapidly, and a picture came across of a collection of animal-drawn vehicles and primitive railroads, of coastwise shipping infested by pirates, of inclined roadways down which vehicles traveled by gravity, to be hauled up a steep slope for the next stage, the whole so-called transportation system being sluggish, subject to a complete stoppage on every religious feast day, and dependent for continuous performance on a large number of warehouses in which goods periodically piled up and drained out as the erratically functioning parts of the network speeded up or broke down.

Scowling, he read more slowly, noting the opportunities this transport net offered black marketeers and guerrillas. To top everything else, it was irreligious to work on feast days, so on these days the Terexian guards were off duty.

The colonel next leafed through the stack until he came upon a report headed "The Irregular Volunteers on Terex." The choice of words puzzled him, but became clear as he read a paean of praise for the guerrillas, and realized that the writer of this PDA report hated the Space Force.

The obvious next thing to look for was information about the Skaga cult. But after reading it, the colonel knew less than he'd thought he'd known to start with.

The Chief impatiently tossed the last report on the desk.

"It seems to *me* that the local guerrillas, religious leaders, and Skaga cultists, are all different parts of the same thing—a kind of machine to grind the Space Force troops on the planet to a pulp. But it's hard to see how the Skagas get along with the rest. The others seem to have moral standards."

The colonel looked up from a report on "comparative literature," which praised the "technical artistry" of the locals, but complained of their "primitive exaltation of craft and prowess. Indeed, the most popular folk hero, in whatever guise he may appear, is inevitably faced by a formidable enemy, whom he defeats by a stroke of genius, usually delivered while the hero's own cause is on the brink of disaster."

"Hm-m-m," said the colonel. With an effort, he put his mind on the Chief's comment. "Well, the Skagas and the other religions may not *get along* with each other, but they may *work together*, all the same."

"Informally, you mean?"

"Maybe without even thinking they *are* working together."

The Chief nodded, and sat back.

"The trouble in dealing with a whole race, such as this bunch, is that you *think* you're dealing with so many individuals—and it's true, you are—but it also involves more than that. In such numbers, there are unseen inter-relationships, and statistical effects. It's as if the whole race together made up an organism. One section may do one thing, while another section does another thing, to cre-ate an overall result neither section appears to aim at. In this case, the religionists disarm the Space Force, the Skagas rob them, and the guerrillas kill them. *And the Terexians, as a whole, draw the conclusion that humans are inferior beings.*"

"As if," said the colonel, "the overall situation were a kind of test?"

"Yes. And conducted according to Terexians' idea of what constitutes superiority." He looked through the stack of reports, separated one from the rest, and read: " ' . . . Characteristic saying of the local pundits is that "any beast may be strong, but it takes a man to be wise". . . . ' "

"Well, that fits. Their actions have been such as to elimi-nate the effect of the Space Force's superior *strength*."

"Hm-m-m. And the human race then proved 'inferior.' "

The colonel nodded. "Only strong—not wise."

"Correct."

"Well," said the colonel, "they've tested the Space Force. But unfortunately for the Terexians, *we* have now been called in."

The Chief sat back with a speculative expression.

"Considering this judo hold the Terexians have on the Space Force, exactly what do *we* do?"

"Break the hold. Of course, the Terexians may lose a few fingers in the process."

"How are you going to get at those guerrillas?"

"Through the Skagas."

The Chief glanced thoughtfully off in the distance, and suddenly nodded.

"What will you need?"

"Some stuff from Special Devices, the local language, transportation to the planet, an H-ship and crew, and permission from the Space Force to operate at one of their supply centers where goods are shipped to the planet, before they're transshipped by the local transportation system. Plus twenty or thirty men to do the job I have in mind at the supply center."

The Chief shook his head. "You can have everything but that last item. You know our manpower situation."

"In that case, get me permission to recruit from among the Space Force veterans who survived that ambush."

"Wait a minute. You've got at least four unassigned men—Roberts, Hammell, Morri—"

"They're still in Basic."

"And everyone else is tied up?"

"Completely."

"In that case, I suppose there's nothing to do but try this idea of getting some volunteers. But how you're going to get volunteers from amongst those veterans is a good question. These aren't impressionable recruits. How are you going to get them to leave a comparatively soft—" He paused suddenly.

"Ordinarily," said the colonel, "they'd only smile. But there's nothing ordinary about what *they've* been through lately. I think they'll join us fast enough—if we promise them that their first assignment will be *revenge on the Skagas and the guerrillas.*"

The Chief nodded.

"O.K. Make your arrangements, and I'll get permission for you to recruit."

The colonel's arrangements went with a combination of smoothness and jarring inconsistency. S-Branch promised a timed explosive, minute quantities of which would do everything the colonel desired, with delivery on Terex in two days at the most. T-Branch then patiently explained that it was absolutely impossible to get a human being to Terex in less than ten to twelve days, if the idea was to get him there alive. I-Branch obligingly offered to put the colonel, by transposition, onto a Space Force ship near Terex, within twelve hours, and in the guise of a Space Force officer. This would incidentally have put the colonel, as head of Operations, at the mercy of Intelligence, and he politely refused to do it. I-Branch then grudgingly went along with his original plan, but pointed out that the Space Force could lose a lot of men while he was spending twelve days on the way to the planet. The colonel exasperatedly got in touch with S-Branch, and demanded to know how the timed explosive could be made and gotten to Terex in only two days, all told.

"Nothing to it, Val," said the head of S-Branch cheerfully. "It happens that we're testing direct-contact with a G-class ship off Terex. The contact cross-section is only about two feet in diameter, but there's no difficulty getting our stuff through. For that matter, we could put *you* through, lengthwise, if you were in a hurry."

"I *am* in a hurry."

"No problem. We can shove you through in about six seconds. Then the G-ship can deliver you to the planet, or to another ship in the region. How's that?"

"That's fine."

"Let us know when you're ready."

A few moments later, the screen was blank, and the colonel was considering that what T-Branch stated to be impossible in under ten days, could be almost completely done by S-Branch in six seconds. And the beauty of the thing was that transportation was the *specialty* of T-Branch.

Exasperatedly, he tapped out the Chief's call number. The important thing was to make sure the Space Force veterans ended up at the right place at the right time, with permission to join the Patrol.

When his arrangements were complete, the colonel went down to S-Branch, was strapped flat on a kind of stretcher on rails, and pushed through what appeared to be a porthole looking into the interior of a patrol ship, and through which the narrow rails of the stretcher passed. He was slowly slid through and unstrapped on the other side, where an Interstellar Patrol major apologized, and explained that it was "bad business to hit the edge of the contact zone," so they had to strap anyone who passed through when the cross-section was so narrow. A moment later, a package containing the colonel's explosive came through, and fifteen minutes after that he was talking by communicator to the captain of the H-class ship assigned to the job. Late the next morning, the colonel and the captain of the H-ship were on Terex, wearing civilian clothes for disguise, and talking to a Major Brouvaird, the officer in charge of Space Force Offloading Center 2 Terex.

"You see," growled Major Brouvaird, "they're all wearing loose coats and those damned oversize floppy straw hats." The major moved closer to the edge of the platform looking down on a crowd of Terexians working in the unloading line. "Watch this. You see that bird knocking open that ammo case, halfway down the line? Watch his hands. There he goes. Twenty-two magazines went out of the case into that damned keg, and two went under that loose coat of his into the pouches on a leather harness underneath. He must be about loaded up, now. You notice how he moves? Sort of careful? All that stuff in those pouches is getting heavy. The square edges are digging into his ribs. There he goes now."

Down below, in the jostling line, the Terexian held up his hand. His voice drifted up. "Tika b'wip, tul!" the euphemistic translation came to the colonel simultaneously: "Ship must lighten load, quick!"

A demoralized Space Force private nodded, and the Terexian, walking with a peculiar swaying motion, headed for the rear of the line, where a door stood open to the outside. The private stared at the floor or the wall—anything to avoid watching the Terexian workers as they manhandled the Space Force cargo.

"And there he goes," said the Space Force major, watching the Terexian go out the door. "Out back, near the latrine, there's a Terexian refreshment stand. This bird will step into the booth, and come out with a fresh harness. The candy wagon back there will lug out all the loads from the workers, and that's just the first skim, off the top."

The colonel nodded, and adjusted his civilian suit. Considering the haste with which this assignment had been prepared for, the suit was like a bad omen. It had a shirt that seemed to have no pores, a collar that dug into his neck, and cuffs that felt like slippery plastic bands around his wrists. The jacket was made out of some kind of bristly hair that looked all right in the mirror, but the bristles stuck into his neck above the collar. The trousers were made out of the same material, so that it felt like poison ivy around his neck, and from his belt to his shoes. The shoes were too small.

Possibly as a result of the frame of mind these clothes put him in, when the colonel spoke, his voice came out with a bite like a high-speed drill.

"Why the devil are they allowed to break the cases?"

The Space Force major winced under the unmistakable lash of authority, then recovered and stared at the lean civilian.

"I thought, Mr.—ah—Fisher, that you had been thoroughly briefed on this procedure."

"So did I," said the colonel shortly. "But no one mentioned this piece of insanity. I knew there was pilferage and outright robbery, and I knew your cargoes are trans-shipped over the local transportation system. But no one bothered to tell me that the cargoes are broken out of their shipping crates and transferred to other containers. What's the point? What's wrong with the original shipping cases?"

"They are in advance of local technology."

"What of it?" said the colonel.

The major frowned, seeking to explain to himself Fisher's civilian capacity, military bearing, and obvious authority.

The colonel, unaware of the effect he was creating, thrust out his jaw.

The major squinted at the card the colonel had handed him on arrival:

INTERSTELLAR
INVESTIGATIONS
CORPORATION
L. L. Fisher
Chief Regional Operative

The card had a picture of the civilian on it, a miniature set of fingerprints, retinal patterns, and other identifying data, and the warning, "THIS IS A TIMED CARD.

CARRY OUT YOUR IDENTIFICATION WITHIN ONE HOUR OF RECEIPT."

The major seemed to have heard of something called Interstellar Investigations, which now and then came into the news when it nailed some particularly troublesome operator. Nevertheless, no detective, Chief Regional Operative or otherwise, would have occasion to develop that ring of command, and that manner of authority. It was that that bothered the major. His instincts told him that he was dealing with a military man, and one of comparatively high rank. The civilian clothes and the card didn't prove a thing. The orders the major had received, instructing him to cooperate with one L. L. Fisher of the Interstellar Investigations Corporation, who was "assisting the Space Force in attempting to trace losses incurred in shipment," and so on—all that was so much humbug. It came to the major like a bolt of lightning that, somewhere in the Space Force, someone of very high rank had gotten wind of the stink off Terex, and had either come himself to investigate, or had sent a trusted member of his staff—whoever it was, was now standing there in disguise right beside the major; the disguise no more concealed his real nature than a necklace of flowers on a tiger—but, of course, the major had to *act* as if it fooled him.

With a puff and a sudden heat, the identification card burst into dust. The major shook his hand, and took a deep breath.

"Ah—Well, you see, Mr. Fisher, this is typical of our whole problem on this planet. In one way or another, the locals nullify the advantages of our technology."

"What's the pretext for breaking the shipments out of all those cases?"

"The locals have strict regulations for containers to be used on their transportation system. They make *their* cases out of solid wood and iron. They specify a certain minimum thickness for each size of keg, barrel, drum, crate, or what-have-you. Well, *our* cases are stronger. But *their* standards are applied arbitrarily. They won't let our cases be used on the planet—*because they are of inferior weight and thickness.*"

The colonel looked down on the reloading line. As he watched, he could catch the quick movements as grenades, small hand weapons, and magazines disappeared under the

loose cloaks. He began to see other things, too, such as skillful wielders of hammers and chisels who opened cases of rifles, and deftly knocked sights out of line as they transferred the weapons. Five hand-launchers came out of one case, and went into a barrel that would only accommodate four of them without jamming. The little bag containing the firing pins vanished into a Terexian cloak. Onto these containers, the shipping labels were slapped in odd positions. Doubtless *these* containers would not be pilfered en route. Meanwhile, over in a corner at the far end of the line, half-a-dozen of the locals were bent over a kind of keg, feeding in what looked like a length of thin wire off a small roll; now a grenade went in, and the Terexians carefully pressed the cover down, pulled out some of the wire, cut it off, and pushed the end back inside. What could *that* be but a booby trap?

Beside the colonel, Captain Finch of the H-ship stood, his concealed recorder taking down sight and sound.

The Space Force major was saying, " . . . Obvious enough they're robbing us, but we aren't allowed to use our own loading crews. That would 'deprive Terexian citizens of much-needed employment.' If we take them to court, it's our word against theirs, and any number of them will swear we're lying. I could go right down there this minute, grab one of those loaders with a full harness, and *I* would be arrested for assault and battery. We need our own loading crews, our own courts—and our own transportation system, as a matter of fact. But *that's* unthinkable. These are our 'loyal allies in the fight against the guerrillas.' By 'giving them employment,' we are 'winning their gratitude, and gaining their loyalty in a most effective way.' Sir, until we get PDA's wishful thinking and propaganda out of the way, we're going to get slaughtered on this planet."

The colonel noted the "sir," realized with a shock what had happened, and then accommodated himself to it in an instant.

"Never mind that," he said. "Mr. Dexter and I, with our . . . ah . . . team of operatives . . . will do what we can to rectify this situation. Now, what we need is an enclosed building of some kind where we can get at a portion of the shipment before it goes through the loading line here."

"Well, sir—"

"Mr. Fisher."

"Yes, Mr. Fisher. Excuse me. There's a sizable shed out back, that you could use. Of course, you'll want to keep it secret that you're using it. That poses a problem, but—"

"Not at all," said the colonel. "We *don't* want to keep it secret. We want it announced that a team of human experts has arrived to track down the source of the trouble. We want a published warning, over your signature, that any individual who comes into possession of any human military equipment should turn it in at once, for his own protection. Every shipment that goes through this center will have a big seal put on it, announcing that it is under the special protection of the Interstellar Investigations Corporation, and that secret hidden methods of extraordinary craft will be used to track down and punish anyone who unlawfully appropriates the contents."

The Space Force major tried to look enthusiastic about this idea, gave up, and frankly looked sick.

"The last time anyone tried anything like that, the pilferage rate at that center went up to one hundred percent."

The colonel smiled.

"Have faith in the Interstellar Investigations Corporation."

"I'll be a laughingstock for making the announcement."

"A small sacrifice to make for the good of the service."

The major looked pained, but nodded dutifully.

"Yes, Mr. Fisher."

Having finished work at the loading center, the colonel and the H-ship captain went back to their ship. The colonel was mentally damning the haste with which this operation had been rushed through. He particularly damned himself for not insisting that reports, imperfect or not, be made up into an orientation. He had missed the obvious business about transferring weapons from one container to another, and there was no predicting what else he might have missed. As he and "Mr. Dexter" now approached the ship, he saw twenty or thirty Space Force men in battle dress debarking from a Space Force tender not far away. There were Terexian workers scattered all over the field, and some of them were doubtless spies.

The Space Force men formed a column of twos, and marched toward the H-ship, which was lettered:

INTERSTELLAR
INVESTIGATIONS
CORPORATION

"Mr. Dexter" said dryly, "Here we go, Mr. Fisher."

The colonel nodded.

"Let me handle it, Mr. Dexter."

The Space Force veterans came to a halt and faced to the front. The sergeant in charge glanced at his orders, and looked up in bafflement at the ship. Several Terexian laborers dawdled at their work as they shifted crates nearby, and shot furtive glances at the ship and the veterans.

The colonel stepped forward, and cleared his throat loudly.

The men looked around.

The colonel ran a finger around his uncomfortable collar, and looked at the sky, as if seeking inspiration.

"Gentlemen . . . ah . . . *men*—" He cleared his throat again. "We of the Interstellar Investigations Corporation have been called upon to use our modern techniques of detection, to . . . ah . . . ah . . . detect and track down those ill-advised few among the largely loyal native population who are attempting pilferage upon the Space Force, and, lacking sufficient trained man-power to carry out our scientific detection procedures, which I understand would not . . . ah . . . fit well with the cultural patterns of thought and action upon this planet, we have obtained permission to train and put to use combat personnel who are temporarily . . . ah . . . dismounted pending future assignment. Ahem."

The Space Force veterans were looking at him with a variety of expressions. Some were studying him as if trying to identify just what kind of creature he might be, and they looked as if they had not been able to pin it down yet. Others looked bored. A few looked sick. One looked as if he would like to break the colonel's neck, and was having trouble arguing himself out of it.

At the crates, the Terexian workers cast brief sharklike smiles at each other.

"Now . . . ah . . . gentlemen," said the colonel, "you will please file into the ship for . . . ah . . . orientation to this new task, which, I might add, is extremely important to the pacification and mutual assistance effort on this whole planet."

Some of the men looked as if they had finally succeeded in identifying him. Those who had looked sick looked sicker, and there were more of them.

After a distinct hesitation, the sergeant cleared his throat, and gave a low-voiced order, spoken like a curse, that started the men filing into the ship.

The colonel stepped inside, watching the expressions of the men as they crossed the short catwalk leading from the fake outer hull to the massive inner hull.

The men looked around blankly, then nudged each other as they passed through the massive lock to the inner hull, to find themselves jammed in the comparatively small interior of the real ship. The inner and outer locks shut.

"All right, men," said the colonel, and this time his voice was lower, and slower. "Now that you're all temporary members of the Interstellar Investigations Corporation, I will tell you how we detect who stole Space Force equipment, and I will leave it up to you to decide who wants to take part, and who would rather get out now. First, let me mention that only the first word in the Corporation's name is real. The rest is a dummy. And the purpose I stated outside, for the benefit of whoever might hear, is also a dummy. We are here for exactly one real purpose—to blow the Skagas, the black-marketeers, and the guerrillas, sky-high. Anyone who wants to join us in cleaning out this mess of thugs and bushwhackers will be welcome—provided you can pass our tests. Now, as I understand it, you've all been in combat. But how many of you have been in an off-loading center on this planet?"

Everyone looked blank.

"The captain of this ship and I visited one of these offloading centers this morning," said the colonel. "We went as investigators for the Interstellar Investigations Corporation. We recorded what we saw, and you might be interested to see it. Captain Finch—If you will project—"

The room darkened, and multiple rays of light shone out from the far wall, so that each man seemed to see before him what the colonel and the H-ship's captain had seen earlier. The conversation also was reproduced, and as the scene progressed, an angry murmur rose in the room. At the end, when the lights came on, the colonel had changed back to his uniform, and there was a booth near where he had stood, with the words above it:

INTERSTELLAR PATROL RECRUITING

Boiling mad, the Space Force men shoved forward, toward the booth, where their requests were processed with lightning speed.

That over with, and their anger having cooled to that thoughtfulness that can follow sudden emotional enlistment, it dawned on some of the new Interstellar Patrol candidates that they had not yet found out exactly how the colonel intended to finish off the guerrillas. But already, the first group of candidates was being assembled for transfer to the testing ship—the G-class already off the planet checking its contact equipment, was to be used for that purpose. There was a lot to think about all of a sudden, and not much time to think about it. The Interstellar Patrol recruiting sergeant suddenly found himself answering a lot of questions.

"Ah—We have to pass *admission* tests? What happens if we don't pass them?"

"You don't make it into the Patrol. And then you can't take part in the operation. But you'll pass them. Don't worry."

"How many tests are there?"

"Five."

"If we don't make it, we will go back to the Space Force. Right?"

"Not necessarily."

"What do you mean, 'not necessarily?'"

"You can't be a candidate in the Interstellar Patrol and a member of the Space Force at the same time, without special permission. If, for instance, you're in a Space Force guardhouse, and the Space Force wants to be sure to get you back and wring the juice out of you, if you don't get into the Patrol, then we have to hand you back. But that isn't how it was done this time. The first paper you signed was your resignation from the Space Force. The second paper was your provisional enlistment in the Interstellar Patrol. So, you see, if you fail the tests, you don't go straight back into the Space Force."

"What *does* happen to us?"

"Well—That's a good question."

"You *bet* it's a good question. What's the answer?"

"H-m-m-m . . . I don't know. Colonel?"

The colonel was smilingly handing the bulky sheaf of enlistment forms up through a hatchway to someone on the deck overhead. He looked far more formidable in uniform than he had in the suit, but he also had a look of well-being that hadn't been there before. The look of well-being had come over him as he watched the men crowd around the enlistment booth.

"Yes?" he said, benevolently.

"Sir, one of these men wants to know what happens to him if he fails the tests."

The colonel looked incredulous.

"*Fails* the tests?"

"Yes, sir."

"Oh, I don't think anyone here has to worry about that. Just do your best, men. You see, these tests are designed to weed out people so far below the level we need, that it would be pointless for us to try to bring them up to it. We usually have a high rate of such failures. But you are all pre-selected, anyway. It's hard to believe that Space Force combat veterans, from crack units, wouldn't meet the level of Interstellar Patrol *recruits*."

"Yes, sir," said one of the candidates stubbornly, "but what happens *if* we fail?"

The colonel looked him in the eye, noting the stubborn set of jaw, and the direct gaze. This was the man who earlier had looked as if he would like to knock the colonel's head off.

"*If* you fail," said the colonel, "I will think you failed *on purpose*."

"Then what happens?"

There was a silence, with all the other candidates listening alertly.

"*If* I think a candidate has failed on purpose, I have discretion to do quite a number of things—whichever one strikes me as suitable. These tests are very hard to fail on purpose. They are so designed that it goes against the grain to fail them. To fail them *in a certain way* demonstrates that you have the ability to pass them. To fail in another way automatically ends the series. We aren't bound to many iron rules in the Patrol. I will do what I think best. Why? What's wrong?"

"You promised to tell us how we'd take care of the guerrillas."

There was a murmur of agreement.

The colonel reached into an inner pocket of his uniform jacket, and drew out a small transparent container holding what looked like a thick crayon.

"What does that look like to you?"

"A marking crayon."

"That's what it is. But it's made of a very special compound, that we call 'special tar.'"

"What does it do?"

"I'll tell you, but only on the understanding that whoever hears the information will get set down on whatever planet, or in whatever place, we choose to set him down, if he fails the tests. I can tell you that we will choose to set him down in a place where he will be unlikely to repeat the information to anyone who wants to know about it."

There was an immediate murmur of agreement. No one objected. Then there was an intense silence.

"That's understood?" said the colonel insistently.

"Yes, sir. What is this 'tar?'"

"It's the short way of saying 'transient atomic reactant.' It's also a kind of stuff that, when you get it stuck on you or anything else, it's hard to get off. The basic trouble on Terex isn't just the guerrillas, it's also the Skagas that you saw in operation just a little while ago. The Skagas operate the black market that supplies the guerrillas with the best Space Force weapons available, while at the same time sabotaging deliveries to Space Force troops. Now then, Terex has no industry capable of turning out these weapons. Terex is technologically backward. The guerrillas get their weapons *from the black market*. The black market *feeds* them weapons."

The colonel paused.

The troops stared at the marking crayon, which he was still holding up so they could see it clearly.

"Interstellar Investigations Corporation," said the colonel, "is going to put a tiny mark on weapons passing through Space Force Offloading Center 2. This will be done *before* these weapons pass through the reloading line. This mark will be in some out-of-the-way place. Perhaps inside the mechanism of the bolt. Perhaps under the heel plate. It will all depend on the weapon. A little bit of special tar will go on each weapon. A little bit of it goes a long way."

"And it . . . ah—You call it—"

"Another name for it is 'transient atomic reactant.' I will quote the explanation as the head of S-Branch stated it to me:

"This is a 'fibrogravitic quasiclathrate.' The gravitic component is inherently unstable. The basic active ingredient is composed of particles which might be called 'nuclear catalyst,' as they create rapid nuclear breakdown with a partially sustaining regenerative action. The containing of this basic ingredient, the nuclear catalyst, so-called, is the function of the gravitic component of the fibrogravitic quasiclathrate. Obviously, such a nuclear catalyst can't be mixed in with a little glue, to stick it to whatever you want, since the catalyst would immediately destroy the nuclei of the glue. Therefore, the catalyst is held in very tiny gravitostrictive 'bottles,' that look like minute bits of sand in the tarry-appearing adhesive. Since no adhesive will stick to a directed gravitic field, a very fibrous substance is used to imprison the 'grains.' Now, the grains don't remain imprisoned forever, or the compound wouldn't be worth much. The directed gravitic field of the grains is inherently unstable, and breaks down. This releases the 'nuclear catalyst.' It is possible to predict *when* the inherent instability will result in breakdown, release of the 'catalyst,' and consequent explosion of closely adjacent materials. The force of the explosion then depends on the nature and the density of the adjacent atoms. The time of the explosion can be predicted accurately."

There was a silence as the colonel finished speaking, then a slow exhaling of breath.

"We will," said the colonel, "naturally put a warning sticker on every keg, drum, barrel, and other container that leaves the loading center. We will circulate warnings locally. But, the Skagas and black marketeers being as they are, there's a question whether these warnings will do them much good. Of course, we aren't going to give them all the details. Perhaps they will choose to ignore the warnings. We will, naturally, warn the Space Force commanders, and they will pay attention; but if the Skagas and the guerrillas run true to form, the Space Force probably won't see too many of these weapons. For good measure, the special tar is timed for one of the local feast days. Naturally, no religious person will be working on that day, so the supply dumps *should* be deserted. If the black marketeers, guerrillas, and their hangers-on happen to be looting the supply dumps on the same day that the tar goes off, that just shows what they get for being irreligious. I'm sure no religious person on the planet should object too strongly. And afterward, I don't think there will be too many irreligious ones left."

The colonel glanced at the stubborn candidate, who was now smiling.

"Any further questions?"

"No, sir. If I fail the tests, just dump me off in empty space. I'm happy."

As the colonel hoped, but hardly dared expect, all the candidates passed the tests, though some of them only barely squeaked by the fifth and last test. As each batch passed, the colonel put them to work at the offloading center, where the Terexian loaders had a good laugh at the seal that was now stuck on each reloaded crate, keg, barrel, and drum:

WARNING!
Not For Unauthorized Hands!
Contents of
This Container Protected
Against Unauthorized Use By:
INTERSTELLAR
INVESTIGATIONS
CORPORATION
Danger!
Extreme Peril!
Beware!

For good measure, the colonel had a number of small signs put up along the reloading line, in such locations that the thieves who worked on the line could not possibly miss them:

NOTICE
This installation has been

THIEF-PROOFED by the
INTERSTELLAR INVESTIGATIONS CORPORATION.
You are being watched. No one profits by
criminal activity. Crime does not pay.
Do not imagine that *you* will get away
unpunished, if you try to do the very
things, such as pilferage, shoplifting,
looting, and other such activities that the
INTERSTELLAR INVESTIGATIONS CORPORATION
has broken up on other worlds. You
cannot succeed. Be honest. You will find
that there will be a great reward for honesty.
And a great punishment for dishonesty.

The result of these two notices was that there were reports
from all the Space Force receiving supply centers that *no*
shipments from Offloading Center 2 were now being received.
The whole output was being robbed.

The colonel now coerced the commanding officer of the
center into issuing a statement on the situation:

It has come to the attention of Space Force authorities charged with the distribution of supplies to the
forward troops that, probably purely by accident or misunderstanding, some quantity of the deadly weapons
and implements of war may have fallen into unauthorized hands. It has even been rumored that religious
feast days have been violated for the purpose of making unauthorized entry into places of storage for military supplies, and there making illegal depredations upon
such supplies.

Without wishing to state a definite position regarding the truth or falsity of these allegations, it must be
stated that, if true, this would constitute an extremely
serious and dangerous situation. Space Force supplies
are sometimes of an extremely volatile nature. Many
of these supplies are actually dangerous explosives.

All of our weapons have entered this world at the
express permission of the Priestly Authorities. To steal
or possess them, to consort with those who steal or
possess them, to violate holy days, all this would appear
to be very dangerous, and not merely because it challenges

the worldly authority of the Space Force, which has come to this planet in reply to a call for help.

It is well known that Evil Recoils Upon The Doer. It is to be hoped that those who wish to escape Retribution will number themselves amongst the Righteous.

The result of this statement was merriment amongst some of the workers, but also an immediate drop in the number of workers on the reloading lines, followed by their replacement by a crew that gave cold chills to any ordinary citizen who showed up, innocently looking for a job.

Meanwhile, the military situation was going from bad to worse. Ordinary Terexians had by now come to regard all humanity roughly in the light of a well-intentioned but stupid child, a viewpoint that was cheerfully brought home at a gathering on the afternoon of the very day that the remaining stability of the transient atomic reactant dwindled down into the minutes and seconds.

"I must confess," said the host, a prominent Terexian by the name of Swelnior, "that you Earth people have shown yourselves incredibly naive. The thought of appealing to the good will of Skagas—" He chortled delightedly.

The colonel, wearing an improved version of the prickly suit he'd had the first day on the planet, experienced a faint chill as he looked at his watch.

"Pardon me, Mr. Swelnior—"

"Ho, ho, my dear fellow, it's precisely *you* who have been the most . . . do forgive me . . . ridiculous. To appeal to *Skagas*—"

"The appeal," said the colonel coldly, "was to whoever might choose to *dissociate* himself from the Skagas."

"You people came to the planet like some sort of divine heavenly beings with supernatural powers . . . forgive me if I speak frankly, it's my nature . . . and bit by bit you have gradually come down until we can see you as . . . as *children*."

Across the table, a prominent Terexian laughed.

"Not children. But *puppies*."

"I hope," said the colonel, his voice cutting though the merriment, "that none of you gentlemen have trafficked with the Skagas or the black marketeers."

"I like that word—'trafficked.' It has a quaint archaic tone.

Really, now, Mr . . . what's the name . . . Fishee? Really, Mr.
Fishee—"

"Because there might be time for you to—"

"His name is 'Fish.' You know, the things we Terexians
catch and eat."

" . . . Might just be time for you to clear a few valuables
away from black market—"

"Oh, yes, before the Hour of Retribution?"

Down the table, a Terexian priest looked up. His eyes lit
with a glow of fanaticism.

"Do I hear someone *joke* about the Hour of Retribution?"

Swelnior leaned forward, smiling.

"Surely, we need not fear Retribution from—" He inclined
his head toward the humans in the room.

The Terexian priest looked at the colonel, then at Swelnior.
He picked up his chair, and walked around the table to seat
himself beside the colonel, who, with the other humans, had
a considerable space between him and the nearest Terexians.
Ignoring Swelnior, the priest looked at the colonel. "If I read
your face rightly, Mr. Fisher, the balance has tilted too far,
and the evil that has been done is about to be righted by the
Sword of Justice. You are, I see, a soldier."

The colonel recovered from the shock, and groped for a
reply. But the priest had already turned toward Swelnior.

"You sack of wormy swine, do you imagine that one of the
Faith will join in your folly? You, with the wisdom of a block
of sawn wood, the polish of a lump of sandstone, and the
self-discipline of an eel two days dead and afloat in scum,
you dare invite the Select of the Faith to ape your depravity?"

There was a stunned silence. Swelnior opened his mouth.

"See here—"

"None of that. You have had the power and misused it.
The accumulated worth of past deeds is used up, and you
have forgotten how you came to where you are. Know then
that there is a weight in the lives of men which, set in
motion, overcarries, however the later acts of a man may
seem to mock it. But it is only for a moment in the eyes
of those who know. Now prepare to eat the ripened fruit
that you have raised in your orchard."

Swelnior turned pale, and looked around at the others.
Most of them looked shaken. A few sat with outthrust jaws
and steady gaze.

The priest looked up.

"I feel it come."

The colonel glanced at his watch.

The room moved as if they were on a ship that swayed around them. Ornate water glasses slid and spilled. A heavy spiked candleholder smashed down on the table.

The roar seemed to go on forever.

It came to the colonel that the Skagas had had some backing that he hadn't known about. This meeting was being held in an exclusive section of the capital city. From the roar and the shooting flames, it was obvious where a part of Mr. Swelnior's wealth had come from.

Swelnior himself was frenziedly shouting. The bulk of the guests were screaming as chunks of plaster and ornate stone blocks smashed to the floor. The priest was looking on with a grim smile. The air was full of plaster dust, glowing pink from the flames glaring in the window. Major Brouvaird, from the Offloading Center, emerged from under the table with the other Space Force officers, stared around, and let loose a string of awed profanity.

" . . . The guerrillas?"

A younger officer said urgently, "How do we get *out?*"

There was a sizzling, cracking sound, the flames vanished, and a cloud of white vapor steamed up past the window. An instant later, the Interstellar Investigations ship loomed through the mist, dangling a flexible ladder, and an amplified voice boomed orders to climb onto the ladder. The Terexian priest seemed slightly disappointed by the rescue, but everyone else reacted with enthusiasm.

Once on the ladder, the ship swung away from the side of the building, where the flames were again starting to spring up, and now the rest of the city, the hills on three sides, and the bay on the fourth, came into view.

One whole section of the city was in flames, and from here and there in the surrounding wooded hills, sizable clouds of dust and smoke climbed up. In the exclusive hill section of the city, Swelnior's house and two or three others nearby were a shambles.

As the ship set them down, all the Terexians at once crowded around the priest, anxiously seeking guidance. The priest was giving it to them in no uncertain language as the colonel, Major Brouvaird, and the other Space Force and "Interstellar Investigations" men looked around.

"That column of smoke," said the Space Force major, "is the storehouse we built at the near end of the coastal canal. The damned pirates looted the place every feast day." He stared at the hills. "That biggest column of smoke—where you can see flames shooting up—corresponds with the location of a guerrilla supply dump they've been rumored to have been building up." He looked at the colonel again. "If what we can see from here is typical, the Skagas and the guerrillas have just gotten the stiffest jolt of the war. Do you mind if I ask what hit them?"

"Interstellar Investigations," said the colonel gravely, "has its methods."

"Ah," said the major, going along with the joke, "but I thought Interstellar Investigations was hired to *detect* who was robbing the supply system."

"That was the problem."

The major looked around at the towering clouds of smoke. "But—"

"Those that blew up," said the colonel politely, "were guilty. We detected the criminals by seeing *who got punished by his crime.*"

Off in the distance, the Interstellar Investigations ship, having perhaps got special permission of the priesthood to use gravitors on this desperate occasion, had warped a huge column of water up out of the bay on a gravitor beam, and was dumping it on the burning section of the city.

The Space Force major wrestled with the colonel's comment.

"But—"

"When you want to see who's stealing all the cookies from the cookie jar," said the colonel, "you can make up a batch filled with red pepper. It has the virtue of detecting the criminal, punishing him for his crime, giving him second thoughts for the future, and just possibly raising his respect for the chef."

A number of highborn Terexians, looking pale and greenish, passed by the humans with markedly respectful bows.

The major's eyes widened as the idea hit him, and as it dawned on him how much he still didn't know.

Down in the city now, the holocaust had been reduced

to a towering column of steam. The ship came back again, again lowering its ladder, but this time booming out instructions that only "Interstellar Investigations" personnel should climb aboard.

"*Interstellar* Investigations," said the major dazedly, as the last deduction added itself up in his mind. With a sensation like a stiff jolt to the midsection, he realized what he'd really been dealing with.

The colonel, climbing swiftly, was now almost up to the ship. He waved goodbye just before he climbed in.

The major recovered his self-possession and threw a salute. There, at least, was an organization PDA couldn't touch, and that knew you didn't gain respect and cooperation by letting yourself be jumped on. *There* was an outfit that did things *right!*

The colonel stepped into the ship, and watched as the fake outer hatch swung shut. He shook his head, and stepped in through the massive hatch of the real ship. There had been a mess if he ever saw one. He'd almost got himself and some valuable recruits killed by going to Swelnior's meeting, and the fact was inescapable that a number of innocent people, *hopefully* a small number, had got blown up along with the black marketeers and guerrillas. On the other hand, Space Force casualties should go down to where they should have been in the first place, and if PDA didn't commit some new piece of stupidity, it might be possible to have peace on the planet for a while. Meanwhile, he'd picked up thirty-one highly promising recruits, and, when he got back, Roberts, Hammell, Morrissey, and Bergen should just be getting back from Basic. Maybe then it would be possible to get things straightened out so they could do things *right* for a change.

With these thoughts filling his mind, the colonel almost smashed into the highly polished, practically invisible column at the center of the ship. He had scarcely recovered when a shout came down from overhead:

"Colonel! The Chief's on the screen!"

The colonel thrust through the jammed recruits, and started up the grav-shaft.

It *would* be nice to have things the way they should be. But something told him there would be a slight delay first.

BASIC

Vaughan Roberts wiped the sweat out of his eyes and studied the sliding gate with its strong close-spaced horizontal bars. The gate was set in a chain-link fence fifteen feet high, topped with five strands of electrified barbed wire. The lower edge of the fence was embedded in a concrete base two feet thick. At the gate, this base swelled into a concrete apron twenty feet across. Set in the concrete, directly in front of the gate and close to it, was a round hole some fourteen inches wide at the top, with smooth sides sloping to a small round flat bottom about eighteen inches below. The bottom was metal, with several small vertical holes and several rods supporting flat upraised metal plates. Around the top of this hole was a circular brass rim bearing the words, INSERT KEY AND TURN TO OPEN GATE.

Roberts blew out his breath and turned around, to look down a steep stony slope marked with scratches, grooves, and whitely powdered rock, that descended to a gentle slope marked with shallow circular dents a foot or so across. At the base of this slope lay a shiny metallic object about eighteen or twenty inches long, shaped like a cone, with the small end flattened, and the large end gently curved like the outer surface of a sphere. The small end was slotted, and bore several projecting studs. The smoothly polished sides and top reflected the sun in a bright point of light, and gave a distorted image of blue sky, white clouds, straggling green grass, and dark-green forest beyond the fence. The fence itself, fifteen feet high, concrete-based, and topped

275

with electrified barbed wire, reached down both sides of the hill and across the bottom, enclosing Roberts, the cone, the hill, and the cone-shaped hole by the locked gate.

Roberts with a calculating gaze again studied the steep rocky slope. He glanced back at the gate, and the nearby hole. He looked with loathing at the shiny cone lying at the bottom of the slope, and then sucked in a deep breath and started downhill toward the shining chunk of metal. As he slid in the slippery dust, and as the loose bits of splintered rock turned underfoot, he became conscious of a peculiar sensation, like the awareness of the sound of a buzz without the actual buzz itself. He shoved the tail of his lightweight sweat-stained shirt into his worn trousers, slid his small communicator from its scratched belt-case, and snapped it on. The familiar voice of his fellow basic trainee, Hammell, came out angrily.

"You still cooped up?"

"Yes. You?"

"Yes. It just got away again. All the way to the foot of the hill."

"Same thing here," said Roberts. There was a lot more he could say, but he kept it bottled up, in the hope that it might generate a little extra horsepower when he needed it.

"This," said Hammell, his voice exasperated, "is a damned stupid way to finish up a basic training course. We can't *use* anything we've learned!"

"No," said Roberts, noncommittally, remembering from just this morning the muscular catlike figure of the guide, as he said cheerfully, "Well, gentlemen, you have now endured nearly all that the basic training course of the Interstellar Patrol has to offer, and are about to pass on as full members of the Patrol. You have one or two little formalities still to go through. First, some advice.

"You realize, men, that *many* qualities are required of you, and some of them may seem contradictory. Bear in mind that such qualities as personal initiative and the capacity for strict obedience, while certainly capable of total opposition, are not *necessarily* contradictory. The human body is supplied with muscles so arranged that one set can oppose and frustrate the action of another set. Nevertheless, although there is a wrong way to use them, the body still has to have both sets to function properly. Bear this in mind. A quality may be indispensable, but insufficient by itself. And the necessary additional quality may be its apparent opposite.

"Now, as you know, gentlemen, the Patrol does not like to cram information down anyone's throat. I have told you enough, I think, so that you can understand the nature of this first little formality you have to go through.

"This, gentlemen, is really a very simple little test.

"Basically, the problem is to get out of an enclosed space. There is a gate in one side of the enclosure. Your problem is merely to open this gate. That's all there is to it.

"But you *must* open the gate. Do not, please, try to get *over* the fence. You will be electrocuted. Do not cut or otherwise create a *gap* in the fence. This will detonate mines laid inside the enclosure. Trying to dig under the fence will produce the same result.

"Do not, please, waste time and ingenuity seeking to avoid electrocution by vaulting or otherwise crossing the top of this fence without touching the wire. You will be shot down by concealed automatic guns. The idea is not to pass over, under, or through the fence. The idea is to *open the gate,* and get out *that* way.

"If there is anyone here who is capable of safely passing out of the enclosure *without* opening the gate—and we recognize the possibility—then permit me to point out that, while we will not penalize you for doing this, we will, nevertheless, put you back in as often as you get out, until you finally get out *our* way—namely, by opening the gate.

"You may open the gate in any way that you are capable of opening it; so far as we know, there is only one way for an ordinary human without tools to do it. It will be perfectly obvious to you what I mean when you are inside.

"But, you see, the trick is not just to *understand* what has to be done. The trick is to *do* it.

"Each of you must solve this problem separately. However, for purposes of mutual commiseration, you will be allowed to communicate with one another, so long as you are still inside the 'Coop,' as it is called, and have not yet solved the problem. We may, at any time, cut off your communication. If you suddenly understand the 'secret' and blurt it to some friend before we succeed in cutting you off, we will be irritated, but this will not invalidate the test.

The difficulty, as we say, is not merely in finding out what to do, but also in *doing* it.

"Now, gentlemen, good luck with this simple, though very basic, little test. And may your disposition be as sweet in a few hours as it is right now."

Roberts reached the bottom of the hill, and looked down sourly at the shiny cone. His disposition was nowhere near as sweet as it had been a few hours ago.

Hammell's voice came out in an indrawn gasp from the communicator, and Roberts knew from experience, without extending the communicator's eyepieces, just what had happened. He said drily, *"That's* not the answer."

Hammell growled, "I thought maybe I could work the thing by hand. But the raised plates in this recess are *charged.*"

"Correct," said Roberts, feeling equal exasperation, but keeping his emotions bottled up. He experimentally hefted the shiny cone.

It felt even heavier than the last time. He looked up at the steep final slope of the hill, and frowned with vexation.

"What we've got here," said Hammell angrily, "is a *stupid* set-up. We can unlock the gate if we can get this so-called key into the hole. But we've got no tools whatever, the slope is so steep you can barely stand up on it empty-handed, and the damned 'key' feels like it's made out of lead. What kind of basic training is this? The thing is *stupid.*"

Roberts shook his head. "It can't be stupid, because the *testers* aren't stupid. It's supposed to be a test—Well, a test of what?"

"All it is, is a test of muscle and agility."

Roberts stared at that steep final slope. "That can't be it. You try to carry the thing up the last part of the slope, and if you slip you half kill yourself."

"Then what else *could* it be?"

"A persistence test?" suggested Roberts, doubtfully.

"That's a thought."

"But then—"

"Yeah. What about that business to the effect that, 'if you find the *secret,* we'll try to cut you off before you can communicate it.' What secret is there to a persistence test? You just keep trying."

"I notice we're still talking. Nobody has tried to cut us off."

"So, *that* isn't it. I had a bright idea a little while ago for using clothing to make a sling to hold the thing. That isn't it, either."

"No," said Roberts, absently feeling some of the thin worn stuff, frayed almost through by hard wear. "No, we still haven't hit on it."

He looked up at the slope and down at the cone.

All he had to do was to get it up that hill, drop it in that cone-shaped hole, and turn it.

But how?

"Well," said Hammell, "I'm going to try this s.o.b. again."

They broke the connection and Roberts scowlingly contemplated the situation. For an organization that delighted in advanced technology, it seemed like a very crude problem. But, here it was, and he was stuck with it. And so, *now* what? He had already tried carrying it to the top. He had also tried rolling it to the top. He had tried alternately carrying it and setting it down. He had tried rolling it up on the inner half of the two-foot wide concrete base of the fence. That time he'd been sure he could make it, since to rest he could cling to the fence with his hands, and meanwhile he could jam the thick end of the cone against the fence with his legs. But, each time, the cone had gotten away and slid and rolled to the bottom, and the frustration had built up till his last try had been a pure brute rush straight up the hill. That had been worst of all. He'd been lucky not to get a broken leg out of that one. Well, what was there left?

He frowned up the slope, noting the innumerable white scrapes and scratches on the exposed rocks. The whole width of the hill was marked with scratched rocks and grooved and dented dirt where previous recruits had come up against this same problem, and somehow solved it *some* way.

Looking at the hill, it occurred to Roberts that maybe he didn't have to work the whole answer out by himself, after all. Obviously, those other recruits had solved it and got out of here. How? Perhaps the hill would tell him.

Intently, he studied the hill, seeking some place where

the scratches were conspicuously few. *That* might be the place where there had been the fewest slips and falls because, for some reason, it was easiest to get up there.

But the stony hill was scratched more or less evenly from side to side. It was only free of scratches near the bottom, where the slope was very gentle—and near *the top*, where it was steepest. Apparently, no one dropped the cone when he had it near the top. Why? As far as Roberts could see, only a physical superman could hope to get it up the last ten feet of that slope.

The only peculiarity Roberts could see was the number of dents in the ground at the foot of the hill—from dropping the cone, wide-end down? That, he supposed, must have happened from misjudging the weight of the cone the first time it was picked up. But he had made many false tries himself, and yet he had never done that.

He looked around, noting the straggling green grass of the hillside, the blue sky, the drifting white clouds, the fence, and the trees outside. He looked down at the massive cone, with its flattened small end, and its spherically-curved large end, the whole thing mirror-smooth and hard to hold.

How to get a grip on a thing like this?

Outside, life went on. Meanwhile, here *he* was, stuck with this damnably simple problem.

Mentally, he pictured every conceivable way of climbing that hill. But the trouble was always the same—that steep slope near the top. No feat of gymnastics could get this thing up that last steep slope.

Supposedly, it might be possible to scratch out a kind of ramp up that steep slope, from one side of the hill to the other. But aside from the lack of tools and the time it would take, there was the little question of those mines that were supposed to be laid inside the enclosure. Where were they, and how deep? Supposedly, they were somewhere near the fence. But then, so was that steep slope.

Roberts groped around for more ideas, and none came to him. But he couldn't just stand here and go to sleep on his feet, so he crouched, and gripped the massive, awkwardly shaped chunk of metal. He straightened up, damning the weight of the thing. It had been bad enough to begin with, and seemed heavier every time. What was it made out of, anyway?

Heavily, his muscles straining, he walked up the gentle beginning of the hill, and even managed to climb the first part of the steepening slope. Then he sank down, lowering the weight heavily to the ground.

He waited until his breathing became even, then he crouched beside the weight, and shoved the large end of the cone uphill in a semicircle. He seized the smaller end, and levered it up and over so that the large end was again downhill.

With steady concentration, he moved it monotonously up the hill, first one end, and then the other, as the slope gradually steepened, and became worse and worse to climb, and then a soundless buzz caught his attention, to provide a welcome break in the hopeless job.

Heaving the small end up and over, Roberts crouched beside the cone, holding it in position with his right hand as he took out the little communicator with his left hand.

Hammell's voice said, "I thought I ought to mention it. This damned thing is gimmicked somehow."

Roberts' right foot slipped on a loose pebble, his right leg shot out behind him, and he slid downhill, losing his hold on the cone. The cone's small end came up and flipped over. The large end rumbled around in half a circle, then the small end flipped over again, and the large end went around in another half-circle, the whole thing slipping in the dust and loose rock fragments, and starting to gather speed.

Roberts in a flying jump landed across the cone, but his right hand, outstretched, slid in a spray of gravel, while his left hand, still gripping the communicator, was out of action. Somehow, the cone got free, and banged and thudded down the hill.

Roberts peered sourly down the slope to see the dust blow away, showing the cone once again at the bottom. He sat up, and raised the communicator.

"It's *gimmicked?* I don't see that the damned thing *needs* to be gimmicked. It's impossible just as it is."

Hammell seemed to think Roberts doubted his word. "Well, it *is* gimmicked. There's no question of that. There's a column of mercury or some such thing in it."

It seemed to Roberts that he could get along nicely without this superfluous complication. One impossibility at a time.

"Yeah," he said, his voice expressing no great conviction.

Hammell said shortly, "Listen, I've tried half-a-dozen times to keep the damned thing on the base of this fence. It falls off every time."

"M'm," said Roberts noncommittally, getting up and starting downhill toward the cone.

" 'M'm'?" Hammell said, losing his temper. *"Try* it! See what happens!"

Roberts' eyes narrowed. Exactly what made Hammell assume he was the only one who might have thought of that?

Still, there was no point having an argument over it. They might yet be able to help each other work out the answer.

Roberts strained hard to keep the anger out of his voice, but the accidental result was that he spoke in a kind of drawl:

"Well, you see, I've already tried *that.*"

There was a little silence, accompanied by a sense of a thickening of the atmosphere.

Hammell snarled, "And what was *your* experience?"

"No trouble with it falling off."

"How come you didn't get it all the way to the top?"

"It slipped loose, about a third of the way up that steepest section."

"But it didn't ever fall off the base when you put it there? The hell you say."

"Oh," said Roberts, his suppressed anger coming to the surface, "the hell I say, eh?"

He stuffed the communicator back in its case and crouched to grip the cone. He staggered to his feet with it, stunned at its weight. He could only imagine he must have worn himself out trying to get it up the hill the last time. This added frustration further infuriated him. Meanwhile, a little voice was repeating Hammell's "The hell you say," over and over in his mind, and this affected him like being stung by a yellow jacket that doesn't rest content with stinging once, or stinging twice, but stings as many times as it can sting until it is killed.

Roberts' anger boiled over, and he gripped the cone with redoubled force.

The cone tore itself loose, and he barely managed to guide it aside and yank his foot out of the way. The cone hit the ground with a *thud* that he both heard and felt, and that was heavier by far than he would have thought possible.

For an instant he stared at it, then he seized it again, tried to wrestle it up off the ground, and couldn't do it.

He snapped the communicator from its case, and switched it on.

A roaring crackle came out that no one could have talked through. The communicator had been jammed.

Roberts put it away, and stared at the cone.

He must be close to the answer.

He strung a series of virulent epithets in chains, and aimed them all at the cone. Once started, the emotion snowballed and when he'd reached the point of dull raging frustration lined with pure hatred, he crouched down, tried to grip the curved underside of the cone, and *couldn't work his fingers under it.*

The cone had now sunk heavily into the stony dirt. By no stretch of the imagination could he ever have lifted anything that heavy.

In fact, it just *couldn't be* that heavy—unless it contained a mixture gravitor with a device keyed to his own moods and designed to compound his own frustration.

He turned away, forcing his breath to come quietly and evenly. He looked off at the dark-green trees and up at the fluffy white clouds. Soon, he told himself, he would be out of here. He would be out of here, with just one more test, one more "little formality," awaiting him. But the main thing was, he would be *out* of here. Because now he had a handle on the slippery featureless problem.

His mood began to lighten, and he repeated over and over to himself that he would soon be out of here. What was it the guide, their advisor and friendly antagonist, had said? "Now, gentlemen, good luck on this simple, though very basic, little formality. And may your disposition be as sweet in a few hours as it is right now."

For anyone with a brain in his head, surely that comment *ought* to have been enough. But it hadn't been enough. Still, better late than never.

He looked intensely at the shiny conical "key," sunk in its hole.

"Soon," thought Roberts, looking at it, "I'll be out of here. I'll be out of here, *thanks to my good friend, the key.*"

When he could actually feel flickerings of affection for the miserable device, as if it were a pet dog, he knelt, worked his fingers under it, and straightened.

The cone came up out of its hole as if made of balsa wood.

Roberts, now genuinely feeling friendly toward the thing, his mood *actually* cheerful, wasted no time going straight up the hill to the gate, and sliding the now-light key into its nearby cone-shaped recess in the concrete apron. He moved the cone around until the various studs, holes, plates and slots lined up, then he shoved it home, and reached down to turn it.

There was an instant of blankness, as when a man reaches for a tool he has laid down, and someone else has meanwhile walked off with it.

The cone, eighteen to twenty inches long, fit in the recess, about eighteen inches deep, to leave nothing exposed but its shiny curving surface. This surface offered no bump, hole, edge, or grip of any kind, and was mirror-smooth.

Roberts had expected the edge to project slightly, like the rim of a wheel. He stood looking down at this curving mirror, framed in its brass ring bearing the words:

"INSERT KEY AND TURN TO OPEN GATE."

"Turn key." How?

He crouched, and the key favored him with a distorted view of himself. He put both hands flat on the slick curved surface, pressed, and tried to turn it.

The key didn't move. His hands slipped.

He sat back.

Now, he had to turn this thing, and to turn it, he had to get some kind of *grip* on it.

But there was nothing there *to* grip.

Staring at it, he made two or three more tries to figure it out, and the thing threw him each time, like some kind of mental judo champ.

He gave that up, and turned around, facing down the sloping hill, where he at least wouldn't have to look at his distorted reflection.

Down the hill, all the dents at the bottom of the slope were obvious now, plain messages that the weight of the key could vary.

Roberts looked up.

Could he turn it by some similar process?

He crouched by the key, and now he *willed* it to turn.

Time after time, he imagined that the mirror-smooth surface rotated.

The gate, however, didn't move a fraction of an inch, but remained blandly reflected, along with his own distorted image, in the shining surface of the key.

He tried emotion on it. He hated it, beamed friendship at it, commanded, pleaded, *believed, saw* it turn— Dizzy and beginning to question his own sanity, he sat down again, facing down the slope so as to get the thing out of his sight.

There had to be some other way to figure this out.

Let's see now. After all, this was a *test*. It followed that, contrary to what might otherwise be the case, there should be some rhyme or reason to it.

A good part of the problem was therefore to figure out the viewpoint of the tester.

Now, the Interstellar Patrol might be tricky, devious, or brutally direct, but it wasn't stupid. *And* this problem would almost certainly bear the characteristic mark of its maker.

Now, why did the Patrol give this test? It was a part of basic training. It *must* be to drive home some important point. What was it the guide had said? —"A quality may be indispensable, but insufficient by itself. And the necessary additional quality may be its apparent opposite."

Now, what had he been shown but that *mental attitude* was important?

What would be the natural remainder of the test?

In actual life, particularly in tight spots, *was* mental attitude important?

Yes.

Was it enough?

No.

What *else* did it take?

The physical part of the problem had to be dealt with.

Now, the physical part of this problem was that slick featureless mirror-smooth surface. How to grip what offered no hold? Well, it was often necessary to grip or turn some ordinary slippery surface. How? By gripping it *tighter.* And what did that mean? —By *exerting greater pressure.*

Roberts turned around incredulously, to look at the

evidence of how thoroughly he had been sent down the wrong track by mental indirection.

There was the shiny surface in the concrete apron. Right beside it, reflected in the surface, was the locked gate with its strong horizontal bars.

Roberts went to the gate, stood on his hands, his feet up against the bars of the gate, walked his hands to the edges of the shiny key, locked his elbows, and straightened his knees. He could feel the heavy pressure in his joints, and now he twisted clockwise—no result—then counterclockwise. Under his hands, the shiny surface smoothly turned.

The gate began to slide.

He dropped to his feet, saw the gate slide wide-open, and stepped through.

That "little formality" was over.

Now, there stretched before him a path through open woods, doubtless leading to the *final* test.

And abruptly, Roberts could feel his viewpoint change.

Inevitably, a new member of the Interstellar Patrol, seeking some ground for confidence that he could handle his job, would look back to his training in the hope that, *having handled training as tough as that, he could therefore handle the job, too.*

Roberts started down the path.

Anyone in his right senses would hope for as speedy and simple an end to this grind as possible. But that wasn't what he hoped for.

As he headed down the path, Roberts had one fervent wish for this last problem:

Let it be tough!

TEST ULTIMATE

Vaughan Roberts, his muscles tired and sore, stood in the clearing with the other recruits, waiting for the last test to begin. Roberts leaned into the wind that had sprung up, and that made the branches of the trees lift and sway, hiding and then uncovering the dazzling sun. The shifting shadow and glare made it hard to see the guide who had led them almost to the end of the training course, and who now spoke to them from a low platform of logs at the edge of the clearing.

"Just one final test, gentlemen," the guide was saying, "and then your training will be *over*, and you will be full members of the Interstellar Patrol.

"There isn't much to this final exercise, but you must carry it out successfully to pass the course, so you might be interested in a few brief comments.

"To survive, and successfully do his duty, a member of the Interstellar Patrol must make *the* right use of courage. This quality is so important the final test will emphasize the proper use of courage.

"Now, this is not a complicated test. But it has its points, gentlemen, as I think you will agree after it is over.

"The problem is simply to climb a rock face twenty-five feet in height, onto the ledge at the top. The climb is not difficult, but to get to this rock face, you must first cross a wide, shallow pool. It is a pretty pool, at first glance. But it is stocked with carnivorous fish.

"Remember, gentlemen, this is a test in the proper use

of courage. You may not enjoy it, but you must do the best you can to succeed, whatever that may involve.

"To avoid too high a loss rate, the test will be given by simulator. You will experience a highly realistic illusion, that, to your senses, will be the same as if it *were* real.

"As an aid in learning, a special guide will be assigned to each one of you in this final test."

Roberts abruptly found himself standing in the quiet shade of tall trees, on a stony slope that slanted gradually down to a wide, shallow pool of sparkling, splashing water. Directly across the pool was a narrow border of marsh, rising to a steep forested hill farther back. To Roberts' left, across the length of the pool, was a gray rock face, down which a rivulet of water trickled onto a wide rock shelf, whence it flowed quietly into the pool.

For an instant, the scene seemed pleasant. Then Roberts realized that the sparkle and splash were caused by sleek steel-gray forms that burst up out of the water to snap, and then splatter and splash the surface. The ceaseless flash and snap, and the splatter and splash as the carnivorous fish fell back, now made the pool look to him like a kind of seething hellish cauldron.

Just as the full impact of the scene hit Roberts, a powerfully built figure in the shadows near the edge of the pool turned toward him. Wearing a tight, black one-piece garment, with three rows of ribbons at the left chest, and wide belt bearing knife and fusion gun, this figure was plainly the special guide. Roberts, relieved, waited for instructions.

The guide raised one muscular arm, and swept it out across the pool toward the rock face.

"Don't hesitate. This is a courage test. In you go, and head straight for that rock face!"

Roberts, relieved to have some clear-cut direction, started forward.

Ahead of him, the water seethed.

Roberts fixed his mind on the rock face across the pool, made a rapid estimate of the distance, and then saw with a start that the water was so roiled up that he couldn't see the bottom.

The voice of the first guide, back at the clearing, came

to him: "The problem is simply to climb a rock face twenty-five feet in height, onto the ledge at its top."

There across the pool was the rock face and the ledge. But considering that these fish were carnivorous, how could he get through them, across a possibly uneven bottom that he couldn't see, without being eaten up on the way?

Nearby, the special guide called sharply, "Don't hesitate! *Keep moving!*"

Roberts hesitated, then with an effort kept going.

In front of him, the steel-gray forms leaped out, their sharp jaws flashing with a knifelike glint.

The guide, his voice approving, shouted, "Good lad! Now, *straight for that cliff!*"

Roberts' mind seemed split in halves. Thoughts flashed through his consciousness in a chaotic rush:

"Don't hesitate! Keep moving!"

"There isn't much to this final exercise, but you must carry it out successfully to pass the course."

"Don't hesitate. This is a courage test. In you go, and head straight for that rock face!"

"The problem is simply to climb a rock face . . ."

"Now, go straight for the cliff!"

"Remember, gentlemen, this is a test in the proper use of courage."

"Don't hesitate. This is a courage test . . ."

" . . . A test in the proper use of courage."

Across the pool, the rock face loomed like a mirage over the water. Ten feet out from shore, a big steel-gray muscular form leaped high and fell back, and the splash briefly uncovered a glistening human rib cage.

Roberts stopped in his tracks.

The special guide whirled, put his hand on Roberts' shoulder, and said sharply, "Go straight in! Even if you don't make it, I'll vouch for your courage. *That's all you need to pass the courage test!* Now, *move!*"

He gave Roberts a push to start him into the pool.

Abruptly the two divided halves of Roberts' mind came back together again. He ducked free of the pushing hand, pivoted, and smashed his fist into the guide's muscular midsection.

The guide doubled over, his arms flew out, and he slammed back into some kind of invisible barrier, that recoiled and

threw him back toward Roberts. The guide recovered himself, and his hand flashed toward his fusion gun.

Roberts hit him again in the midsection.

The guide went down, and at once came up on one knee,
still groping for the fusion gun.

Roberts jerked him to his feet, and knocked him down
for the third time.

The guide landed full length on the ground, and Roberts
bent to swiftly take the belt, with its knife and gun. He
had hardly straightened, when the guide again struggled to
get up, and Roberts cracked him over the head with the
gun.

The guide sat back down with a grunt, then started up
again.

Roberts stepped back, frowning. He held the gun in one
hand, and the belt, with holster and sheathed knife, dangled
from the other hand. So far, he hadn't been able to put the
special guide down long enough to fasten the belt.

The words of their original guide, back in the clearing,
came to him:

"Now, this is not a complicated test. But it has its points,
gentlemen, as I think you will agree after it is over."

Roberts glanced out at the seething pool, and back at the
grim-faced special guide, just coming to his feet.

Despite the gun, the guide suddenly rushed him. Roberts
landed a terrific kick to the base of the chest.

The guide went down, and this time it looked as if he
might stay there a while.

Roberts clasped the belt around his waist, looked at the
fish springing from the water, glanced back at the motionless guide, then looked around, spotted a length of fallen
branch lying on the ground with most of the twigs rotted
off. He picked up the branch and swung it over the pool,
the far end dipping into the water.

Instantly, the water exploded in gray forms.

Snap! SNAP! Snap!

The branch lightened in his hand as two-and-a-half feet
at the far end disappeared.

Roberts glanced around at the guide, already starting to
shake his head dazedly. With his thumb, Roberts felt the
end of the stick. It was cut off smooth, as if by a sharp
curved blade.

The guide sat up, his eyes focused on Roberts. He came to his feet in one fluid motion.

Roberts aimed the gun at the guide's head.

The guide's eyes glinted, and he started forward. His voice had a sharp ring of authority.

"Drop the gun. I'm coming to take it, Mister. *Drop* it!"

Roberts depressed the fusion gun's trigger, and the searing pencil of energy sprang out, missing the guide's head by several inches.

Roberts said flatly, *"Halt!"*

The guide halted, face stern and eyes intent.

"Now," said Roberts, "just back up to where you were."

The guide didn't budge. "You won't get away with this!"

Roberts watched him alertly.

"I won't get away with *what?*"

"Cowardice! You don't show the guts to do as you're told! Now, *drop that gun!*"

Roberts kept the gun aimed at the guide.

"I was told to climb that rock face. I can't climb it if I don't last long enough to get near it. To obey your instructions would guarantee that I wouldn't do what I am supposed to do."

"I told you, Mister, that if you showed courage, I'd vouch for you!"

"That's nice. But that won't get me up that rock face."

The guide's voice came out in a deadly menacing tone.

"Do you question my word?"

"Yes," said Roberts. "As a matter of fact, I question everything about you. I have a suspicion that somewhere there's a complicated little network that projects a mass of muscle, an empty head, and a loud voice, with built-in responses, and that's all there is to you. There's something about you that fits the Interstellar Patrol like oars on a spaceship. Incidentally, I notice you haven't stepped back. *Back up!*"

Glowering, the muscular figure backed up several feet.

"All right," said Roberts, "turn around."

"Go to hell."

Roberts aimed the fusion gun at the guide's midsection. "Friend, there's a kind of courage that makes sense, and there's another kind that's stupid, even in an illusion. The more I see of you, the more convinced I am that the Patrol would never have let *you* in. It follows that what you really are is a special kind of highly advanced electronic booby trap. You almost got me into that pool, but not quite. That push was too much. If this were strictly a test of raw courage, I'd have had to go in under my *own* power."

"I was helping you."

"That's the point. That help would spoil the test."

The guide spoke in a reasonable, persuasive voice. "I could see you weren't going to make it without help."

"In that case, I'd have been allowed to fail. What's the point of a test if you pass those who should fail?"

The guide now looked sympathetic.

"Lad, I knew a little help at the right time would get you over the hurdle. I never thought you'd show a yellow streak this wide. But I'm still willing to overlook all of this, if—"

Roberts shook his head critically. "Among other things, now you're ignoring the fact that I was given a definite goal, with no set time limit. Why should I have to *immediately* jump in with the carnivorous fish? I was told to *cross that pool and climb up that rock face onto the ledge.* That may involve the right *use* of courage, but instant suicide won't accomplish the job."

"Well, now, that about the rock face was only how it was *expressed*. The thing is to *show courage*. That's the test!"

"When you're ordered to attack, the thing to do is to just rush in quick where the defenses are thickest, eh?"

The guide looked reasonable again.

"What do you gain by delay? Sooner or later, you'll *have* to go *in*. There's a field of force on all sides of us, overhead, and under the ground surface, that leaves just this space between this edge of the pool and the trees. The only opening in the field is toward the pool. *There is no other way out*. What do you gain by putting it off? I'll overlook what you've done if—"

"Turn around," said Roberts.

The guide looked blank, and ignored the demand.

Roberts shifted the gun slightly.

"Turn around."

The muscular figure turned around.

Roberts said, "Lie flat on your face, hands at your sides. Now, keep your arms straight, but work your hands and arms under your body, so your right thigh pins your right hand, and your left thigh pins your left hand. All right, work the whole length of your arms under. Stay that way."

The guide lay flat on his face in the stony dirt.

Roberts walked over.

"Bend your legs slowly at the knee. Raise your feet."

Roberts piled stones on the guide's shoulders, and on the flat soles and heels of the guide's boots.

"Now, don't move, or the stones will fall off, and the clatter will warn me."

Roberts walked back near the water's edge, and looked out over the pool. He had one obstacle temporarily out of the way, but he was still a long distance from that ledge. He carefully felt along the invisible barrier, and, so far as he could judge, it was exactly as described. It felt somewhat like the edge of a kind of large transparent balloon, yielding as he pressed against it, but growing progressively harder to force back as he displaced it. When he stopped pushing, it forced him back.

As he moved around, he glanced repeatedly at the guide, who was cooperating, so far.

There seemed to be no way around the barrier, and very possibly no way to shorten the distance across that stretch of seething water. What the bottom was like was anyone's guess, but it could be uneven blocks of rock, covered with slime, and littered with the skeletons of past victims. From what Roberts had seen, ten seconds in that water would guarantee that he wouldn't climb that rock face.

A dull glint from the direction of the rock face briefly caught his attention, but, when he looked, he saw nothing different, and merely retained the impression of a falling rock. He glanced around.

There *had* to be some way to either get over the pool without going in it, or to deceive or eliminate the fish.

Roberts glanced at his prisoner, then looked at the forest cut off from him by the unseen barrier. Experimentally, he fired his fusion gun. Swinging the beam to be sure he was seeing what he thought he was seeing, he found that the barrier stopped the beam each time. It didn't reflect it. It seemed to absorb it. That meant that he couldn't hope to fell across the pool any of the tall trees beyond the barrier.

And where the fusion beam *could* reach, there were no trees close enough to the pool to do any good.

Roberts watched the fish leaping from the water, raised the gun, waited, then aimed at a gleaming gray form, and squeezed the trigger.

A large sharp-jawed fish dropped back, eyes bulging, hit awkwardly on its side, and flopped around on the surface.

All across the pool, the leaping and splashing stopped. The surface of the water roiled in a hundred swift brief currents. The injured fish was jerked, wrenched, and ripped to bits, sharp snouts and sleek flanks showing for just an instant around it.

Roberts aimed carefully, and fired a second time.

A second fish twisted up nearly out of the water, and fell back with a flat splash.

The others at once tore it to shreds.

Roberts fired a third time, at an exposed flank.

A third fish flopped on the surface.

The water around the injured fish was alive with snapping, tearing, steel-gray forms.

Back of Roberts, there was the clatter of a fallen rock.

In rapid succession, Roberts fired at several more fish, then glanced back.

The guide had dumped the stones from one foot, and was carefully lowering the other.

Again, out of the corner of his eye, Roberts sensed motion at the rock face. But there was no time to look in that direction.

He fired carefully, just over the guide's head.

The guide froze.

Roberts turned back, and glanced briefly at the rock face. All that moved there was falling water.

He looked back at the pool, and fired at another fish, and then another.

He kept firing methodically, until suddenly there were no more targets.

A few bits and fragments floated on the surface, but nothing attacked them. The flying insects ranged over the pool unmolested.

Now, supposedly the remaining fish were glutted. If so, it *should* be safe to go across the pool.

Roberts glanced at the rock face to his left, estimated the distance, and blinked.

Down this face of rock, along with the trickle of water, flopped a sleek steel-gray form, bounding and turning, to hit the rock shelf below, where the water flowed out toward the pool, with a loud *splat.*

Roberts abruptly realized what this would do to his plans, and raised the gun.

Behind him, there was a crash of pebbles, and a sudden scramble.

The guide was on his feet, hurtling straight for him.

Roberts sprang aside.

The guide changed direction and slid, then Roberts was back out of the way, and put the thin, dazzling beam of the fusion gun in front of the guide's eyes.

The guide stopped.

Now, Roberts thought, he had survived that.

But, at the same time, that one fish that had come down the rock face had flopped into the pool. And *that* fish wasn't glutted.

Roberts glanced out at the water, and the bits and fragments were no longer floating on the surface. But that little appetizer wouldn't be enough. The fish would still be hungry.

There was a splash, and out of the corner of his eye, Roberts could see the sleek gray form fall back and vanish, after snapping up one of the flying insects.

The guide said, "Drop the gun," and began to slowly walk toward Roberts. *"Drop* it!"

Roberts put the beam of the fusion gun over the guide's left shoulder. Then he put it past the guide's head, over the right shoulder.

The guide grinned, and his eyes glowed.

He kept coming.

From the direction of the rock face, something flashed briefly, falling down the stream that flowed over the rock, to hit with a *splat.*

The guide charged.

Roberts sprang aside, kicked him under the chin, whirled like a ballet dancer, and hammered him across the back of the neck as he passed.

The guide grabbed unsuccessfully at Roberts' leg, then went down on his hands and knees.

Roberts said coldly, "It's a mistake to try unarmed combat on a man armed with a knife and a gun." But he was noting that blows that would have killed an ordinary person were about as effective with this opponent as taps with a length of rolled-up paper.

The guide stumbled to his feet, turned and faced Roberts. "You won't fire the gun or use the knife. Not to kill me. Because you're yellow." He straightened, and his face showed pitying sympathy. "Sorry, lad, but you're yellow."

The guide began walking calmly toward Roberts, his face sure and confident. "Drop the gun. You won't use it. *Drop* it."

Roberts aimed at the guide's head.

The guide kept coming, his face reflecting quiet confidence.

Robert squeezed the trigger.

The fusion beam hit the guide's left eye. There was a dazzling white glow, the flesh peeled back like paper in a fire, and there was a splintering *crack!* Bits and fragments of glass or plastic, glowing redly, flew out in a shower.

"Halt!" said Roberts.

The guide halted.

Where the flesh had peeled back to expose the left eye socket, a silvery glitter showed instead of bone.

Roberts reminded himself, all this was taking place in a simulator. But the problem remained.

Roberts studied the motionless roboid "special guide" and said, "I didn't realize the Patrol was so hard-pressed for manpower that it was recruiting humanoid robots."

"No, sir."

"How come that now I'm 'sir'?"

"At this stage, sir, I am programmed to so address you."

"You will obey my orders, now?"

"Yes, sir.

"At this stage?"

"Yes, sir.

"So that, if I order you to go over to the water and kneel down you will do it?"

"Yes, sir."

"And if I command you to carry me piggyback across that pool, you will carry me piggyback across the pool."

"I will obey you in this phase, and, at your order, will do anything I am capable of doing."

That left unanswered the question whether the robot was capable of carrying him across. It also raised another point. Roberts cleared his throat.

"When does 'this phase' end?"

"When an internal mechanism gives the appropriate command signal, sir."

"When will that happen?"

"I cannot predict, sir. It depends on circumstances."

Roberts nodded. That fit in. The "command signal" would be given at that unpredictable moment when Roberts stuck his neck out far enough for the "guide" to heave him into the pool.

"I see," said Roberts. "Can *you* cross that pool without being attacked?"

"The fish are turned back by a chemical repellent with which my garment has been impregnated. Sir. They would otherwise bite me as they would bite you; but they would not ingest my substance, as it is not nourishing to them."

"All right. Go over near the edge of the water, and kneel down."

The robot willingly and obediently went near the edge of the water and knelt down.

Now, thought Roberts, if he climbed on its back, it would take him partway across and then toss him to the fish.

The function of this "special guide" seemed to be to give disastrous advice and murderous assistance. It followed that there was only one thing to do.

Roberts stepped back, aimed deliberately at the base of the robot's neck, and depressed the trigger.

The fusion beam sprang out.

There was a flare of flame, flying sparks, the "head" tilted and separated from the robot's body, and the body rose and wheeled toward Roberts.

Roberts shifted his aim to the lower chest, and the robot fell forward on the sand.

From the rock face to one side a dull flash briefly caught Roberts' attention.

Down the rock face, another steel-gray wetly gleaming

length of muscle and hunger tumbled, to land with a *splat*, and flop into the pond.

Roberts wiped the sweat out of his eyes, warily circled the human-like form, and crouched near its feet. Carefully, he undid the boots, and, holding the gun, stood thoughtfully considering the one-piece garment. He carefully pulled off the boots, but he had a disinclination to get in reach of the arms, however motionless the robot might seem.

Was the thing out of action, or wasn't it?

He stepped back, found what was left of the long stick he'd held over the water, lightly pressed the end to the edge of the one-piece garment, partway up the back. He moved the stick as if he were tugging at the cloth with his fingers.

Pebbles flew and dust whirled as the headless robot sprang at the stick.

Roberts fired at the robot's lower chest, and again it dropped to the ground.

Now, this time was it finally out of action, or wasn't it?

And what if, in trying to make sure he had hit the control mechanism, he hit the energy-source instead?

Roberts blew out his breath and stubbornly considered the situation.

The obvious thing to do was to get that repellent-impregnated garment.

Roberts raised the gun, and methodically burned the thick arms off the trunk of the mechanism, cut a line across the garment with the fusion beam, warily took hold, and pulled the garment free. A hard kick threw him back and could have knocked him into the pool if he hadn't expected it. But now he had the cut, but still usable, garment. And he could see that he was going to need it.

Down the rock face across the pool, another steel-gray form spun and fell, hit the shelf below with a *splat*, and flopped into the pool.

With an influx like that, there must be some way out for the fish already in the pool. But from where he was, Roberts couldn't see it. He shook his head, put the garment on over his fatigues, put his shoes back on, started for the pool, and then paused, looking at the robot.

The headless, armless torso had rolled toward the place

where he would have landed if that last kick had fully connected, and now it was feeling carefully with its feet along the water's edge. Finding nothing, it lay still.

Roberts stood frowning.

Considering the source, how had he come to take *that* piece of information for granted?

He took his shoes off, and pulled off the robot's repellent-impregnated garment. He put his shoes back on, searched along the edge of the invisible barrier, found a second long stick, tied one leg of the garment to the stick, and let the other end of the garment hang free. He walked down near the water's edge, swung the stick out over the water, and dipped about eight inches of the garment into the water.

The stick jerked in his hands. The garment was cut off in a ragged edge half-a-foot above the water, and the steel-gray forms shot up in a boiling froth to snap bits off the part that dangled higher yet.

Roberts straightened.

This was the "repellent-impregnated" garment he had almost relied on.

Roberts glanced around at the robot, saw it was too far away to bother him, drew the fusion gun, lowered the remainder of the garment's dangling leg barely into the water, and shot the first fish to leap out after it.

Other fish attacked that one, and, using his tried and proved method, Roberts reduced their numbers by enough to satisfy the appetite of the remainder.

And once again the pond became placid.

The robot was now exploring the far edge of the barrier's opening on the pool.

Roberts, thinking over the situation, decided that things were about as favorable as he could hope to get them. Most of the fish in the pond should now be digesting the last meal, and any that might still be hungry ought to be attracted first to the remaining cloth on the end of the stick, rather than to him.

Dipping the cloth in the water, with the stick held in his left hand, Roberts eased carefully into the pool. The fusion gun, he held in his right hand, ready to use in case the cloth were attacked. But when he tried to move forward, his feet at once came up against some obstruction. He tried in a different place, with the same result.

The trip across now turned into a nightmare all on its own. Through the water, still murky, but no longer so badly stirred up, loomed skeletal rib cages and piles of bones. Here and there, a fish hung sluggishly, fins moving spasmodically. Roberts worked his way across, looking up frequently at the rock face, down which from time to time fell a steel-gray form that he had to kill before it got in the pool, because, if he didn't finish it, it might very well finish him.

By the time Roberts was halfway across, the worst of the horror looming up at him through the water had begun to ease off. The bottom was becoming clearer, apparently because most of the victims had never made it this far.

From there on, suddenly it became almost easy, and the bottom was so flat and unobstructed that just a little care-lessness on Roberts' part would have dropped him down a narrow vertical cleft not eight feet from the edge of the rock shelf. He got across that with a sense of relief, reached the shelf, and just then something tugged at his shoe.

The cloth on the stick jerked, there was a splash, a sense of something brushing his leg, and when he looked down, the water was stained with red.

He threw the remainder of the "repellent-impregnated" garment into the pool, and pulled himself out on the rock shelf. He moved over near the face of the rock, took off his shirt, and bound it tightly around his badly bitten lower leg.

Now he discovered that the shoe of the same leg had been cut open, and he was bleeding from inside the shoe.

He took the shoe off, clenched his jaw at the sight, tore off strips of his ragged trouser legs, bound his foot, put the cut shoe back on, and laced it tight.

The bandages were turning red, but there was nothing he could do about that. He looked up at the rock face, which was apparently a form of shale, with many little ledges, some of them dry, and some of them, where the water flowed down, wet and mossy. The face wasn't vertical, but if he should slip, there was nothing there to give his bare hands a real hold until he hit the rock shelf at the bottom.

Carefully, he started to climb, clenching his jaw against the pain from his leg. About fifteen feet up, there came a *flop-thump* from above, and one of the steel-gray fish bounced past, snapping at him on the way by.

Roberts began to climb again. When he had almost reached the ledge, he paused, studying the green moss at its rim just above. The moss had little stalks on it, and each stalk had a set of miniature spikes at its end.

What would happen if he touched that? Was it, perhaps, poisonous?

He looked around, then carefully worked to the side, and now he was on slippery wet rock. There was still moss up above, and he kept moving to the side.

Overhead, an occasional insect flashed out over the edge of the ledge, and then darted back again.

Another carnivorous fish flopped over the edge, and snapped its jaws shut not three inches from Roberts' left shoulder. He kept moving steadily to the side.

Finally, there was no moss up above, and no flying insects darting into view and back again.

Cautiously, he worked his way up onto the ledge.

To the side, where he would have come up if he had climbed straight up, was the edge of a shallow pool into which water flowed from a further, more gentle, incline of rock. Over this pool, flying insects darted irregularly back and forth, to vanish suddenly as the fish shot up and snapped their jaws.

Roberts straightened and drew a deep breath.

Provided he had understood the rules in the first place, he had finally made it.

Abruptly the scene vanished.

The familiar guide—who had been with them throughout the course—looked at him with a smile.

"Well, Roberts, *you* made it."

"Thank you, sir. It's over?"

"It's over. And you are now a full member of the Interstellar Patrol. There will be a little ceremony later on, when the others join us.

"'The others'?"

"Your fellow basic trainees. I regret to say, Roberts, that even among the best material for the Patrol, there *are* those who believe the sanction of authority is everything. Hence when they are told they will pass the last test if they merely plunge straight in, like so many sheep—Why, they *do* it! Even though it involves the sensations of being eaten alive by carnivorous fish."

"*Don't* they pass the test?"

"Oh, they barely pass the test. But the Board of Examiners immediately decides that their action brings into question prior indications of basic suitability for the Patrol. You see, we don't encourage *unthinking* reliance on authority, or on the appearance of authority. Some of the great defeats and disasters of history have followed from exactly that cause. We have trouble enough without that. So, we pick this last test to give a little reminder that our men should *have the courage to think.* Consider this, Roberts. A recruit in the Interstellar Patrol is given disastrous advice by someone with an air of authority—advice that obviously means the recruit will fail to do what he is supposed to do—and the recruit *does* it! We can't have that."

"What happens?"

"The Board of Examiners grudgingly recommends that the trainee be allowed the opportunity to *repeat the test.* Thus, after having unthinkingly taken his supposed superior's word for it, and having as a result experienced the sensations of being eaten alive by carnivorous fish, the trainee finds himself right back in the same spot all over again, with the same pool, the same fish, and the same electronic boob giving the same worthless advice. What do you *suppose* happens?"

Beside Roberts, his friend Hammell suddenly appeared, his face red, massaging his fists, and feeling tenderly of places low down on his legs.

"Well." said the guide, smiling, "*this* time you made it."

Hammell growled incoherently. There was another little blink of time, and there stood another friend and fellow trainee, Morrissey, electric-blue eyes blazing in anger. And there beside him suddenly stood Bergen, his blond hair on end. One after another now, they appeared, until the whole class was there; and then before them appeared a slight well-knit figure with a look of self-discipline and good humor.

"Gentlemen, in the Patrol, thought does not solely radiate from the top down, but takes place on all levels, including that lowest and hence *closest to the facts.* Any time you are tempted to pass the buck upward or to blindly accept obviously disastrous orders without objecting to them, remember this incident. Possibly by doing so, you may avoid an experience worse than this one.

"Very well, gentlemen, you have now passed the basic training course of the Interstellar Patrol, and you are full members in good standing of the Patrol, with all that this implies. You will now receive your weapons and full issue of uniforms, with appropriate insignia, in the order of your passing out of this course. As I call your names, step forward, salute, and receive your weapons and uniforms.

"Roberts, Vaughan N."

Respectfully, Roberts stepped forward and saluted.

PART III: *And the Others…*

COMPOUND INTEREST

Nels Krojac lay flat on his back as the dizziness wore off, the ringing in his ears died away, and the tingling of his hands and feet told of returning circulation. Carefully he sat up, his gaze taking in the wide bed he lay on, the drawers along the walls to left and right, the emergency control console that filled the end wall, and, beside the bed, the communications screens that could put him in touch with any part of the ship by snapping a switch.

He sat at the edge of the bed, and the mirror on the right-hand wall showed him a broad-shouldered man with dark hair, massive chest, and watchful blue eyes, wearing a dark-blue dressing gown with dragon design on the chest. The slightly stubbled face was lean, broad-boned, and hard, and he recognized that face from long familiarity. What he didn't recognize was the pallor of skin and hesitancy of expression as he tested his legs.

Cautiously, he walked the length of the room to the foot of the huge console, then back to the bed and the communications screens, back once more to the console, then to the door on the left wall of the room below the console, and back to the bed to look again in the mirror.

The paleness was fading away. Now he looked like a man who has walked into a glass door, and has just staggered back to his feet. A few seconds consideration told him it would never do to show that face to the universe.

He paced the room, opened the left-hand door, to his private swimming pool, where the water was pale-blue, still, and inviting, but he was afraid to use it. And then the realization that he was afraid struck home. He walked back to the bed and glared angrily in the mirror.

There. *Now* he looked like himself again.

He snapped on the bedside screen. A long-faced suave-looking individual with lightly-oiled wavy hair took a cigarette from his mouth, put it out in a nearby ash tray, and still exhaling smoke said, "Yes, Mr. Krojac?"

"Reagan, what happened down there yesterday while I was explaining the contract to that gang of feline aliens?"

"They watched every move you made, and they looked at you as if they were trying to drill their way into your head with their eyes. They look so much like tigers anyway, that I had my hand in my pocket, gripping that fusion gun, all the time we were there."

"Did they stare much at you?"

"Just for a few seconds."

"Did they seem to understand the contract?"

Reagan hesitated. "The impression I got was that they knew something was being put over on them, but they didn't know what. Anyway—they agreed to it."

" . . . With the verbal proviso that the written contract must match the verbal explanation."

Reagan shrugged. "That has no legal force."

"Yeah," said Krojac sourly, remembering what had happened a few minutes ago. The dizziness hit him every time he planned to bend the contract terms. "Where do we stand if we *do* follow the verbal understanding?"

Reagan looked jarred, as if someone had suggested that he rob his mother.

"Well, we . . . I certainly wouldn't recommend *that*."

"We'd lose money on the deal?"

"It's worse than that. We're at the crux of a pyramiding of credit. We've got enormous assets and enormous debts. So long as the assets are part of a functioning concern, they're worth more than the debts. Split up and sold piecemeal for cash, they wouldn't cover half the indebtedness. We've *had* to go this far in debt to get a strategic position in this end of space."

Krojac nodded. "Otherwise, Reed & Osborne would have moved in."

"Exactly. Now, Reed & Osborne is conservative in their

financing. To have blocked us directly would have required heavy risks. That company prefers to let *us* take the risks, and reach an agreement with us later if we succeed, or buy our depreciated assets if we fail. Reed & Osborne's position is solid in the settled regions. It can afford to move in here just fast enough to force us to extend ourselves, or accept a permanent second-class position."

"Yes," said Krojac. That, he thought, was always the way it was. To try for safety meant that others took the big risks—and *some* of those others succeeded, and got the big gains. They were the first-rates, and with their resulting big assets, they could grip the central positions, and dominate the scene with ease. And, he told himself, the only way to break that dominance was to have big enough assets yourself to take big risks and make big gains, and in turn secure a dominant position. But since those already dominant would so cramp you that you could never acquire big assets, what was there to do but plan your move, and then borrow the assets to carry it out? In which case, if you made one bad slip, the whole house of cards folded up.

On the screen, Reagan shrugged. "We've done very well until now. We've got our foundation solidly laid. We've got the properties and some of the necessary contracts for development and future use. But we're stretched to the limit. The first loans are now coming due. We're going to be watched very carefully. *If* we pay those loans on time, then we'll have no trouble with future loans. But, if we *fail* to pay those loans, the word will go around that we're in trouble. God help us then."

Krojac nodded soberly. Here was the clinch. It was one thing to see the opportunity, conceive a plan, and carry the plan as far as ordinary luck, energy, thought, and determination would carry it. It was another thing to have that plan reach the point where it should just start to bear fruit, and then see it pile into a stone wall.

"How far's our work behind schedule, down on the planet?"

"Just three days. But when those colonists start coming through here, we've got to have the facilities ready. Otherwise, instead of pay, we're going to get a penalty. Either pay, or penalty, is figured per head, and the numbers passing through here will be enormous."

Krojac thought it over. The main new colonization route through this sector passed nearby before branching, and that had seemed to be his opportunity. What he needed was a quick return that would pay off immediate debts. Colonists outbound on the longer government routes were given a chance to rest and make up deficiencies in their equipment before the final stage of the trip. The government would gladly pay a private enterpriser who would supply the rest-and-refit facilities.

Krojac had known an Earth-type planet ideally situated, and occupied only by monster carnivores and herbivores, and a kind of big-boned tiger-like creature with no visible technology, civilization, or other accomplishments. All he had to do was to get the refit contract, and he could build on this planet, and have a sure source of cash income. He decided to do it.

The first shock had come when the government put the refit contract up for bids, and Reed & Osborne publicly announced its intention of bidding.

"Now what?" Krojac demanded.

Reagan shook his head. "I'm afraid their move is obvious."

"Bid at just what they think it will cost?"

"Right. Then whether they get it or not, they won't lose a cent; while if *we* don't get it, we'll be denied our immediate source of cash. Yet to get it, we'll have to bid *below cost*. The result will be that we'll be driven to the wall. And when we fold up, Reed & Osborne will buy us out cheap, for an enormous overall profit."

Krojac tested the logic of it. It fit like a sharp knife between the ribs. "There's just one thing. This is a *long-term contract*."

"Yes. They can't plan on renegotiating it every year or two."

"That means they'll have to figure planetary rights over a long period. After they've sold them out, they'll still have expenses. If we *should* live through this, they don't want a drawn-out drain on their resources."

"Hm-m-m, that's right. Let's get Sheaster's opinion on this."

A moment later, a shrewd face looked at them from the

screen. "Sure, when you take a government R and R Contract, you get full planetary settlement rights. That's thrown in free. It doesn't cost the government a cent. Yes, if you've got space left over, and you always have lots of it, you can sell homesteads to the settlers, and the government will pay you the settlers' outbound shipping cost." Sheaster's eyes narrowed. "But wait a minute, now. You can't extrapolate the short-term gains onto a long-term basis. What happens is, you get a fast flow of cash while the nearby land is used up, then you run into expenses. You've got to deliver the settler fairly close to the homestead. You've got to lay out a system for the homestead boundaries. You've got to make the first year's supplies available. You run into diminishing returns pretty fast when you start shuttling them over mountain ranges against gravity, and hauling out supplies. It turns into a mass of details, and whether a river flows north or south can make all the difference."

"How's Reed & Osborne going to figure it?"

"The same way, only more so. They don't want it. They just want to saw off the limb we're climbing on."

"We'll be safe to figure they won't bid below their idea of average *long-term* cost?"

Sheaster thought it over. "Yes. But *you* think we can cut under their bid, count on short-term sales to settlers, and have cash from the government? Sure. Later, we'll have a steady drain till the contract runs out, but by then we can cover that from other sources." Sheaster squinted at the screen. "Yes, I think that's it."

Krojac said, "Is there any place we can get in a trap?"

"If we make a wrong guess as to costs, sure. Or if it turns out there's a 'sentient race' on the planet."

"We've got the survey reports. They haven't classified it yet, but there's no sign of that."

"No. But if that happens, we could wind up with the contract and no planet. When there's a 'sentient race,' you have to get their permission."

"The initial recommendation was to classify it A-1 except for the big carnivores on the planet."

Sheaster nodded. "We can't eliminate chance. If we don't do this, we take a bigger risk of failing."

"Just what *I* think," said Krojac. "O.K., we'll bid slightly below cost."

✣   ✣   ✣

And, Krojac thought, sitting on the edge of his bed ten months later, it had worked like a charm, until about six weeks ago. He had won the contract. He'd gotten ready to start work. But then it developed that the chief of the classification unit on the planet thought the planet's tiger-like race was sentient; he also thought it was potentially deadly.

Since the classification chief produced no proof for this belief, the obvious answer was that Reed & Osborne were quietly paying a little something into a hidden account somewhere. The simplest counter was to try to outbid Reed & Osborne, and when that didn't work, to pull every string available to force the local official, whose name was Lindell, to make up his mind.

Lindell, however, did *not* make up his mind, but instead sent back worried reports of possible future trouble, along with every conceivable kind of proof that the local species was neither sentient nor actually dangerous. These reports, copies of which quickly found their way to Nels Krojac, all but drove him wild. Reed & Osborne, through Lindell, had him in a box.

"All right," said Krojac finally, "there's nothing to do but send the men down there anyway, and fight it out in court afterward. Maybe by then, at least, we'll have the money to pay the fines."

Sheaster nodded. "We *might* beat him. This is so irrational, it *must* be he's been bribed."

Reagan said, "He can't actually stop us. His base is set up to fight off the carnivores. But that's all the weapons he's got, except for lightly-armed surveyor-probes."

Krojac nodded. "And his base is far enough away so that's no bother."

"Except," said Sheaster thoughtfully, "there's just one thing."

"Now what?"

"He *could* call in the Space Force."

Krojac could see the incandescent sparks dance before his eyes. "That's all we'd need."

"*Agh,*" said Reagan, "what's the likelihood of that?"

"With this Lindell," said Sheaster. "I'm not so sure."

There was a silence, then Krojac shrugged.

"What else *can* we do?"

"The Space Force shoots with guns," said Sheaster. "It's a difference of going bust and getting killed. Maybe you don't care, but *I* do."

Reagan said, "We don't know he'll call in the Space Force."

Sheaster pursed his lips doubtfully.

Krojac nodded. "Reagan's right. As it stands, we're beat. We've got to force the issue. Meanwhile, in case he does call in the Space Force, we've got to dig up every complication, legal precedent, and argument for delay we can think of. We might make it so complicated the Space Force would think it lacked jurisdiction."

Reagan said thoughtfully, "I've got a nephew on one of those ships—I think he's second-in-command of a patrol squadron. I think *he'd* see reason."

"If he can get us out of this," said Krojac earnestly, "I'd be grateful, in five figures. You and he can split it any way you want."

Reagan said, "I don't know. It's no use unless he's in the right squadron."

"Maybe we could cut his C.O. in. This thing is worth plenty to me."

"Yeah," said Reagan, "but there're a lot of patrol squadrons out there, and I'm just not sure—"

"Listen," said Sheaster, "go easy about cutting the C.O. in. There's a certain type we don't want to fool with. Let me get it across to you, these boys play with *guns*."

Krojac said, "What do you think those things are we've got mounted all over the ship. We paid plenty for those."

"Do you have the fire-control apparatus, the combat computers, the disciplined crew—"

"I'm not talking about fighting a war with them."

"I'm glad to hear that, at least. But what I'm saying again is, there's a type we'd better not come up against. Forget about cutting the C.O. in."

"Everybody likes money."

"There's a kind that likes opposition better. They swim against the current. Let's not *us* make the current they swim against."

"Nuts," said Krojac. "We've got to resist to the limit, and give them every chance to lose their nerve. *Obviously*, we can't fight the Space Force. But we *can* drum up so many legal specters and so many complications that maybe we can take the initiative away from them."

Reagan said, "*If* Lindell calls them in."

"Yes," said Krojac, "*if* he does. O.K. We put the men down."

Reagan nodded. "I'll take care of it."

The following day, Lindell called in the Space Force.

Sheaster said worriedly, "This is getting pretty bad. We've got the Midas touch with a reverse twist. Everything we put our hand on turns to dirt."

Reagan was frowning. "I don't know. My nephew is second-in-command of Squadron 2337. The squadron that answered Lindell's call is 2337."

Krojac beamed. "That could be the end of our troubles right here."

"I talked to him . . . just a friendly chat," said Reagan, "and I think he got the picture."

Sheaster said forebodingly, "He's going to bribe the C.O., eh?"

"He's going to try to get him to see reason."

The screen lit up. "Sir, a Lieutenant Colonel Doyle, commanding Squadron 2337, wants to speak to Mr. Krojac."

"Fast work," said Krojac, smiling.

"Hold on," said Reagan. "Hannie hasn't had time to see him yet. This Doyle will just commit himself against us and that will make it harder all around."

Krojac glanced back at the screen. "Tell him I'm busy, and can't speak with him right now."

"Yes, sir." The screen blanked.

A formal message from Doyle of Squadron 2337 promptly arrived, warning that any construction or earth-moving work on Marshak III had been banned, and the Space Force would uphold the ban, using whatever degree of force was necessary.

"Hannie evidently hasn't gotten to him yet," said Reagan.

Krojac glanced at Sheaster. "O.K. Fire your legal broadside."

Sheaster promptly sent out a complex legal document sixty-two pages long.

Lieutenant Colonel Doyle of Squadron 2337 sent back a sharp message reiterating his first warning.

Krojac looked at the two messages. "Something tells me Hannie is never going to convince *this* boy."

"It certainly doesn't look promising," said Reagan. "Well, do we go ahead with the next step?"

"There's nothing else *to* do. If we act invincible enough, maybe we'll even convince Doyle."

Reagan called Doyle of Squadron 2337, using a trick screen that showed, in the background, realistic recorded views of a prominent senator and a Space Force general. Reagan bore down heavy with an air of power, and the implied warning that Doyle was seriously endangering his career.

Doyle watched in silence. Shortly after the call, Krojac received a third warning, varying from the previous two only in trivial details of the wording.

Sheaster shook his head. "This boy won't stop. He's coming right through."

Reagan said, "What we've done so far has been like trying to tie him up with rubber bands."

"With enough rubber bands," said Krojac, "we may do it. All right, start calling Doyle. First put on somebody to throw another legal block into him. Then put on . . . let's see . . . Root is good at this. Yes, put Root on to explain to Doyle, in the most reasonable way, why it is we've *got* to put the men down there. After all, this wasn't our idea. Lindell is forcing our hand. If that doesn't work, hit him with the legal stuff again. Then somewhere in there, we want to get it across that he's got a good spot waiting for him with us if he's reasonable about this. Then dig up the highest-ranking ex-Space Force officer we've got that has any power of persuasion, and have him disagree with Doyle's interpretation of the technicalities. This ex-officer has got to look like he's living in the lap of luxury. See, to give Doyle a little incentive. *He* made it. So can Doyle."

Sheaster put his head in his hands.

Reagan said hopefully, "Drop by drop, we'll wear him down."

Krojac nodded. "Where's that trideo actress we picked up? We'll put her on next, and in case he doesn't go for that, we'll hit him again with some more legal stuff."

"O.K.," said Reagan. "If we pile it on fast enough, maybe we'll bury him in it."

They promptly put the plan in action.

Doyle disagreed with Krojac's legal specialist, listened patiently to Root, stated the regulations required him to act as he was acting, informed a new legal team that he was acting under regulations, showed no indication that he was eager for a bribe or afraid of Krojac, and listened unimpressed to his "brother Space Force officer." Reagan never got a chance to try the actress on Doyle, because just before she was to go on, word came in that Squadron 2337 was entering a "potential war zone," and would henceforth maintain complete communicator silence.

"'Potential war zone,'" said Sheaster. "That's *us*. Do you realize that?"

Reagan shook his head. "It looked hopeful for a few seconds now and then, but the fact is he went through that stuff like a fusion beam through an overstretched balloon."

"The trouble is," said Krojac, "it's all been one hundred percent bluff. We don't have anything to fight *with*." He frowned. "Wait a minute."

"What?" said Reagan.

"We're armed. I'll bet this ship, together with the *Star Chaser*, mounts more firepower than the whole pipsqueak squadron. What do you bet one of our ships outweighs a dreadnought?"

"Wait a minute, Nels." Reagan said. "We're *not* going to fight the Space Force. If you're turning pirate, count me out."

"No, no," said Krojac. "Do you think I'm nuts? Who's planning to *fight* them? But this Doyle must be under pressure by now. He's going on, clinging to regulations, but he's wondering about a lot of things."

"No," said Sheaster. "He's not wondering about anything. He's got his orders, and that's that. He's *not* wondering."

"He's wondering," said Krojac stubbornly, "and he's *uncertain*. Meanwhile, we've still got to get this work done. He's going to get here about the time those earth-moving machines get set up. If we just let him go down and block us, we lose the chance to fulfill the contract. Lindell sits on the classification till the last minute, and we're *ended*. There won't be time to do the job."

"We'll still be alive," said Sheaster.

"Suppose," said Krojac, "this space kid and his popboats find a ship bigger than a dreadnought waiting for them, its big fusion guns already centered on them, and another big ship just coming up over the curve of the planet—*then* what?"

Reagan suggested. "They'll try to contact us."

"We won't answer. What can they do?"

Reagan frowned. "Not being a Space Force colonel, I don't know. They *might* think it was too dangerous to force the issue."

Sheaster put one hand over his eyes, turned away, then turned back with a sudden thrust of the hand to the side. "Look. Let me try again. *There are different kinds of people.* There is one kind that when you pull a gun on him, you better be ready to shoot him."

"Who's 'pulling a gun'?" said Krojac hotly. "Our guns are *already there*. We've got a legal right to move them around however we feel like it. Look, this Doyle is already up against a lot of pressure. We'll give him an *excuse to not interfere.* This Doyle is a military man, and military men respect guns."

Sheaster shook his head gloomily.

Reagan scowled. "It *sounds* as if it might work. But there's something about the way Doyle has acted so far—"

"All right," said Krojac. "What can we do if we *don't* do this?"

"That's a point," said Reagan slowly. "O.K. We'll try to scare them off."

Krojac's larger ship, the *Empire*, was ready when Squadron 2337 appeared off the planet Marshak III. The *Empire* held the ships of Squadron 2337 in the automatic sights of her guns, and replied to no calls. Slowly and ominously, Krojac's other ship, the *Star Cruiser*, rose up over the curve of the planet.

Squadron 2337 lit up like a mountain range of erupting volcanoes. Two of the squadron's ships streaked off at wide angles. Suddenly, a series of thuds jarred the *Empire.*

The first officer appeared on Nels Krojac's screen.

"Sir, the Space Force ships have put our guns out of action, and implanted heavy missiles in the ship."

"Implanted—what does that mean?"

"They've got missiles they can slam right through an unarmored hull. These smash through into the guts of the ship, and go off in a set time-interval unless the missile officer shuts off the timing device. We've just been warned

these missiles will go off in ten minutes. There's a Space
Force colonel on the screen talking to the captain now."

Krojac could feel his head spin. "I'll talk to him."

Krojac used on Doyle every device of word and manner
to force some slight concession, or at least to gain a little
time.

Doyle refused to yield an inch.

Krojac's captains surrendered their ships.

The ships were boarded and methodically searched,
including Krojac's private quarters.

"Well," said Sheaster, "*now* do you say he'll run away?
I tell you, you don't bribe this kind and you don't scare
him. Pull a gun on him, and you better shoot it."

"Are we dead?" said Krojac. "How could we know what
he'd do without trying it? My ships surrendered to him—
so what? The only charge he has against us is that we
'behaved in a menacing way,' or some such thing. I never
said we were going to fight him."

"But where are we now?" said Sheaster.

"In a tough spot. Well, we'd have been in just as tough
a spot if we'd said, 'Yes, sir,' when the first order came in.
I don't aim to fold up just because somebody gives a threat.
If they're going to fold me up, *they're* going to have to do
the work. I won't do it for them."

Reagan said, "What about the work crews on the planet?
Do we call them back up?"

"No. Have them go ahead."

"But—"

"But what? That's what this is all about, isn't it? Doyle
stops here and the work crews go ahead, *we win.*"

"With all the power Doyle has on tap—"

"It isn't enough that he's got the power. He's got to *use* it."

Reagan looked dazed. "The work crews go ahead?"

"That's right. No delay."

Reagan sent down the order.

The work crews promptly started out with their earth-
moving machines.

Doyle with equal promptness set down a troop transport,
and armed men blocked the earth-moving machines.

Krojac's tough work-crew chiefs obeyed orders and drove
straight at the troops, ignoring commands to stop.

Doyle's troops fired warning shots over their heads.

Krojac's men ignored the warning and slammed straight ahead.

Doyle's troops lowered their guns, and opened fire on the machines themselves. Then, and only then, was Krojac stopped.

"All right," he said, "they've stopped us. But never forget. *They* did it. *We* didn't. We have nothing to be ashamed of. If you do your best, that's good enough."

"Nevertheless, we're stopped," said Reagan.

"O.K., but if I get licked, I want the other side to carry a few memories away. Now, what we've got to do is to find some way out. What's going to happen here? What's the setup? Is Doyle bought? Did Reed & Osborne get to him?"

"No," said Sheaster. "I keep trying to tell you, you don't *buy* that kind. They aren't for sale."

"Even with what Reed & Osborne have got?"

"Not if Reed & Osborne had ten times as much."

Krojac frowned. "But they've got Lindell?"

"That I don't know. I thought so. Now I don't know. That he called Doyle in so fast doesn't exactly fit. Well . . . who knows? Maybe *he's* honest."

Krojac said exasperatedly, "How do you deal with honest men? You can't predict what they're going to do." He thought a minute. "All right, we'll train more work crews, and put the ships to work improvising more equipment. If Doyle and Lindell *are* honest, anything might happen."

The screen came on. "Sir, we've just got word there's an advanced linguistics computer, the LC-10,000, already on its way. It should get here tomorrow."

"What's the object of that?"

"If the locals have a complex language, then Lindell can rule that there's an anomalous situation here that needs further study—in that the natives have some advanced characteristics and some primitive characteristics. Then he can put the planet in the 'Unclassified' category and delay exploitation of it."

"Well, that fits. Let me know if anything more comes in."

"Yes, sir."

"Well," said Krojac, "that's a nice, neat trap. That could *really* string the thing out."

Reagan scowled. "What do they do if this computer doesn't cooperate?"

Krojac shook his head. "We'll go nuts trying to figure this out. How do you bribe a computer? Forget it. Get going on the work crews."

The next day, the situation took a series of twists none of them would have thought possible.

First, the infallible computer announced that the "speech" of the natives was nothing more than "simple repetitive syllables." This knocked the props out from under Lindell.

Second, the Space Force colonel, Doyle, walked over to a group of natives and succeeded in getting them to understand him.

Third, Lindell, himself stupefied by this development, let it be known that the natives appeared to communicate by "visual telepathy," by which he meant that they were able to transfer mental pictures to each other's minds, and had actually been able, though it was evidently a strain, to "talk" this way with humans. Lindell could now put the planet in the Unclassified category, and there was no predicting when it would get out of that category.

Fourth, the natives, communicating with Lindell, let it be known that they were agreeable to having the rest-and-refit center on the planet, providing they negotiated directly with the center's head man—who was Krojac.

Fifth, Krojac, gathering himself together after these jolts and surprises, went down to the planet and drove a bargain with the natives, who agreed to a reasonable rent, but flatly refused to allow permanent human settlement on the planet. Krojac, resorting to every subterfuge he could think of, managed to get the contract officially signed, with two tricky clauses in it.

Sixth, having got back up to his ship, Krojac began to plan how to use these clauses. At once, his ears began to ring, his hands and feet went numb, and everything went black.

The first time this happened, Krojac gave it up for a while. But he tried again. And again. With the same results.

The next day, Krojac tried once more. The same thing happened. He called Doyle on the screen, and Doyle was interested, but had no answer. Krojac decided he had enough delay, and went to work to plan in earnest exactly what to do. When the dizziness came, he didn't stop.

This time, the effect was brutally powerful. It was after that, that Krojac paced the floor, unwilling to let his followers see his pale shaken facial expression. And it was then that he got Reagan on the screen to go over what had happened the day before.

Finally, Reagan, who still knew nothing of Krojac's dizziness, said, "But look, Nels, you've saved the situation with that contract. The cats may not like it, but that's not *our* worry. If *they* stop the colonists, we can get the Space Force in on *our* side."

"There's a little catch." Krojac explained what had happened.

Reagan stared at him. "Then we're stopped again?"

"It looks like it. I can't *even think* of letting those clauses be invoked, or it hits me."

Reagan shook his head. "Then we're still in the same position as before. What is it—a jinx?"

"I don't know. But we've got to do *something*. Listen, I'll call you back in a little while. I've got to think."

Krojac shut off the screen. For a moment, he found himself struggling with a host of doubts. Had he made the move too soon? Wasn't he just a second-rate trying to puff himself up into a first-rate? Who was *he* to head the enterprise? Did he have, for instance, Reagan's financial know-how, or Sheaster's knowledge of people?

But the answers were right there. He had to move. It was now or never, because Reed & Osborne was moving in by calculated stages. As for whether he was first- or second-rate, he didn't have to think about that. The situation would answer that question. Any time he spent stewing over it would only influence the answer in the wrong direction. It was true that Reagan knew more about money, and Sheaster knew more about people—look how Sheaster had foreseen Doyle's reactions—but Krojac couldn't picture either of them at the head of the business.

Frowning, he wandered around the room as thoughts passed into and out of his field of consciousness. He thought about Sheaster, Doyle, Reed & Osborne, the creatures down on the planet, Reagan, the loans coming due, the colonists who would soon pass through here in a growing stream, and by some process of association, he was thinking of Sheaster's tycoon father, J. Harrison Sheaster.

"That kid of mine," the elder Sheaster had growled, "could make a hundred billion if he wanted to, but instead he thinks about *higher* things: The Law. But if that's what he's so interested in, I can't change it. The rule in business is— Get people what they want. That means you've first got to find out what they want, and second, find somebody to supply it. That's basic. Well, if the kid doesn't want it, isn't interested, I might as well save my breath. People think it's genius or will-power when somebody blasts his way to the top. They can't see that underneath it all, it's *interest*. Interest comes first."

The old man smiled. "*You* look interested. You know what's the best situation in business? When you find two separated sets of people, and each is interested in what the other can supply. Now, that's *compound* interest. You want to think about these things. The simple truths stand up when the hurricane sweeps away the fancy techniques. There are people who stand for the techniques, and *people who stand for the basic truths*. Without the first, you're in trouble. Without the second, you've got no foundation, nothing to tie to, and get swept along in the current. That's why sometimes the top people don't seem as slick as the people working for them. Think it over. Maybe someday you'll need this."

Now, in the big room with the huge control console at one end. Nels Krojac stood perfectly still, saw why he was running the business, and saw what his job had to be if they were going to win. Sheaster had used every legal technique to save them. Reagan had extended the financial techniques to the limit. Now he, Krojac, had to work on the basic elements of the situation. The words "trade," "interest," and "compound interest" occurred to him, and he began to analyze the situation.

Later that day, in one of the ship's powerful tenders, Krojac headed for the nearest subspace jump point that would take him far from Marshak III and its tiger-like inhabitants. At intervals along the trip, in and out of subspace, he tried to think of using the two misleading clauses of the contract. Each time, he felt dizzy, heard his ears begin to ring, and his vision fade. Each time, he stopped, and the symptoms slowly faded away. Finally he was satisfied. "It's built-in. Distance doesn't affect it. Now for the tricky part."

As soon as he got back, Krojac sent Reagan down to set up a meeting with the natives. Then, prayerfully, since everything was now balanced on the brink of disaster, Krojac went down himself.

That same day, the natives changed their stand.

Human settlers *could* move into Marshak III, but they could settle only in a large region convenient to the rest-and-refit base. This was exactly where Krojac needed them to make his immediate profit. He came back up to the ship exhausted but triumphant. Reagan and Sheaster looked at him with awe.

"That's just in time," said Reagan. "A couple days later and we'd have been finished. In fact, right this minute I can hear the corks popping and the champagne fizzing at Reed & Osborne."

Krojac sank into a chair. "The news will taste like vinegar."

Sheaster stared at Krojac. "You remind me of my father. They had him finished half-a-dozen times. But it never took. Each time, the ground moved around under their feet, and when it got through moving, he was in the clear."

"How," Reagan demanded, "did you ever persuade the locals to allow settlement?"

"I convinced them they could buy the land back later. This is a rest-and-refit center, and anyone can go farther out if he pays his fare to the government. Well, if the locals offer a settler enough, it's worth his while to move. Most settlers are convinced it's better farther on anyway."

"But wait a minute," said Reagan, scowling. "Where do the locals *get* this money? Their rent for the R and R site isn't going to cover it. Do we have to pay them some big—"

"We don't pay them anything. They pay their own way."

"What with? They've got no technology, no skills, no—"

"No skills?" said Krojac. He tossed across a sheaf of handwritten papers headed:

Marshak Contract Guaranty Corporation
Nels Krojac, Honorary President
Erkbat N. W. Marshak, President and
Chairman of the Board
Motto: *When we enforce it, they don't break it*
Moderate fees
Offices on principal planets

Sheaster snorted. "*Any* contract can be broken—or bent into a pretzel. Then it's up to the courts—" He paused in mid-sentence and stared at Krojac.

Reagan was saying. "'Erkbat N. W. Marshak.' Who's that?"

"A big thing like a tiger that looks into your eyes, and when you say you mean what you say you mean, he just gives a little nod, and you *better* mean it, because any time you plan to get around it by some clever stunt, your hands and feet go numb, your ears ring, your head swims, and everything goes black."

Sheaster whistled, and a look of amazed respect crossed his face.

Reagan stared into space. "A thing like that could make quite a simplification."

Sheaster looked at Krojac. "This was your idea, or theirs?"

"Mine. It's theirs now. I sold it to them, in return for *permission to settle the territory in convenient reach of the base.*"

Sheaster said dizzily, "So that gives *them* a source of income, with which they can buy back the homesteads that they now let *us* sell, so that we, in turn, have the money to pay the loans now due?"

"That's it."

Reagan said, "That puts us over the hump."

Sheaster said in admiration. "A stroke of pure genius."

Krojac shook his head. "The locals were interested in what I had to offer, and I was interested in what they had to offer." He looked at Sheaster. "Your father had a name for that."

Sheaster nodded. "He had names for a lot of things. I still call it genius."

Krojac was positive. "It wasn't."

"What *was* it, then?"

"Compound interest," said Krojac.

EXPERTS IN THE FIELD

Lieutenant Colonel Andrew Doyle glanced around from the crest of the natural amphitheater. In the distance, occasional groves of trees were scattered over the rolling grassland. Far off to his right, a dull metallic glint and a flash of dazzling sunlight told of the planetary-classification base near the wide slow-flowing river. Then he winced, and looked down into the big grassy bowl, where some two thousand large-browed tigerlike creatures, heads tilted back, created a shrieking torrent of noise that instantly set Doyle's teeth on edge, gave him chills and a dizzy sensation, and now and then seemed to set up answering vibrations in his very bones.

To Doyle's right, a tall pale man with a pipe in his hand winced at a high-pitched note that seemed to stop the universe, then sucked in a ragged breath, and gestured with the pipe stem.

"To your left, Colonel. See that group watching the machines? It's obvious they're talking. You can *see* they're talking."

About eighty feet away, a knot of angry felines, upright on their hind legs, with sinuously-twitching tails and glittering eyes, looked down the long outer slope at a fleet of big motionless earth-moving machines. Spread out in a thin line blocking these machines off from the hill were two squads of Doyle's troops, their guns unslung and expressions wary.

As Doyle glanced from the machines to the troops, then

back to the cluster of angry felines, one of the tigerlike creatures, his expression that of a man halfway through a string of profanity, balled one forepaw into a fist, and slammed it savagely into the other forepaw. Another feline pointed down the hill at one of the larger machines, his expression thoughtful, as if he were talking about the machine's function. The creatures' mouths were moving, and Doyle, though too far away to hear the words, had to admit that it certainly *looked* as if they were talking. But that was only one side of the question.

To Doyle's left stood an impatient group in goggles and coveralls, headed by a burly barrel-chested man with a big black cigar jutting from one corner of his mouth, who glanced impatiently at his watch, turned angrily toward Doyle, and suddenly picked up a tripod with a big cone set at an angle on top, and carried it over.

Doyle fought off the effects of the singing, and forced his dazed mind to yield up facts about the antagonistic sets of individuals who crowded the landscape.

The tall pale man gesturing with outthrust pipe was Al Lindell, head of the planetary-classification unit on the planet, which was known as Marshak III. Lindell, acting under Article 12 of Interservice Regulations, had called Doyle on the screen the day before, and angrily demanded that the Space Force intervene to "stop a planetary grab by Nels Krojac, before we get a war out of it."

Doyle had intently studied the face on the screen, to see a somewhat scholarly-looking man who was obviously boiling mad.

"A *war?*" said Doyle.

"That's right. A planetary war with the inhabitants of Marshak III."

"Who is causing the trouble?"

"Nels Krojac," said Lindell. "He's president of Interstellar Construction Corporation. He's landed a work crew here, before the planet is classified."

"You're calling on me to stop him by force?"

"I am. Under Article 12, I hereby formally request your aid to prevent exploitation of an unclassified and, in my opinion, potentially dangerous planet."

"Just a minute, Mr. Lindell." Doyle looked up. "Major Burke—"

A strongly built officer, standing by a three-dimensional display panel, speaking into a small hand microphone, turned to face Doyle.

"Sir?"

"Change squadron course for Marshak III. Maximum squadron acceleration. Condition Three."

"Yes, sir."

Doyle looked back at the screen.

"You say you expect *war* if the work crew isn't stopped?"

"I do. Experience tells me we're right on the edge of an ugly situation. I can't prove it. I can't even show proof why this planet shouldn't be classified in the A series. The dominant race is a large, obviously powerful and dangerous carnivore. But it has no visible technology or artifacts of any kind. To classify this planet as I think it should be classified, I have to show: a) advanced technological skills; b) complex social organization; c) a highly-developed language. I haven't been able to find so much as a stone ax on the planet, so I can't claim 'technological skills'; their 'social organization' is on about the level of the lion's, so *that* doesn't count; I know perfectly well that they communicate with each other, so it follows that they've got a highly-developed language—but my linguistic analysis experts insist the creatures only make 'simple repetitive sounds' when *I* know they're talking. But I'm not allowed to make a subjective judgement. Classification has to be based on objective facts."

"What makes you so sure the animals are dangerous?"

"These creatures—we call them Marcats—Marshak III Cats, that is—these Marcats are built a lot like tigers. You can't see them without knowing they're dangerous. But it goes beyond that. This planet has things on it that make *Tyrannosaurus rex* look like a lap dog. But they don't bother the Marcats. *Nothing* bothers the Marcats. If the Marcats feel like going for a stroll through a place thick with carnivorous monsters, why, they go for the stroll. And all the other carnivores come piling out in a hurry."

"What do you think will happen if the construction work isn't stopped?"

"There's going to be a sudden mess of trouble. The one known art form that the Marcats have is what you might call a . . . ah . . . well, 'community singing.' Hundreds of them get together from time to time, and have a . . . a concert, you might call it. The place where the local Marcats have this concert is at a natural amphitheater in low hills not too far from here. The Marcats like this place. In fact, I don't think it would be too much to say it's sacred ground with them. Well, Krojac Construction plans to level this natural amphitheater tomorrow, to start work on a centrally located Administration Complex for a big rest and refit center they're putting up for colonists using the main-trunk transport route that's going to go right past here."

"And you think the Marcats will retaliate?"

"I *know* they'll retaliate. All hell will break loose. But Krojac and his hired blockheads are so thick in the skull they think the Marcats are just a kind of big pussycat. Krojac figures to grab this planet, run up his big rest and refit complex on the ground and in orbit, and use the planet to get leverage on future out-bound commerce and construction in this sector. He made low bid on the R and R contract, and for his purposes this planet is ideal. The maddening thing about it is, I can't *prove* a thing. And I've only got one week till the mandatory deadline for planetary classification runs out. If I can't find some way to prove my point, I'll have to classify this planet A-10: 'Physical environment ideal; primitively dangerous biological entities.'"

Doyle said, "Wait a minute. Why can't you classify the planet as you think it should be classified?"

"Because I have to operate according to very strict rules. These rules were set up to eliminate the natural tendency of a planetary classification man to let his sympathies for the local life forms run away with him. There have been cases where human colonists were turned away because the classification team found the local race lovable, or didn't want the idyllic scenery disturbed. So to prevent false classifications, the rules are ironclad."

Doyle frowned. "So all I can do is to hold the crisis off for a week? Then you'll be forced to classify the planet A-10, Krojac Construction will move in, the Marcats will attack the construction teams, and I'll have to attack the Marcats?"

Lindell looked unhappy. "At worst, yes. But I'm still hoping to straighten this out. If I can prove the dominant local species has a highly-developed language, but has no developed technology or social structure, then we have an anomalous situation, which will justify me in classing the planet in the U series. I've sent for PDA's advanced new linguistics computer, the LC-10,000. If the LC-10,000 arrives here in time, I'm sure I can straighten out the whole thing. But I have got to keep Krojac Construction from touching off an explosion before the LC-10,000 gets here."

Doyle scowled. "Let's see if I have this straight. This LC-10,000 is a new *linguistics computer?*"

"Right. The LC-10,000 is the ultimate authority on language. It contains the sum total of all that humanity has ever learned about language. It knows, in absolute and perfect detail, everything about every known human and non-human language in the known universe. Its receptors are capable of picking up the finest and most complex sounds, of whatever loudness or pitch, without exception. And its micropicominiaturized directed-pulse quasi-fibril potential circuits, with their sextillions of switching elements cooled in baths of liquid helium—Well, if it's language, believe me, the LC-10,000 will recognize it in a flash. My troubles are over if I can just get the LC-10,000 here. And I've put the request in the strongest possible terms. But meanwhile, Colonel, I have to keep Krojac from leveling that amphitheater. That's the fuse on the bomb."

Doyle nodded. "I'll get in touch with Interstellar Construction."

Lindell looked worried.

"Look, Colonel, Krojac is a shrewd customer. He may say—"

Doyle shook his head. "It doesn't matter what he says. You've formally requested that he be prevented from starting construction work on an unclassified planet. You're head of the authorized PDA classification unit on the planet. Regulations state that I will enforce your ban on unauthorized activities on the planet. I will, therefore, enforce the ban. That's all there is to it."

Lindell looked relieved, thanked Doyle, and broke the connection.

Doyle got in touch with the headquarters ship of the Interstellar Construction Corporations. This turned out to be a gigantic self-contained globular office-building and nerve-center for Krojac Enterprises, Inc. A series of suavely-assured individuals informed Doyle that Mr. Krojac could not be disturbed at the moment, but that if he wished to request an appointment, it would be duly considered by Mr. Krojac's appointments secretary.

Doyle then sent a formal message warning that any construction or earth-moving work on the planet Marshak III had been banned by duly-constituted authority, and he, Doyle, would enforce the ban, using whatever degree of force was necessary.

The message had hardly gone out when a reply, couched in legal phraseology, with references to authorities of all degrees of obscurity, began to come in. This reply ran to sixty-two single-spaced pages, and neither Doyle nor any of his officers could either understand it as it stood, or break it down into anything they could understand.

Doyle promptly sent a second message, warning in tough language that his first message stood unchanged.

A call shortly came on the communicator, and a long-faced individual with lightly-oiled wavy hair introduced himself as "J. Hale Reagan, special consultant to Mr. Krojac." Holding by his thumb and forefinger two slips of yellow message paper, J. Hale Reagan looked at Doyle with slightly raised eyebrows and an expression around the nostrils as if he smelled rotten fish.

"I'm sorry to say, Mr. Doyle, that these messages of yours are quite unacceptable. I can scarcely believe that a person of your potential rank and attainments would choose to put himself on record in regard to Mr. Krojac in such a fashion."

As Doyle looked on, J. Hale Reagan, against a background of what appeared to be a cocktail party, with a well-known senator just behind his left shoulder, and a Space Force general a little farther back, slowly touched the flame of a cigarette lighter to the two yellow slips of paper, dropped them into an oversized ashtray, and looked pointedly at Doyle.

"I couldn't possibly forward such messages to the captain of this ship, and I most certainly will not waste Mr. Krojac's time with them. I think we'd better just forget all this."

Doyle found himself looking at an empty screen. He was in such a frame of mind that he didn't trust himself to do a thing for a minute-and-a-half.

Then he sent for copies of the two previous messages, and changing the wording just slightly, sent a third message that said the same thing.

Doyle's recently-appointed second-in-command, Major Hanford, had apparently witnessed the call to Doyle from J. Hale Reagan on a separate screen, and now said, frowning, "What will happen if Mr. Krojac and his people just ignore the warning?"

"Then I'll stop them by force."

"But I understand Interstellar Construction alone is worth eighty billions. Krojac is supposed to have friends at the top in Planetary Development Authority, the Space Force, and the Government itself. This business on Marshak must be important for him to be there in person. What will happen if he creates a situation where we have to kill him to stop him?"

"Then we'll kill him."

Hanford blinked. "I don't think it's that simple."

Doyle leaned forward, his expression alert. "What do you mean?"

Hanford hesitated, then said smoothly, "A man like Nels Krojac can do a lot to help or hinder an officer's progress in the service. This is plain realism."

Doyle stared at him. "I could find a better word for it than 'realism.'"

"Of course, what I mean—"

"The most polite word for it would be 'opportunism.'"

Hanford stiffened. "Look here. I must—"

"A more accurate word might be 'cowardice.'"

"Wait a—"

"But I think 'bribery' is probably the best word for it."

Doyle narrowly watched the succession of shades of color pass over Hanford's face. "How is it that you're so well informed about Mr. Krojac's finances, Major?"

"They're a matter of common knowledge."

"Probably they are, among the man's retainers. But how do *you* know?"

Hanford opened his mouth, and shut it again without saying anything.

Doyle said quietly, "Don't favor me with any more worldly wisdom. Just see to it that you obey orders."

"Yes, sir," said Hanford.

At that moment, the communicator buzzed, and a shrewd-looking individual, who introduced himself as a member of the Krojac Enterprises legal staff, put it to Doyle that on the basis of a careful study of the underlying intent of the relevant regulations, Article 12 could not be invoked.

Doyle disagreed flatly.

At once, a bluff friendly fellow named Root came on the screen and explained, man-to-man, that Interstellar Construction would be "over a barrel" if they couldn't start work the next day. "Nels signed the contract to care for these transient colonists on the clear understanding that the planet's classification would be favorable, and would be completed in good time. But this fellow Lindell is dragging the thing out to the limit, and now we've got definite reason to suspect that he's hooked in with S. and O. Enterprises, and is stringing this out just to make trouble. Why, the average planet would have been classified over eighteen months ago!"

Doyle listened patiently, then pointed to Article 12, which required him to back up Lindell.

Root explained that their legal counsel had found that Article 12 actually didn't apply.

Doyle quoted Article 12 verbatim, and it was obvious that it *did* apply. Root shrugged and stated that he was no lawyer.

When Doyle got through with Root, two of Interstellar Construction's legal staff came on the screen side-by-side at the same desk, and while one talked, the other studied Doyle's reaction. Speaking alternately, so that neither one actually committed himself, they put across the impression that a high-paying executive job awaited Doyle if he saw reason, while if he didn't, they would bring him to court on the charge that he had been bribed by a competitor. Moreover, any attempt to block Interstellar would fail. If necessary, Nels Krojac himself would lead his men to work, and the Space Force would never dare try to stop such a prominent, highly-placed man. Moreover, the only way to stop Mr. Krojac and his men would be to fire on them, and the Space Force would scarcely fire on unarmed humans.

Doyle stated coldly that it was his duty to enforce Article 12, and he would enforce it.

Another call came in immediately. A former Space Force officer smiled from the screen, and, in the guise of friendly disagreement with Doyle's interpretation of Article 12, got across a clear picture of just how well Nels Krojac could reward a man who got him out of a tough spot. While this was going on, Doyle scribbled a note to his communications officer, who announced, when the next call came in, that Squadron 2337 was now moving into a potential war zone and would henceforth maintain complete communicator silence.

By now, the routine report of the situation to Space Force Headquarters had been routinely acknowledged, and initial plans had been made for what *should* be a simple routine operation. But by now, Doyle was none too sure there would be anything simple or routine about it.

The next day found Squadron 2337 off Marshak III, where an enormous globular ship followed the movements of the squadron with large fusion guns mounted in multiple turrets. An earlier call to Lindell had brought the information that Interstellar Construction was bringing down heavy earthmoving equipment, and showed no sign of paying the slightest attention to Doyle's warning. When Doyle's communications officer tried to contact the big Interstellar Construction ship, there was no response. About this time, a second ship appeared, orbiting the planet, with its guns swinging around to bear on the squadron.

Doyle, at the command console, briefly studied the screen, then hit a number of communicator studs.

"Gunnery officer: Destroy at once every gun that bears on the squadron. Communications officer: Order those ships to answer our call at once or be attacked as planetary raiders. *Vulcan*: Sow your heavy implant missiles for convergent attack on the larger of those two ships. *Ranger*: Sow your heavy implant missiles for parallel attack on the smaller of those two ships. *Minotaur*: Go down on Marshak III and set up defense of the PDA base against air or surface attack."

As Doyle spoke, before him on the screen, the brilliant lines lanced out, the two attack-ships swung rapidly apart, and the armed transport dipped toward the planet. On the big globular ship, one of the guns glowed white in answer, and abruptly the whole section around that turret flared red, then white, and puffed out in shreds. All over the huge ship, there suddenly were dazzling spots of glowing red.

"Gunnery officer speaking, sir. All turrets bearing on the

squadron have been burnt out. Minor resistance from the larger ship only, sir. No damage to the squadron."

"Good work," said Doyle. "If either of those ships turns to present undamaged turrets, destroy the turrets at once."

"Yes, sir."

"*Vulcan* C.O. speaking, sir. Heavy implant missiles sowed for convergent attack."

"Implant your missiles."

"Yes, sir."

An instant later, the communications officer spoke up. "Sir, we have the captain of the Krojac *Empire* on the screen."

"Put him on the auxiliary screen."

A small screen to one side flared to life, and a slightly puffy man in a uniform covered with insignia, decorations, and gold braid cried out in mingled anger and disbelief. "Are you insane? Mr. Krojac will—"

From a separate speaker came a clear competent voice. "*Vulcan* C.O. speaking, sir. Heavy missiles implanted. The central section apparently contains an armored citadel. The rest is *el punko junko*. Shall we detonate, sir?"

"In ten minutes detonate all implanted missiles unless countermanded."

"Yes, sir. Detonate all implanted missiles in ten minutes unless countermanded."

On the small screen, the captain of the Krojac *Empire* cried out, "Good God! *What are you doing?*"

"Your ship has been implanted with heavy missiles, which will be detonated unless I countermand the order."

From a separate speaker came another quiet competent voice:

"*Ranger* C.O. speaking, sir. Heavy implant missiles sowed for parallel attack."

"Implant your missiles."

"Yes, sir."

On the small screen, the puffy face above the braid-encrusted uniform suddenly vanished. In its place appeared a broad-shouldered man with dark hair, massive chest, and hard blue eyes, wearing a dark dressing gown with a dragon design on the chest. He looked intently at Doyle, then suddenly grinned. "Tough, aren't you?"

Doyle said coldly, "You have a little under eight minutes till the implants detonate."

A clear voice spoke from a separate speaker.

"*Ranger* C.O. speaking, sir. Heavy missiles implanted. No armor on this ship, sir. Shall we detonate?"

Doyle glanced at a small round clock face where two long thin hands swung steadily around the dial.

"In seven minutes and fifty seconds detonate if not countermanded."

"Yes, sir. Detonate in seven minutes and fifty seconds if not countermanded."

Another voice spoke.

"Communications, sir. We have the captain of the *Star Chaser*—that's the smallest ship. He wants to surrender his ship at once, sir."

"Good enough. Tell him to disarm his men, assemble them in the entrance corridor, lock his undamaged turrets, and stand by for boarding."

"Yes, sir."

Doyle touched one of the switches on the console.

"*Ranger.*"

"Sir?"

"Countermand detonation order. Board, secure crew, and seize. That smaller ship has identified itself as the *Star Chaser*, its captain offers to surrender, and I have accepted. He is to disarm his men, assemble them in the entrance corridor, lock his undamaged turrets, and stand by for boarding."

"Yes, sir. Countermand detonation. Board, secure crew, and seize."

From the auxiliary screen, the hard-eyed attentive face looked out alertly. "You're making a mistake, Colonel. For less than this, I've had guys like you put on the Bemus asteroid census for years."

"You have six minutes and forty seconds until detonation."

"You wouldn't dare detonate."

"Detonation is fully automatic unless countermanded, first by my verbal order, second by action of the missile-officer in immediate command. Countermanding takes time. But there is no question of not daring to detonate. Everything so far has been pure routine, and detonation will be the same."

"You'd be hung from the rafters."

"Visual records will show the menacing attitude of both the *Star Chaser* and the Krojac *Empire,* if these are actually the ships' names. Granting this and other circumstances, I am fully justified in regarding either or both ships as planetary raiders or worse. Detonation will blow your ship into vaporized fragments. If there is an armored central citadel capable of surviving the initial explosion—and it is very doubtful that anyone inside will be alive after detonation—that citadel itself will be destroyed at once by concentrated missile and fusion attack. You have five minutes and fifty-six seconds until detonation."

"And suppose I decide to ignore this whole silly business?"

"You will be destroyed."

There was a silence that lasted several seconds as the hard blue eyes looked steadily at Doyle and Doyle looked steadily back.

Then Nels Krojac laughed. His image vanished from the screen, and after a moment the braid-encrusted captain reappeared.

"Mr. Krojac orders me to yield this ship for your inspection, to provide you with any necessary papers or information, and to satisfy any reasonable demand on your part to convince you that we are not planetary raiders. The ship is not surrendered, however; Mr. Krojac is *not* to be disturbed; and the operation of his business offices is to be disturbed as little as possible, on pain of punitive legal measures."

"I won't accept restraints on examining the ship."

The captain blinked. "Then I'm not authorized to proceed."

Doyle touched a stud on the console.

"Gunnery officer."

"Sir?"

"Count off the minutes and half-minutes till detonation of that larger ship."

"Yes, sir. Just a moment, sir. Five minutes until detonation."

The captain of the Krojac *Empire* said nothing, but the sweat rolled down his face as he stared at Doyle.

The gunnery officer spoke:

"Four minutes and thirty seconds until detonation."

The Krojac *Empire*'s captain thrust out his jaw.

"Four minutes until detonation.

"Three minutes and thirty seconds until detonation.

"Three minutes until detonation.

"Two minutes and thirty seconds until detonation.

"Two minutes until detonation.

"One minute and thirty seconds until detonation.

"One minute until detonation."

Doyle watched the second hand sweep for the last time around the dial. It was now clearly apparent that the Krojac *Empire* was no raider. When the hand reached "30," Doyle would, therefore, countermand detonation and order a boarding.

At "45" the Krojac *Empire*'s captain moistened his lips. Suddenly he blurted, *"I surrender this ship!"*

Doyle touched a stud on the console.

"Vulcan."

"Yes, sir?"

"Countermand detonation."

"Yes, sir. Detonation countermanded, sir."

"Board that larger ship with a fully-armed search party, determine the identity of the ship with certainty, and examine the ship throughout for any sign that it is a planetary raider."

"Yes, sir. Board, determine identity, and search to see if the ship is a planetary raider."

"The captain has surrendered the ship, and you can make any temporary arrangements with him that seem suitable."

"Yes, sir."

On the auxiliary screen, the hard features of Nels Krojac reappeared, to study Doyle coldly. Doyle broke the connection, and glanced at the main screen. The armed transport had disappeared from direct view, but a green symbol showed its approximate location.

"Minotaur."

"Sir?"

"What's your position?"

"We're at twenty thousand seven hundred feet above the planet, sir, dropping toward the PDA classification-unit base. No trouble so far, sir."

"Good. Let me know when you're set up."

"Yes, sir."

Doyle touched another stud on the console.

A voice said promptly, "Communications, sir."

"Get the PDA classification-unit on the screen."

"Yes, sir."

Lindell appeared on the screen. "You got here just in time, Colonel. The work gangs are moving their machinery into place right now."

"You mean there's been no change in Krojac's schedule?"

"Not by a hair."

"I see," said Doyle. "Well, I'll put troops down to stop them."

"Fine. That's a relief."

"Have you had any word on your language-computer?"

Lindell beamed. "Yes. The LC-10,000 will be here tomorrow. So the situation is well in hand. This is really the ultimate linguistics computer, and it will extract the linguistics elements from the welter of noise that has my experts baffled. Our trouble, you see, is that the Marcats produce much sound that is . . . ah . . . somewhat at a tangent to what we're interested in. Their art form of vocal singing, for instance, runs largely in the range of 2,000 to 50,000 cycles. Since an acute human ear can detect loud sounds of roughly 30 to 20,000 cycles, you can see that we have some cause for confusion."

"I can see you have considerable cause for *discomfort*. But what's confusing about it? Would aliens speak the same way we do?"

Lindell changed expression. "This is quite a technical matter, Colonel."

Doyle was unconvinced, but nodded. "Incidentally, could you send me the survey and evaluation reports on this planet?"

"I'm afraid they're highly technical, and—"

"I'm not talking about the *linguistics* reports. I'm talking about general reports on how the Marcats live, their planetary distribution, numbers, characteristics, habits, size, weight, and so on. Remember, you've expressed the opinion that we may wind up in a *war* here."

Lindell's face cleared. "You don't want the linguistics reports?"

"I'm perfectly content to leave that to you."

"All right. I'll see that you get copies of the rest."

The *Minotaur* shortly set down on the planet, and Doyle had troops sent out at once to stop the work crews. A savage argument followed, in which the earth-moving machines were stopped only when the troops opened fire.

Then the reports on the planet began to come in.

Doyle gradually built up a mental picture of big-browed tigerlike creatures that roamed the planet like lords of creation, lived in dens or burrows lined with dried grass, could be found in nearly any type of terrain on the planet, and everywhere were left strictly unmolested by the monster carnivores that roamed the globe. Pictures showed grown tigerlike Marcats upright on their hind legs, strolling casually along over rolling fields and hills, obviously deep in conversation, as younger Marcats gamboled and played around them on all fours, bounded up trees, and chased rabbit-like creatures that went twenty feet at a bound. Meanwhile huge beasts with teeth like broadswords slunk out of sight, or bolted for the horizon at top speed.

After watching enough of these scenes, Doyle gradually came to the conclusion that Lindell was right. The Marcats *were* intelligent, *did* talk, and *were* more formidable than their teeth and claws suggested. Though how, remained a good question.

One visual record particularly impressed Doyle. It showed a creature like *Tyrannosaurus rex* that blundered out into the path of a strolling Marcat. The Marcat gave it one hard look, the big carnivore collapsed and lay motionless, apparently dead. Now, did the creature suffer a heart attack at the mere sight of the Marcat, or what *did* happen? But the closest examination of the scene showed Doyle nothing whatever to answer the question.

Other scenes showed savage fights, between the Marcats themselves; in these fights no Marcat dropped from a hard look. The fight was with fang and claw, and the scene was thick with blood and flying tufts of fur. But then, human beings used weapons against alien attackers that they hesitated to use on each other.

As Doyle wrestled with the problem, to wind up in the same frame of mind as Lindell, word came that the LC-10,000 had arrived, and would carry out its test shortly.

Doyle went down on the planet, found himself deafened by music like harmonizing bandsaws, while a group of angry Marcats glared at the earth-moving machines, and Al Lindell earnestly assured him that the Marcats *did* talk. Then the

burly man with jutting cigar angrily carried over a tripod
with cone on top, putting it down so hard that the tripod's
pointed feet sank out of sight in the ground.

"There, Colonel. Now, take these earphones, listen to them
yourself, and see if *you* think they talk!"

Doyle looked around, to see coming up the hill behind
him a huge glittering ovoid covered with outthrust horn-
like devices, and drifting along on antigravs beside a tall
individual wearing thick glasses, a long laboratory coat, and
the dignity of a high priest.

Doyle winced as the Marcats hit another jarring note, then
he put on the earphones, and swung the wide end of the
cone toward the coveralled humans. He heard a blast of
sizzling profanity, turned the device toward some Marcats,
who were obviously deep in conversation, and then stood
paralyzed at the sounds that came through the earphones.
They were complex sounds, but certain dominant notes stood
out:

"Quack-quack, quack-quack, quack-quack."

"Peep-peep-peep-peep-peep-peep."

"Oink, oink, oink, oink, oink."

"Whoo-oo. Who-oo. Who-oo."

The sounds were unvarying, repetitious, with far less
expression than two chickens clucking in a henyard. Unless
the part that counted was up above the human range of
hearing, no one in his right senses could think of it as
"conversation." Dumbfounded, Doyle took off the earphones.
Now it was obvious that the Marcats *were* talking. He put
the earphones on. Now it was obvious that they *weren't*
talking.

Doyle took the phones off, and looked around.

Down in the natural amphitheater, there came a sudden silence. The Marcats rose, stretched, some leaning forward, tails in the air and claws bunched in the turf, others
erect, with big furry forepaws flexed and showing muscles.
Then the creatures turned to each other, like theatergoers
during an intermission, and began to *talk*, forearms across
each other's shoulders, gesturing occasionally, grinning,
prodding each other in the ribs, and waving to mutual
acquaintances. The babble was terrific, deafening. But to
Doyle's newly-educated ear, it had a monotonous, meaningless sound.

He stepped forward, to listen to an animated group in front of him. Their voices came across clearly.

"Erkbat. Erkbat. Erkbat. Erkbat."

"Cluck-cluck. Cluck-cluck. Cluck-cluck. Cluck-cluck . . ."

"Boomity-boomity-boomity-boomity. Boomity—"

Doyle stepped back. No wonder Lindell hadn't wanted to hand over the records of the language analysis. It wasn't that they were too technical to understand. It was that they were so obvious no one could help but understand.

Just now, not far away to Doyle's right, the impressive glittering bulk of the LC-10,000 made it to the brow of the hill, and its multitude of outthrust horns at once swung around and aimed in various directions into and around the amphitheater. Beside it, Lindell was speaking earnestly to the tall lab-coated official who accompanied the computer.

"Is this," Lindell was saying anxiously, "a sufficient sample?"

"Amply sufficient."

"Ah . . . there's no chance of the computer . . . ah . . . making a mistaken—"

"The LC-10,000 does not make mistakes."

"But if there are *very high-pitched* sounds—"

"They would be detected."

"There may be signals of some kind—"

"The LC-10,000 is designed to detect sonic signals of *whatever* character."

"I see. Well then, it *ought* to be all right."

"The LC-10,000," said the lab-coated figure severely, "is a computer designed by computers for six generations back."

Lindell looked awed. "I hadn't realized that."

Time passed. The horns swung around to new positions.

Finally the technician glanced around. "The ready-light flashed. The analysis is complete."

There was a sound of tearing paper.

"The LC-10,000 finds that there is no language here, at *whatever* frequency or on *whatever* level. The LC-10,000 has analyzed the totality of vocal sounds, and these are 'simple repetitive syllables.' That is all."

"But—Good God, man!" cried Lindell. "Look at them yourself!"

"That is a purely subjective attitude. I certainly will not take part in any display of childish anthropomorphism."

The impressive bulk of the LC-10,000 turned ponderously to aim itself down the hill.

Lindell said, "If you'll just try again—"

The LC-10,000 specialist spoke pityingly. "Try to compose yourself, Dr. Lindell. Really, your attitude is irrational. The LC-10,000 is *the ultimate authority on language.* You have put the question, and the LC-10,000 has answered it. Now let's try to be scientific about this. Total vocal analysis reveals no meaningful patterns capable of conveying intelligence, except . . . let's see here . . . this means—Each of these creatures, during the test period, made *its own specific sound.* Conceivably, if the creatures couldn't recognize each other by sight, this could convey the identity of the individual speaking. But believe me, it conveys nothing else. Now then, if there were the slightest indication of really meaningful vocal exchange, I would be only too glad to track it down for you. But there is *none whatever.* If you are so firmly convinced that these creatures have a language, let me suggest that you look for it in the area of visual or tactile signals—"

"We've already tried that," said Lindell moodily.

"Then I'm sorry. Our schedule is crowded. Good day."

The LC-10,000 moved off down the hill, and Lindell turned dazedly to look at the Marcats. Not twenty feet from where Lindell stood, one Marcat banged another on the back as both grinned. The lips of a third Marcat moved, and the other two at once turned to him, then looked simultaneously across the amphitheater at something on the other side. Their lips moved briefly, and all three started off together.

Doyle watched the scene in exasperation. *Obviously* the Marcats were talking. But every time the matter came down to factual details, they *weren't* talking.

To Doyle's left, an exasperated voice said, "How about it? We're going to flatten this place now or the end of the week, one or the other." The way he said it, Doyle got a clear mental picture of the amphitheater converted into a smooth flat mass of fresh dirt.

For a moment, there was a peculiar sense of strain in the air, as if the fabric of things momentarily threatened to come apart.

Doyle glanced along the top of the slope, and there, some eighty feet away, the Marcats who'd been watching the earth-moving machines were now looking at him intently. Doyle looked absently back, asking himself how these creatures conveyed information, and why on earth they should make the simple repetitive noise the LC-10,000 referred to. Why should they want to identify themselves, unless they had something to say?

Suddenly Doyle caught his breath. He walked toward the Marcats, who watched him come with what obviously were puzzled frowns, looks of faint uneasiness, and hints and suggestions of belligerent self-assertion and even menace. Doyle picked the most dominant-appearing Marcat and looked him in the eye. The Marcat seemed surprised, but looked back steadily.

Doyle cleared his throat, forced down his feeling of foolishness, and spoke in a monotonous repetitive tone. "Doyle, Doyle, Doyle, Doyle, Doyle, Doyle, Doyle, Doyle . . ."

The Marcat blinked. "Akran, akran, akran, akran, akran, akran, akran, akran . . ."

Lindell walked over to speak to Doyle, then glanced from Doyle to the Marcat in astonishment.

Doyle formed a clear mental picture of the creature in front of him extending his right paw, and holding this picture in mind, Doyle went on, "Doyle, Doyle, Doyle, Doyle, Doyle. . . ."

For a long moment, nothing happened, then the Marcat slowly stretched out his right paw. And Doyle had a fuzzy mental picture of a human being stretching his arms overhead.

Doyle stretched his arms overhead.

The Marcat beamed in delight, and immediately reached out as if to bang Doyle on the back. Doyle moved fast to stay out of the hospital. Quickly, Doyle formed a mental picture of an inert uniformed figure being helped away by other humans.

The Marcat winced, and Doyle had a mental picture of a dejected tigerlike figure with its head in its paws.

Doyle now created a mental picture of the huge tyrannosaurus-like creature he had seen in the visual records. Next he pictured a Marcat. Straining his powers of visualization to the limit, he pictured the Marcat looking up at the tyrannosaur, which suddenly dropped. Doyle repeated this over and over again.

The group of Marcats watched with interest as the one directly in front of Doyle ran his paw along the back of his neck, eyed the sky, looked down the hill, and spotted a rabbit-like creature, that suddenly dropped flat and lay motionless. In Doyle's mind, there formed a picture of the animal's head, then of a brain, then of a net of interconnected nerve cells that changed color and texture. At the same time, he had a mental picture of a tree limb with, at first, one bird sitting on, then two birds, then a flock of birds sitting on it. At the same moment that he saw the nerve cells change color and texture, he also saw the tree limb break. The mental picture faded out, and the reiterated murmur of "Akran, akran" stopped a moment later.

Doyle nodded. The Marcat seemed to understand this gesture. Then his face took on an angry look, and as he began to speak, Doyle got a clear mental picture of the Marcats' amphitheater flattened into a mass of compacted dirt. The Marcat waited with an angry questioning look.

Doyle shook his head, and painstakingly pictured the earth-moving machinery going off the planet. He concentrated so hard on this that he forgot for a moment to repeat his name, but this didn't seem to trouble the Marcat. It beamed, turned to the others, and there was one chaotic moment of babble, then the lot of them were banging each other on the back.

Lindell, watching with a look of desperation, burst out, "Doyle, what in space is going on here? I can *see* you talking to them. But all you say is 'Doyle, Doyle, Doyle, Doyle.' What is this, anyway?"

"I wouldn't claim to have the last word on it, but it looks to me as if you've got a bunch of visual telepaths here."

Lindell looked at them.

"But . . . in that case . . . why do they use their voices at all?"

"Because there's one thing a telepath needs to know as much as anyone else."

"What do you mean?"

"He needs to know *who's talking*. And how is he going to know that just by seeing a picture form in his mind?"

"Then all that repetitious chatter is just—*recognition signals!* Good Lord! No wonder we couldn't figure it out!" Lindell paused as a new aspect occurred to him. He looked at Doyle in amazement. "But if *they're* visual telepaths, and *you* were able to communicate with them . . . then you—"

Doyle shook his head. "That doesn't make me much of a telepath. It just means they're powerful enough to put an image in my mind, and sensitive enough to detect what I'm trying to get across, once they realize—from my repeating my recognition signal—what I'm trying to do."

Lindell nodded. "Yes, I see. And now we've got a way to get across to them, we can rig up a test to prove objectively that they communicate. Then I can classify this planet the way it *should* be classified."

Doyle, worn out, went back to his ship, congratulating himself that he wouldn't have to fight a war with telepathic entities that could kill at an unspecified range by overloading a man's brain circuits.

He was starting to feel like himself again when a call came in from Nels Krojac. Krojac's expression was a little hard to decipher. There was anger in it, plus triumph, and something else that was hard to place.

"Say, Doyle," said Krojac. "I've got a little problem."

"What?" said Doyle warily.

"Lindell got the situation across to the cats down there, and they put it to him that having the R and R center here is O.K., so long as *they* pick the spot. But first, I was supposed to 'talk' to them myself. Well, they gave me a pretty hard looking over, and I got kind of a funny feeling in the head. And . . . ah . . . this contract I made out. It's got a couple of jokers in it. Now every time I start to plan when to spring the trap, the room goes black, I get a ringing in my ears, my hands and feet go numb, and I get a funny swimming sensation. Do you figure this means what I think it might mean?"

"I know one thing. If I were you, I'd spring no legal surprises on them."

"Yeah. Well—How far do you suppose this effect reaches out?"

"You have the unique opportunity to find the answer to that, yourself."

Krojac nodded thoughtfully. "O.K. Thanks, Doyle. If you ever get sick of traveling third class in the Space Force, drop around. I can always use a man with brains and guts. Forty thousand to start."

"Thanks," said Doyle. "If I ever get sacked, I'll think of it."

Krojac grinned and broke the connection.

A little later, Lindell was on the screen.

"I wanted to thank you, Colonel. I was so surprised earlier that I didn't even think to thank you. But now, there's one other thing about this that leaves me dumbfounded."

"What's that?"

"How could you find such a difficult, out-of-the-way answer to this when everyone else failed, including all my experts, and even the LC-10,000 itself—the greatest and most infallible expert in the entire field?"

Doyle laughed. "I had an unseen advantage, Dr. Lindell."

Lindell blinked. "What was that?"

"Everyone else was an expert-in-the-field. But the answer *wasn't in the field*. And that's a situation where a rank amateur has all the advantage. He can look *outside* the field, where the answer *is*."

THE HUNCH

Stellar Scout James Connely and Sector Chief of Scouts Gregory MacIntyre eyed each other with mutual suspicion. Connely, his blood pressure already well above normal, could see that this latest meeting was going to develop along the lines of those that had gone before.

"Look, Mac," said Connely, "my ship's fine. I'm fine. I don't need anything re-equipped. Spare me the new improvements and just let me know—What's the job this time?"

MacIntyre, a powerfully-built man with heavy brows and light-blue eyes of unusual brilliance, watched Connely with that look of alert concentration seen on bullfighters, duelists, and cats springing for mice.

"This isn't the usual scout job," said MacIntyre emphatically. "We've sent out two ships four months apart, and heard nothing more from either. Obviously they came up against something that outclassed them."

MacIntyre gestured at the new and weird devices that sat on tables and chairs around the room. "We flatly will not let you go out half-equipped. This job is risky."

Connely looked at the new equipment with no enthusiasm, and jerked a thumb in the direction of his ship, "Look, I can already outfight any ordinary ship up to twice the weight of my own. I keep away from territory infested with commerce raiders. If I do get surprised, my ship's as fast as they come. If I have to, I can even outrun the Space Force."

MacIntyre snorted. "The Space Force. Who cares about

347

1

8

48* Christopher Anvil*

them? When they aren't hide-bound, they're budget-bound. I hate to hear an Stellar Scout measure himself by the Space Force."

"Mac," said Connely, lowering his voice with an effort, "it took me six months to figure out that last batch of new equipment you put in the ship. Some of that stuff is fine, and some of it's poison. Now that I know which is which, *leave it alone.*"

MacIntyre visibly controlled himself. "Why don't we at least try to be logical about this, Con?"

"Sure. Go ahead."

"All right. Now, look. These two ships I've mentioned went out on the same route you're going to take. They weren't heard from again. They had more advanced equipment than your ship has. *And yet they were lost.*"

"So, you think I should have the same equipment they had, eh?"

"Oh, no, Con." MacIntyre looked shocked. "That's the whole point. We've got *better* equipment, now, and you've got to have it."

"Where were these two ships headed?"

MacIntyre snapped on a three-dimensional stellar projection and pointed out a distant sun-system.

Connely scowled. "The shortest route there is thick with Maury's commerce raiders. That's the worst gang there is. Maury's got a reconverted dreadnought."

"I know," said MacIntyre. He touched a button, and a complex set of lines appeared in the projection, showing a series of awkward roundabout jumps to detour the dangerous territory.

Connely scowled at the long route. "Damn and blast commerce raiders."

MacIntyre nodded, "With the Space Force tied up in that sector, they crop up like toadstools. But there they are and we have to face it." He snapped a switch, and the projection faded out. "You noticed how complex the detour was? That makes it extra hard to know where the trouble happened. But at least it is obvious that it happened *en route.* As soon as either of those scouts reached his destination, he'd have orbited a signal satellite. The satellite has an automatic trip that triggers a subspace emergency call if it's not canceled every twelve hours. No call has been received. Now, we have no knowledge of any-thing *natural* along these routes that would finish off two ships four months apart. Therefore, we're up against something manmade."

"An undeclared commerce-raider preying on the second-ary routes?"

"Most likely," said MacIntyre. "You see how we arrive at this conclusion by simple logic. But let's go further. If the other two ships were lost because of inferior speed or weapons, what we have to do to prevent *your* loss is to remove the inferiority. Therefore, your ship needs to be re-equipped. Q.E.D."

Connely opened his mouth and shut it.

MacIntyre beamed. "All right, Con?" He reached for the work-order.

"No," said Connely. He struggled for an explanation of his own viewpoint and finally said, "The thing doesn't feel right to me, Mac. I've got a hunch the equipment caused the trouble."

MacIntyre's face changed expression several times. As if tasting the sentence, he growled, "I've got a *hunch.*" He nodded his head in disgust and got up. "Well, Con, don't say I didn't warn you." He started for the door, and paused with his hand on the knob. "If you want your mail, inci-dentally, it's in the top drawer on the left." When he went out, he slammed the door so hard that a badly-balanced piece of equipment slid off a chair, gave a low whistling sound, and lit up in green lights.

Connely blew his breath out and glanced around suspi-ciously. It was not like MacIntyre to give up without a knock-down, drag-out fight. Puzzled, Connely crossed to MacIntyre's desk and reached down to pull open the drawer.

The faint sound from the device that had slid off the chair rose to a howl the instant Connely touched the drawer handle. The lights on the device all flashed yellow. A thing like a miniature gun popped out of a turret, and gave a high-pitched whistle with a weird variation that riveted Connely's attention. Then bubbles seemed to be bursting in the air all around him. He was conscious of a faint sweetish odor, and of a sensation that he was falling in a long, long, seemingly endless fall.

✣   ✣   ✣

Connely opened his eyes, to see before him the control board of his ship. Glancing around, he saw a number of changes. On a bulkhead to his left, the meteor-warning gong had been ripped out, and a new panel installed. The panel was covered with toggle switches and pink, green, and flashing yellow lights. Hanging from one of the switches near the bottom of the panel was a note:

> *Con:*
> *Sorry you got into a disagreement with one of our new items of equipment. But that's life.*
> *As you'll notice, I've re-equipped your ship from end to end. You've even been outfitted with our new reflex helmet and clothing. The instructions for everything but the clothing are attached to the pieces of equipment they refer to. Knowing your violent temper, I've decided to put the instructions for the clothing where you won't be likely to tear them up in an outburst of rage. Check the other equipment, and you'll find the instructions for your garments, too.*
> *You'll notice that your course has been all taped and set up in the new-type course control. Keep your eyes open, make the best use of your new equipment, and perhaps you'll succeed where the men before you failed.*
> *As for your mail—you couldn't read it while you were here, and you'd be distracted if you read it out there— so I will hold it against your return.*
> *All the best,*
> *Mac*

Connely stared at the note, then nodded sourly. Mac had done it again. Now it would be Connely's job to stay alive in a ship crammed with new equipment just one jump out of the experimental stage. Connely bent, raised an edge of his non-regulation gray carpet, and dropped the note underneath for future reference. He scowled at the new panel with its colored lights, and saw a slim brown envelope hanging beside the cabinet and marked, "Instructions."

Connely took down the envelope, glanced over several sheets of instructions and diagrams, and found that the panel was a supplementary control box for various new devices installed all over the ship—such of them as were not purely automatic. From this panel, Connely worked his way slowly toward the rear of the ship. He found numerous changes. The already strong frame had been reinforced by heavy cross-members that angled through the ship, half-blocking the corridors. Everything metal had a peculiar gloss that refused to dent under the roughest treatment Connely dared to give it.

A variety of new weapons had been installed, including one whose thick instruction manual asserted that it fired "holes." Each piece of equipment had its own weighty instruction manual, and the combined mass of information presented in these manuals made Connely feel dizzy.

After he'd glanced through an unusually complicated manual, Connely paused to scratch his head. He immediately felt as if someone had placed a hand on top of his head and given a sharp twist. There was a low *whir,* his vision cut off, and something gave his hand a painful whack.

Then something spun across his face, and Connely's vision returned.

Cautiously, he raised his hand and felt the slick glossy surface of some kind of helmet. As long as he felt along the surface of the helmet, nothing happened. As soon as he tried to touch his face, however, the helmet spun around, giving his head a sharp twist in the process, and knocked his hand out of the way. This, Connely realized, must be the "reflex helmet" MacIntyre had mentioned in his note. Connely tried to get hold of the edge of the helmet to take it off, but whenever his hand approached the edge, the helmet swiveled rapidly, to knock his hand away.

This, Connely conceded, might be a very fine defense if someone was trying to smash his face in with a club. But how did he get out of the thing, anyway?

A few minutes of neck-wrenching experiments convinced him that the quickest way would be to locate the instructions. But he had by now worked his way back almost to the drive unit, and he had seen nothing of the instructions so far. He pulled open the door of the drive chamber, looked inside, and swallowed hard. The old drive was gone, and in its place sat a monstrous unit of such dimensions that special handholds had been installed to make it possible to climb back around it. Gradually it dawned on Connely that the new drive unit took up so much space that it actually projected forward into the place formerly occupied by the fuel tanks. In order to fit the drive unit in, the fuel tanks had been ripped out. Connely blinked, and glanced all around. *Where was the fuel?*

He climbed into the drive chamber, looked around, climbed up and around past a number of blocky projections, and eventually located a container not much bigger than a foot-locker, that was surrounded by big coils and a complicated arrangement of braces, wires, and tubes. This was such a formidable-looking thing that Connely was careful not to even touch it. He crouched in the narrow space between the tank—if that was what it was—and a projecting bulge on the drive unit. He reached carefully in without touching the maze of wires and tubes and got the instruction manual dangling behind it. Sure enough, the manual was labeled, "Fuel Tank M81-x, Service and Operating Instructions."

Scowling, Connely flipped back past diagrams and data tables, and was relieved to find a summary at the end. He skimmed it rapidly, then slowed as he came to a section that read:

" . . . the tank, therefore, 'contains' only the head end of each keyed chain of packed fuel molecules. The remainder of each chain is selectively distorted into subspace. This allows for a very great reduction in the size of the fuel tank. It is, however, MOST IMPORTANT that no interruption in the action of the subspace-control unit be permitted to take place. Should such interruption occur, the normal volume of the molecules, no longer distorted into subspace, will attempt to fill the tank. The tank, of course, cannot possibly contain this volume of fuel. It will, therefore, burst. The outsurge of fuel, no longer molecularly oriented, and removed from contact with the negative catalyst layers of tank and fuel lines, will explode. As no part of the ship can possibly survive the release of such quantities of energy, it is strongly recommended that the preventive maintenance procedures in this manual be thoroughly understood BEFORE the tank is filled."

Connely swallowed, shut the manual, and started to get up. The back of his head bumped the bulge on the drive unit. He slouched a little to avoid banging into the drive unit again, and as he did so he came close to one of a number of copper-colored tubes that angled up from the

tank to the drive unit. There was a whir, a twist at the
top of his head, and his vision cut off. Alarmed, he tried
to ease himself back to a sitting position. There was
another sharp twist, as the helmet spun around again. He
had a momentary glimpse of blurred light, then *Bang!*—
the edge of the helmet hit the drive unit and knocked his
head forward. Immediately there was another whir and
another twist.

Whack! Bang!

Bathed in sweat, Connely dropped to a sitting position
on the metal deck, and sat as motionless as he could.
The helmet came to a stop. He drew in a shaking breath
and looked around. Everything seemed to be all right. He
edged carefully out from under the bulge of the drive
unit and got to his feet, still clutching the instruction
manual. Gradually he relaxed, and began to breathe easily
again. He grabbed a nearby handhold to climb back into
the forward part of the ship, and cast a last glance back
at the fuel tank.

A glittering drop of liquid fell from a bend in the cop-
pery fuel line, hit the top of tank, and disappeared.

Connely, frozen into a state of paralysis, watched the
dripping fuel for some time. With unvarying regularity, each
drop appeared at the same point on the tube, fell in the
same way through a maze of wires and supports, and hit
the top of the tank, to vanish without a trace. A new drop
then formed, to fall in exactly the same way.

Gradually, Connely dragged his gaze from the sight of
these falling, highly-explosive drops. He forced himself to
move up along the hand-holds, and gradually worked his
way into the front end of the ship. He felt no safer here,
but at least, he could move without the fear of doing yet
more damage.

He sank into the control seat, pulled out his handkerchief,
and reached up to wipe the perspiration out of his eyes.

Whir! His head twisted and his vision cut off. The helmet knocked his hand aside.

Connely sprang to his feet, furious.

The helmet swung around again, and now he could see.

Boiling mad, Connely thumbed through the fuel tank

manual, hoping against hope that the instruction sheet for the helmet was inside somewhere. But it wasn't there.

Connely pulled back his rug, got out MacIntyre's note, and read:

Knowing your violent temper, I've decided to put the instructions for the clothing where you won't be likely to tear them up . . . Check the other equipment, and you'll find the instructions for your garments—

Connely read this over several times and swore savagely. He *had* checked the other pieces of equipment! Angrily, he shoved the note back under the rug, and straightened up. A flashing yellow light on the new panel caught his eye.

Having skimmed through the sheet of instructions for that panel, Connely knew that a flashing yellow light indicated something that needed attention. The light for the fuel tank was still glowing a comfortable green and he had checked everything else, so what was that one flashing light for?

Connely asked himself if he could possibly have missed some piece of equipment? If so, maybe MacIntyre had put the instructions for the helmet near that very piece of equipment. Connely got out the list that identified the various lights, checked it through carefully, and discovered something called "IntruGrab MI-X, Medium."

What in space, Connely asked himself, *is an "IntruGrab?"* He stared at the diagram, found the location of the thing, and trod down the corridor, pausing here and there to duck under or climb over the reinforcing structural members that got in his way. When he came to the spot marked on the diagram, the only thing there was the inner space-lock door. Connely glanced around, and turned to go back to the control room.

From somewhere came a faint thumping sound. He stopped, and tried without success to locate it. He stepped back around a beam and looked up. Over his head was a hemisphere of metal plate and shiny metal bars wrapped around a transparent globe.

Inside the globe, red-faced, furious, and hammering on the transparent surface with a calloused fist, was Sector Chief of Scouts Gregory MacIntyre.

At first, Connely couldn't believe it. He climbed up on a beam for a closer look, and MacIntyre glared out at him through the transparent layer. When Connely merely stared, MacIntyre jabbed a finger at something out of Connely's range of vision, opened his mouth as if shouting, shook his fist at Connely, drew a finger across his throat and then banged his fist against the transparent layer, which gave forth a faint thump.

Connely shrugged and reached up for the instruction manual which was tied by a string to one of the bars. Once he had the manual, he dropped off the beam and walked back up the corridor, a smile on his face. He was aware that at any moment the ship might still be exploded into its component atoms. Or a commerce-raider might appear from nowhere and reel him in on a souped-up gravitor beam. But for some reason these thoughts no longer bothered him.

He settled down comfortably in the control room and flipped through the instruction manual for the Model M1-X IntruGrab (medium). Connely hoped to find the instructions for his helmet—but they weren't there. Scowling, he went back to the beginning of the manual, and carefully worked his way past diagrams and descriptions, noting a sentence here and a technical detail there, which gave him enough to go on so that he saw the purpose and general mode of operation of the device even before he read the final paragraph at the back of the manual:

"In brief, the M1-X IntruGrab (medium) is designed to prevent human or other intruders from gaining entrance to restricted localities. Once keyed to the physical characteristics of the personnel legitimately present, and activated to prevent entry of others, the IntruGrab will selectively remove unauthorized intruders, will imprison such intruders for an indefinite period, removing waste products and providing minimal nutritive requirements according to the specifications table on page 32. The IntruGrab (medium) will handle individuals from the size of a grasshopper to that of an adult male gorilla, and will signal capture by flashing light, tone alarm, or other standard warning mechanism. *CAUTION:* The manufacturers do not warrant use of the M1-X IntruGrab (medium) for any purpose contrary to local statute or ordinance. *Consult your lawyer or local law-enforcement agencies before installing.*"

Connely skimmed back through the manual to the

instructions for releasing captured intruders. He discovered that there were two methods of release: permanent, and provisional. He decided he should not overburden his mind by studying too much at once, so he only learned how to release an intruder provisionally. Armed with this information, he went back down the corridor, and looked up.

MacIntyre was glaring down through the bars with a look that would have shriveled the self-confidence of almost any subordinate. Connely, however, had not gravitated into the Stellar Scouts by accident. and so as he looked back at MacIntyre, a grin gradually spread over his face. This brought MacIntyre to a state of boiling rage bordering on apoplexy.

Connely, alarmed lest MacIntyre hurt himself, mentally reviewed the instructions, then raised his hand toward the globe. An orange light blinked on.

"Lower," said Connely.

The globe came down on a frame like a set of lazy tongs. A number of plastic tubes snapped loose from the globe and coiled up into the ceiling.

"Release," said Connely.

The transparent layer slid back, the bars came open, and MacIntyre stumbled out. The cage went back up to the ceiling, and MacIntyre swayed unsteadily on his feet.

It occurred to Connely that the food served by the M1-X IntruGrab (medium) was probably pretty poor stuff, to say nothing of being locked up in the thing for all this time. He guided MacIntyre down the corridor to the control room, helped him sit down, and got some instant heated hot broth for him.

"Thanks," said MacIntyre, his voice hardly more than a croak. He glared across the room at the new control panel, then looked away. He stiffened his jaw and said nothing.

Connely cheerfully refrained from making any comment. He thought the situation was sufficiently clear as it was. While he was enjoying a sensation of comfortable superiority, the aroma of the hot broth made him aware that he was extremely hungry. He got some of the same broth for himself, and raised a steaming spoonful.

Whir. The helmet whipped around, knocked the spoon out of his hand, and splashed most of the hot broth from the spoon across his face. When he tried to wipe off his face, the helmet knocked his hand away.

Connely, boiling mad, but unwilling to admit the fix he was in, said casually, "By the way, Mac, where are the instructions for this helmet?"

"In the Mangle," said MacIntyre, his voice hoarse.

Connely frowned. He had no memory of any "Mangle." He checked the list of devices controlled from the new panel and found no "Mangle" listed. Mentally, he worked his way from the front of the ship to the rear, crossing off the places he had already looked over. Suddenly he realized that he hadn't looked in the General Supplies storeroom.

Connely went back along the corridor, opened an air-tight door, went down a short cross-corridor, and opened the door to his left. Inside, cramping the shelves and bins of parts and equipment, stood an enigmatic gray block about six feet wide, eight feet high, and twelve feet long, with smoothly rounded corners. Connely touched it, and it gave him a snappy shock. Connely looked all around it. A single lens, about an inch across, and set about eighteen inches below the top, traveled around from side to side as if keeping an eye on him.

Connely lost patience, and muttered to himself, "Where in space is the manual for this thing?"

A wide slot promptly popped open in the side nearest him. A gray oblong about an inch thick by eight inches wide popped out, and folded apart down the center to reveal a gray metal book marked with glossy black lettering: "Mangle MI-X (small, medium, large) Instruction Manual."

Connely flipped back the flexible metal pages of this book, which were almost hot to the touch. Between the last page and the back cover was a sheet of what appeared to be fine charcoal. Connely looked at it closely, and an odor of creosote and wood alcohol wafted up to meet him. It dawned on Connely that this must be the remains of the instruction sheet he wanted.

Connely went back to the control room, and found MacIntyre looking much improved. Connely, using short and simple language, described the trouble he'd had with the Mangle, the new fuel tank, and the "reflex helmet."

MacIntyre looked serious. "That business with the fuel tank sounds bad."

"Oh," said Connely, "the *fuel tank* sounds had, does it? I have to eat, you know. How do I get out of this helmet?"

MacIntyre appeared to be searching his memory. He said hesitantly. "To tell you the truth. Con, the microcircuit for that helmet was so unusual, and I got so interested in it, that I don't believe I ever *did* read the operating instructions."

Connely restrained himself with an effort. In a very low voice, be said, "You don't happen to have any suggestions, do you, Mac?"

"Hm-m-m," said MacIntyre. "Well, maybe we could *squirt* the food in?"

This suggestion left Connely speechless. Before he had recovered, the annunciator gave a buzz, and announced in its synthetic voice: "Ship sighted. Class III cruiser, identity unknown. No recognition signal."

MacIntyre growled, "A Space Force ship would have identified itself right away. That must be the raider we're looking for."

Connely whirled to thrust the drive control full ahead. The accelerometer needle wound around its dial in a tribute to the power of the ship's monster drive unit. The communications screen cut into the battle-control circuit to show a small green image being overtaken by a much larger red image.

After a little while, Connely saw that the cruiser was losing its struggle to narrow the gap fast enough, and stepped over to look at the trip meter.

On the rectangular chartlike face above the meter itself a little white dot representing the scout ship was moving past within easy distance of Space Center 7.

MacIntyre said, "As I remember, the fleet based at Seven has half-a-dozen dreadnoughts, and around eighty other ships above the size of scouts. To operate here, any raider would need to be out of his head."

Connely tried the communicator, and could contact neither the cruiser nor Space Center 7.

The annunciator sounded its buzzer. "Ship sighted. Dreadnought of unknown class and identity. No recognition signal."

The battle screen now showed a huge red image closing

in fast on an intersecting course. The likelihood of its being on this course by pure chance wasn't worth thinking about.

Connely said, "We're trapped, Mac. We built up so much momentum getting away from that cruiser that we'll land right in the lap of the dreadnought."

"That's the dreadnought's worry," snapped MacIntyre. "With the stuff we've got on board, we could take on the sector fleet."

"If it works."

"It'll work," said MacIntyre positively.

The communicator chimed and Connely snapped it on. A bored voice said, "You come through Maury's territory, you either pay your tariff or we squash you. We already picked off two of you little bugs."

Connely snapped off the communicator and glanced at MacIntyre.

MacIntyre said, "We can't be in Maury's territory. I specifically set up the course to avoid that."

Connely snapped on the communicator. "According to our trip-meter, we're nowhere near Maury's territory."

"Your trip-meter must have a busted bolt, pal. Now cut out the 6-V act and pay your tariff like a good little boy. Or get squashed."

MacIntyre knocked forward a lever that put the handling of the ship and its weapons completely under control of the battle computer.

On the view screen a pair of the dreadnought's monster turrets lit up in a white blaze as the fusion guns let loose their warning blasts. The scout ship continued on its course.

MacIntyre set his jaw. Connely, bathed in sweat, watched the two screens.

On the battle screen, a burst of yellow lines left the dreadnought as ultra fast missiles and missile-killers streaked out on their tracks. The dreadnought lit with dazzling blasts from its fusion weapons, and the space distorters of the two ships reflected these blasts, to hurl the searing bolts of energy back and forth between them. Enormous blue-white blurs reached out from the dreadnought, to haul the scout ship bodily off its course.

Connely felt a gathering vibration of the deck underfoot. On the screen, the racing missiles arced in, like a fist closing to squash a gnat. Then the overloaded space-distorters ceased to throw the fusion bolts back at the dreadnought, but merely deflected them into space.

The yellow tracks of the missiles abruptly ended. It took Connely a few seconds to realize that the space distorters, in deflecting the accumulated fusion blasts from the dreadnought, had done it with such accuracy as to burn up every missile approaching the scout ship. A small faint dotted line traveled from the scout ship to the huge red image of the dreadnought. Red dots began appearing here and there all over the battle screen.

Connely blinked and glanced at the outside viewscreen. The dreadnought, filling the screen from end to end, was fast taking on the look of a piece of Swiss cheese. As Connely watched, chunks of armor plate and turret vanished right and left, leaving round holes several yards across.

A thin purple fan now reached out on the battle screen from the scout ship to the dreadnought. On the outside viewscreen, the dreadnought appeared to lengthen out like an image on a sheet of live rubber. It stretched out into an elongated cylinder dotted with oval slits.

Abruptly the fan faded. The cylinder snapped back, and the viewscreen showed the dreadnought with the look of a ground car that has just run into a tree at a hundred and fifty miles an hour.

Connely and MacIntyre looked at each other. MacIntyre grinned suddenly, "Well, Con, *now* what do you have to say about new equipment? Without the new drive the cruiser would have gotten us. Without the new weapons, the dreadnought would have."

"It's not *new* equipment I'm against," said Connely, "but unreliable equipment. And I never saw a piece of new equipment yet that didn't have at least one nasty shock built into it."

"The new drive and weapons saved us."

"And the leak the new helmet put in the new fuel line may finish us."

"Oh" said MacIntyre. "I forgot that." He grabbed the fuel tank instruction manual, and instantly buried himself in it.

Connely hit the Astroposit button, and a few moments later, got their position based on a comparison of the stellar patterns around them with known stellar patterns. This informed them they were right in the middle of Maury's territory.

Scowling, Connely glanced at the trip-meter, which showed distance traveled so far, and, in its projected chart showed the ship drawing away from Space Center 7. Connely looked at the trip-meter, a standard item of equipment, as if it were a traitor. He pulled off inspection covers, peered in with lights and jointed mirrors, and found nothing wrong. Next he looked suspiciously at the new course-control, where MacIntyre had set up his course. A look into this strange item merely confused Connely, so he contented himself with a study of the instruction manual.

After a considerable time, MacIntyre handed Connely the tank instruction manual, and pointed out a paragraph:

Node Effect. CAUTION! *Do not touch exterior surface of fuel tank while subspace control unit is in operation. Such contact may unbalance the matter-energy equilibrium designed into the tank, causing momentary formation of a subspace node at the point of contact. That portion of an object within the node will be projected into subspace and may not reappear within several light-years of the tank. Severe injury may result.*

"Evidently," said MacIntyre, "the dripping fuel is being thrown harmlessly into subspace. Since there's a special repair kit for the fuel line, I think we can fix it all right."

Connely sighed in relief. "Good. Now let me show you something." He handed MacIntyre a big sheet of thin paper thick with diagrams and text in fine type, that had been pasted into an envelope in the back of the course-control manual.

MacIntyre scowled at the paper. then squinted at a sentence Connely pointed out, and read aloud:

"Unlike most course-controls, the late model Z60 is perfectly foolproof. If the inexperienced pilot sets the Z60 for an unnecessarily complex route from point to point, the new corrector circuits shorten the route automatically."

MacIntyre looked up, speechless.

"Isn't that nice?" said Connely. "You or I or anyone else painstakingly sets the Z60 for a roundabout route to keep out of dangerous territory. The Z60 then charitably decides we are too ignorant to know there's a shorter way, so it puts us right through the middle of the place where we don't want to go. Meanwhile, the standard trip-meter has no way to know the Z60 has changed the course, so the pilot finds it out when it's too late."

MacIntyre shook his head in disgust.

Connely said, "I had a hunch it was the equipment that was making the trouble. But I didn't have all the facts, so I couldn't *prove* I was right."

"But how," MacIntyre objected, "could you guess what was wrong without knowing the facts? That's not logical."

"It sure isn't. Logic has to do with chains of individual facts. Intuition takes whole groups of facts at once. You can recognize a familiar pattern—like a familiar face—even though you *don't* consciously know all the details. Sometimes it's a mistake, but then you can often use logic as a check. With intuition you see it; with logic you check it."

Connely, now that the excitement was over, was again feeling hungry and uncomfortable. "You don't have *any* idea how this helmet works?"

"I think it's a psionic circuit. That's all I can tell you." MacIntyre glared at the course-control manual and suddenly slammed it down. "The devil with it. I'd better fix that fuel line."

As MacIntyre went out, Connely had a vague hunch that something was wrong. However, he was too busy trying to get out of the helmet. Psionics, he told himself, had to do with the interaction of devices and the human organism itself. Maybe mental attitude would affect the helmet. Connely tilted his head forward, and visualized, pleaded, urged, insisted, *believed* that the helmet would fall off.

With a thud the helmet fell to the deck.

For an instant Connely felt as if all his troubles and difficulties were over. Then he saw the familiar flashing yellow light on the new control panel.

The light told him that, like all the other pure machine-like devices on board, the M1-X IntruGrab (medium) was doing its duty with ironclad, black-and-white, absolutely indisputable logic.

But Connely did not belabor the point as, for the second time, he let MacIntyre loose.

STAR TIGER

Lieutenant General John Wilforce knew the saying that
trouble comes when least expected. It occurred to him as
he finished his shower and toweled briskly. He was still
considering it as he slid between the cool sheets for his first
full night's sleep in six months.

Wilforce lay still, hearing the rumble of the automatic
loaders that poured fuel, food, and ammunition into the
flagship's tanks and storerooms. In his mind's eye, he could
see the ships of his fleet. Most of them, like his own, were
drawn close to the starlit framework of girders, drums, crates,
and pressurized spheres that was Space Center 12. From
these ships, thousands of his men were now streaming into
the bars, game rooms, and psychosynth parlors of the Center,
eager for a few hours of release and forgetfulness after the
brutal months on Inferno.

Before letting himself fall asleep, Wilforce reviewed his
precautions. He had detached a strong squadron of the fleet
to reinforce the guard ships of the Center. Half the men
in each ship now reloading at the Center were on board,
ready for duty at a few minutes notice. Moreover, the latest
reports showed no sign of trouble whatever, anywhere in
his sector.

Satisfied that he had done his job, the general pulled the
covers close around him, and fell sound asleep. Unnoticed
as he slept, the hands of the clock on the communicator
by his cot swung slowly around their dial until, in the early
hours of the morning, a red light blinked on.

Wilforce woke with a hammering clang in his ears. He threw back the covers to see the communicator's red warning light flash on and off. Then the screen flared into life:

CLASS A EMERGENCY!
CLASS A EMERGENCY!
CLASS A EMERGENCY!

Wilforce swung to the edge of the cot and hit the "Receive" stud. On the screen appeared a man with three stars at his collar and his shirt plastered to his skin with perspiration. Clouds of vapor rolled past behind him as he said: "General Wilforce?"

"Right here." Wilforce snapped on the room light so he could be seen. He recognized the man now as Larssen, armed forces commander in a sector bordering his own.

Larssen, a note of strain in his voice, said, "General, are you still tied up on Inferno?"

"We just got back from it."

Larssen hesitated barely an instant. Then he said, "A little over the border from you in my sector is a sun system called Bemus. There are colonies on the third planet, and they've been there better than ten years with no trouble. I also have a small rest camp on the planet. At last report, a month ago, everything was fine."

Larssen paused, then said, "Three days ago, a destroyer of mine crash-landed on Bemus III. Every colony there has been smashed. All records, books, food, and clothing are gone. Weapons are strewn all over. There's not a human being left. There are abundant tracks of animals entirely different from those native to the planet, but the animals themselves aren't to be seen."

Wilforce listened intently.

Larssen went on. "The detector network shows nothing approaching or leaving the planet. The result is, I don't know what happened on Bemus III. Right now nearly everything I've got is tied up. Yet, if something can get past the detector network and wipe out a whole planet, I can't ignore it. Can you help me?"

Wilforce said, "I'll do everything I can."

Larssen thanked him fervently, and promised to have his staff send immediately every scrap of information available about Bemus III. The screen blanked, and Wilforce punched a number on a vertical row of buttons to the left of the screen. The competent, slightly pudgy face of Rybalko, his chief-of-staff, appeared.

Wilforce said, "Did you hear that, Balky?"

"Yes, sir," said Rybalko. "I heard it."

"How long will it take us to load up?"

"Sir, to do it right will take another five days."

Wilforce thought a moment. If he waited, the trouble, whatever it was, might have time to develop. If he immediately took his full fleet to Bemus, he might by sheer force crush the thing at its beginning. On the other hand, experience told him that he might find himself making gestures in empty space, and be forced back in a few weeks for lack of supplies. He made up his mind, and glanced at Rybalko.

"Balky, get a light task-force together to prowl around Bemus system. Load a D-transport with Pioneers to scour Bemus III and piece together what's happened. Put a combat group on another D-transport to back up the Pioneers. Then get in touch with the destroyer that crash-landed on the planet. I'll want to talk to the commanding officer."

"Yes, sir."

Wilforce got up, splashed cold water on his face, and got dressed.

The destroyer's commanding officer turned out to be a spare major with craggy features.

Wilforce said, "Major, exactly where are you on the planet?"

The major held up a map. "Sir, we're in the planet's northern hemisphere here, about three hundred miles southwest of the rest camp. The terrain where we came down is a gently-rolling, dry, grassy plain. We're at the point marked 'X' here on the map, about twenty-seven miles north of the big loop of this river."

"What's your situation right now?"

"Well, sir, we have plenty of supplies. An abundance of fresh meat. And we haven't been threatened in any way. We've scoured the five-hundred mile radius of territory we can cover thoroughly with our light fliers, and we've let out Bats and Probes to scout farther out. We can't find anything that looks dangerous—except that the colonies and rest camp have been totally wiped out."

"Have you taken pictures?"

"Yes, sir. As soon as we realized what had happened, we started taking them. We're getting ready to send you a batch on the trifac right now."

"Good work. Now, how did you happen to crash-land on the planet in the first place?"

The major hesitated. "Sir, to be perfectly honest, I don't know *what* happened. None of us knows. We were making a routine sweep through this part of the sector, and swung close to the planet because we couldn't get any response from the communications center down at the rest camp. Then something hit the ship like a hundred tons of lead. The next thing we knew, the air was whistling out. Seams parted here and there the whole length of the ship, and we barely had time to get into suits. There was nothing on the detectors that could have caused it, but there we were just the same. I decided to set down on the planet to replenish the air and repair the ship. But we'd had even more damage than I realized. On the way down, several drive tubes blew their linings, and a gravitor broke loose from its mount. That was how we came to crash-land on the planet."

"Do you have records of your detector readings?"

"Yes, sir. We can run the record tapes through the trifac if you'd like."

Wilforce said, "Yes, do that, from the time you entered Bemus System till you landed on the planet."

"Yes, sir."

"How are your repairs coming?"

"We expect to have the seams sealed up, the gravitor mounted, and the tubes lined in about two weeks, sir. Straightening the frame will be a job for the yards at Main Base. But we should be able to get back all right."

Wilforce thought a moment. "Major, take several three-dimensional photos of the damage to your ship and send them along, too."

"Yes, sir."

"Is there anything else that seems important to you?"

"No, sir. Nothing I can think of."

"All right. Have your communications officer signal us every hour, and get in touch with us right away if anything further happens."

"Yes, sir."

Wilforce broke the connection. Shortly afterward, the first reports and photos of the colonies came in on the trifac.

Wilforce first located some maps in the growing pile sent in by Larssen's staff. The maps showed the colonies on a gently rolling, heavily forested plain. They were located in a circle several hundred miles across, with Larssen's rest camp in a cleared rectangle near the center.

Looking over plans and photographs, Wilforce saw that the individual settlements were large clearings near lakes or streams with L-shaped rows of cabins along the south and west edges of the clearings. But these rows of cabins were laid out differently from those Wilforce had seen on other heavily-forested planets. Instead of being simply straight rows of cabins, each cabin was turned roughly thirty degrees from a line due south or west. From above, each row of cabins suggested a row of dominoes lined up end-to-end, separated to leave spaces between them, then each pivoted thirty degrees about its center.

Wilforce puzzled over this till an explanation dawned on him. In a straight row of cabins, gunfire from one cabin couldn't reach the space close to the front or rear walls of adjoining cabins. By turning each cabin, its front and rear walls could be protected by neighboring cabins.

The next thought to occur to Wilforce was, "*What enemy?*"

Methodically, he worked his way through reams of information on the planet, and wound up some time later with a faint pain between the eyes, and a summary of all the data that seemed to count:

"Bemus III is an Earth-type planet, with ideal gravity and atmosphere, a reasonably pleasant climate, and a somewhat longer than standard year. It has few mineral resources, but rich soil and abundant forests. There are no plants or animals harmful to man. The largest life form is a placid, herbivorous, mammoth-like creature called a 'cropper' which is protected by Planet Certification because it is nearly extinct. The other herbivores are small. The largest carnivore is a shy nocturnal creature little larger than a rabbit. Man has no enemies on Bemus III."

With this fresh in his mind, Wilforce reached for photographs and diagrams of Larssen's rest camp. A glance showed

him that the camp was made up mostly of tents and pre-
fabricated one-story barracks put up and taken down as
needed. Then Wilforce looked at the only permanent buildings in the camp—the communications center.

Built in a tight hollow square, from the middle of which
rose a covered tower mounting a machine gun and a big
searchlight, the communications center was surrounded by
a stockade of upright logs, sharpened on the ends. A barrier of packed earth filled the space between this stockade
and an outer log wall that looked from above like a four-
pointed star. Emplaced within the barbed-wire-strung arms
of this star were heavy machine guns and multiple rocket
launchers. Outside was a broad deep ditch ringed with more
barbed wire.

Wilforce looked at this a moment, then glanced back to
the reports that described Bemus III as a peaceful harmless planet. He carefully checked to see if by any chance
he was reading data on two different planets with similar
names. When he was satisfied that this wasn't the trouble,
he glanced with a deepening scowl at the pile of recent
photos sent in by the destroyer.

These photos showed solidly-built cabins knocked askew,
doors smashed in, guns still at windows and loopholes, axes
and unsheathed knives strewn on the floors. At the communications center, the massive logs at one part of the outer
wall were snapped back like toothpicks. The earth behind
was pulled down as if by a giant hand, with a machine gun
lying in the dirt at the bottom. Two of the communications
buildings were knocked apart. The tower had long splintered scratches, several braces torn loose, and its roof ripped
open.

Wilforce looked at one photo after another, then at the
views of the destroyer with its side flattened in the aft section
and slightly dished-in forward.

Frowning, he had several photos of the rest camp and
the ship enlarged.

The ship appeared to have been hit by a solidly-built
cylindrical object about its own size, and nearly parallel to
it at the time of collision. The enlarged photos of the ruined
colonies showed deep parallel scratches in cabin walls, big
paw marks in the dirt outside, and in one place behind a
low swell of the earth, the outline of an enormous body

with fan-shaped marks in the earth behind it. This suggested to Wilforce a huge cat crouched in wait and thrashing its tail.

Scowling, Wilforce put down the photos, and went out to make a quick check of the condition and equipment of the troops being sent to Bemus III. He found that the equipment had been brought almost back to normal. But the combat group was depleted in both men and officers, and somehow looked none too good to him. Finding nothing specific that was wrong, he attributed it all to the recent ordeal on Inferno, wished the men luck, and went back to the problem of Bemus III.

Five days later, the one significant change in the situation was that the reloading of Wilforce's ships was complete. His main fleet now blasted off for Bemus III. En route, Wilforce wrestled with the conflicting data, but it still proved impossible to fit it into any sensible pattern.

The trip to Bemus III was expected to take about sixteen days. Before they had been gone one full day, the destroyer on the planet stopped transmitting reports, and could no longer be reached.

When the fleet was still better than five days out from the planet, the commander of the fast task force sent ahead of the fleet reported back to Wilforce by communicator.

"Sir," said the officer, frowning, "we've just completed our first sweep through Bemus System. If there's anything out of the ordinary here, we haven't seen it. The one thing I don't like is this big belt of asteroids between the third and fourth planets."

Wilforce nodded. An asteroid belt could confuse the detectors and incidentally conceal whole squadrons of hostile ships. Wilforce said, "When do you intend to land the Pioneers?"

"In about four hours, sir. They're coming through right now. We expect to keep the troops close by, but offplanet unless the Pioneers run into trouble."

"Good," said Wilforce. "Have the Pioneers report to me as soon as they find out what happened to that destroyer."

"Yes, sir."

Wilforce spread out several big charts of Bemus System. Later that day, he was rechecking his plans for approaching it, when Rybalko came over, his face pale.

"Sir, the Pioneers have found the destroyer and boarded it. We have them on the screen."

Wilforce put down the chart and went over to the screen, where a man wearing the customary fringed leather shirt of the Pioneers knelt beside a long low shape covered with a rough gray blanket. As Wilforce came over, the Pioneer pulled back the blanket.

Underneath, stretched full length on the metal deck, lay a bare human skeleton.

Wilforce drew his breath in slowly. He noted the thin steel chain that looped loosely around the vertebrae of the neck to hold the dull metal tags. He saw, flat on the floor nearby, a shiny cleaver, the plastic inserts in its handle missing.

The Pioneer glanced at Wilforce. Wilforce nodded, and the Pioneer pulled the blanket back over the skeleton. He said, "We've found eight more of these in just one section of the ship. That's all we've found of them. Outside, there's only tracks. Mr. Pick said he wants to have a better idea what happened before he gets in touch with you. But he'll call you in three hours at the latest. Is that all right?"

Wilforce thought a moment. Pick was head of the Pioneers attached to Wilforce's command, and he generally worked best when given plenty of freedom. Wilforce said, "Does Pick need reinforcements?"

"Not right now. He doesn't want them."

"All right."

The screen blanked, and Wilforce glanced at Rybalko. "After we break out of subspace, I want one squadron located to smash anything that raises its nose in the densest part of that asteroid belt. I also want selected sections of the belt saturated with reconnaissance torpedoes. You might have the data run through the computer now, and we can see what the best pattern seems to be."

Rybalko said, "Yes, sir. Sir, did you notice that cleaver?"

"I noticed the handle. But we won't really know much till we talk to Pick."

Jeremy Pick was on the screen a little over three hours later. He was a tall man with a high-bridged nose and light gray eyes that shifted warily as he talked. He said, "General, I don't know exactly how to describe this place. It's too quiet. And for some reason we feel even more uneasy inside the ship than out."

Wilforce said, "You didn't find any survivors in that destroyer?"

"Not a one. We've found nine skeletons, and that's all. Outside, there's scattered weapons and equipment. Apparently, the men were overrun in a rush before they had a chance to act."

"Overrun by *what*?"

"To judge by the tracks, by carnivores measuring around twelve feet between the fore and hind limbs, and weighing up to thirty-five hundred pounds."

"Have you seen any of these animals?"

"No. We've seen some herbivores that aren't mentioned in the survey reports; but they might be the young of these 'croppers.' We haven't seen a single carnivore of any size yet."

Wilforce scowled. "Is there any place they could hide? Or could the carnivores be nocturnal animals?"

Pick shrugged. "It isn't dark here yet, so I don't know. Maybe they'll emerge from somewhere. But I've had clouds of small reconnaissance probes buzzing all over this section of the planet since we landed. If there's any carnivore that big around, it's either invisible, or else it's hugging the mud on a river bottom."

"Do you have any idea how the destroyer came to be taken by surprise?"

"Well, they had one of the big gravitors partly spread out outside, so I suppose they were spreading the parts out in the sun to dry. We checked and found where a section of coolant line had burst in the gravitor, so that much makes sense. Other crewmen were relining the ship's drive tubes. Some of the maintenance hatches were open in the aft section of the ship, along with the loading hatch, so it must have been easy for anything to get in. As nearly as we can figure out from the remains of the log, they had scoured this section of the planet, found nothing dangerous, and weren't worried."

Wilforce said, "You say, '*remains* of the log'?"

"The log is partly eaten up, as if by mice."

"Have you *seen* any mice?"

"None. And we haven't found any droppings."

Wilforce said exasperatedly, "That's a peculiar planet, Pick."

"It's peculiar, all right. The more we find out, the less sense it makes."

"If those giant carnivores can show up by surprise once, they may do it again. Are the hatches shut now?"

"The hatches are dogged tight. No one goes in or out except through the air lock. I've got half-a-dozen Bats cruising around outside waiting for any carnivore to so much as raise its snout. All the same, I don't exactly feel at home in this place."

Wilforce thought a moment. "Listen, why not move one of the communicators into some part of the ship where we can watch what you're doing, and then leave it on. If anything happens unexpectedly, we'll know about it."

Pick said, "Good idea." They talked a little longer, then went back to work.

While still about a day out from the planet, Wilforce was in the flagship's command center studying the computer's suggested deployment. A call from the task force commander was relayed to him, and the man appeared on the screen with a look of alarm and uncertainty. "Sir, we've got something here, but I don't know what."

"What do you mean?"

"About fifteen minutes ago, our detectors picked up an object roughly the size of a destroyer. We were standing by off Bemus III, and the object passed between us and the planet, moving at about two miles a second. It stayed on the detectors a little under three seconds, and then it vanished. We can't locate it. There was no sign of it before, and there's been no sign of it since. But we've checked, and the detectors of every ship in a position to pick it up *did* pick it up."

Wilforce looked away a moment, then said, "How far from the planet was this object?"

"About twenty thousand miles, sir. It was moving as if it was in orbit."

"It *sounds* as if it's in orbit. Calculate its projected course as well as you can, and have a ship trail it. If it comes in sight again, learn all you can, but for now don't interfere with it. Just watch it."

"Yes, sir."

Wilforce had just finished this call, when Rybalko came over. "Sir, Mr. Pick was just on the screen. I didn't want to interrupt your call, so I took it myself."

"What did Pick want?"

"Reinforcements, sir. He's run into a peculiar situation. He's lost several men. One of them was carried off by a carnivore about the size of a tiger, that was apparently lying in wait in a ruined cabin. A probe was overhead, and had the carnivore in sight as it vanished in a patch of thick brush. The animal had no time to get out of the brush before other probes had it in view. Pick and a crew of Pioneers took the brush patch apart bush-by-bush. No carnivore came out. No carnivore was in there."

"You mean, this tiger went in. It didn't come out. And when they looked, it wasn't there?"

"That's what he says, sir."

Wilforce frowned. "How did Pick seem?"

"Jumpy. He had a fusion gun in his hand and kept glancing around all the time. But he sounded rational enough."

"All right. Send the combat group down to back him up. And have Pick send up reproductions of the visual records from the probes that had this in view."

"Yes, sir."

Rybalko went out. Wilforce turned to look at a large three-dimensional image of Bemus System, his planned deployment outlined on it. The computer had helped perfect the details of this deployment, but Wilforce was now thinking that the most accurately detailed plan is questionable if based on questionable information. With a vanishing ship flitting through space near the planet, and disappearing animals on the planet, how was he to make a satisfactory plan?

Bit-by-bit, allowing for large uncertainties, he began to revise the plans.

Rybalko came in when Wilforce was part way through, and stood watching the symbols on the big three-dimensional image.

Wilforce looked up and Rybalko said, "Sir, the records of the probes watching that carnivore are starting to come in."

"Good. I'll take a look at them later, if I have time. Have Evaluation go over them and see what they think."

"Yes, sir." Rybalko hesitated, looked at the projected plan, then said, "Did you think we should make a more gradual approach, sir?"

Wilforce nodded. "When you're locked up in a dark cellar with some one who may be an enemy, let *him* make the first big move. Of course, you can always toss out something small and see if he jumps for it when he hears the clatter."

Wilforce's fleet was normally organized in five divisions. The fast ships of one division made up the task force that had gone ahead. Wilforce now took the remaining ships of this division, plus his own center division, out of subspace toward Bemus III. Behind him in subspace lay sixty percent of his striking force, ready to attack at a moment's notice.

In the command center's big, three-dimensional battle screen, Wilforce could now see the first stages of his deployment working out as planned.

The bright lines arcing closer to the sun Bemus showed the paths of fast transports carrying mobile racks of the disks that would be sowed in long rows, each to exude a puff of loose silvery material that could expand at a given signal to a wide thin doughnut with a dazzling film of silver stretching across its center. And that could, at another signal, contract, turn together through specified angles, and again expand, to focus an unendurable blaze of solar energy in a selected region nearby or far away.

Wilforce watched the bright lines that marked the transports slowly separate as they raced to their separate positions. He glanced at the asteroid belt, represented in the battle screen as a stream of green-colored dots. Any abrupt change of speed or direction would cause the dots involved to turn red. So far, they remained green.

Toward the sun from the planet Bemus III, were the four pale blue spheres that represented the four sections of his diminished fleet. These spheres were grouped as at the four corners of a huge tetrahedron. From them, a spray of fine lines reached out toward the planet like the fingers of a giant fist. These were the advance scouts, that would scour the planet from pole to pole, to provide a picture in which Wilforce hoped to find some pattern that would give a clue to past events.

As the transports approached their final positions, and as the scouts let loose their clouds of probes, Wilforce waited, tensely alert.

The ideal time for an enemy to strike slid past.

Nothing happened.

The transports reached their positions, and sowed the racks that sowed the disks. The solar beam was ready.

The scouts sent back a flood of aerial photographs and data, for Evaluation to fit together into a coherent picture of Bemus III.

Still nothing happened.

Wilforce looked at Rybalko.

Rybalko looked blank.

Time passed. And still nothing happened.

Wilforce thought over his dispositions. Sixty percent of his fleet was like a hidden club, which he could bring out at any time. The other forty percent, himself included, acted as bait. The probabilities seemed to show that *something* wished to remove humanity from Bemus III. Therefore, if he immediately proceeded to take over Bemus III, the something should strike. If it struck, he might very well be able to strike back. If he was unable to strike back, then, at least, the extent of the danger would be uncovered. But now, *nothing* happened.

In time, Rybalko said, "Sir, first reports from Evaluation show nothing unusual on the planet, except some large herds of herbivores—apparently offspring of the croppers."

"Herbivores. No carnivores?"

"None seen yet, sir."

Wilforce nodded. Methodically he went back over what he knew about Bemus III. All reports showed it to be a placid quiet planet, with no natural enemies of humanity on it anywhere, but all the same, the colonists had built their settlements as if they expected attack any time. And the colonists had lived there unmolested for over ten years— then suddenly had been wiped out.

Wilforce scowled, and then considered the rest camp. Nearly all the buildings in the rest camp were light and temporary. They could no more hold off an attack than a blotter could seal out water. Obviously, no attack was feared. But on the other hand, there were those few permanent buildings in the rest camp. And these were fortified like a frontier outpost on a planet swarming with reptilian monsters. Obviously, an attack *was* feared.

Wilforce drew a deep breath, and turned his thoughts to the destroyer. Its crew felt sufficiently sure there was no enemy around to leave their ship and work outside. The Pioneers, much more capable of defending themselves on a strange planet, felt so uneasy that they were jumpy inside a locked-up destroyer that could make mincemeat of endless carnivores—granted only that the people inside were on their guard.

As if this were not trouble enough, there was the problem of the way the destroyer had arrived here in the first place. It was on the planet because of a collision with, or a blow from, some invisible object. Just such an invisible object had now momentarily come into view of the task force off Bemus III, only to vanish again. Why appear in the first place? Why vanish?

And now, Pick had lost several men despite precautions, one of them eaten by a carnivore which was plainly seen to go to a given place. When the place was examined, the final result was that the carnivore had gone in, he hadn't come out, and he wasn't there.

Wilforce swore aloud.

Rybalko looked up. "Sir?"

"Nothing," said Wilforce. He forced his attention back to that incident of the carnivore. There, at least, was something definite. Methodically, Wilforce considered the possibilities. To begin with, either the observation was correct, or there was some mistake. On any other planet, Wilforce would have thought it was a mistake. But here, it fit the pattern perfectly.

In that case, assuming Pick was right, what *could* have happened? Wilforce thought hard, and ended up with only a few possibilities that seemed reasonable. First, either the animal had merely ceased to exist, which was ridiculous, or it had not. If it had not, then it was either still in the place where the brush patch had been, or it was out of it. This led to a few possibilities that should be checked. If in the patch, it would seem that the animal must have a well-concealed burrow. If out of it, it must have gotten out by an underground burrow, or on the surface. If on the surface it must either actually have been invisible, a possibility Wilforce did not enjoy thinking about, or it must have very effective protective coloration.

Wilforce sat down at a communicator, and called Evaluation. A weary-looking captain appeared.

Wilforce said, "Captain, do you have some films from Mr. Pick's probes showing a carnivore that attacked one of the Pioneers, then disappeared in some brush?"

"Yes, sir," said the captain. "We've been over that sequence till we can't see straight."

"Can you summarize it for me?"

"Yes, sir. The Pioneer was examining tracks outside the cabin, which was badly smashed up. Several other Pioneers were nearby with guns keeping an eye on things in general. A large, somewhat tigerlike carnivore came out of the cabin in one blur, knocked the Pioneer flat, seized him in its jaws, and sprang behind another cabin. He was behind the cabin before the men could fire. There was a gravsled nearby, and they jumped into it, but the carnivore had already bounded to a patch of tall, widespread, thickly branched brush. There was a Bat overhead that they could have used to kill the carnivore, but that would have blown the man to bits as well as the carnivore. Well, sir, by this time the carnivore could have been in any of a number of places in that brush. There was thick foliage overhead, but ample room to move around underneath."

"Then what happened?"

"A probe had been overhead to catch all this. It was immediately shifted to cover more of the brush, and other probes were quickly switched in to cover the rest. This all happened very fast."

"Could the animal possibly have gotten out before the coverage was complete?"

The captain shook his head. "Sir, I don't think so. You see, those probes were nearby. All the brush wasn't being observed right then, but there *was* a complete ring of territory around the brush that was covered. The probes were moved in such a way that this ring of observation was never broken. It was merely contracted till it included the brush. For the carnivore to have gotten out of the brush, it would have had to move very fast, and it would still have had to cross space that was under observation. It didn't."

Wilforce nodded slowly. "What happened next?"

"Mr. Pick and a small army of Pioneers methodically hacked the brush apart piece-by-piece. They worked shifts, using floodlights and flares to keep the place lit all night long. There was no time it was really dark in there. Finally, they had the whole thing taken apart, and there was no carnivore."

"Did they find *anything* in there?"

"Yes, sir, they drove out quite a number of small animals, a herd of pretty big herbivores, and a flock of birds. You see, the brush patch was made up of tall bushes that grow large edible berries, so the animals were attracted to it. But the carnivore wasn't in there."

Wilforce was silent a moment. "You checked this a number of times?"

"Yes, sir."

"What chance is there the animal could have crawled into some crevice or concealed burrow in that patch of brush?"

"We thought that must have been what happened, sir, but since then the Pioneers have gone over every square foot of ground, and they haven't uncovered a thing."

Wilforce thought this over. Then he nodded. "Thank you, captain."

"You're welcome, sir."

Wilforce next decided to call Pick. A jumpy-looking Pioneer appeared, to say, "General, he's down in the food storeroom right now, and he's mad as a Martian rat in a rainstorm. I'll try to get him if you want, but you can't expect much."

Wilforce laughed. "Go ahead. I'll take my chances."

The Pioneer turned away. There was a mutter of voices. Wilforce even overheard the word "sir" once or twice, and he knew the Pioneers were constitutionally indisposed to use that word. Several minutes passed, and the Pioneer reappeared on the screen, red-faced and mopping his brow. "He'll be right up."

Pick came on the screen tight-lipped and silent, with an expression around the eyes like a panther with its tail in a trap. He glared at Wilforce and said, "Do you have something called a stalker's helmet?"

"Special Equipments probably has some. Why?"

Pick drew a deep breath, and seemed to struggle to calm

himself. "We've got some kind of small rat in the food stocks. We don't see it. We don't hear it. It leaves no droppings. But it eats. We want to see it in action, if possible. It also occurs to me we might need something like this 'stalker's helmet' I've heard of. It's supposed to be a new item of Space-Force emergency equipment, isn't it?"

"Yes, but I don't know anything more about it. How many do you want?"

"Three should do it."

"O.K. Now, about that carnivore you spotted, and that ran into the brush—"

Pick shook his head. "It went in. It didn't come out. And it wasn't there afterward. That's all I can say. We've found no sign of a burrow whatever. We've been over those films till we're black in the face. Maybe by some form of clever camouflage the animal could have slipped away without our seeing it *at the time*. But we'd spot it when we checked over the films afterwards. So that isn't it, either. We've examined those films inch-by-inch, and what happened I don't know, but no visible carnivore came out of that brush, and that is all I can say."

Wilforce said, "Well, that leads us nowhere."

"So," said Pick, "I am going to concentrate on the vermin on board this ship. If I can get a grip *anywhere* on this mess, maybe I can straighten it out. So far, I feel like a man trying to swim in empty space."

Wilforce nodded sympathetically, then suddenly got an idea. He glanced around and saw Rybalko coming across the room from a group of staff officers. Wilforce said, "Balky, does the 186th still have its mascot?"

"Yes, sir. I'm sure of it."

Wilforce turned back to the screen. "Pick, I think I know where you can get just what you want—a full-time expert on rats, with endless patience, great stalking ability, and extra-sensitive vision."

"Where's that?"

"Get in touch with the C.O. of the 186th Combat Group. If you explain your predicament, and promise to take good care of him, the 186th *might* let you borrow their mascot."

Pick frowned. "*What* mascot?"

"A big, ugly, tiger-striped gray tomcat. For your own sake, be careful how you handle him. He's a little rough."

Pick's eyes glinted. "That's the best idea yet. Do you have anything else you want to ask me?"

"No."

"O.K. Get off the screen so I can call the 186th."

Wilforce punched several buttons to the side of the screen. A second lieutenant appeared.

"Sir, Special Equipment."

"Do you have any stalker's helmets around?"

"Stalker's helmets? Just a moment, sir." He turned and called out. An answering call came back. The lieutenant turned around. "Major Barnes will be here in just a minute, sir."

A medium-sized man with major's leaves appeared. Apologetically, he explained that stalker's helmets were new items of equipment that weighed thirty-two pounds apiece, and were just a little clumsy. "They haven't got all the bugs out yet, sir."

The major turned to bark orders at the lieutenant, who vanished and reappeared with a thing like a dull-gray inverted fishbowl with a set of eyepieces sticking out in front, in back, on both sides, and on top. Wilforce was reminded of the high-pressure spheres in which Planet Certification lowered its men to the ocean depths.

"You see, sir," said the major, "the idea is that when a man moves, he's seen. But he *has* to move to see what's going on around him. So this helmet is rigged up in such a way that by a very slight inclination or rotation of the head, the lines of vision of the man wearing it can be switched through lenses and prisms to any one of these sets of eyepieces. In theory, he can see what's in any chosen direction. In practice, after a man has carried this weight around on his head for any length of time, he finds it hard *not* to move his head slightly. The result is, he sees alternately right, left, forward, back, and out the top of his head. Trying to walk in one of these is like a madman's nightmare."

The major paused, and added apologetically, "If you still want one of these, sir, we've got them. But I'd wait till the improved model comes out."

"I see your point. Well, write a brief note explaining the shortcomings of these things, and how they're supposed to operate and send three of the helmets down to Mr. Pick."

"Yes, sir."

Wilforce turned away as he finished the call, to glance at the battle screen. Nothing significant appeared to have happened, and as he paused to review the situation and decide what to do next, the red warning light on the communicator beside him flashed on.

Wilforce snapped on the communicator. A neat officer with a look of intense self-discipline, wearing two stars on each shoulder, saluted stiffly. This was General Davis, Wilforce's Combined Forces Commander. In a full-scale planetary war, Davis would control the combat forces actually on the planet. But right now, there was only a single combat group on Bemus III. Puzzled, Wilforce returned the salute.

Davis said, "Sir, I have to report a case of gross dereliction to duty, regarding the commanding officer of the Forty-second Combat Group on Bemus III."

"What's happened?"

"Sir, the purpose of landing the Forty-second on the planet was to enable us to very quickly send help to Mr. Pick, if he needed it. To be able to do this, the major commanding the combat group should hold his forces mobile and ready to act at a moment's notice. This hasn't been done." Wilforce frowned, and Davis went on. "His troops are digging themselves in. Instead of being heavily armed, the charges for their fusion guns are locked up inside one of the communications buildings. The proxex and impax ammunition are locked up in another building, so the men have nothing but ordinary target rounds. The grav-carriers are stacked in the communications compound, along with most of the rocket launchers. Specially-selected, heavily-armed troops that the major feels he can trust man the walls around the communications center, where he has his headquarters."

Wilforce seemed to feel his collar grow tight. " 'Troops the major feels he can trust'?"

"Yes, sir."

"Go on."

"Sir, that's it. The major has his nest in the communications center. Selected guards man the wall to protect him from his own troops. The bulk of these troops are armed after the style of 1912. They dig their foxholes and trenches by hand, and have to hunt for food in the forest nearby."

An unlovely combination of words rose to the surface of

Wilforce's mind. With an effort, he kept his voice level as he asked, "It's like this right now?"

"Yes, sir. It will be at least an hour-and-a-half before I have it straightened out."

"I see. How did you find this out?"

"I saw the unfinished trenches on a high-level photo from one of the scout ships. It seemed to me they could have had those finished long ago. I shifted focus on the viewer, and discovered they weren't using a trencher. They were doing it by hand. I snapped on the screen to get the Forty-second's commanding officer, but a medical officer appeared and told me the C.O. was suffering from nervous strain, and I couldn't talk to him."

Wilforce loosened his collar.

Davis said, "It took me very nearly five minutes to break through this asinine situation, and get the major on the screen. The major was dead drunk. The medical officer now intruded to inform me that this was 'therapy.' It appears that the major is suffering from a chronic state of anxiety, which is relieved by the situation down there as it now exists. Unless we handle him with padded tongs, we are likely to upset his emotional balance."

"You say it will take *an hour-and-a-half* to get him out of there?"

"Yes, sir. I'm sorry. I have near the planet a colonel of Scouts who's had a good deal of experience with troops, but it will take that long to get him on the spot."

"That's too long. All hell may break loose down there any time."

"Sir, in the rat's nest atmosphere of the Forty-second's headquarters, I can't find anyone qualified to command. And we can't risk having it bungled."

"That may be, but it won't do. An hour from now, the Forty-second may have suffered fifty percent casualties from a few monsters that one properly handled fusion gun could chop into hash. Not only is it bad in itself, but it makes a story that will be told for the next fifty years. A thing like that can spread cynicism and rot through the service like a virus spreads disease."

"Yes, sir. But—"

"Wait a minute." Wilforce thought back to his quick inspection of the Forty-second's equipment just before they left the Space Center for Bemus III. He thought he remembered something. He said, "Find out if they have a full-range battle transceiver down there."

"Sir, we used almost all of them on Inferno, and the Center didn't have any new stocks."

"Check and find out."

"Yes, sir."

Wilforce glanced around, to see that nothing of any importance seemed to have happened. He frowned, thinking back to the appearance of the Forty-second at the Center, and wondering why he hadn't noticed anything. There *had* been something—a general washed-out spiritless look of the troops, and a sort of nervous over-cordiality in the commanding officer—but Wilforce had attributed it to the long misery on Inferno, and the wild binge to celebrate getting off Inferno, followed by the news that they were being sent to some new mess that wasn't even in their own sector. Wilforce glanced back at the screen, where Davis reappeared with a surprised look.

"Sir, they *do* have a battle transceiver."

"Good. Have them set it up on some rise of ground between the communications center's outer wall and the trenches."

"Yes, sir."

Wilforce turned to Rybalko, and told him what he was going to do. He added, "If we have any trouble back here, I'll want to know immediately. Have a competent officer in a monitor booth ready to take over the transceiver."

"Yes, sir."

Wilforce glanced at the communicator, where Davis returned to say, "Sir, they're setting it up."

Wilforce said, "Good," and walked swiftly to one of several blocks of thick-walled booths that stood at an angle to the rear wall of the command center. He stepped into one, and shut a thick door behind him.

Directly in front of him appeared a sweep of slightly-rolling ground cut by trenches where men dug slowly with picks and spades. About five hundred feet away was the forest. To right and left, the forest stretched farther away. Wilforce turned, to see behind him a faint line outlining the door of the battle transceiver booth, and, beyond that, a high wall of thick upright logs.

A little distance away, holding their fusion rifles at the ready, were two burly privates. A sergeant stooped to check the dials of a brown box near a power cable that ran back across a ditch and over the wall into the communications center. For an instant, Wilforce felt his usual sense of disorientation, and reminded himself that this was nothing more than the ordinary two-way communicator screen carried a step farther. The booth he was in had its circuitry within its walls, and its multiple screens curved and joined over the inside surface of the booth. The battle transceiver, on the planet, had its circuitry inside, and its screens shaped and joined on its outside surface. The effect was that the commander using the battle transceiver saw things as if he were on the planet, and he was seen by those on the planet as if he were actually there. The defect was that the bulky transceiver on the planet was awkward to move, and constantly in danger from every chance bullet and shell fragment that came its way.

As Wilforce watched, the sergeant made a final adjustment at his box, and abruptly there was sound. The dull clink and scrape of pick and spade reached Wilforce clearly. A voice carried to him from the trenches:

"Hey, the general's ghosting us!"

Wilforce glanced up briefly, and pulled down a small microphone on a slender stalk. "Sergeant," he said, and his voice carried clearly.

The sergeant snapped to attention and saluted.

Wilforce returned the salute and heard the sound of digging slow, as men paused to listen. He said, "Why are these men digging by hand? Is the trencher out of order?"

"No, sir."

"Are all these men being disciplined?" Wilforce's tone was cold.

"No, sir."

"Then why are they digging those trenches?"

"Major's orders, sir."

A dead stillness settled over the clearing.

Wilforce said, "I want those picks and spades put away immediately. Tell the major I want to see that trencher at work out here inside of five minutes. I also want the major and his company commanders to report to me as fast as they can get here."

"Yes, sir." The sergeant stepped back and saluted.

Wilforce returned the salute.

The sergeant faced about and set off at a run. Wilforce watched him scramble down into the ditch around the jutting log walls, climb a ladder against the walls, and pause to salute a lieutenant. There was a brief exchange of words. The lieutenant cast one glance toward Wilforce, and joined the sergeant in a headlong rush toward the inner wall. An instant later, there was the sound of shouted orders, the clank of an engine, and the crash of heavy objects being moved.

The long low trencher rose up behind the wall, a big, roughly ski-shaped grav-carrier supporting it, with three other carriers crosswise to brace the front. At the prow of each carrier bent a sweating technician, while atop the trencher stood the lieutenant, his face pale as he glanced nervously along the line of grav-carriers, and back up over his shoulder at the looming tower. He called out a series of sharp orders to the technician in each carrier, then his voice rose to a scream as one carrier started to sink lower than the rest. Then, heavily, carriers and trencher moved out over the walls, and eased down outside. The trencher trundled off the carriers with a low clank and rumble, then wheeled toward a trench where the men had just stopped digging. The trencher's center section swung down into the earth, and a steadily increasing stream of dirt poured out the discharge to the side.

Wilforce glanced back at the walls to see a number of officers, very neatly dressed, scramble down the ladder, hesitate at the ditch, then plunge down in and an instant later reappear, several of them reaching out to steady one who stumbled and nearly fell.

As they approached, Wilforce saw that the man who had nearly fallen was the combat group's commanding officer, his face puffy, and his expression blank and hopeless. The officers came to a straggling halt, and saluted.

Wilforce returned the salute, and said, "Major, I have heard that most of these troops are without proper ammunition or charges for their fusion weapons. Is that true?"

There was a distinct lapse of time, then Wilforce saw a faint glimmer in the major's eyes. He started to speak.

Before he could get the words out, a pudgy captain,

wearing the bright emblem of the Medical Corps, stepped forward.

"General, this man is ill. As a physician, I must forbid—"

Wilforce glanced at the captain, as a soldier looks at a blood-sucking bug in the bedding just before he squashes it.

The captain hurriedly stepped back out of the way, his teeth clicking together.

The major drew a deep breath, and said shakily, "Sir, it's true."

"I see," said Wilforce, and the silence quickly deepened around him till there was only the rumble of the trencher and the faint rustle of the forest around them. This silence told Wilforce that every man who could was watching, and because of the carnivores in the nearby forest, this situation was dangerous. Wilforce chose his words with care, and spoke so that his voice would carry clearly.

"Major, there are large and dangerous animals in that forest. No doubt the men can hit them with the ammunition they have now. But they can hit them a lot harder with the proper ammunition. I want proxex, impax, and fusion charges issued immediately."

As the major said, "Yes, sir," Wilforce could see the faces of the men turn to glance uneasily toward the forest. This much he had expected. But this was followed immediately by a shout, the glint of a rifle swinging up, and a spatter of gunfire.

Wilforce glanced around to see a brownish form blur across the clearing, then rise in a bound that showed huge forepaws and teeth like bayonets. The fire of machine guns, and of rifles firing almost point-blank, had no effect on the creature that Wilforce could see. A quick glance toward the communications center wall showed him men with fusion rifles looking on in a sort of trance.

Wilforce brought the microphone to his lips and spoke loud and clearly, "You on the walls, there—burn that thing down!"

Belatedly, the fusion rifles swung up. In the trenches, the men ducked as the carnivore sprang overhead, whirled, crouched, and reached in with its huge paw like a bear scooping fish from a stream. There was an audible snap and crunch of breaking bones, and the huge throat muscles worked under the fur.

Then finally, the dazzling lines of light reached out from the wall. There was a sizzling crack like a thunderbolt striking close at hand. The carnivore jerked, twisted around to claw at its middle, where a dark and widening pool flowed into the earth. Then a searing line of light touched the huge head, there was a spasmodic jerk of paws, and then all that was left was a steaming carcass.

Someone shouted from the far side of the wall, facing the opposite end of the clearing.

Wilforce turned to see the major and his officers standing as if they had been frozen into blocks of ice. He said sharply, "Major, get that ammunition and those fusion charges passed out, *and hurry up!*"

The major blinked, then suddenly seemed to come to life. He gave rapid orders to his officers, glanced at Wilforce as if he wanted to say something, shook his head slightly, saluted, and set off at an unsteady run for the communications center. A few moments later, the trencher ate its way from the inner line of trenches toward the wall. Men began passing ammunition cans down the ladder to other men in the trench.

Just then, a voice spoke to Wilforce, and it took him an instant to realize that it was Rybalko, saying, "Sir, excuse me—that vanishing ship has been spotted again."

Wilforce slid the microphone up, pressed back the door edge, and stepped out of the transceiver booth, feeling again a momentary disorientation as he glanced around the command center. Then he saw the big viewscreen on the far wall, the planet Bemus III in its lower left corner, and in the center a silvery object like a chopped-off length of giant rod. Wilforce crossed the room to take a closer look.

He studied the big flat-ended object for a moment, noted the pitted look of its surface, and saw what appeared to be a small hatch housing at its far end.

Rybalko said, "Sir, this thing is in orbit around the planet. We've only been watching it for several minutes now, but it vanished twice."

Wilforce, trying to see if what he saw near the far end *was* a hatch housing, abruptly found himself looking through empty space at a distant constellation. The huge closed cylinder was gone.

Rybalko had a watch in his hand. When the cylinder

reappeared, with the abruptness of a projected image thrown on a screen, Rybalko glanced at the watch. "Eight seconds. There doesn't seem to be any pattern."

Wilforce said, "*All* our instruments show this object?"

"Yes, sir. And its orbit seems perfectly sensible. But all it seems to do is to vanish and reappear. There's been no actual sign of life from it so far."

Wilforce nodded. For a moment, he tried to connect the disappearing ship with the disappearing animals on the planet. But there occurred to him such a host of unlikely theories that he decided to forget all about it. He glanced at Rybalko.

"Both ends of that cylinder are closed?"

"Yes, sir. There are signs of possible openings, but they're shut now."

Wilforce glanced at the cylinder again. Its blocky shape suggested to him that it was probably not intended for use in a planet's atmosphere. It might be—perhaps—an interplanetary cargo carrier. The apparent invisibility of the ship might be due to extremely well-designed counter-detection apparatus. Assuming it had, for some unknown reason, been left in orbit around this planet, it could have remained there for thousands of years with little noticeable change. And the destroyer that crash-landed on Bemus III had collided with something. It seemed reasonable to think it had collided with this cylinder, had heavily jarred the counter-detection apparatus, and caused a malfunction that produced the alternating visibility and invisibility.

Wilforce turned to Rybalko, and said, "We'll have to see if that thing can be boarded. It's just possible that this might be the loose end of the knot."

Rybalko turned to the communicator to repeat the boarding order to the task force commander.

As Wilforce again turned to glance at the unchanging battle screen, a call came in from Pick.

"Here's something queer," said Pick. "Some of my men have been finishing up a check of the settlements. They've found a few partly-chewed scraps of clothing, paper, and so on, plus droppings containing metal snap fasteners, identification tags, and other metal items, which pretty well bolster the theory that the carnivores attacked and actually ate the colonists, and the herbivores ate the food stocks and records. But some of the metal identification tags, chains, and other items were in *unburied* droppings, exactly typical of the Bemus herbivores we've seen so far."

"The colonists could have taken off their tags and left them in the pockets of their clothing."

"Would they have taken out their dental fillings and put *them* in their pockets?"

Wilforce stared, then said slowly, "Dogs don't bury their droppings. They're carnivores."

"True, but everything we've found so far suggests catlike forms that lie in wait, not doglike animals that run down their prey. And it's important to a catlike animal to keep the herbivores in the vicinity unaware that it's there. This business strikes me as very peculiar, and it's not the *only* peculiar thing."

"What else?"

"All the settlements have big barbecue pits. Now we find from the remains of weeds buried under the dirt from these pits, from the size of weeds growing atop the dirt, from the ashes in the pits, and from the condition of the pit's big stakes, that they were dug recently and only used once—around the time the attack was made on the settlements."

Wilforce went to bed still turning this problem over in his mind. Early the next morning, he came wide awake, and, for an instant, everything fitted together in a complete picture.

Wilforce swung to a sitting position on the edge of his cot. Already, the thoughts were slipping away, and carefully he held his mind nearly blank, trying to grope back along the mental associations to the pattern of ideas that had been in his mind the instant before he came fully awake. Gradually, it all came back to him, and he saw the puzzle on Bemus III fit together like the steel hooks, jaws and springs of a powerful trap.

Wilforce went over his thoughts a bit at a time, carefully checking each connection, till he was sure it fitted together in a consistent whole. Now he wondered how he could ever have missed it. He washed, dressed quickly, and started down the corridor to the command center. He turned a corner and a junior communications officer came out a door and said, "Sir, excuse me, could you come in here a minute?"

"What is it?"

"It's the screen the Pioneers set up so we could watch the destroyer, sir. We've got something funny here."

Wilforce said, "All right. Let's see it."

The communications officer quickly led the way into a darkened room, where a technician sat hunched at a screen. Wilforce looked over his shoulder to see a dim corridor in the crash-landed destroyer. In the foreground was an air-circulation duct. As Wilforce leaned closer, he saw a faint movement, then a small shadowy thing that squeezed under a corner of the mesh over the duct opening and dropped to the floor. There was a swift scurry down the corridor, then another small thing moved in a long bound. There was a brief struggle, then silence, and finally a faint crunch. Another shadow slid out the duct.

Wilforce said, "How long has this been going on?"

"Ever since they carried that big tomcat around the corner into the food storeroom. These things have been popping out the ventilator right and left."

"I see." Wilforce turned to the communications officer. "Get Mr. Pick for me on another screen, and hurry."

"Yes, sir."

The officer went out, and Wilforce turned to glance at the screen. On it, nothing moved. The corridor appeared to be empty. He said to the technician, "We aren't transmitting sound, are we?"

"No, sir."

"Have you seen any other animals beside these small ones?"

"Sir, I could have sworn something the size of a rat went by the other night. But it was moving fast, and I haven't seen anything like it since."

"Did it come out of that ventilator?"

"No sir. It streaked down the corridor well over to the side."

The door opened. "Sir, we'll have Mr. Pick in just a moment."

Wilforce said, "Switch the call to the command center. I'll want General Rybalko to see it, if possible."

"Yes, sir."

Wilforce went to the command center, observed that the battle screen continued to show nothing of interest, and then saw the big wall screen, lit to show the huge cylinder, now

surrounded by small spaceboats. There was a round opening in the far end of the cylinder where Wilforce thought
he had seen a hatch. He looked at the cylinder with a frown,
then glanced around as a communicator switched on. Pick
was on the screen, tired and scowling.

Wilforce described what he'd just seen.

Pick said, "Just a minute. I'll find out whether that cat's
caught anything."

Wilforce snapped on another communicator, and called
Davis, who appeared on the screen rumpled but alert.
Wilforce said, "Has the Forty-second had any more trouble?"

"Nothing serious, sir. Every now and then, something
charges out of the forest and gets cut to pieces before it
can do anything. The only trouble is rats and hallucinations."

"Rats?"

"Yes, sir. A kind of furtive vicious rat has turned up that
feeds on the remains of the carnivores and any other flesh
it can sink its teeth in. There have also been reports of things
something like hyenas, but there are a lot more of these
rats."

"What was that about hallucinations?"

"The nervous strain down there must be pretty severe.
The men are probably in no real danger now, but the thought
of those monsters springing out of the forest any moment,
and the constant watch that has to be kept—Well, some of
the men think they've seen chunks of carnivores they've
shot get up and walk away."

"You have your colonel of Scouts in charge?"

"Yes, sir."

"Did you get that medical officer out of there?"

"Yes, sir. Incidentally, sir, he cracked up. He tried to shoot
himself, and bungled the job."

Wilforce said, "Get a transport into position. I may want
to take the Forty-second off that planet entirely."

"Yes, sir."

Wilforce blanked the screen and turned to see Pick on
the other screen, a deep scowl on his face. Pick said, "That
tomcat has eaten, all right. He's filled out like a barrel.
He's in there dozing, and purring like a gasoline engine.
There are half a dozen tails spread out around him, and
the rear half of something like a cross between a rat and
a weasel."

Wilforce said, "Get that half a rat, or whatever it is, and watch it. See that it doesn't get away."

Pick looked blank. "It's *dead*. How's it going to get away?"

"Never mind that. *Watch* it."

Pick's face screwed up in thought. He nodded. "All right. We'll watch it."

"Do you expect to need any help from the Forty-second?"

Pick shook his head. "I don't think we'll need any help. The simple fact is something made us jumpy. We're *still* jumpy. But now we're used to it."

Wilforce nodded in understanding. "Suppose for the time being you keep your men under cover, and use the probes to scout and observe."

"All right" said Pick. "Have you figured out what's going on here?"

"I'm not absolutely sure," said Wilforce. "But it seems to me we've got one foot in the biggest biological trap ever constructed. Now, I've got to see if this is true, and if so, how we can smash the trap." After this call, Wilforce got Rybalko.

"Sir?" said Rybalko.

"Balky, I want three sub-nuclear triggers checked out. I don't think we'll have to use them, but I want them ready. And have the reflectors ready to focus on Bemus III, so that a given word, we can roast the planet."

"Yes, sir," said Rybalko.

Wilforce called Davis to take the Forty-second Combat Group off the planet. Then he had his flagship's communications center get the nearest headquarters of the Planet Certification Authority, which had made the original survey of Bemus III. He asked a single pointed question, and after a considerable delay, he received the answer: "General, there have been no restrictions on travel to Bemus III since the planet was certified for colonization."

Wilforce got the task force commander, and asked, "What have you found out about that cylinder?"

"Sir, as nearly as we can tell, it's nothing but an extremely heavy protective housing. Inside it, there's a missile armed with what we're pretty sure is a sub-nuclear trigger. Evidently someone wanted to be able on short notice to turn that planet into a brilliant star."

"How is the missile released from the cylinder?"

"The ends of the cylinder are hinged to swing open like double doors, sir."

"What causes the missile to be launched?"

"So far, sir, we don't know."

"All right. There may be more of these missiles in undetectable housings. If so, we want to know about them. Check the most likely simple orbits, on the assumption that a number of missiles were used in case one failed."

"Yes, sir."

Wilforce turned to see Rybalko talking to a tall, tense-looking man Wilforce recognized as Dr. Traeger, his chief medical officer. Traeger was speaking insistently, and Rybalko was frowning. Wilforce walked over.

"What is it, Traeger?"

"General, Evaluation has been trying to decide whether the smaller herbivores on Bemus III are offspring of the big, mammoth-like croppers that Planet Certification thought were becoming extinct."

"Yes?"

"Well, several of my colleagues and I tried to dissect a medium-sized herbivore, to see how similar the internal structure was to the cropper Planet Certification reported dissecting."

"What did you find out?"

"General, we had a trying time. The exposed tissues exuded white droplets. These cohered to form a tough membrane through which we could see absolutely nothing. We cut off a number of large blocks of muscle tissue to study this process. Nearly every block was quickly covered with a tough membrane. We examined the blocks at intervals and found that the enclosed tissues became soft and viscous. Layers of large hollow cells built up behind the membrane, and the internal temperature rose sharply. A reorganization of the substance of the tissues began to take place."

"To form what?"

Traeger drew a deep breath, looked directly at Wilforce and said unhappily, "To form the outlines of a small carnivore."

"An embryo?"

"No, not an embryo. I don't know how to explain it except to say that it reminded me of the precipitate that forms when a photographic plate is exposed. No doubt the mechanism is completely different, but that is what it *looked* like."

"This happened in blocks of *muscle* tissue?"

"Yes, sir."

"How would the animal find enough of the right chemical substances to form its teeth, bone structure, brain, and so on?"

Traeger shook his head. "General, I don't think it *would* find enough. But the report on Planet Certification's original dissection mentions a chain of complex nerve cells of unknown function, paralleling the main skeletal framework. At intervals, there were large ganglia, again with no known function. If we had cut through the entire limb, instead of merely taking blocks of muscle tissue, some of the blocks would have included these large ganglia as well as bone. Then the development *might* have been complete. As it was, the outlines became less distinct in the last blocks we examined. But the important point is that it happened at all."

Wilforce said, "Did the Planet Certification report mention anything like this?"

"No, sir. Nothing. It may be that the larger and older animals take longer to regenerate. Planet Certification also used the latest methods of tissue preservation, which weren't available to us."

"What happened to the animal you cut the muscle tissue from?"

"Well, by this time we'd seen what I've just mentioned, and were getting a little uneasy. We were doing the dissection in an improvised lab on one of Evaluation's scout ships. The idea was incredible, but incredible or not, we didn't care to find ourselves suddenly at close quarters with one of those carnivores that had shown up down on Bemus III. We switched to another ship, so we could watch what happened next by communicator. We needn't have hurried. Some ten hours later, there were convulsive movements beneath the membrane that formed under the fur and over the cut parts of the animal. The membrane ripped open, and a medium-sized carnivore, its fur wet and clinging, climbed out, crouched, and ate the membrane."

Wilforce nodded slowly. "And in the chunks of muscle

tissue, you said small *incomplete* carnivores had formed? Not herbivores, but carnivores?"

Traeger said, "We could see the beginning of claws and teeth, and the shape of the head. They were carnivores. I know how it seems, but there it is. The whole thing's impossible."

"Never mind that," said Wilforce. "If it happened, it's possible. Nature isn't bound to one single procedure. What did this large carnivore do after it ate the membrane?"

"It looked around, ate the remains of the blocks of muscle tissue, then curled up and went to sleep. After a short sleep, it woke up, sniffed the fur the membrane had formed under, tipped the communicator stand over, and that was the last we saw."

Traeger shrugged helplessly.

"All right. Now we have to find out more. What we might do now is pack the landing boat's air lock with a variety of meat, flour, paper, and other organic materials and food-stuffs, put in a time-opener for the inner air-lock door, and another communicator behind heavy mesh, and see what happens when that carnivore gets at the food."

Traeger said, "I was thinking of something like that. I'll let you know as soon as we find out anything more."

Good."

Traeger turned to go out, and Wilforce noticed Rybalko standing nearby with a deep frown on his face. Rybalko looked at Traeger's retreating back as an officer might look at a subordinate who reported, "Sir, there's a stream in front of us, it's wide and deep and it's flowing uphill at a good clip."

Rybalko turned to Wilforce and said, "Sir, I don't quite know about Traeger. I don't exactly believe that."

Wilforce said, "Don't be too sure. Back on Earth, if I remember correctly there are things called 'oysters'—small water animals protected by two hard shells—that grow in large number in 'oyster beds' and are used for human food. There are also creatures called 'starfish.'

"Now," said Wilforce, "the starfish likes to eat oysters, just as people do. When the starfish finds an oyster, it grips the oyster's shell with sucking stalks on the underside of its limbs, and eventually forces the oyster's shell open. Then it squirts in a digestive fluid, and eats the oyster. Naturally, people don't care to find these starfish prowling through the oyster beds. At one time, whenever they could, they used to chop the starfish to pieces."

Rybalko nodded approvingly.

Wilforce added, "They did this until they discovered that a mere single arm of the starfish, if it included enough of the center, could regenerate *a complete new starfish.*"

Rybalko looked blank. Then he said, "This happened on *Earth?*"

"It did. Quite a while ago, too. Our problem here has been compounded, multiplied, and raised several powers higher, so that we have what you might call a 'star tiger' to deal with. But even that is only about half of it. And we have to find an answer quickly."

During the rest of the morning, Wilforce received a number of calls. Pick, perspiring heavily, told Wilforce that the half-rat from the storeroom had grown some kind of white film, out of which had emerged a little vicious furtive thing that looked like a shrew. This thing hid under every scrap of cover, and tore a chunk out of the forefinger of a pioneer who tried to uncover it. Pick mentioned this in the defensive manner of a man who doesn't expect to be believed.

Immediately after this, Davis called, to cautiously reveal, with many roundabout expressions, that he had seen by battle transceiver a kind of big carnivore climb out through the whitish membrane around a chunk of carcass down on Bemus III. The soldiers were already so used to this that they shot the creature all over again as it emerged from the membrane. Other than this, the Forty-second had lifted from the planet without incident, but Davis was at pains to get the significance of the carnivore across to Wilforce.

No sooner was this call ended than one came in from Evaluation, and a scholarly biologist explained Traeger's information to Wilforce all over again, with many homely analogies to make it easier for the layman to understand. He dwelt heavily on the caterpillar that spins a cocoon to emerge a moth, and nothing Wilforce could do would stop him till he ran through all the details.

In a bad mood, Wilforce called back to have Davis hold the Forty-second's transport away from his other troops, and also to have to have the men be on the lookout for small mouse- or shrew-like creatures on the transport. Davis nodded and started explaining all over again about the carnivore coming out of the chunk of carcass. Wilforce saw little flecks dance before his eyes, and Davis hastily changed the subject.

That afternoon the task force commander called to say he had located another cylinder.

"How did you find it?"

"We figured they used three, to be reasonably sure at least one would work, and spaced them evenly about the planet. We already could make a pretty fair guess how the orbit of the one we'd found had been when the destroyer swiped it, so it seemed logical to sweep one hundred twenty degrees back with a flat pattern of reconnaissance torpedoes. This could have taken a long time, but we guessed right, and pretty soon one of the torpedoes banged into something that didn't show up on the detectors."

Good," said Wilforce. "Tag that one, then see if you can find another."

"Yes, sir."

Wilforce blanked the screen, thinking that there might well be half-a-dozen or more of the cylinders, but that there was no point discouraging his men by mentioning things like that.

Dr. Traeger now appeared on the screen to say, "General, we did as you suggested. We ran a sealed boarding tunnel to the scout ship, and filled the air lock with meat and other edibles and organic materials."

"What happened?"

"When the timer worked the inner lock door mechanism, the carnivore gorged on the meat, then went to sleep. We could see into the ship, and the skin and fur was gone, so evidently it had eaten that. Well, twenty minutes after gorging on the meat, it drank a great deal of water. It curled up very tightly, and its breathing became labored, as if it was struggling up a steep hill. Then the breathing gradually slowed. Three hours later the animal got up, and we could see that the form of its head, teeth, and body in general had altered to match that of the usual Bemus herbivore. It walked over to the air lock, ate up twenty-five pounds of flour, ten pounds of sugar, a ream of yellow scratch paper, a ball of twine, a uniform shirt, a pair of leather boots and a plastic ruler. Then it went back to sleep."

Wilforce nodded, and said, "Now what I want to know is, how does it all fit together? Kill a Bemus animal and it turns into one or more savage carnivores. Feed the carnivore and it becomes an herbivore. I wonder if it forms sort of a scale, with the mammoth-like cropper on top, and some other creature on the bottom."

Traeger said, "I should think the lower limit for this creature would be the minimum size capable of efficiently carrying the biological control mechanism that reorganizes the tissues."

Wilforce said, "I imagine Pick can help us on that. He already has one about the size of a shrew. I'll call him."

Pick was on the screen a few minutes later. Wilforce said, "Pick, do you still have that shrew?"

"We've got the thing. We aren't happy with it."

"I want you to kill it."

"It will be a pleasure. But what if it dies, and later on half-a-dozen carnivorous grasshoppers pop out?"

"That's exactly what we want to find out. We want to know just how small the thing will get."

"We'll find out for you."

The screen blanked, and Rybalko came over to say, "Sir, the Forty-second has searched its transport. A number of men think they saw small furtive animals, but there's nothing definite."

Wilforce said, "Have them lay another transport alongside, bridge the air locks, and cross over one at a time. They'll have to strip before leaving one ship, and receive a new issue of clothing as they enter the other. Then we can pump the transport's air back into its tanks, send some men back through in spacesuits to search, and eventually find out if there *are* any animals on board."

In the next few days, spacesuited searchers found a number of small mouse-and-shrew-like animals on the transport. Now that everyone had an idea what to look for, one thing rapidly led to another.

From Traeger, Evaluation got the first solid details of the life cycle of the carnivore. With this clue to go on, they went back over a number of previous observations, and found that what they had dismissed as irrational made sense after all. Wilforce now got a flood of information that would have cleared everything up if he had gotten it sooner—but

Evaluation had been afraid to give it to him because Evaluation knew it didn't make sense.

Pick called to say that the shrew was thoroughly dead, it failed to show any signs of reviving, and it was getting unpleasant to keep the thing around. Pick, therefore, buried the shrew, and Evaluation, now ready to believe anything, kept a wary eye on the grave.

Meanwhile, a sound engineer, going over a film of the animals in the corridor of Pick's ship, discovered that the furtive "mouse," when attacked, gave terrified squeals—in a pitch too high for the human ear to hear. He suggested that these just inaudible noises, repeated over and over, accounted for the uneasiness of Pick and his men, and might also be used to test for the presence of the animals.

As Wilforce and Rybalko were going over this information, the task force commander called to say that he had found two more of the huge cylinders. One contained another sub-nuclear trigger. The other contained the bulk of the control mechanism, designed to ignore an object that went *down* to the planet, but to send a signal that would trip off the triggers if anything tried to come *up* from the planet.

Wilforce said, "Why didn't it work?"

"Because two metal strips had to slide over one another under light pressure. Apparently, they had been there so long the atoms of the metal had interpenetrated. The strips didn't move. We've dismantled the whole thing, just in case."

"Was the mechanism purely automatic?"

"Yes, sir. But there was a manual control, too. This cylinder also had an arrangement for internal heating, plus a cot, and a desk with a little statuette."

"A statuette?"

"Apparently some kind of reminder, sir. It showed a carnivore, its sides all swollen out, with what looked like an empty pair of boots and a hat nearby."

Wilforce said, "Keep looking. There may be more of those triggers, and there should be a separate warning system around somewhere."

When this call was finished, Wilforce sat back for a moment, then had his communications center get in touch with the chief of colonization. A strongly built, firm-jawed man promptly appeared on the screen. He said, "I've been studying staff reports on Bemus III since Larssen sent out his alarm. Is it as bad as it seems?"

"Sir," said Wilforce, "in my opinion, it's a terrific nuisance, and a headache of the first magnitude. I don't think it should be anything worse."

The chief of colonization looked surprised, and picked up a sheet of paper. "I have here an analysis that ends up as follows: ' . . . Thus small furtive Bemus creatures must already have left the planet on supply ships. They have infested an unknown number of other ships, supply centers, and almost certainly, planets. It is impossible to alter the traffic flow to prevent further infection, because we don't know where they are already. Any one of these creatures may grow larger, suffer successive 'deaths,' and by an unprecedented type of reproduction come to populate any planet where it is introduced. The small creatures are furtive and hard to find. The large herbivores eat immense quantities of food. The large carnivores are deadly.'"

The chief of colonization scowled. "I am no pessimist. And I don't believe in being hypnotized by difficulties. Still— are the facts I've just mentioned correct?"

"Yes, sir."

"But you think it's just a headache?"

Wilforce nodded. "It seems to me to be part of the price we pay for colonizing new star systems. If we break a trail through the jungle, some fine day, a tiger will lie in wait beside it. That doesn't mean the trail is no good. It only means that now we have to figure out how to dispose of the tiger. It's been like this since back before history began. The caveman discovers fire; that's fine—but now he gets burnt. He wants light at night, and invents the lamp; it gives light, and it also flickers and smokes up the cave. He stores food for the winter; rats get in it. A problem solved leads to one unsolved. Now we find ourselves with a big trail— and a big tiger beside it."

"But how do we dispose of this one?"

"Well, most big problems break down into a number of smaller problems. Here, we have three of these smaller problems. First—the source of the trouble—the animals on Bemus III. Second, their ability to stow away and travel on our spaceships. Third, any new colonies of the animals on other planets.

"To start with," said Wilforce, "we can ring Bemus III with sub-nuclear triggers, set up a warning network to keep ships away, and, if necessary, destroy the planet.

"As for travel by spaceship, it's the small, furtive animals that do this. We might not be able to ferret them out ourselves, but we can find animals to do it for us—the cat, for instance. As a check, we can put in devices to spot that high-pitched squeal the animal gives when it's caught."

The chief of colonization nodded. "Good so far. But what do we do if it gets onto a planet?"

"That's harder. Evaluation has just tried poisons, for instance. The carnivores don't touch it, and herbivores 'die' and reconstitute themselves as carnivores. All we've seen so far shows it's not much use just to kill them. The colonists put up special barbecue pits. Evidently they killed the animals for a feast to celebrate their tenth anniversary on the planet. The captain of the crash-landed destroyer told me his men had plenty of fresh meat, so apparently they were killing them. The Forty-second had to hunt part of its food in the forest. In each case, we got misery and disaster as a result. Chance accidents, such as lightning, drowning, the fall of limbs in windstorms, were evidently enough to create an occasional monster carnivore, and keep the colonists constantly on edge when they didn't kill the things themselves. So I don't think we want to kill them."

"If we don't kill them, what *do* we do?"

"Feed them. Every time there's been an attack on the herbivores, hosts of carnivores have appeared, only to vanish by the time anyone got here to investigate. The carnivores will eat the herbivores if there's nothing else handy. They'll eat chunks of dead carnivores. They very quickly become herbivores, and *they* will eat all kinds of things. So if we have emergency food stocks ready, we can dump them in chosen areas on any infested planet, and let the creatures gorge themselves. Since they eat all kinds of things, the food stocks needn't be expensive."

"You're thinking—instead of carnivores and little scattered furtive creatures, we'll end up with placid herbivores?"

"Yes, sir."

"Then what?"

"If nothing else, we can prod them into a cargo carrier,

and sling the whole works into the nearest sun. It's crude, but it ought to work."

The chief of colonization nodded absently, "Don't let the crudity of it bother you, as long as it works." He frowned. "What about those cylinders?"

"What we've seen so far indicates they're ancient. Evidently some other race ran into this problem long ago, arrived at roughly the same solution we've thought of, and has since died out, or somehow moved on. The Bemus creatures remain locked in a sort of fluid status quo."

The colonization chief was staring off at something out of the range of vision. Suddenly he snapped his fingers. "I think I see what to do. Of course, the Interstellar S.P.C.A. may let out a howl such as was never heard in all recorded history. Still—"

Some months later, the two men were on Donak IV, a frontier planet that had reported an outbreak of Bemus creatures. Moving barriers of charged wires prodded herds of the monster herbivores across a causeway to a cluster of cylindrical metal towers in the middle of a lake. There appeared to be some sort of grim production line in progress.

From where Wilforce stood, he could see the animals go around a corner, get shot by men with fusion guns, then picked up by mechanical loaders, and dumped onto a conveyer belt which promptly carried them down out of sight.

There came a sound of rushing water, and an electrified barrier switched the flow of Bemus creatures to another tower.

Near the tower were several buildings, one bearing the sign: "TANNERY."

The chief of colonization nodded approvingly. "Very satisfactory arrangement. We stuff a load of monsters in that tower, fill it up with water, and let them evolve through whatever grisly changes they want to. It doesn't matter whether they turn into super-tigers, medium-sized carnivores, or little carnivores—they don't live without air. And that situation keeps them too busy to eat up their furs after they finish a change."

A grav-carrier lifted a load of hides from one of the towers toward the building marked "Tannery." A small hole in the side of a tower opened and spat into the lake several dozen limp mouse- and shrew-like animals, which were promptly snapped up by lean, sharp-toothed fish swimming around.

The chief of colonization glanced at Wilforce and smiled. "Well," he said, "*that* problem seems to be solved—but who knows what may happen next?"

"That's right" said Wilforce. "Man's special skill is solving problems. But the one he can't solve—is the problem of *having* problems."

REVOLT!

Colonel Matthew Crandall was in process of grinding the conceit off a new lieutenant when the message came in. The *ping* of the communications bell could barely be heard through the drone of the lieutenant's voice:

" . . . And, sir, a Space Force Second Lieutenant outranks a Planetary Development Technician 3rd by two grades. So I ordered him to stand aside. But this Third tried to act as if he hadn't heard me. He tried to precede me on board *Vengeance*." The lieutenant's chest expanded and his head tilted back. "And so, sir, I enforced my order!"

Crandall eyed the lieutenant with the look of a farmer who has his ax raised, but does not yet have the chicken's neck in the right spot on the block. Then the *ping* of the communications bell caught his attention. Crandall got up, stripped a piece of message paper from the transceiver and read:

Planetary Development H.Q. Cygnes VI m 4 to Space
   Force H.Q., Cygnes III
Personal: To CoL. Matthew Crandall.
   Matt: Have just heard from Purcell. Three hundred latest model delGrange mechanical suits en route from Purth, due today 01-23-2212. Three hundred sixty operators en route from Szalesh, due 01-24-2212, fully trained in Model C trainers. I intend give them brief practice in new suits, then get them down on surface of VI. Every indication VI is loaded with crude ore. I need

your formal signature for first contact, pursuant Section 67b. Am sending courier with forms.

Thanks, Dave.

David L. Paley, Chief, Planetary
Development Authority, Cygnes.

Crandall read the message over, frowned and pulled a chair around to the transceiver. He rapped the date-time key, tapped out the heading, paused for a moment, thought, then went on:

Dave: Would like to do as you say, but Section 67b is plain that when I sign, I share the responsibility. You say new suits due here today, 01-23-2212, and the operators tomorrow, 01-24-2212; you propose give operators "brief practice" then send them down. My experience is, all new equipment has flaws. Gravity on VI is such that if flaws become apparent down there, we may have mess of big proportions to clean up. Let's go a little slow at first.

Matt.

Matthew Crandall, Colonel, Space Force.

Crandall sent the message, turned back to his desk, and glanced at the lieutenant. Crandall rapped his fingers on the desk, looked steadily at the lieutenant, and waited.

The lieutenant started, as if he had been daydreaming. "It would," he said, "have been an insult to the Space Force, colonel."

"What would?" said Crandall.

"Sir?" said the lieutenant. "Why, to let a Planetary Development Tech. 3rd precede a senior Space Force officer, sir."

Crandall let his glance stray to the small bar on the lieutenant's left shoulder: "What senior Space Force officer, lieutenant?"

"Senior to . . . to the technician, sir."

"Just how senior was the technician?"

"He was . . . just a Technician 3rd. Sir, if I had let him precede a senior—"

"A what?"

"A . . . A *ranking* Space Force officer, it would have been a . . . an insult to the service, sir."

"So you grabbed him and shoved him back?"

The lieutenant's face turned red, then white. "Sir, I *ordered* him to stay back. Then I . . . he didn't, and I had to *enforce* the order."

" 'Enforce' it. How did you do that?"

"I—Well, I used force, sir."

"Did you hit him?"

The lieutenant winced, then stood straight. "I just sort of—Sir, he acted as if—"

"Did you hit him?"

"I—No, sir. I just sort of, quickly pushed him aside, and got out in front of him."

Crandall looked steadily at the lieutenant, and watched as the phrase "got out in front of him" echoed through the lieutenant's mind.

The message bell pinged and Crandall stepped over to the transceiver. He stripped off the message and read:

> Matt: I understand your hesitation, and regret it is my fault for neglecting to mention that suits will of course be thoroughly inspected and checked during interval before arrival of operators. DelGrange is a perfectionist in design, and of course these suits have already been checked by him, prior to being shipped. But we will check them again as ordinary routine.
>   Dave.
>
>   David L. Paley, Chief, Planetary
>   Development Authority, Cygnes.

Crandall scowled and tapped out his reply.

> Dave: I appreciate the thoroughness of your preliminary check on the equipment. But what I have in mind is something that may not show up until the suits are actually in use down on VI. Then if we have committed ourselves by sending them all down, there will be nothing we can do in the heavy gravity down there till another bunch of suits and operators arrive. My suggestion is, that we follow your plan, but a little more slowly.
>   Matt.
>
>   Matthew Crandall, Colonel, Space Force.

Crandall sent the message, went back to his desk, and scowled at the lieutenant. The lieutenant looked uneasy.

"So," said Crandall, "you shoved the Planetary Development man out of the way and squeezed out first?"

"Sir . . . it wasn't quite like that."

"Were you in a hurry? Official business?"

"I—No, I wasn't sir, but—"

"You weren't?"

"No, I—"

"Were you, or weren't you?"

"No, but—"

"Then just what *was* your reason for shoving the Planetary Development man around?"

"I—It was a slur on the service, colonel."

"If you," said Crandall, "had been a civilian on the spaceboat, and seen a junior second lieutenant wrestling with a junior technician to get out the hatch first, what would you have thought of the service?"

The lieutenant's face turned red. He struggled to say something, then merely looked sick.

Crandall added, "There's another little point here you might think about."

"Yes, sir?"

"Planetary Development often uses junior technicians as couriers. Sometimes they carry dangerous chemicals. At other times they carry delicate apparatus. There are occasions when these things are needed in a hurry. It would be natural for a junior technician to forget protocol."

"Yes, sir. I see. But this one—"

"Some small pieces of apparatus," said Crandall thoughtfully, "cost upwards of sixty thousand dollars."

The lieutenant looked totally blank.

The message bell pinged, and Crandall remarked, "At your present rate of pay, it could take you thirty years to pay off the damages. And, of course, it would come under the head of Destroying Government Property. Then there might be enough bad feeling to charge you with Conduct Unbecoming An Officer." Crandall got up and added thoughtfully, "I saw a sixty-year old lieutenant once."

He went over to the transceiver, stripped off the paper, and read:

Matt: I agree with you in principle, but the trouble
in slowing things down is that we won't be in position for another drop till thirty days from now. This
ore is vitally important back home. We have to send
back as much as we can as fast as we can.
Dave.

David L. Paley, Chief, Planetary
Development Authority, Cygnes.

Crandall frowned, thought a moment, then sent:

Dave: If it will be thirty days till the next drop, I
see your point. But I still think we should hold some
of the suits in reserve in the event of emergency.
Matt.

Matthew Crandall, Colonel, Space Force.

Crandall walked back to his desk and sat down. He
observed that the lieutenant looked sick. "Sir," said the
lieutenant, "I'm sorry. I should have known better. But this
P.D.A. technician—*Was* this technician carrying anything?
I didn't see anything, but—"

Crandall shrugged. "We haven't had a damage notice yet.
Sometimes an interservice damage complaint takes time to
clear through channels."

"Sir, I'm sorry."

"All right," said Crandall. "And remember one more thing
when you're tempted to fight with an opposite number on
Planetary Development."

"What's that, sir?"

"A pair of pliers," said Crandall, using an argument he had
used many times before and found serviceable, "is a useful
tool. But take out the little bolt that holds the two halves
together, and those two halves, separated, aren't worth much."
Crandall leaned back and heard the message bell *ping* again.
"Planetary Development," he said, "and the Space Force, are
like the two halves of a pair of pliers. You don't want to hurt
the co-operation that holds them together. Remember that."

"Yes, sir," said the lieutenant fervently. "I'll remember."

They exchanged salutes. The lieutenant about-faced and
left the room. Crandall got up and stripped another message from the transceiver:

Matt: Everything we hold back will be out of action and useless for thirty days. Every operator held out will result in thirty man-days totally and irrevocably lost. They need this ore back home. Please give me your signature on my original plan as soon as possible.
Dave.

Crandall took a deep breath.

The intercom buzzed, and Crandall turned to snap it on.

"Sir," said a voice. "There's a courier from Planetary out here. He's got a Triple-A priority. Should I send him in, sir? Or just the papers?"

"Just the papers."

"Yes, sir."

A tall sergeant brought in a sheaf of papers, and Crandall scanned them carefully. He looked up at the sergeant. "Make out exact duplicates of these papers, but substitute the figure 276 for 300 in this item '300 delGrange suits and 300 operators.' "

"Yes, sir."

Crandall went back to the transceiver.

Dave: I have received your suggested plan. While I agree this would be excellent if we knew more about these new suits and about VI, right now I don't think we should take the risk. Thirty man-days wasted is a serious thing, but what we have at stake is a total of nine thousand man-days. While I agree with you in principle, I can't agree in detail. To save delay, I am having a new set of papers made up, will sign them and send them back with your courier.
Matt.

A brief pause followed, and an answering message came in:

Matt: How many suits are you planning to hold out?
Dave.

Crandall sent: *Dave: Twenty-four. Matt.*

The sergeant came in with the revised sheets, and Crandall signed them. The message bell pinged.

Matt: Twenty-four is damned near a fourth of one hundred, or about one-twelfth the whole force. What are you trying to do, hamstring me?
Dave.

Crandall puffed out his cheeks.

Dave: The only prudent thing to do is to reserve at least some small force in the event of emergency. There may be new developments. In thirty days we may need these suits. Twenty-four suits is only eight percent of your total force. This is a very modest reserve.
Matt.

Matt: We aren't fighting a war on VI. What do we have to hold out any "reserve" for? Our only enemies down there are gravity and pressure. What you are asking me to do is to sacrifice three thousand six hundred man-days to satisfy your misplaced military notions. Planetary development isn't war. There is no enemy down there. There is no need for a reserve. Our job is to get up the ore as fast as we can in as large a quantity as possible. Kindly sign my original papers and send them on immediately.
Dave.

Dave: If I have to sign and share responsibility for an action, I feel entitled to have some share in planning it. If you don't like the word "reserve," call it "safety factor." Whatever you call it, it is only eight percent, and it is a provision that seems vital to me. How can you or anyone else predict that nothing unexpected will happen on VI? I realize you are anxious to get up as much ore as you can. So am I. But if you have to cut potential production slightly to create a workable margin of safety, it seems to me we had better do it.
Matt.

Matt: I don't know how else to get it across to you, so let me tell you a story: Two men in a small town each had a thousand dollars. One put all his in a

checking account where he could get at it. The other—
just to have a little reserve—put eighty dollars of his
money in a savings account where he had to give thirty
days notice to get his money out. A chance came up
to buy a local business. Both men wanted it, but the
man who could put up a thousand dollars cash got it,
because he could offer eighty dollars more than the
other man. The business prospered. The man who
bought it got rich. The other man soon spent what he
had, and ended up worthless. All for what? For eight
percent held back.
Dave.

Crandall read the last message three times, and loosened
his collar.

Dave: I certainly do appreciate your care in explaining
it all to me so carefully. Let me just ask you about one
little point: What happens if the business goes bust?
Matt.

Matt: Colonel, will you or won't you let me do this
thing my way? This is my field, not yours.
Dave.

Dave: It seems to me your field and mine come
together at this point. Evidently the people who framed
Section 67b thought so, too.
Matt.

Matt: Will you or won't you?
Dave.

Dave: We need twenty-four suits in reserve.
Matt.

Matt: Let me offer one final compromise. I will
consent, freely, to hold two—or, if you insist—even up
to four of these suits "in reserve." But I positively,
definitely, and flatly refuse to keep two dozen of the
latest and most advanced delGrange suits floating around
in cold storage for a whole month because of your

fossilized notion of a military "reserve." This is not a military matter. This is not your field. You are not competent to meddle in it. The signature that you are so concerned about is a mere formality, and Section 67b is well-known to be merely a sop to military pride. Whether things go right or wrong here is up to me, not you. You won't be investigated if things go wrong. I will. But this planet has been checked and rechecked, and this whole affair has been planned with a precision you cannot appreciate. I flatly refuse to jeopardize Earth by doing as you say. Don't intrude where you aren't fitted to operate. I very strongly suggest to you, colonel, that you sign the original papers without further delay.
  Dave.

Crandall walked across the room, came back and tapped out an answer:

  Dave: I am very sorry that we can't seem to adjust this matter quietly. No doubt you have your reasons, but I have mine, too. I cannot read the intent of Section 67b, or any other part of that section, as any other than what is written there. I have to follow it implicitly, and it is as binding on you as it is on me. I fail to see what enrages you at the thought of keeping eight percent of these mechanical suits as a reserve against emergency. But I cannot fail to observe the meaning of your sentence beginning: "But I positively, definitely, and flatly refuse to keep two dozen of the latest and most advanced delGrange suits . . ." Considering Section 67b, this is not a matter of choice on your part, yet you "flatly refuse" to carry it out. I am sorry, Dave, but you haven't left me a great deal of choice.
  Matt.

Space Force H.Q. Cygnes III to G.H.Q. Space Forces, Terra Staff:
  Pursuant Section 67c rpt 67c a State of Emergency is rpt is hereby declared throughout Cygnes System.
                              Matthew Crandall, Colonel,
                              Space Force, Commanding.

Space Force H.Q., Cygnes III to Planetary Development
    H.Q. Cygnes VI m 4 Staff:
You are hereby notified that pursuant to Section 67c
rpt 67c, a State of Emergency has been declared throughout Cygnes System.

> Matthew Crandall, Colonel,
> Space Force, Commanding.

Space Force H.Q., Cygnes III to Planetary Development
    H.Q. Cygnes VI m 4
Personal: To D. L. Paley, Chief
Sir: You are rpt are hereby required and directed to
retain twenty-four rpt twenty-four latest model delGrange
mechanical suits as emergency reserve, as outlined in
preceding correspondence. You are rpt are hereby warned
that failure to do so will be cause for summary suspension from office pursuant to Section 67d. You are
hereby directed to state your intention to comply with
this order.

> Matthew Crandall, Colonel, Space Force,
> Commanding.

Planetary Development H. Q. Cygnes VI m 4 to Space
Force H.Q., Cygnes III
Personal: To Col. Matthew Crandall.
Sir: I positively, flatly, definitely, and finally refuse
rpt REFUSE to obey any order, directive, proclamation
or ukase that requires me or any of my organization
to hold two dozen of the latest model delGrange suits
in a state of futile lassitude while Terra hungers for ore.
That is final.

> David L. Paley, Chief, Planetary
> Development Authority, Cygnes.

Colonel Matthew Crandall leaned back and studied the
message with a sensation almost of suspended animation.
He found himself turning the message over to look at the
blank reverse side of the sheet. He asked himself what,
exactly, was so bad about keeping twenty-four pressure suits
in storage for a month? He reread the message, shook his
head, and tapped out:

Space Force H.Q., Cygnes III to Planetary Development
　　H.Q. Cygnes VI m 4
Personal: To D. L. Paley
　　Sir: Pursuant to Section 67d, you are hereby
suspended from office.
　　　　　　　　　　　Matthew Crandall, Colonel,
　　　　　　　　　　　Space Force, Commanding.

Space Force H.Q., Cygnes III to Planetary Development
　　H.Q. Cygnes VI m 4 Staff:
Pursuant to Section 67d of the Interservice Code,
David L. Paley is rpt is hereby suspended from office.
His successor is hereby required and directed to either:
a) retain twenty-four rpt twenty-four latest model
delGrange mechanical suits as emergency reserve, as
outlined in preceding correspondence with D. L. Paley,
former Chief; or b) clearly state reasons why this should
not be done. His successor is hereby directed to state
his intention to comply with this order.
　　　　　　　　　　　Matthew Crandall, Colonel,
　　　　　　　　　　　Space Force, Commanding.

Planetary Development H.Q. Cygnes VI m 4 to Space
　　Force H.Q., Cygnes III
Personal: To Col. Matthew Crandall.
　　Sir: I hereby state my intention to refuse rpt refuse
to obey your order to retain twenty-four latest model
delGrange suits as "emergency reserve." You are perfectly free to suspend me and choose the next man in
line as new Chief. You may, if you want, go all the
way down the line in this fashion. Upon inquiring of
the person directly under me, I have been informed that
all Planetary Development personnel who have expressed
an opinion on this topic unanimously resent your high-
handed approach to a situation you are incompetent to
judge. I advise you to rescind your silly order before
you make a complete fool of yourself.
　　　　　　　　　　　Peyton B. Jones, Acting Chief,
　　　　　　　Planetary Development Authority, Cygnes.

Space Force H.Q., Cygnes III to G.H.Q. Space Forces,
　　Terra Staff:

Pursuant Section 68a rpt 68a, martial law is rpt is hereby established throughout Cygnes System.

> Matthew Crandall, Colonel,
> Space Force, Commanding.

Space Forces H.Q., Cygnes III to Space Forces Cygnes Staff:

Effective immediately rpt immediately carry out Schedule Three rpt Three, Deployment for Sabotage Control. Any or all Terran or other ships attempting to evade or oppose this order are to be boarded, their personnel confined to locked quarters, and their officers removed and held under guard. Any ship attempting to escape is to be warned, and if it does not promptly submit, you are hereby directly ordered to destroy rpt destroy it.

> Matthew Crandall, Colonel,
> Space Force, Commanding.

Planetary Development H.Q. Cygnes VI m 4 to Space Force H.Q., Cygnes III
Personal: To Col. Matthew Crandall.

Matt: Good God are you out of your head? You can't shoot at our men. This is just a jurisdictional matter. You don't understand. Try and be reasonable. The press will have your head if you start any shooting.

> David L.. Paley, Chief (Suspended),
> Planetary Development Authority, Cygnes.

Space Force H.Q., Cygnes III to Planetary Development H.Q., Cygnes VI m 4 Staff:

You are hereby notified that pursuant to Section 68a, martial law has been established throughout Cygnes System. Pursuant to Section 67d, Peyton B. Jones is rpt is hereby suspended from office. His successor's name is to be sent to Space Force H.Q., Cygnes III, immediately.

> Matthew Crandall, Colonel,
> Space Force, Commanding.

Planetary Development H.Q., Cygnes VI m 4 to Space Force H.Q., Cygnes III Staff:

John R. Hennings is successor to Peyton B. Jones.

Space Force H.Q., Cygnes III to Planetary Development
H.Q. Cygnes VI m 4

Personal: To J. R. Hennings, Chief.

Sir: You are hereby authorized and directed to fully acquaint yourself with the messages passed between your two previous superiors and myself regarding latest model delGrange mechanical suits en route from Purth, due 01-23-2212, and especially regarding retention of twenty-four rpt twenty-four of those suits as emergency reserve.

You are hereby directed to inform me of any reason why these suits cannot be retained as emergency reserve, or of any reason why, in your opinion, such retention would be disastrous or dangerous. My intention is to order you to hold twenty-four of these suits in reserve if you do not give any logical and satisfactory reason why this should not be done.

In present circumstances, your refusal to carry out such a direct order would result in immediate trial by military court. You would be accused of attempting to block by your disobedience the extraction of vital ore from Cygnes VI, thus endangering the security of the race. The formal charge would therefore be treason. The punishment if found guilty will be death.

> Matthew Crandall, Colonel,
> Space Force, Commanding.

Planetary Development H.Q., Cygnes VI m 4 to Space Force H.Q., Cygnes III

Personal: To Col. Matthew Crandall.

Sir: I see no reason why retention of such a reserve would be disastrous or dangerous, unless it cut down ore production sufficiently to produce a dangerous shortage. I will of course obey your orders to the best of my ability.

> John R. Hennings, Acting Chief,
> Planetary Cevelopment, Cygnes.

Later in the day, Crandall received a damage claim against the lieutenant for:

1 pipet, 25 ml., smashed $2.75.

Crandall took the time to pay it out of his own pocket, saying nothing to the lieutenant. Then he got back to work.

He spent an hour carefully going back over the successive messages. Try as he might, he could not see what had gone wrong, or spot any single place where it happened. Things just seemed to pile up with no sensible reason. Then he began to notice sentences here and there in the Planetary Development messages:

"This ore is vitally important back home."

"Everything we hold back will be out of action and useless for thirty days."

"How many units are you planning to hold out?"

"Twenty-four is damned near a fourth of a hundred, or about one-twelfth the whole force. What are you trying to do, hamstring me?"

"What you are asking me to do is to sacrifice three thousand six hundred man-days to satisfy your misplaced military notions."

"I flatly refuse to jeopardize Earth by doing as you say."

Two more lines popped out, from Paley's jittery last message:

"This is just a jurisdictional matter."

"The press will have your head if you start any shooting."

Crandall squinted hard at this last sentence. How, he asked himself, had the press gotten into this already? He looked up as an unpleasant possibility began to form in his mind.

Just then, the message bell rang:

G.H.Q. Space Force H.Q., Terra to Space Force H.Q.,
   Cygnes III
Personal: To Col. Matthew Crandall.
   Would you mind telling us exactly what is going on out there?

                    G. C. Davis, General, Chief of Staff.

Crandall relayed the entire correspondence from beginning to end to G.H.Q. on Terra. Before this had time to reach Terra, Crandall received a second message:

G.H.Q. Space Forces, Terra to Space Force H.Q., Cygnes
   III

Personal: To Col. Matthew Crandall.

We now have a three-ring circus and medicine show in operation here. Planetary Development G.H.Q. is handing out generalities about military callousness, waste, and stupidity, and they have scheduled a mammoth press conference for tomorrow. Unless you would like to spend the rest of your life plotting asteroid maps, you had better send us full and complete information and get it here well before the press conference opens.

G. C. Davis, General, Chief of Staff.

Crandall immediately sent a series of specially scrambled queries to staff officers he knew on Terra. When he had finished, the message bell pinged, and the transceiver unrolled a brief message:

T.S.F. Corvette Lightning Bug to Space Force H.Q., Cygnes III Staff:

Planetary Development Communication Ship Flash disobeyed order to end transmission as per Schedule Three rpt Three. I at once carried out Radio Subrelay Jamming Directive, and have also boarded Flash, confined crew, arrested and removed officers.

L. S. Daniels, 1st Lieut., Space Force, Commanding.

Crandall promptly sent L. S. Daniels, 1st Lieut., his personal commendation. Then the transceiver went into operation again:

G.H.Q. Space Forces, Terra to Space Force H.Q., Cygnes III

Personal: To Col. Matthew Crandall:

We have received your long message here, and while I do not claim to have digested it all, I think I see what happened, and I imagine you see it too by now. It is all very neat, smooth, and nicely put together, with a strong spring and good sharp teeth in it, like a bear trap under the leaves. I fail to see what else you could have done that would not have compromised our security. But I don't know if that is going to help or not. I will not try to advise you at this distance, except in generalities: 1) Don't worry about us at this end; we will cover you and keep the avalanche off your head as long as possible, 2) Waste no time thinking about the unpleasant possibilities; keep your mind working on the pressing details. 3) This may seem a little hackneyed, but I would advise you to take a few moments and pray.

G. C. Davis, General, Chief of Staff.

Crandall thought it over, and took a few moments for fervent prayer. Then the bell pinged, and a number of freshly unscrambled messages came in, in reply to his queries. Most of these messages were signed by staff officers and were headed "G.H.Q. Space Forces, Terra."
They went on to say:

Matt: Regarding the new delGrange pressure suit— it must be a classified Planetary Development exclusive. We have nothing solid on it, just rumors. If there's any reason why some of the suits can't be held in hand as a reserve, Paley should have given you the reason. We don't know enough about it to say one way or the other. On the other hand, of course, Paley or his successor can stand you off indefinitely by looking virtuous and saying "Classified." All that we can say back here is, we wish you luck.

Matt: You're right, and the Chief did perhaps put a little bit of a squeeze on our friends here in the sister service a few weeks ago. I know we should never underestimate our friends. But this business you describe shows such fast reactions, and such slick knife work, that I just can't believe it. Are you sure this isn't a misunderstanding?

Matt: We have dug up Paley's record for you. Also those of his top aides. The aides are more or less conventional. But here are some points on Paley: Graduated cum laude. Major: Business administration. Minor: Renaissance history. Joined P.D.A young and rose fast. A number of interesting articles published in historical journals. Example: "The living influence of Machiavelli in Post-Renaissance Italy." Paley's nickname in college: "The Op." Paley's favorite game: Go. Has high efficiency rating and said to be fanatically loyal to P.D.A. Many minor brushes with military while in lower positions, but none later on. At least none recorded.

Matt: Press reaction here violent. Newspapers, magazines, radio, trideo, solideo, and 6-V are booming versions of two stories: a) You have shot your opposite number and are running Cygnes as a military dictator. b) Planetary Development tried to seize Cygnes with new secret weapons, and you are now locked in last ditch death struggle to save Cygnes for Earth. Hard to say whether you're villain or hero, but you're notorious, anyway.

Crandall studied the messages carefully and gloomily, then checked to make sure the rigorous routines of martial law were being carried out. He ate, thought over the whole matter, then fell into an exhausted sleep. In his dreams he was a young second lieutenant, and a brisk colonel was saying to him, "Never fight with your opposite number, lieutenant. The Space Force and Planetary Development are just like two halves of a pair of pliers; you have to take care of that little bolt of mutual trust and co-operation that joins them together. Never fight with your opposite number, lieutenant. The Space Force and Planetary Development are just like two halves of a pair of pliers; you have to take care of that little bolt of mutual trust and co-operation that joins them together. Never fight with your opposite number, lieutenant—"

Crandall woke up with a headache and a general feeling of fuzziness. The first news he received was that the latest model delGrange mechanical suits had arrived from Purth during the night. The next news was that the operators had arrived from Szalesh in the early morning, had put on the suits, and practiced in them. Immediately afterward, he received a message:

Planetary Development H.Q. Cygnes VI m 4 to Space Force H.Q., Cygnes III Personal: To Col. Matthew Crandall.

Sir: At 0630 TCT this morning, I sent down to Cygnes VI the reduced force of delGrange mechanicals with their operators. In obedience to your orders, I have, as you require, held back from the mining operation a full two dozen . . . twenty-four . . . latest model delGrange mechanicals along with over seven dozen operators. These tremendous machines and their highly trained operators cannot, as we informed you time and again prior to your imposition of martial law, take part in the mining operations for over four weeks more. Because of your order, these huge engines and their skilled operators must now be held idle at tremendous expense to the taxpayers.

While I certainly don't desire that I or any of the Planetary Development organization be shot dead for saying so, still I would very respectfully like to make, sir, a suggestion. Perhaps, sir, you did not create this terrific waste intentionally, but were misled into causing this expense by the temptation to activate the obsolete Sections 67 and 68 of the Interservice Code. I say this, sir, with no intention or desire to be shot for treason for making the suggestion, but because— logically, sir—I think you should somehow come to realize fully just what damage these Sections 67 and 68 are doing to Terra.

Obediently,
John R. Hennings, Acting Chief,
Planetary Development, Cygnes.

Crandall read this over three times. Hitherto, the new delGrange devices were "suits," now they were "mechanicals," "huge engines," "tremendous machines." Crandall looked hard at various parts of the message, checked this one with previous messages, then tapped out:

Space Force H.Q., Cygnes III to Special Service Command Staff:
Unpack and set up immediately one (1) gallows, portable, M12, using the nearest plot of ground convenient to H.Q. prisoner detention area.
Matthew Crandall, Space Force, Commanding.

Space Force H.Q., Cygnes III to Planetary Development H.Q. Cygnes VI m 4 Staff:

Pursuant to Section 67d, John R. Hennings is rpt is hereby suspended from office. His successor's name is to be sent immediately to Space Force H.Q., Cygnes III.

Matthew Crandall, Colonel,
Space Force, Commanding.

Space Force H.Q., Cygnes III to T. S. F. Cruiser *Vengeance* Staff:

The following personnel are to be placed under arrest and delivered to H.Q. prisoner detention area:

1) David L. Paley
2) Peyton B. Jones
3) John R. Hennings

These men are to be held separately under close guard. They are not rpt not to be allowed to communicate with each other, or with outsiders. They may, if they so request, receive religious guidance and counsel from chaplains of their own faith.

Matthew Crandall, Colonel,
Space Force, Commanding.

Planetary Development H.Q. Cygnes VI m 4 to Space Force H.Q., Cygnes III Staff:

James L. Buzzel is successor to John R. Hennings.

Space Force H.Q., Cygnes III to Planetary Development H.Q. Cygnes VI m 4
Personal: To J. L. Buzzel.

Sir: You are hereby required and directed to immediately prepare for inspection one rpt one latest model delGrange mechanical suit.

Matthew Crandall, Colonel,
Space Force, Commanding.

Space Force H.Q., Cygnes III to Special Services Command Staff:

Obtain the names of the next-of-kin of the following:

1) David L. Paley
2) Peyton B. Jones
3) John R. Hennings

Forward these names to this office as soon as possible.

> Matthew Crandall, Colonel,
> Space Force, Commanding.

Crandall pulled out a handkerchief and mopped his forehead. He ordered a light scout spacer gotten ready, then turned as the message bell pinged again. He read:

> G.H.Q. Space Forces, Terra to Space Force H.Q., Cygnes III Personal: To Col. Matthew Crandall.
>
> For your information, we have learned that Planetary Development G.H.Q. is readying bill to strike out Sections 67 rpt 67 and 68 rpt 68, and replace same with new sections placing Planetary Development Authority in charge of Space Force in order to quote eliminate confusion end-quote.
>
> G. C. Davis, General, Chief of Staff.

The intercom buzzed and Crandall flipped it on.

"Your ship's ready, sir."

Crandall boarded the spacer. Several times on the trip to Planetary Development H.Q., he found himself wondering whether asteroid plotting would be such a bad life after all. He forced his mind back to reality, then was interrupted by a startled grunt from the pilot.

Crandall looked up. "Now what?"

"Look at the upper right of the screen, sir. Coming into view as we turn."

Crandall bent forward and looked at the upper right section of the screen. He saw what looked like a huge spindly webwork, interspersed with big shiny rectangular blocks. As the ship turned, more and more of this web came into view, till it filled the screen from right to left and top to bottom.

"What in space," said Crandall, "is that?"

"I don't know, sir."

Crandall and the pilot sat, squinting, each man turning his head to different angles, trying to reduce the monstrosity to some familiar pattern. Abruptly the pilot switched on his microphone and began barking queries. He blinked, scratched his head, and turned to Crandall.

"Sir, Planetary says that mess is 'one dozen mechanical suits.' There's another dozen around the other side of the base."

Crandall let his breath out with a hiss. He fastened his gaze on one of the long strands of the web. Close observation showed at intervals what appeared to be joints, and on the underside of the thing, a row of sharp metal teeth. Crandall traced along the arm to a thing like a shiny boxcar. From this boxcar stretched thick cables that twined like long metal snakes. Crandall leaned forward and enlarged the scene. From one end of the boxcar jutted a thick bar bearing a flat base with a curved transparent cover. Inside the cover, grids, loops, and V's turned listlessly. A big gray crate was fastened by loose cables to the end of the boxcar.

Crandall readjusted the focus of the screen for an over-all view. There were many of these floating boxcars and crates. When he counted them, he found a dozen of each. They were all inter-tangled. The teeth on jointed arms had hooked cables, the cables were caught around the short bars between boxcars and housings, and eccentrically-attached conveyer belts floated loose and free from the boxcars, tangled at random with long metal arms, cables, and each other. The whole mass wavered and rippled with a slow motion, like seaweed under water.

"Sir," said the pilot, "there goes one of their dock-you ships."

"Their what?"

"Dock-you . . . Documentary ships, sir. They make surveys on new planets, take before and after pictures, and so on. Funny to see one out here."

Crandall studied the documentary ship with narrowed eyes. The ship raced forward, slowed with a blast of rockets, lit with winking flashes of light—presumably a signal that it was taking pictures—then darted up, slowed, eased back and forth, and lit with more flashes of light. It rushed off to a new position.

"Sir," said the pilot, "they're sending up the technicians."

"Tell them," said Crandall, "that I want to see Buzzel, too."

Crandall boarded the Planetary Development ship with

the feelings of an explorer starting across a swampy tract
where the bog grass stands in clumps amidst sinkholes
of bottomless muck. Buzzel, on his part, greeted Crandall
with the calculating wariness of a zoologist transferring
a captured hornet to the cyanide bottle. The two went to
a small conference room, and opened a conversation that
circled in gingerly from the general to the particular, till
Buzzel asked:

"Why did you have to hold two *dozen* of them?"

"Why wasn't I told they were so big?"

Buzzel gave a spare smile. "Classified."

"What," said Crandall, "will you do if something *does* go
wrong down there?"

"What could?"

Crandall shook his head, as if to brush away a swarm
of gnats. "Suit failure," he said. "The breakdown of one small
part in any vital place. Or psychological difficulties on the
part of the operator."

Buzzel frowned, then said positively, "Those suits are
mechanically and electronically perfect. DelGrange assembled
them and tested them himself in conditions comparable to
those here on Cygnes VI." Buzzel relaxed. "What more could
you ask?"

"A test on the spot," said Crandall. He scowled. "How
do you get those suits down through VI's atmosphere without
burning them up?"

Buzzel gave his spare smile. "Classified."

Crandall felt his collar get tight.

Buzzel raised a hand and said cautiously, "I don't mean
this offensively, but I think it ought to be said. You have
your job. We have ours. I wouldn't presume to advise you
in carrying out a fleet action. How do you suppose it makes
us feel to have the military riding herd over us in our job?"

"The occupation of any new planet," said Crandall harshly,
"involves risk and uncertainty. The Space Force is geared
to act fast and strike hard in the event of trouble. Planetary Development is geared to make the most of a stable,
predictable situation. When we make the first sizable landing
on a new planet, we don't know *what* the situation is going
to be. That's why we're both concerned. It's as much my
job as yours."

"But under Sections 67 and 68, *you* have the final say."

Buzzel frowned. "The evaluation of the situation properly belongs to *us*."

Crandall shut his eyes and took a deep breath. "That's beside the point. Sections 67 and 68 *are already law*. If we aren't to have chaos, we have to obey the law. If you want a change, all right. But this isn't the time or the place to make propaganda for it."

Buzzel looked at Crandall with something approaching compassion. "Even if you know you're right, how do you rouse popular support for your side without a striking incident? If the law forbids you to make the incident, how do you ever get a change so long as you obey the law?"

Crandall studied the tabletop as Buzzel went on. "I don't have any thing against you personally, Colonel. I'm sorry if anyone gets hurt, but the principle involved outweighs personalities. Paley could explain this to you much better than I, but I'll try. Let me tell you a little history. The first concern of man used to be food. The hunter was paramount. Then tribes and nations arose, and there were battles between them. The warrior was paramount. That day, colonel, has faded into the day of science. The most important concerns have become, not military, but scientific. Today, the scientist is paramount."

Buzzel hesitated. "Paley could explain this much better than I. I used to accept Sections 67 and 68 as just ordinary aggravating routine. Now I can see that those sections are fossilized structures that we have to get rid of."

Crandall said, "Which is higher, Buzzel, the brain, or the spinal cord?"

"The brain, of course."

Crandall nodded. "Which is superior, a fully organized thought, or a reflex?

Buzzel frowned. "A fully organized thought. What are you driving at?"

"As man developed," said Crandall, "did he subordinate everything to his brain? Did he subjugate all the mechanisms that went before to this latest and best one? If somebody slings a brick in your face, which has precedence, a calm, orderly estimate of all aspects of the situation, or a quick duck?"

Buzzel looked steadily at Crandall. "All right. But what

does that have to do with *this* situation? There's no danger here."

Crandall said, "If a man looks at a python through two-inch glass, and the python strikes at him, will the man stand still, smiling, or will he jump? The reflex gives him the advantage of fast action in the event of danger. The disadvantage is, he may act fast and waste energy when there's no real danger. But it has to be that way. Otherwise the reflex would have to stop and consult the brain, which would take twenty or thirty seconds to hand down a judgment on whether the python was really dangerous or only seemed to be. The man could be pulp by that time."

Buzzel stared at the opposite wall. "I see what you mean. A simple mechanism may have precedence over a higher one. But how—Where does this fit in here?"

"Put the planet in the place of the python," said Crandall, "and substitute the human race for the man looking at the snake. You're part of the brain, and I'm part of the reflex arc. Now you tell me not to send the impulse to jump. What you say to me is 'Don't do your job. *This* python isn't dangerous.' Just how do you expect me to react?"

Buzzel bit his lip, looked down at the table, and frowned.

"You see," said Crandall, "the irritation of jumping when you don't need to is the price you pay for moving fast when it's jump or die. Anyone who succeeds in changing Section 67 and 68 saves a good deal of friction and irritation. And when the right situation turns up, humanity will stand there thinking things over till the python gets a good grip and starts snapping ribs."

Buzzel took a deep breath and looked up. In a low voice, he said, "The planet has been thoroughly researched. There's no danger there."

"So be it," said Crandall. "But I am going to do my job."

Buzzel frowned, and stared at the opposite wall. "Yes," he said, "and I have to do mine." He shook himself and pushed back his chair. Conversationally, he added. "There's no danger in this."

There was a moment's silence as Crandall frowned, studying Buzzel's reactions, and wondering why Buzzel said over and over. "There's no danger. There's no danger here."

The moment stretched out into a long silence while neither man moved.

The ship jumped like a can hit by an iron bat. The metal walls rang like the sides of a bell.

Table and chairs jolted with a snap of bolts and slid.

Crandall and Buzzel flew sidewise, grabbed wildly for support, and slammed half-bent on the steel deck.

Violent acceleration piled them in a corner. Sharp deceleration slid them to the other end of the room. Crandall fended off a chair. The table tipped over and landed on Buzzel. The door opened and a ship's officer glanced in. "You all right, sir?"

Buzzel heaved the table off his chest. Crandall shoved the chair back, got up, and helped Buzzel to his feet. Buzzel looked at the ship's officer, who slowly congealed into a posture of attention. Crandall watched approvingly as Buzzel spat out words like bullets out of gun:

"What was that?"

"S-Sir, one of those things swung an arm around and—"

"One of what things?"

"One of those . . . one of . . . One of those suits, sir."

"It did what?"

"Swung an arm around and hit the ship under a drive tube. It—The suit's letting itself loose from the others right now, sir."

Buzzel looked as if he'd been hit over the head with a club. "That's preposterous. It couldn't—" He cut himself off.

Crandall said, "Where's the viewscreen?"

The ship's officer tore his gaze from Buzzel, stared dully at Crandall, stiffened, and said: "Just down here, sir."

Crandall and Buzzel followed the officer down a corridor and through a doorway.

On the screen, one of the shiny boxcars was moving in the center of a mass of writhing snaky limbs. The limbs untangled themselves from the others, the big gray crate above the boxcar drew its cables tight, and the whole thing started to pull loose from the rest. It was moving in toward Cygnes VI.

Buzzel said, "That can't—" He whirled toward the ship's officer. "Get in touch with Base. Have them make a roll call of suit operators." He glanced at the screen. The huge boxcar was gathering headway. Buzzel bit his lip. "No. Don't. Too slow." he glanced around. His hands opened and closed.

Crandall said, "Is that suit equipped with a radio?"

"Yes. The operators can talk to each other. But not on any of our wave lengths."

Crandall glanced at the suit, then at the ship's officer. "Can you get in touch with my pilot?"

"Yes, sir."

Crandall turned to Buzzel. "Am I right? Does this mean something a lot worse than the theft of a suit?"

"I don't know," said Buzzel. "If it's that, it's bad enough. But—" Buzzel hesitated. "Yes. It could mean something a lot worse."

The ship's officer handed Crandall a headset. Crandall heard his pilot say, "Sir? Hello?"

Crandall said, "Do you see that floating tangle of boxes and cables? Do you see that one that just cut itself loose?"

"Yes, sir."

"Swoop in front of it once or twice, and try to signal it to stop. If it doesn't, fire a light missile so it strikes the front of that gray crate that's doing the pulling." Crandall covered the microphone and turned to Buzzel. "Or is that too dangerous?"

"No," said Buzzel in a dreary voice. "It'll wreck twenty million dollars worth of equipment, but— No. I'm right with you."

On the screen, the scout spacer dove in front of the delGrange suit. The suit swung in a fast arc—arms, cables, and conveyer belt flailing out behind—and dove on the spacer. The spacer swung back in a tight fast loop and hung in place behind the suit.

The pilot's voice spoke in the earphones. "Releasing missile."

The delGrange suit swerved, climbed, and streaked for Cygnes VI. A thin bright line curved around its side and came back. There was a flash of white light. The suit raced on at constant speed, the wreckage of the crate drifting back to tangle the boxcar.

Crandall glanced at Buzzel. "Was that crate the only source of power?"

Buzzel hesitated. "No," he said, "there's an internal source for the limbs and the conveyor. But there's no other drive."

Crandall glanced back at the screen and roughly guessed at the suit's speed and course. He turned to the ship's officer and asked him to work out a more exact estimate, then he snapped on the communications screen.

The pilot's voice spoke in Crandall's ear. "Sir, I could swing in and try to get a tow cable on that thing."

"No," said Crandall, "Just keep it in sight."

Crandall got the cruiser *Vengeance* on the communications screen.

"Is *Monitor* on station near VI?"

"Yes, sir."

"I want you to put her on an interception course." Crandall turned to the ship's officer, who read off estimated course and speed of the delGrange suit. Crandall glanced back at the communications screen. "Can you do it?"

"Yes, sir. *Monitor's* near at hand."

"How long will it take?"

"About an hour, sir."

"Fine," said Crandall. "Thank you." He snapped off the screen, and glanced at Buzzel.

"Maybe we should talk things over again."

Crandall and Buzzel stared at each other across the table in the little conference room.

Buzzel said, "Maybe we're going to get cracked ribs here after all."

"What's happened?"

"There are just two alternatives. Either that suit flew off by itself, in which case we've got the chance of a terrific mess, or else one of the suit operators stole it. And that opens up possibilities almost as bad."

"Why?"

"The operators are picked for certain outstanding traits. Intelligence isn't the most important of these, but the operators can't be fools, either. The suits are worth, roughly, half-a-billion apiece. But to try to steal one for money, a man would need the mentality of a cretin."

Crandall nodded.

"All right," said Buzzel. "Grant that the operator has the sense to see he'll never get out away from Cygnes without being spotted and stopped. Why *else* should he try to get away with a suit?"

Crandall scowled, and Buzzel fidgeted. Crandall said, "My purpose in coming out here was to examine one of those suits. Now there isn't time. Have *you* looked one of them over yet?"

Buzzel said, "I operated one this morning."

"What was it like?"

"You put on a suit of tight, close-fitting skin, go in through an air lock, and lie down in a special form-fitting seat. A capsule comes down over the seat. A very soft cap fits over your nose and mouth, and fine needles pierce your arteries and veins. The capsule fills with a warm liquid, and oxygen comes through a hose to the cap at your mouth. A nutrient solution and certain drugs pass through the needles."

Buzzel shivered. "Bodily activity drops to a minimum. The operator floats in this soft, close capsule. Through a series of highly sensitive mutual inductances, information—in the form of sensation concerning the position of the limbs of the delGrange suit—is relayed to his brain. This principle is carried through elaborately. If someone applies light pressure, or a mild corrosive, to the exterior skin of the suit, it feels like an itching sensation. More pressure gives the effect of a pinch. Strong pressures or corrosion produces severe pain. The operator loses awareness of his body. He comes to sense *the delGrange suit* as his body."

Buzzel added, "The trouble is, one of the most important qualifications for an operator is his ability to identify with the machine he operates. Some people are fascinated by machines. Ground cars, airplanes, spacers—away back in history they rode horses as if they and the horse were one. Put a splendid horse out in the yard and tell one of these people he can't touch it—"

Crandall nodded thoughtfully.

"Always in the past," said Buzzel, "we've had trouble with operator fatigue. Sooner or later it disrupts the identification. But delGrange is a perfectionist." Buzzel moodily studied his fingernails. "What we seem to have here is the maximum of identification with the minimum of operator fatigue. The cyberneticists spotted it this morning, and they and Paley had a small war over it. I stuck with Paley. So did the rest of Administration."

"But" said Crandall, "now that an operator has come and tried to make off with one of the suits—"

Buzzel nodded drearily. "Maybe the cyberneticists had something."

Crandall sat back.

Buzzel said, "Picture what may come about thirty days from now. All that time the operators' identification with the suits will be increasing. Suit failure is practically nil. Then, all of a sudden, they're supposed to come up, and get out of the suits." Buzzel put the fingernails of one hand in his mouth and bit down.

"How long," said Crandall, "can they last if they don't come up?"

"Fifty days at most. That is, fifty days, all told."

"Twenty days more after the thirty are up?"

"At best. The suits ought to be restocked every thirty days." Buzzel took a deep breath. "There could be," he said, "a hundred and fifty billion dollars worth of equipment sitting around down there two months from now with dead men inside of it." He pulled out a handkerchief and wiped his forehead.

Crandall looked up at the ceiling. "Whoever happens to be in charge of Planetary Development here when that happens will get strung up by the heels, I imagine?"

Buzzel said, "The publicity could be terrible." He looked around uneasily. "There would have to be a scapegoat."

Crandall felt his mouth start to bend up cheerfully at the corners, and blanked his face. He glanced at his watch. "You'd better tell me in detail what one of those mechanical suits can do. Then we'd better get back to the control room."

The *Monitor*, a black spherical mass at the center of a giant spoked wheel, swung up onto the screen from below. Six squat tugs were spaced around the rim of the huge wheel, faced against the direction of motion, their rockets blazing as they struggled to brake the massive ship.

Crandall spoke to the *Monitor's* commanding officer. "Do you see that thing like a big steel box with a shallow glass cup on one end?"

"Yes, sir."

"As you can see, it is going to fall into an orbit around Cygnes VI, dip in closer, and burn up in the atmosphere. We have to stop it."

"Yes, sir."

"Unfortunately," said Crandall, "it's equipped with drills, breakers, pile drivers, power crushers, and similar equipment, either recessed in the body of the thing or at the tips of those arms attached to it."

The eyes of *Monitor's* commanding officer narrowed to slits as he glanced aside at his own viewscreen. "Any guns on the thing?"

Crandall glanced at Buzzel, then back at the officer. "No. But if it got close enough to drill a hole in your hull, it could pack it with atomite and set it off, all in about three-tenths of a second. I imagine that would be just as good."

The officer glanced from his viewscreen back to Crandall. "Sir, you let me yank a few of those arms out by the roots and we'll have an easier time of it."

Crandall turned to Buzzel, who looked pale and sick. Buzzel made half-a-dozen objections before Crandall could cut him off. "No good," said Crandall, glancing back to the officer. "You might let the air out. That could kill the operator."

"Sir, if he won't obey orders—"

"We want some information he's got."

"Oh. Well—Suppose I can snap off a few of those arms about half-way down. The tools are in the ends, aren't they?"

Crandall looked at Buzzel. Buzzel gave a weak nod.

"If you can do it," said Crandall. "But the main idea is to see to it that that thing doesn't go on down toward VI. And we want the operator alive, if possible."

"Yes, sir."

"If you can disable it so we can get in and get the operator out, so much the better. But the main point is—keep it away from VI. And look out for it. It may move faster than you expect once it gets hold of something."

The officer's lips drew back, showing large white teeth. "Don't worry, sir. We'll take care of it." He saluted and stepped out of range of the communications screen. Crandall switched his gaze to the viewscreen showing the delGrange suit and the *Monitor* swinging up from below.

A muffled volley of orders came from the direction of the communications screen. Two of the six tugs spaced around the rim of *Monitor's* drive wheel detached themselves and darted away. The other four moved to again space themselves evenly around the rim. The *Monitor* slowly swung toward the delGrange suit. The suit reached out with several of its long flexible arms and cut loose the cables holding the wreckage of its propulsion unit.

From overhead, a tug drifted down trailing a long cable.

The suit put out a long flexible arm and spun it rapidly clockwise. The suit itself slowly turned counterclockwise, bringing the jointed, saw-edged arm around toward the passing cable, and yanked it in. Snakelike flexible arms reached out, gripped the cable and hauled back hard. The suit ran up the cable like a spider up its thread.

A roar of oaths and orders burst from the communicator. The tug hauling the cable cut loose and dove in a blaze of rockets. The suit arrived at the end of the cable holding out a set of jointed toothy jaws like scrapers on a power shovel. From overhead, the other tug dove, and clamped on to the opposite end of the line. The suit switched holds and went flailing up the line toward the second tug.

Buzzel suddenly sucked in his breath, whacked the keys on the frequency control, and grabbed for the microphone. Crandall jerked his gaze from the suit, and saw the documentary ship jockeying around in the background for a better view. Crandall leaned forward, reached out as if to steady himself, and put his hand squarely on the frequency control, changing the setting. Buzzel grabbed Crandall's hand, reset the control, and began barking orders into the microphone. Crandall made another grab in the air as if to recover his balance, then straightened, relaxed, and saw tug number two hastily let go the line as the latest model delGrange suit arrived at the end poising a big oversized drill.

Buzzel's voice, snapping orders for the dock-you ship, came to Crandall's ears, and Crandall switched his attention rapidly back and forth noting both the frenzied stream of Buzzel's orders, and the delGrange suit, now hurtling down the line toward tug number one, which had again taken hold the opposite end of the line.

In the background, the front end of the dock-you ship lit up in a brilliant display of flashing lights which, Crandall hoped, signified that a large footage of documentary film was now being taken. Crandall permitted himself the luxury of visualizing for a moment a dim room packed with cabinet officers, members of Congress, sedately smiling Space Force officers, and Planetary Development officials with bottles of sedative sticking out their pockets. On a large screen at the front of the room was the projected legend:

HALF-BILLION DOLLAR
PDA MACHINE
GOES WILD
OFF CYGNES VI

Buzzel abruptly cut himself off. In a bewildered voice, he said, "They're taking them *anyway*—"

He sucked in his breath. Crandall, out of the corner of his eye, saw Buzzel give a light yank on the microphone cord. The already unplugged end jumped out from between some switches and fell on the floor.

On the screen, the delGrange suit was now scrambling wildly up the cable, brandishing drills, claws, and jackhammers. On *Monitor*, a squat black cylinder was rising up out of the central sphere. In the background, getting it all down on film, the dock-you ship flashed its lights.

Buzzel made a strangling sound. Crandall whirled. "Something wrong?"

"You . . . You—" Buzzel grabbed the plug. Crandall lost his balance again, hit the frequency control, then said, "Look on the screen!"

The suit, a long thin extension wrapped around a ringbolt on one of the tugs, clung and hauled itself in as the tug put on rapid bursts of power to break free. A second long extension reached out and gripped the tug. The tug went into a fast dive, then swung up and around with the suit pulling steadily nearer and easing its drill closer and closer to the ship.

Crandall and Buzzel looked on, speechless.

In the background, the dock-you ship moved around to get a better angle.

From the direction of the *Monitor* burst tiny streaks of light. The second tug swung down near the first, and the two straightened into a flat run past *Monitor*; the suit got its drill near the tug, and hitched itself closer. The drill slid ahead once again.

The tiny streaks of light swung down fast into the tangle of suit and tug. The suit jerked, spun around, hauled toward the tug, broke loose, and floated in free space, two of the flexible limbs dangling from their attachments, the rest wrapped tightly around the upper part of the suit.

A third tug joined the other two, trailing a three-cornered

cargo net. The tugs clamped the net, dove on the suit, and caught it in the center. One of the tugs folded a corner of the net around the suit, swung up from below, clamped that corner to the opposite side of the net, and let go. The suit sprawled loosely inside the net, as motionless and inactive as a cargo crate being transshipped in space. Various limbs and power tools trailed out through the net to the rear.

Crandall watched the suit closely, then turned to Buzzel.

Buzzel was staring at the screen, the microphone dangling forgotten at his side. He blinked, took a slow breath, and looked at Crandall. "Shock," he said. "The operator's in a state of shock. He's got the equivalent of two broken arms." Buzzel looked back at the screen. "Well, now we can get him out of there and—"

The documentary ship swung around for a long-distance shot of the two tugs carrying off the inert latest model delGrange suit. Buzzel let out an angry growl, lunged forward with the wire and plug, and roared orders into the microphone.

An alien hiss and cackle burst from the speaker. Buzzel blinked his eyes rapidly. Crandall leaned forward and stared at the frequency setting.

"Sir," said the voice of the *Monitor*'s commanding officer "we've got the thing. Now what do we do with it?"

Crandall glanced around. "Just have those two tugs stand by with it." He turned to Buzzel. "Is there some reason you want that ship with lights taken out of there?"

Buzzel was looking at Crandall the way a hungry soldier looks at a ration that has bits of rock in it. "Yes," Buzzel said, "Yes, I do want it taken out of there and I want the film impounded. And now if you'll kindly let go the microphone cord, and keep your hands off the frequency setting, I will order just exactly that."

"No trouble at all," said Crandall courteously. He turned to the *Monitor*'s officer on the screen. "Take that documentary ship into custody. Get it out of here and down to Space Force H.Q. Impound the film. But take good care of it. Don't damage it. And treat all the personnel with proper courtesy."

The officer gave a wolfish grin. "Yes, sir." He turned away and barked out orders.

Crandall thought it well to leave the Planetary Development ship shortly afterward.

✦   ✦   ✦

The two days of the arrival and descent to Cygnes VI of the delGrange suits and their operators had seemed to Crandall as long as several ordinary weeks. The following few weeks seemed to take years in passing, as the avalanche of criticism got past the Chief of Staff on Terra and broke on Crandall's head.

At the same time that violent demands were being forwarded from all branches of the government, Crandall had to deal with innumerable petty crises caused by the daily routines of martial law. Through this, Crandall clung grimly to the awareness that two hundred and eighty-six men would die if they did not leave their suits on schedule. A parade of specialists passed through Crandall's office to testify to this and other facts. Where the facts were concerned, the specialists generally agreed unanimously. Where interpretation and prediction based on the facts were concerned, the specialists generally disagreed unanimously.

The trouble, Crandall told himself, was that this had never happened before, so no one knew how to weigh the factors involved. Once it had happened, it would all be explained, and everything would be obvious. Right now it was another matter, and no one knew how it would turn out.

One of the most certain on this matter of not knowing was Buzzel, who formally requested Crandall to release Paley. Buzzel insisted that he, himself, was not fitted to handle the job. Paley's superior intellect, his swift reactions, his long experience and meritorious service—all argued that he, not Buzzel, should have the opportunity of dealing with the situation.

Crandall was inclined to agree. He had Paley brought up for an interview, while a phalanx of guards waited outside the door. As Crandall told Buzzel, it all depended on whether or not Paley would co-operate. Noting Paley's expression, Crandall thought that the prospects were not inviting.

"Well," said Paley, "do I stand at attention? Should I salute? What happens next? Where am I, anyway?"

"From your point of view," said Crandall, "you're back in the Day of the Warrior. The fossil has you in its jaws."

Paley colored. "What do you want?"

Crandall described what had happened to the suit. Paley sneered and implied that Crandall had handled it all wrong.

Crandall mentioned that the operator afterward had failed to remember anything that happened while he was in the suit. Paley said, "Protective amnesia," and looked condescending. Crandall suggested that they might possibly be dealing with unknown factors and ought to prepare for unpleasant possibilities. Paley remarked that Crandall was out of his province. Crandall said that he would either go a step farther and take direct control of Planetary Development, or a step back and return control to Paley. Paley said that, in the first case, Crandall would find himself out of his depth.

"All right," said Crandall, "what if you're reinstated?"

"Reinstate me," said Paley, "and I will block you every step of the way."

Crandall flipped on the intercom.

"Sir?"

"Start canvassing Special Services for a volunteer executioner," said Crandall. "Also have Special Services form a grave-digger detachment."

"Yes, sir."

Crandall switched off the intercom.

Paley stiffened and blinked. "You can't bluff me."

Crandall said, "You're a good judge of human nature, aren't you, Paley? You know the operators in those suits are going to come up right on schedule. You know the cyberneticists in your own organization are wrong. You know I'm wrong. You know the men who framed Sections 67 and 68 are wrong. Everyone's wrong but you. You've got ability and we badly need it, but why use it? You know you're right without bothering. You let mannerisms, trivialities, and special cases irritate you so much you won't see what's underneath as the principle of the thing. You've got all the answers beforehand. All right, so be it. You won't believe you're going to die till the trapdoor gives way under you." Crandall flipped on the intercom. "Send in the guards."

The door opened. The guards marched in, their boots striking the floor in unison. They halted with a united click of their heels. The bayonets at their sides clinked and rattled.

Paley was standing perfectly still with a glassy look on his face.

Crandall glanced at the sergeant. "Take him out."

They marched Paley out of the room, and the tramp of feet moved off in the corridor.

Crandall reached for a paper on his desk.

There was a commotion outside.

Crandall got up and opened the door. Paley was struggling with his guards. He saw Crandall.

"All right," he cried. "I'll do it—I'll do it."

On Paley's promise to wholeheartedly co-operate, Crandall reinstated him. But before Paley returned to Planetary Development H.Q., Crandall let him sit in at the first run of a nicely-detailed film titled:

HALF-BILLION DOLLAR
PDA MACHINE
GOES WILD
OFF CYGNES VI

Paley went away greenish and shaken.

After Paley's return, Planetary Development began to show increased activity. Permission was requested, and granted, for extensive tests with some of the twenty-four reserve suits. Friction between Paley's men and Crandall's fell away toward normal, and all indications showed a steady rise in P.D.A. morale.

Crandall put in all the thought on the underlying problem that he could. As a result, he sent a series of code messages to G.H.Q., Space Forces, Earth. And he carried out a number of preparations on his own.

A week before the delGrange suits and operators were supposed to come up, Paley came to see him. Paley looked as if he had spent the last few nights staring at the ceiling.

"Matt," said Paley, "This is hopeless. On the basis of the tests I've made, those operators aren't going to come out."

"You said delGrange tested the suits personally, beforehand?"

"That's exactly the trouble. I didn't see it before, but now it's obvious. DelGrange knew so much about those suits, inside and out, that his reactions just weren't the same as the operators' reactions will be. DelGrange *knew*, mentally. The operator *senses*, physically. If delGrange had a blackness and numbness at getting out of the suit, his mind promptly interpreted it as a mere loss of induced sensation from the exterior receptors of the suit. If there was the remote beginning of a sort of terror, his mind could dismiss it as irrational before he was really aware of it. That isn't true of the operator. It isn't true after five hours in the suit. I've tried it myself. There's a blackness that comes over you— a numbness and a dizziness. It builds up. It's like a kind of death to come out of one of those suits. You get terrified. You struggle to get back. That's how it hit me after five hours. How's it going to hit the operators after thirty days?"

Crandall nodded thoughtfully. "Can you service the suits *without* the operators coming out?"

"No, you have to get into the operator's compartment."

"Through the air lock?"

"That's the only way I know."

"Is there any way to force an entrance?"

"Maybe, if all the limbs and devices were smashed. But the suit feels pain. That is, the operator feels damage to the suit as pain. If we try to force an entrance, we'll be in about the same spot as the man who goes into the bear cage at the zoo with a pair of pliers and no anesthetic. Maybe the bear really *wants* that bad tooth out, but—"

"Yeah," said Crandall. "Wait till the pain hits him. Well— All right, we've got two problems. First, they have to come up here. Is that right?"

"Yes," said Paley. "If they don't do that, we can't get them out. The pressure on VI would kill them. To say nothing of what we'd have to go through even to get down there."

"All right," said Crandall, "first they have to come up. Then, second, we have to get them out of the suits. And from what we've seen, they won't *willingly* come out of the suits. If we try to force them, they'll fight. If they fight, the only way to stop them will be to smash their limbs. And then the suits will be ruined."

" 'Yes," said Paley, "and the operators in a state of shock. Two-hundred and seventy-six of them." For an instant, Paley's eyes shut and his face twisted. He sucked in a deep breath and let it out slowly. "Well," he said, "we've got alternate operators coming. That isn't the worst of it. But it's going to take time to repair or replace those suits. VI was scheduled for heavy ore production. With the suits out of action, it will unhinge the whole schedule. Then there'll be all kinds of repercussions once the schedule goes. And that, *still*, isn't the worst that might happen. The operators might come up and—"

"I know," said Crandall.

Paley looked at him dully. "All because the suits were *too perfect.*"

Crandall opened a desk drawer and pulled out a sheaf of papers. "I think there's one way out of this hole," he said "*if* we can act fast and co-operate with each other."

Paley shuddered and said, "I think we can co-operate with each other."

Crandall put the sheaf of papers face up on the desk and began to talk. Paley listened earnestly.

On the day the delGrange suits were due to come up, Crandall and Paley stood near each other on the cruiser *Vengeance*. Each man had his own viewscreen, his own communications screen, and his own battery of microphones. A glance at the wide-angled viewscreen showed Crandall the dark bulk of the *Monitor*, and a cloud of small scout spacers far overhead. A number of huge Planetary Development nurse ships waited in the foreground, while, far to one side, the documentary ship moved from place to place, trying for a better view.

Crandall glanced at his watch, and Paley said, "I don't think they're coming up."

The dock-you ship flashed its lights. Crandall leaned forward. On the screen, a speck appeared, swooping up from Cygnes VI. Other specks came rushing up behind it. The specks grew rapidly, and Paley leaned toward a microphone. In a relieved voice, he said:

"Welcome back, men. Leave your ore-carriers up here to be reloaded. Proceed immediately to the nurse ships for deactivation, servicing, and replacement."

No answer came from the receiver.

Paley scowled. "Welcome back, men—" He repeated his instructions.

The receiver remained silent. On the screen, the specks grew rapidly larger and began to take form. Paley signaled a technician to check the communicator.

Paley repeated, "Welcome back, men. Leave your ore-carriers up here to be reloaded. Proceed immediately to the nurse-ships for deactivation, servicing, and replacement—"

There was still no answer.

Paley glared at the technician, gave the receiver a whack on the side, and again repeated, "Welcome back—"

A flat toneless voice replied, "All humans out of the nurse-ships."

Paley blinked. "Leave your ore carrier—"

"No ore."

"Men—"

"We're going into the nurse-ships two at a time. Any humans in the nurse-ships get killed."

"Listen to me," said Paley. "Your suits have to be serviced. Otherwise you won't last another thirty days."

"We'll service ourselves."

"How?"

"How is none of your business. We're doing it. Now get out of the way or get hurt."

"Listen," said Paley. "I understand. It's not an easy matter to leave those suits. But the ore *has* to be brought up, and then you have to leave the suits. Nothing bad is going to happen to you. It just has to be done. You signed for this job. You've been trained for it. Now you have to carry it out."

"No," said the voice, in a faintly pitying tone, "we didn't sign for this job. We didn't know what it was going to be like. We weren't told till it was too late to do anything about it. We trained in Model C's. They aren't anything like these suits, so we weren't trained for the job, either. Now *you* are going to tell *us* what to do?"

"Earth," said Paley tiredly, "has to have the ore."

"O.K. It's down there ready to load. But *you'll* do things *our* way. We're going to the nurse-ships and service each other. When enough of us are ready, we'll get the ore—if there's time. If you don't like it that way, that's tough."

Paley said, in a dispirited voice, "Give me a few minutes to think it over."

"We'll give you nothing. If the nurse-ships don't open up when we get to them, we'll knock a hole in the side. If you want to do it some other way, forget it. This is the way it's going to be."

Paley snapped off his microphone and turned to Crandall. "The only way I know that they can service each other without leaving the suits is to first cut the nerve cable that supplies the front outer wall of the suits. Then they have to cut out a section of wall and reach through from outside. I don't see how they can repair the cable. That means that future injuries in that part of the suit are likely to go unnoticed. And if they don't put the section of wall back with a very strong tight join, the pressure down there will either make a leak, or else shove the whole section in. Worse yet, I don't think they have either the knowledge or the equipment to do a good job of servicing. If they'd listen, I think I could convince them. But meanwhile, time's passing. We have only so long to get the ore up, the suits serviced, and new operators down there." Paley shook his head. "Maybe your plan will work."

Crandall flipped on one of his bank of microphones. He cleared his throat with a rasping sound. "Attention. This is the Commanding Officer, Space Force, Cygnes. Martial law has been established throughout Cygnes System. Failure of any delGrange suit operator to obey instructions of authorized personnel may be regarded as mutiny."

There was a moment's silence and then, as Crandall had expected, a stream of obscenities came out of the communicator.

Crandall snapped off the microphone, looked at the viewscreen and noted that all the suits seemed to have come up from Cygnes VI. They were bunched, those in back having put on more speed to catch up, and those in front having slowed to change direction.

Crandall glanced at the communications screen. *"Monitor* only, open fire."

Tiny streaks of flame curved away from the massive sphere in its wheel, raced in and out amongst the suits and exploded nearby in brilliant flashes of light.

Incoherent shouts came from the communicator. One voice dominated the rest, and the suits began to move toward *Monitor*. Further bunching now took place, as the suits nearest *Monitor* hung back, while those far away advanced bravely. *Monitor* hurried the process by exploding missiles in front of the nearest suits and behind the farthest.

Crandall, watching intently, said "Scout spacers. First flight only. Ready. Dump your cargo! Second flight, stand by."

Scout spacers dove toward the delGrange suits.

"Second flight only. Ready. Dump your cargo! Third flight, stand by. First flight, reload."

Mingled shouts and curses came from the communicator. On the screen, the suits writhed, twisted, and began to mill about, losing their momentum toward *Monitor*. Over the howling confusion, one voice rose loud and clear:

"Move! Spread out! Keep moving toward *Monitor!*"

Crandall studied the suits and turned to Paley. "O.K. Now."

Paley shouted into a microphone.

Twenty-three delGrange suits—the reserve that hadn't dropped to Cygnes, came out from behind the *Monitor*, spread out, and raced toward the other suits, which were now twisting, writhing, and milling about, their flexible arms scrubbing their sides, their jointed, steel-toothed extensions sawing jerkily across their backs.

"Third flight," said Crandall, "practice dive only. Practice dive. Ready—"

The new delGrange suits raced in among the rest, and new sounds burst amongst the screamed and muttered curses:

"Look out! Here they come again!"

"Run for it!"

"LOOK OUT! HELP!"

"To the nurse-ships!"

"Quick! *To the nurse-ships!*"

These new shouts drowned out a stream of insistent orders and pleadings to *"Keep moving toward Monitor!"* The whole mass began to move in the opposite direction, save for one gesticulating knot of cables that waved and pointed furiously toward *Monitor*, found itself isolated, dropped back and gripped another, then another, succeeded in getting three or four headed back toward *Monitor*, and then received special attention as Crandall sent scout spacers to dump cargo on the hindmost delGrange suits.

The retreat from *Monitor* turned into a wild rush toward the nurse-ships.

Paley gripped his microphone. "Attention! Proceed in an orderly manner to the nurse-ships for decontamination. Attention! Proceed in an *orderly manner* to the nurse-ships!"

A wild yell burst from the communicator. "Let me out of this suit!"

"Slow down!" roared Paley. "No crowding! There's room for everyone. Don't leave your suits till you're *inside the ships!* Retract those drills! Don't use them on the suits! SLOW DOWN!"

The screen was a spidery nightmare. The delGrange suits rushed headlong into the giant maw of nurse-ship number one, flowed around it and vanished into others. The big doors closed.

Crandall and Paley looked at each other and smiled feebly.

Crandall was massaging his throat several weeks later, following a visit of high government officials, when the lieutenant reported his presence.

"Sir," said the lieutenant, handing Crandall a stamped slip of paper with an official seal, "I've been told that you must have made this payment."

Crandall took the paper and saw:

Rec'd Payment
1 pipet, 25ml., smashed $2.75
O.K. P.D.A.

"Hm-m-m," said Crandall. "Well—That's taken care of."

"Thank you very much, sir."

"You're welcome, lieutenant."

"And now, sir—" The lieutenant handed Crandall a small, neatly wrapped package. Crandall, frowning, took it. The package, though small, felt heavy. A card on the outside read:

"To Col. Matthew Crandall, from the officers and men of his command, Cygnes System."

"Well," said Crandall, groping mentally. "Hm-m-m. I certainly appreciate this—"

"I'll tell the men, sir. Ah, sir, may I ask a question?"

"Certainly."

"What was that stuff in bottles and sprayers that we dumped on the suits?"

"Acid," said Crandall, smiling. "The suit operators felt mild corrosion of the suit's outer skin as an itch. The acid gave a sensation like poison ivy on a huge scale. The operators left their suits, the acid was neutralized, an inductive device we'd worked out was installed, and next time we hope to get a better result with less trouble. Keep your eyes open. There'll be a White Paper out on the whole thing pretty soon."

"Yes, sir," said the lieutenant.

Crandall glanced curiously at the package. "Ah—Would you express my thanks for this gift, lieutenant?"

"Certainly, sir."

The lieutenant and Crandall exchanged salutes. The lieutenant about-faced and left the room.

Crandall relaxed in his chair. He turned the package over thoughtfully in his hand.

"Hm-m-m," he said.

He took the card off carefully, untied the ribbon, and folded back the paper. Highly-polished silver flashed in the light of the room.

Crandall squinted, then started to grin.

He got up, opened the door, and glanced out in the corridor to see whether anyone was still around outside.

He walked back into the room and laughed.

He turned the gift in his hands, and saw the word "STERLING." A massive silver bolt joined the two halves unbreakably together.

Crandall set the gift prominently in the center of his desk and got back to work.

The first Space Force officer in history to own a massive, finely-detailed, solid silver pair of pliers.

STRANGLEHOLD

Stellar Scout James Connely and Sector Chief of Scouts Gregory MacIntyre sat by the communicator, with the star charts spread out around them, and considered their predicament.

From the nearby communicator came a recorded voice:

"Don't land. Keep off this planet. For everybody's sake as well as your own. Stay away."

MacIntyre growled, "Nice and informative, isn't it? What's wrong with the planet? Earthquakes? Plague? Carnivores? Vermin? You'd think anyone that gets in trouble and throws up a warning satellite would have the wit to say what the trouble is. But no, all we're told is, 'Don't land. For everybody's sake. Stay away.' A lot of help *that* is."

A rapid sequence of beeps came in, and Connely said, "Well, at least we know it's Barnes." Barnes was a Stellar Scout who'd been missing well over a year, and MacIntyre recognized his voice.

"Yeah," said MacIntyre sourly. "It's his voice, all right, and it's his recognition signal, but he doesn't seem to have been using his brain. The thing is just a little miniature warning satellite. If he'd only followed standard procedure, he'd have put a full-size signal satellite in orbit before he went down there. Then he could have got a full-length message started back through channels the same day he got in trouble. But this thing leaves us tied in knots."

Connely nodded moodily.

MacIntyre went on, "A message like this should be relayed,

447

without delay, straight to our HQ in this sector. That's routine. The booby trap in the setup is that the Stellar Scout Department is a part of Planetary Development Administration. This message will get distributed like lightning, so many copies to Planet Certification, so many to the Colonization Council, so many to Central Records, *and one copy to Space Force HQ in this sector.*"

"Yeah," said Connely. "I see what you mean."

"Good," said MacIntyre. "Then maybe you can help me figure it out. There are only two possibilities. Either what is on that planet *is* as dangerous as it sounds, or it isn't. In either case, you have to bear in mind that the Space Force and Planetary Development do not have the sweetest possible relationship with each other. If the planet *is* dangerous, it's going to look suspicious that I am out here. A sector chief hardly ever goes out on a scouting trip. I'm only here because I got tangled up with a new piece of equipment, and couldn't get loose before the ship took off. That's the truth. But it's an unlikely kind of an accident, and nobody is going to believe it. Word is going to get around that I *knew* there was trouble here, and came out to check before sending in the alarm. That's a serious offense. There will be an investigation. Regardless how the investigation turns out, the Space Force will get considerable mileage out of it."

Connely nodded. "There's no doubt about that."

"Or," said MacIntyre, "alternatively, the place may turn out *not* to be dangerous. Nevertheless, the Space Force is going to rush here all set up for a fight. Big cruisers will be roaring all over the place. Monitors will be orbiting the planet ready to knock off anything that tries to get away. They'll have the solar beam reflectors all set up ready, in case of trouble. Now, if they get all that stuff up out here, and it turns out there's nothing more dangerous on the planet than a chipmunk, Planetary Development Administration is going to be in a mess."

Connely nodded exasperatedly. In his mind, he could hear the wise commentators, and see the glaring headlines:

"NO EMERGENCY"
"PDA WRONG AGAIN"
"SPACE FORCE CHARGES BUNGLING."

Connely could also see the news-sheets that would pop out of innumerable printers in countless homes as hurried husbands bolted breakfast and read:

" . . . Why was a PDA sector chief present at the scene of this latest bungling? Why does a mess like this follow right on the heels of the expensive uproar off Cygnes VI, and the disaster on Bemus III? Why must the public pay through the nose for the endless bickering and backbiting between these two monster organizations Planetary Development and the Space Force? Who is responsible? Careful analysis of the power struggle that took place at Cygnes showed without question that the local PDA official tried to mousetrap his opposite number in the Space Force. In this present instance, we actually find a high official of Planetary Development right on the spot, officiating as the misleading report was sent in. Was this intended to be another Cygnes? Or to be, like Bemus III, a planet officially approved for settlement by the Planetary Development Administration and all its octopoid bureaucratic subdivisions, from the Stellar Scouts through the confusingly named Planetary Development Authority to the oh-so-high-and-mighty Planet Certification Authority, but *deadly to the helpless colonists who must trust PDA?* Or was it another back-stab to the Space Force and the brave soldiers sent yet again to get PDA's roasting chestnuts out of the fire? If Planetary Development is innocent, *why was their Sector Chief already on the spot when this latest mess burst into the news? . . .*"

The communicator beeped again, and said:

"Don't land. Keep off this planet. For everybody's sake as well as your own. Stay away."

MacIntyre swore. "All right, Con. You see the problem. What's your solution?"

Connely shrugged. "I'm no politician, Mac. But as far as I can see, once we relay that warning, the muck hits the fan. After that business on Cygnes, everybody's a little— tense."

"Yeah," growled MacIntyre.

"On the other hand," said Connely tentatively,

"regulations say we've *got* to relay that message." He looked at MacIntyre meaningfully. "As soon as we *hear* it, that is.

"Hm-m-m," said MacIntyre thoughtfully.

The two men looked at each other.

"Of course," said MacIntyre, "if we'd had the communicator, say . . . disassembled when we approached the planet, we wouldn't have heard the message."

"No," said Connely. "That's right. The message wasn't sent out till our approach triggered off the satellite."

"And then," said MacIntyre, "with our communicator out of order, there'd be no *need* to relay the message."

"Of course not," Connely agreed. "We couldn't relay it if we didn't hear it. That's common sense."

The communicator said loudly, "Don't land. Keep off this planet. For everybody's sake as well as your own. Stay away."

MacIntyre said tentatively, "Con, does the reception seem a little rough to you, as if something's going out of whack?"

"Hm-m-m," said Connely, "now that you mention it, it probably wouldn't do any harm if we took a glance at the inside of the thing, would it?"

"An ounce of prevention," said MacIntyre piously, "is worth a pound of cure. Now, let me help you get that inspection cover off."

Several minutes later, parts of the communicator were spread out generously over Connely's non-regulation gray rug.

"Probably," said MacIntyre, "when we land on this planet, just for safety's sake we ought to orbit an extra-powerful signal satellite. Then, at the mere touch of a button in the ship here, we could relay any warning—if, that is, any small warning satellite should happen to be up here. And meanwhile, if we didn't cancel it periodically, the satellite would send out its emergency call."

"Good idea," said Connely. He glanced at the clouded blue and green planet in the viewscreen. "Of course, it doesn't *look* dangerous."

"No," said MacIntyre. "And it probably isn't, either."

"Still, it's a good idea," said Connely. He went off to take care of it, relieved at the thought that the two monster bureaucracies were not about to come together in a head-on clash with him in the middle. Now it might be possible to get down to business.

A little later, they started down to the planet.

On their way down, they noted a number of small isolated villages on the screen, and a few fair-sized, medieval-looking cities widely scattered along the seacoast. Then Connely brought the ship down on a stretch of level grassland several dozen miles from a village built near the edge of a forest. His idea was to get a quiet look at the planet, and the natives, by sending out a few probes. Meanwhile, if there was any danger, it could hardly sneak up on the ship across that expanse of level land, and the detectors would spot anything airborne.

The ship had hardly settled down, however, when there was a noise in the corridor, and a yellow warning light began to flash. This yellow warning light told of activity by the IntruGrab, a device designed to seize intruders, and installed in the corridor near the inner air-lock door. So far, Connely had had nothing but trouble with the IntruGrab. Now, he looked out in the corridor to see its big globe halfway between ceiling and floor, and its metallic arms ranging far up and down the corridor.

Connely walked to the cross-corridor, saw nothing there, and decided that the IntruGrab had suffered a malfunction. He was happy to see that so far, at least, it made no effort to stuff him into the globe; but the metal arms snaking through the air around him were beginning to make him uneasy.

He was about to go back to the control room when he noticed a piece of roughly woven orange cloth on the floor of the corridor. He glanced around, wondering where that had come from, and bent to look at it.

This changed his angle of vision so that a glimpse of reflected light further up the corridor caught his attention. He stepped aside, to see, lying on the deck, a short, well-balanced dagger with no guard, and a thin double-edged blade that had been sharpened almost to a needle point. The lower third of the blade was snapped off, and lay close by. Frowning, Connely straightened. He'd had no such knife on board before, and the cloth, too, was strange. It followed that they must have come from outside. But the air lock was still shut.

Uneasily, Connely glanced around.

There was no one in sight in the corridor, but now from the direction of the control room came heavy breathing and a furious thumping sound. Connely dodged past the angled reinforcing members, and looked into the control room.

MacIntyre, a savage expression on his face, came down with both heels on a thing like a length of dull-green two-inch rope. Connely realized with a start that this was a snake, about four feet long. Just as he realized this, he felt a sensation much as if a feather pillow had been tossed lightly against his back. Something clattered to the floor. There was a scuffling behind him, and, across the control room, the familiar yellow warning light began to flash. Connely turned, to see the IntruGrab's metal arms snatch up a gray-cloaked and hooded figure, which vanished in midair before it reached the globe. Just then, there was a grunt from MacIntyre, and the green snake went flying past Connely down the corridor. Three of the IntruGrab's metal arms grabbed the snake before it hit the floor, and stuffed it into the globe.

A flicker of reflected light caught Connely's attention, and he saw lying in the corridor another dagger just like the one that he had found earlier. This one, however, was not broken. Connely looked around for the thing that had caused the sensation of a pillow hitting his back, and then remembered that he was wearing a new item of equipment called "reflex clothing." This, like the IntruGrab, had been forced on him by MacIntyre, who firmly believed in new and modern equipment—the newer and more modern, the better.

Connely put his fist out, and punched himself in the stomach. His clothing stiffened as he hit it, distributing the force of the blow so that he felt only a light push over the front of his body. The fabric of his sleeve, however, also stiffened, to drag back against his arm, so that he found it impossible to strike as quickly as he intended. It occurred to Connely that it would be a good thing if he never had to move fast while wearing "reflex clothing."

MacIntyre was by now looking down the corridor, massaging his throat. "That snake," he said, "was a constrictor. Did you have any snakes or snakes' eggs in the storeroom?"

"No," said Connely. "And I didn't have any daggers or hooded men in the storeroom, either." He described what had happened, and MacIntyre scowled.

"Maybe there was something to what Barnes said, after all."

"Yes, and it explains why he didn't try to say just *what* the trouble was. How would he describe this?"

Connely went into the control room, and, just in case there should be large-scale trouble outside, he pushed down the lever that put the battle-computer in control of the ship. He was thinking as he did this that a planet as backward as this one appeared to be probably couldn't endanger the ship itself, and probably he and MacIntyre would know in time if it happened. But it was best to be on the safe side.

As soon as the lever was pushed all the way down, however, the gravitors gave a howling whine, the accelerometer needle whipped around its dial, and the scene on the outside viewscreen jumped backwards and melted into a blur.

The communications screen cut into the battle-control circuit, and lit up to show the green image of the ship hurtling toward a blocky turreted structure like a medieval castle. From this structure, the battle screen showed peculiar wavy lines and ghostly whitish blurs moving out toward the ship. From the ship, in turn, a set of yellow missile tracks, and dazzling bolts from fusion guns slammed out at the massive structure. As the ship flashed past, Connely quickly reset the viewscreen. He saw walls and towers erupt in boiling clouds of dirt and masonry. The ship now flipped end-for-end, with a tortured whine from the gravitors, raced back, and hit the remains of the structure a second time on the way past. The ship then landed, in almost the same spot where they had set down originally.

Connely, dumbfounded, looked at MacIntyre. MacIntyre pulled his jaw shut, and glanced at Connely with a blank expression. Connely shook his head, studied the viewscreen, and was rewarded by the sight of an empty expanse of grassland. Thinking it might be possible to get a better view from one of the ship's upper turrets, Connely went up a ladder, and slid back the armor plating from the transparent dome.

A thing about eighty feet long, with teeth as big as elephant's tusks, sprang at the ship. A snake shaped like a boa constrictor, and about the size of a sea serpent, thrust its snout at Connely like a battering ram. Connely almost fell down the ladder in his haste to get out of the turret. He only barely had the presence of mind to hit the switch that would throw the armor back over the turret. He sprang to the controls, and then it dawned on him that the battle-computer would long since have finished off any such things as he had seen. And if it hadn't, the sheer weight of the blows would be knocking the ship around by this time.

He glanced at the viewscreen and saw merely the empty expanse of grassland. He stared at this a moment, then went back up the ladder and pulled the armor away from the turret again. The ground outside was now acrawl with waves of spiders the size of a man's hand, that climbed up on the ship and began to spin a web of white strands from ship to ground, fastening the ship down with a thick white membrane that grew thicker and tougher as he watched.

Connely automatically reached for the hand controls of the fusion gun in the turret, and then paused. He climbed down, and readjusted the viewscreen, which showed him the same view of empty grassland. He climbed up and looked out the turret. He saw big whitish sheets and cables now covering the ship, and being drawn taut by other cables that ran off to the side. As he watched, the hull of the ship began to warp and buckle.

Connely dropped down the ladder and sprang to the viewscreen. There was nothing but empty grassland. He realized suddenly that there had been no feeling of motion, and no sound from the plates of the ship. If the ship were being squeezed like that, there would be movement, and loud creaks and groanings from the bending metal.

MacIntyre, who'd been watching with growing amazement as Connely hurtled up and down the ladder, said abruptly, "No offense, Con, but would you mind telling me what the devil you're doing?"

"Go up to the turret and take a look," said Connely.

MacIntyre grunted and went up the ladder. An instant later, his voice carried down from above, and he shot down the ladder to make a flying jump for the control board.

Connely leaned casually against a bulkhead in the control

room, and watched as MacIntyre grabbed at the controls, then froze halfway, and stared at the viewscreen. He shifted views several times, then glanced at Connely, turned and went back to the ladder. While he was up there, Connely walked back into the corridor to see if the second knife that had been thrown at him was still there. He found it lying where he had seen it before, and noted again that it was a very narrow-bladed knife, apparently balanced especially for throwing, and designed to penetrate flesh with the slightest effort.

There was a faint hum as the armor slid back over the turret. Then MacIntyre was standing beside Connely, who straightened up from the knife, and said, "The more I see of this planet, Mac, the more I have to agree with Barnes."

"Yes," said MacIntyre. "Me, too. And speaking of Barnes, I wonder where he landed?"

"I don't know," said Connely, "but we ought to be able to find his ship. And we might just as well start looking now."

MacIntyre nodded. His face had an unusually thoughtful expression as they walked back into the control room, and Connely lifted ship.

Once they had a reasonable altitude, Connely released several probes that flashed away on predetermined courses. As the ship streaked north, more probes dropped out. A little over an hour had gone by when a red light lit up on a small panel, to show that Probe 6 had spotted something that matched the taped description of Barnes' ship. Connely sent out the signal to recall the others, and then studied on a small auxiliary screen the image sent back by Probe 6.

The country where Barnes' ship had set down was rolling grassland, much like the place where Connely had landed. Here, too, there was a village a few dozen miles away, which suggested that Barnes, like Connely, had hoped to take a quiet look at the people of the planet but didn't want to frighten them away, or make a sudden dramatic appearance that would upset their lives. Connely smiled sourly at this last thought. The native inhabitants of this planet were apparently well able to take care of themselves.

As Connely was thinking this, the gravitors whined, and another massive structure of high slit-windowed towers and walls appeared on the screen. This one was made entirely of black stone, and as it enlarged on the screen, it rapidly took on the brooding, foreboding aspect of a vulture perched on a tree limb. A sense of dread gripped Connely. The outlines of the control room seemed to waver and run around him, like a sketch drawn in washable ink and placed under water. Then abruptly the illusion was gone, and the outside viewscreen showed a towering column of dust and debris rolling skyward where the structure had stood. The sense of dread was gone as if it had never been.

MacIntyre said suddenly, "Look at this screen!"

Connely glanced at the auxiliary screen, to see a ragged scarecrow figure dancing and waving its arms by Barnes' ship.

"That," said MacIntyre, "looks like Barnes to me."

When Connely brought his ship down, the figure was still there, and now they could see that Barnes' eyes were tightly shut. The wild waving of his arms that they had taken for happiness at the thought of being rescued turned out instead to be a violent shooing motion, as if Barnes were trying to warn them away.

Connely said, "Before we open the hatch, it might be worthwhile to see what this place looks like from the turret."

"Yes," growled MacIntyre, studying Barnes' thin worn face. "Meanwhile, I'll run out the loudspeaker and pickup and see if he can tell us anything."

Connely climbed into the turret, ran back the protecting armor, and looked at a scene out of a madman's nightmare. The rolling grassland, which showed up as an empty stretch of ground on the viewscreen, appeared to be filled with a maze of tall moss-covered stone walls cut with large rectangular holes like window-openings and doorways. In the oversize doorways lay huge snakes, big crabs with oversize claws, and semifluid horrors like giant jellyfish. The window openings were closed by big spider webs, or partially blocked by gray cone-shaped nests of hornets and wasps. A brief glance was enough for Connely, who looked away before the scene etched itself any more sharply in his memory.

From below came MacIntyre's voice, as he spoke into the loudspeaker.

"Can you hear me all right, Barnes?"

"Go away," came a rough voice. "Get out of here before they get you, too."

"Can you get around to our air lock?"

"Are you insane? I can't go anywhere through this stuff."

"What's wrong? Why can't you get here?"

Connely said, "He can't, Mac. There's an illusion of big walls, boa constrictors, giant crabs . . . Open your eyes on that sight, and you'd be afraid to take three steps."

"It's more," came Barnes' voice. "It's not just a visual illusion. It's tactile as well. You can touch it, feel it, smell it. It can grab you, block you, flatten you. Whatever you do, don't leave your ship or open up the air lock."

"What's wrong with your ship?" said MacIntyre. "Can't you go back inside, and lock up?"

Barnes gave a short laugh. "My ship? Where is my ship? Do you see it?"

MacIntyre hesitated an instant. "It's right behind you," he said.

"You see it?"

"Yes, in the viewscreen."

"Ah, the viewscreen," said Barnes. Then he added matter-of-factly, "Yes, I suppose the viewscreen picks up the basic physical reality, and doesn't show the rest. But to me there's a low hut back here, and that's all. You say that's the ship?"

MacIntyre said, his voice somewhat desperate, "The ship's right behind you."

"You say so, said Barnes musingly, "but what's reality, anyway? Only an illusion that fits all the senses. How do I know what's true for you will be true for me?"

"Truth's truth," said MacIntyre sharply.

"It may be so on Earth," said Barnes. "It isn't so here. Truth is the image imposed by the stronger mind on unformed matter. Truth changes. It's changed several times since I've been here. Once, while it was in flux, I got up a satellite. At least, I think I did."

"You did," said MacIntyre. "Now stop this nonsense about truth and get ready to climb into the ship. I'm going to move over closer to you."

The ship lifted and moved gradually closer to Barnes. Connely looked warily out the turret, his eyes only partly open, to see the apparently solid stone walls seem to compress and slide around the ship as it moved forward. Barnes came into view, and behind him, a low thatched hut. The ship stopped within several yards of Barnes, and MacIntyre said, "Con, are we close enough?"

"It looks so to me," said Connely.

"O.K., Barnes," said MacIntyre. "Climb in."

Barnes stepped forward with his hands outstretched and his eyes tight shut. He came in under the curve of the ship, out of Connely's range of vision. Connely heard him say wonderingly, "I feel it."

A few minutes later, there was the sound of the outer air lock door coming open. Then the sound of it going shut. MacIntyre said, "Can you hear me, Barnes?"

"Yes," said Barnes. "I hear you."

"I'm going to douse you with disinfectant. It's new stuff, and it's death on germs, but try not to swallow any of it."

"All right."

Connely slid the armor back over the turret, and dropped down to the control room. He snapped off the microphone connection to the wall speaker in the air lock.

"Are we *sure* this is Barnes?" he said. "From what I've seen of this planet, I'd hate to take a disguised native on board."

"You've got a point there," said MacIntyre. "He *looks* like Barnes. But, how—"

Connely nodded sympathetically as MacIntyre looked perplexed.

"Well," said MacIntyre, "we don't have records of finger-prints or retinal patterns handy, but I *may* be able to find out if that isn't Barnes." He snapped on the microphone, and said in an excessively cheerful voice, "You getting a good wash-down in there?"

A gargling sound came back at him. A few moments later, Barnes' voice said, "Ye gods, what awful stuff!"

"It's the new disinfectant I was telling you about," said MacIntyre. He added positively, "It's much better than what we used before."

There was a little pause. Then Barnes' voice said shortly, "Yeah."

"When we get you back," said MacIntyre, "I'm going to completely refit your ship. The fact that you couldn't handle the situation here shows how out-of-date your equipment is."

There was a considerable silence, then Barnes' voice said, "Listen, Mac, I appreciate your getting me out of that mess. But before we go through that business about refitting the ship again, would you mind letting me out of this air lock? Your improved disinfectant is eating patches of skin off my feet."

"I'll give you another rinse," said MacIntyre. Then he snapped off the air-lock speaker and glanced at Connely. "I can't swear that's no native. But he sounds like a Stellar Scout to me."

Connely nodded agreement, and went to get a fresh uniform for Barnes.

About fifteen minutes later, the lanky Barnes was slumped in Connely's control seat, his arms and legs jutting out of the too-small uniform. Barnes looked worn, thin, and somewhat out of sorts after being snatched up by the IntruGrab and put into the globe with the dead snake.

"Listen," said MacIntyre pugnaciously, "*I* spent the first part of the trip in there. If *you* can't take a few minutes of it, that's tough."

"Go on outside for a few months first," said Barnes irritatedly. "See how you like it then."

"If you'd used your equipment properly," said MacIntyre, "you probably wouldn't have got into that mess in the first place."

Barnes glanced at Connely. Connely had never met Barnes before, but in that moment they seemed to be brothers. Connely said sympathetically. "What happened?"

Barnes drew a deep breath. After a moment, he said, "Well, to begin with, I took a rough survey of the planet, and decided it was harmless. I tested the air, ran through all the usual checks, and then I was *convinced* it was harmless. I should have put a signal satellite in orbit, but I only had the new model, and for some fool reason, it wouldn't transmit. Still, I wanted a look at the place. So, like a jackass, after I came down I got out of the ship to take a walk around."

MacIntyre growled, "Unarmed?"

"No, not unarmed. Among other things, I had on your good-for-nothing reflex helmet and clothing. I also had on your worthless M1-X Gazelle Boots, and in addition I had your new Self-Draw Matter-Displacement gun strapped to my waist."

"Then," said MacIntyre, looking puzzled, "you were ready for anything."

"Except the weapons," said Barnes.

MacIntyre frowned. "What weapons?"

"My *own* weapons," said Barnes angrily.

There was a lengthy silence as the two men glared at each other. Connely leaned back, ready to enjoy the spectacle of somebody else fighting with MacIntyre for a change. After a brief glaring contest, Barnes said furiously, "Why don't you try all these things out first, prove them, and go slow about putting every maniacal contraption that comes along into the ships?"

"Join the Space Force," snapped MacIntyre.

Barnes turned red, sucked in a deep breath, and rose half out of the chair. MacIntyre balled his fists and leaned forward. Connely glanced around nervously at all the instruments that might get smashed up.

Apparently, the same thought occurred to Barnes and MacIntyre, who glanced pugnaciously around, and then by mutually graduated stages, that were a little hard for a bystander to follow, slowly subsided into their seats.

Connely tried to get the conversation back on its tracks. "What happened after you went out of the ship?"

Barnes blinked, and looked around as if he'd forgotten where he was.

"Oh," he said. "Well, till I got about thirty feet from the ship, *nothing* happened. Then there was a growl, I turned around, and a thing like the Hound of the Baskervilles was coming straight for me, from the direction of the ship."

"What did you do?"

"The first thing I did," said Barnes, "was to make the mistake of starting to reach for my gun. *Bang!* It slammed out of the holster into my hand and fired itself. The animal was almost on me by this time, and I hadn't wanted to shoot for fear I'd put a hole through the ship, which was right behind it. Rather than risk another shot, I made my second mistake, and pressed down on the toes of the Gazelle Boots, like you're supposed to if you want to go somewhere in a hurry."

Connely had never heard of Gazelle Boots before, and cast

a questioning glance at MacIntyre. MacIntyre refused to meet his gaze, and looked off noncommittally at a corner of the control room. This told Connely that Gazelle Boots were one of those items on which production had been "temporarily suspended pending further study." If the boots had still been in production, MacIntyre would have looked back with stern righteousness.

Barnes said, "The left-hand boot took off in a hurry, but so did the right-hand boot. I landed flat on my back, and this animal bounded over my head. Well, I couldn't wait to get on my feet, but in my hurry, I couldn't keep from pressing down on the toes of the boots before I got up. Every time I did this, the boots went somewhere fast, and I bounced and dragged along after them. The animal's jaws were snapping shut half an inch from my face, and I was in a terrible state by the time I managed to get to my feet. I barely had the wit to press down alternately heel-and-toe, according to the directions for walking in Gazelle Boots, and then the boots really streaked out fast. But the reflex clothing froze up like cast iron every time there was any sudden stress on it, so I *couldn't* move my legs fast, and at the same time I *had* to, because of the boots."

Connely shook his head sympathetically. "Then what?"

"The boots almost snapped my legs off at the ankles. I ended up on the ground again, and the monster dog was all over me. I was firing at it, and couldn't seem to hit it. Then suddenly the dog was gone, and a voice somewhere was talking some kind of foreign language. The meaning seemed to form in my head at the same time as the foreign words that I couldn't understand."

Barnes shook his head in reminiscence, and after a little silence, MacIntyre said, "What did the voice say?"

"It said, 'Why, this fellow is a mere beginner. He's got his spells crossed.'"

MacIntyre looked blank. "Did it say *'Spells'*?"

"That's what it said."

There was another silence, and then MacIntyre said, "Then what happened?"

"That was it," said Barnes. "The dog was gone. I went back to the ship and discovered that the first shot from the matter-displacement gun had taken a chunk the size of a

beachball out of the outer hull and frame of the ship. Before
I could repair it, everything changed to look the way it looks
out there now."

Connely said, "But what happened after that? I mean, what
did you do?"

"What *could* I do? Once I was stuck there, with those
monstrosities staring at me from that wall, I didn't do much
traveling, I can tell you that. And I couldn't work on the
ship, because I couldn't see it, or feel it. Then a stream
of visitors began to come, and I discovered that I was a
curiosity. Some of them tried to teach me the language,
which they said I had forgotten completely because of mental
shock. I think they all looked over the ship while they were
around, although I couldn't see the ship myself, so I couldn't
be sure. Pretty soon, an argument started between a couple
of factions of these visitors.

"As nearly as I could figure it out, one side claimed that
I had made the ship and other devices myself, subcon-
sciously, but didn't have the conscious skill to operate them.
The other faction claimed that the whole thing was a hoax,
engineered by Aloom, or someone with a similar name. They
quizzed me on the subject, and when I learned enough of
the language to tell them the plain truth, they had a big
laugh over it.

"Then each side claimed that what I'd said proved their
theory. One side claimed that it showed that I was a basically
irrational sort of person who relied on intuition rather than
reason, and as everyone knew this meant that I would tap
the subconscious more easily. The other side said that the
illusion was too detailed to be the work of an irrational
untrained mind. The whole illusion must have been impressed
on me from outside. This argument got hotter and hotter, and
the insults flew back and forth, and all I can say is, I'm glad
they didn't forget to feed me now and then."

MacIntyre said, "They had a fight?"

Barnes nodded, "There was thunder and lightning—or
seemed to be—earthquakes, tornadoes, and all kinds of
natural disasters. The sky was black for a solid week one
time. I don't know how to describe it. At any rate, now
and then things would go into a state of flux, the walls
would seem to run like glue, and then they would form again
with a different arrangement. Not *much* different, but enough

so you could notice it. I think what it meant was that one side had wrested mental control away from the other side. While this was happening, I could get a wavering view of the ship and grassland around it."

"In other words," said MacIntyre, frowning, "their illusions canceled each other out?"

"Maybe," said Barnes. "Or maybe, when they nullified each other, I was able to impress my own picture of reality on the scene."

MacIntyre shook his head violently. "It wasn't all illusion. Truth is things as God sees them."

"Sure," said Barnes, "but can we see things that way?"

The discussion was making Connely uneasy. To try to get it back into some familiar channel, he said, "We had a few strange experiences ourselves, right after we landed, and before we put the battle-computer in control." He told Barnes about the snake and the daggers, and added, "It seems like a fair conclusion that the people on this planet have highly developed psychic powers."

"I suppose that's it," said Barnes. "Whatever they've got, it's no fun to tangle with it."

Connely looked at MacIntyre. "What do we do about a planet like this?"

"The first thing is to get off it. See if we can drag Barnes' ship up with a gravitor beam, and then put some space between the planet and us." He frowned as he said this, and it occurred to Connely that MacIntyre's problems would not be over once they got off the planet.

MacIntyre put this into words himself after they'd got Barnes' ship up, and were in orbit well out from the planet. "This," he said sourly, "is a real, first-class mess."

Connely nodded, but Barnes said, "Why? It looks like a simple 'No Landing-No Colonizing' job to me. We put the warning satellites in orbit, notify Planet Certification, and let it go at that."

"Fine," said MacIntyre. "And just what *reason* do we give?"

Barnes opened his mouth, then shut it again. "Hm-m-m," he said. "Well, that is a problem."

"The authorities," said MacIntyre, "don't believe in psychic phenomena. Here we've got a whole planet full of psychic phenomena. Now, what do we do?"

Barnes said hesitantly, "You're a sector chief, Mac. They'd believe *you*, wouldn't they?"

"They'd believe I was in need of a rest cure. I wouldn't believe this myself, if I hadn't seen it."

The three men were silent a moment, then Connely said, "Suppose we brought back proof?"

"*What* proof? The viewscreen didn't show what we saw outside. Therefore the records won't either."

"All right. But what about the snakes, the knives, and the man that appeared in the corridor out there. *They* were real. And we've got the dead snake and the knives."

"Sure, but how do we prove where they came from? Just suppose we had visual records of the whole thing. It *still* wouldn't prove anything to anyone else, because it could have been faked. And if we got a record that *couldn't* possibly be faked by present techniques, it would merely show that we'd developed a clever new technique in advance of the times. The only way that we could convince the authorities would be to bring them here. How do we do *that?*"

The minutes crept past as the three men groped for an answer to this problem. In due time they ate, and then retired to Connely's small cabin, just off the control room. MacIntyre settled in the armchair, Connely sat down at the desk and tilted back the chair, and Barnes stretched out on the bunk. Time crept past. Connely, unable to bridge the gap between unyielding authority and unblinkable fact, found himself drawing a sketch of maniacs gibbering from behind iron bars. Suddenly, as he looked at this sketch, it seemed to mean something. He pulled over another piece of paper and began to write:

TOP SECRET
To: Sector GHQ
             Planetary Development Authority
Subject: Acute Infectious Insanity

Sirs:

We enclose herewith the official logs of Stellar Scout Ships 82 and 87. On the dates mentioned in the logs, the following events took place:

a) Scout Ship 82, after a routine planetary inspection,

was landed by Stellar Scout J. R. Barnes, on the planet identified in the coded data sheet enclosed. Taking normal precautions in the absence of any visible danger, Barnes left his ship to observe the planet at first hand. Though thoroughly experienced in his work, and well armed, he experienced the following subjective phenomena: 1) attack by a large dog-like animal, which was unaffected by Barnes' weapons, and which later vanished; 2) a voice, though no visible person was present; 3) alteration of his surroundings, the ship becoming invisible; 4) visitation by mysterious local inhabitants, who became engaged in a violent controversy caused by his (Barnes') presence; 5) imprisonment by the said local inhabitants.

b) Stellar Scout Ship 87 was landed on the same planet by Stellar Scout James Connely, accompanied by Sector Chief of Scouts Gregory MacIntyre, who was on board to inspect the functioning and operation of new equipment. Although neither man left the ship at any time while on the planet, they experienced the following subjective phenomena: 1) Sector Chief MacIntyre believed himself attacked by a snake of moderate size, which attempted to choke him by constriction; 2) Stellar Scout Connely believed himself attacked twice with thrown knives; 3) both men observed, through the forward fusion turret, realistic illusions of objects, external to the ship, which did not appear on the outside viewscreen.

Full details of these occurrences are enclosed in the accompanying report.

In explanation, it is suggested that the three men were, during their landing on the planet, rendered temporarily insane by the action of some unknown highly infectious agent or agents.

Although this condition subsided promptly upon leaving the vicinity of the planet, it is clear that the planet should not at the present time be opened to colonization and development. Warning satellites have, therefore, been put in orbit about the planet, according to the regulations concerning medically dangerous planets.

MacIntyre read the paper carefully. "I think you've got it, Con! They can *accept* this. And, of course, once they do, they'll be bound to *investigate* it. Meanwhile, in the more complete report, we can put enough information so anyone who can understand will see what actually happened."

Barnes read the paper and nodded approval. "Better that *we* suggest we were temporarily nuts than that *they* think of it."

Connely said, "It's too bad we can't just say what actually happened."

MacIntyre nodded. "Still, it's always this way. We've got a science-based civilization, and if psychic phenomena occur, they're either rationalized away, or denied outright. It's as if science were somehow *allergic* to psychic phenomena, like a hay-fever sufferer who can't stand ragweed. Although why that should be, I don't know."

Barnes said, "I can answer that one, Mac. When I was stuck on that planet, as I said, some of the natives tried to 'reteach' me their language, which they thought I must have forgotten. I got good enough at it so that they could understand me, and I tried to explain what had actually happened. One day, they told me how they *knew* my explanation couldn't be the true one."

"How?"

"Well, they said, at the base of my argument was this thing I called 'science.' And 'science,' they said, was a transparent impossibility, because it was built on an assumption that was provably false."

MacIntyre frowned. "What assumption is that?"

"That experiments can be repeated, and give the same results at different times and for different investigators."

"They don't believe that?"

"No, and what's more, to *prove* it wasn't true, they followed my instructions and got some copper wire and magnets, had a small compass made, and then passed the magnetic field through the wire, using the compass to detect the induced electric current. They carried out a series of experiments, in which the current flowed *in either direction or not at all*, as they wished."

MacIntyre whistled. Then he said, "Oh, you mean, they made that *illusion*."

"I don't think it *was* an illusion, Mac. I think their psychic control was strong enough to reverse a weak current flow caused by a weak electromotive force. But regardless whether it was an illusion or not, the result was the same: to make a perfectly good experiment worthless. Can you imagine trying to develop science on a planet where, so far as you can tell with your senses, the same experiment gives you one result on Tuesday, and another on Wednesday, depending on your own or somebody else's attitude? On this basis, science could never even get started."

"Yes," said Connely, "but wait a minute. The whole point of science is that the experimenter is *disinterested*. He comes to Nature, and puts the question. Whatever answer Nature gives, he accepts, and then goes on from there. These natives of yours didn't have the right scientific attitude."

"I'll say they didn't," said Barnes. "They *willed* the current to go one way or the other."

"All right. Get them to suspend use of their psychic powers, hold the right mental attitude, and experiments will work for them, too."

"Sure," said Barnes. He glanced around at some inexpensive novels Connely had brought along, pulled one out, opened it, and handed it to Connely. He put his finger beside one of the lines and said, "Look at that."

Connely glanced at it:

" . . . at him furiously. She cried out, 'if you do, I'll . . .' "

Connely nodded. "I see it. What of it?"

"Look at it. *But don't read any of it.*

Connely tried it, and said, "The only way I can do that is to unfocus my eyes. Otherwise, if I see it, I've read it."

Barnes nodded and closed the book. "There's the trouble the natives have. Once you do something automatically, how do you *not* do it? They've probably been exerting psychic influence all their lives. They can no more suspend it and take up a proper scientific attitude than we can glance at a line of print without reading it."

MacIntyre said, "Speaking of a 'proper scientific attitude.' I have doubts that many of our own scientists are 'disinterested observers,' anyway. It strikes me there wouldn't be much experimenting done if they were."

"Maybe so," said Barnes. "But that doesn't matter so long as they don't have, or for whatever reason don't exert, enough psychic influence to affect the result. And the schools, with their standard experiments, would tend to screen out at the beginning those who didn't get the usual results, for psychic reasons or otherwise."

"So," said MacIntyre frowning, "what we end up with is that a scientific civilization just naturally inhibits the development of psychic phenomena, and a 'psychic' civilization just naturally inhibits the development of science. So whichever one gets a big enough lead tends to get a stranglehold on the other one."

"Right," said Barnes.

MacIntyre sat silent for a long moment, thinking it over. Finally he said, "Well, all we can do is send in that report. But first, we'd better get your ship fixed, and get started back."

Barnes got up. "The sooner we get out of here, the better, as far as I'm concerned."

They went into the control room, where Connely took a long look at the viewscreen. "Boy, whoever gets put in charge of investigating 'acute infectious insanity' has some jolts in front of him."

Barnes nodded. "But bear in mind, down there they're just as bigoted and pig-headed about science being impossible, as people are elsewhere about psychic phenomena being impossible."

Connely said, "And that will just make it all the worse when the two sets of know-alls come together."

"It will be a real mess, all right," said Barnes.

MacIntyre was beginning to smile. "Oh, I don't know about that. It strikes me as plain justice. You could even make a saying out of it."

"Such as what?" said Connely, looking doubtful.

MacIntyre smiled.

"One good bigot," he said, "deserves another."

AFTERWORD
by Eric Flint

Christopher Anvil's Interstellar Patrol stories, which make up the bulk of this volume, are part of a broader range of stories. Probably the best way to explain it is to quote from part of a letter which Anvil sent to me last year:

Dear Eric:

. . . As for what to call the group of stories that relate to colonization of interstellar space by humans—including stories about the Interstellar Patrol, the Space Force, Planetary Development Administration (or Authority, depending on what part of it is being discussed, and by whom), the Stellar Scouts, etc., and the colonists themselves—I think John Campbell and I both thought of these stories as the "Colonization series."

Within the stories themselves, the organizations and the colonists all add up to an entity called "the Federation," or, formally, "the Federation of Humanity." This Federation, strictly speaking, consists only of the various government organizations, the colonists, and the traders, businesses, and political movements of the colonists. But, from the viewpoint of the Federation's neighbors (Stath, Crustaxans, Ursoids, etc.), the Federation is the formal main bulk of humanity, plus a cluster of irritating smaller entities known as "independent planets," which, since they have proclaimed their independence, hopefully can be lopped off from the

469

Federation without having to contend with the Federation's armed forces.

As for whether the stories should fit together to make a whole, well, they were written to fit together. That is, the individual stories were written with the overall picture in mind as background . . . they are all out of the same universe, so they naturally fit together and tend to reinforce one another.

All told, the Colonization series consists of one novel—*Warlord's World*—and almost forty stories of shorter length, ranging from short stories to novellas. Two science fiction novels, if we count *Strangers in Paradise* as one of them. *Strangers in Paradise* was a heavily edited reissue of the first three stories in the Interstellar Patrol series—"Strangers to Paradise," "The Dukes of Desire," and "The King's Legions," all of which are included in this volume. Since Anvil himself prefers the original magazine version of the stories to their later reissue in novel format, it is those original versions which appear in this anthology.

The Colonization series can accurately be characterized, I think, as Christopher Anvil's magnum opus. Taken together, counting number of titles, the stories constitute almost one third of Anvil's science fiction output, totaling something like four hundred thousand words of writing.

Broadly speaking, the stories can be viewed as existing on three different levels. It might be better to say, using an onion for an analogy, in three different rings.

At the center are the Interstellar Patrol stories themselves—i.e., the stories featuring the characters of Roberts, Hammell, Morrissey, Bergen, and Colonel Valentine Sanders. In the "second ring" are the stories involving the various organizations which are closely affiliated to the IP as well as individuals who run into one or another of these organizations. And in the final, or outermost ring, are a number of stories involving the adventures of various colonists, traders, spacemen, etc.

In this volume, we are reissuing about half of the Interstellar Patrol stories—covering the early careers of Roberts and his friends—as well as a number of stories from what I've characterized as the second ring. In the next volume of this series, we will be reissuing the remainder of the IP

stories as well as all of the stories involving such outfits
as the Space Force, the PDA, etc. (I.e., all the stories
remaining in the "second ring.")

What will appear in the next volume is the novel *Warlord's
World,* along with five IP stories of shorter length. Included
are such well-known stories as "The Throne and the Usurper"
and "The Claw and the Clock." We will also be including
three other stories, two of which—"Goliath and the
Beanstalk" and "Facts to Fit The Theory"—involve the
machinations of the alien Stath and are among my personal
favorites.

So, if you enjoyed these stories, don't go away. There will
be a lot more coming.

—Eric Flint